PRAISE FOR MARYANN CLARKE

"...a unique combination of heartfelt emotion, intoxicating imagery, beautiful locations, and titillating passion. Her ability to pick the reader up and place them down in a small town in France--a country of which this particular reader has zero previous knowledge--and make them feel as they though themselves are there is unmatched. You don't read her books. You experience them..."

Romantically Inclined Reviews for A Forged Affair

"I love everything about this book from the characters to the storyline. It was a pleasure to have the opportunity to read such an amazing book as this one. I just could not put it down once I started reading."

Amazon Reviewer Katie H for Making Room For You

"Want to read a book where the plot [is] crafted in a way that has a grip on your heart, tears in your throat and laughter on your lips? Then this is the book for you. Who doesn't love romance, art history, and family? The plots twists and tension kept me reading well into the night. The Author M A Clarke Scott gives the reader a run for their money. And if you love Italian then you are in high heaven...Makes me want to learn the language. The passion, literally and figuratively, in this book [have to read it to understand that statement best] is well written. Doesn't hurt a bit that strong realistic characters fill this novel from beginning to end."

Goodreads Reviewer Tanya for The Art of Enchantment

BEFORE YOU KNEW ME

BEFORE YOU KNEW ME

HAVING IT ALL BOOK 3

MARYANN CLARKE

WANT TO READ THE FIRST BOOK IN THE HAVING IT ALL SERIES?
FIND A COPY AT books2read.com/beminethistime

WANT TO CONNECT WITH ME?
maryann@maryannclarkescott.com
maryannclarkescott.com

If you enjoy reading this book, please rate it and leave a review wherever you purchased the book. Your opinion can make or break an author's success, and it means the world to me.

"Run from what's comfortable. Forget safety. Live where you fear to live. Destroy your reputation. Be notorious. I have tried prudent planning long enough. From now on I'll be mad." –
Rumi

CHAPTER 1

Sharon Beckett ended the call and allowed herself a tiny smug smile. The opposing counsel's sighing words echoing in her mind, *"You win, Sharon. Again. They accepted your offer."* Her gaze lifted from her sleek orderly desk to bask in the sparkling twenty-second floor panoramic view of Vancouver Harbour on this fine fall day. A fitting reward for a job well done. And a glittering reminder of how far she had climbed.

The art of war. It never got old. Another notch on her belt. Fighting it out in court was fine, and she excelled at that, too, in an efficient, controlled sort of way, but there was nothing so satisfying as a neatly negotiated deal. No muss, no fuss, every I dotted and T crossed. Her diligence paid off.

She stood, closed her laptop, straightened her Montblanc pen in its stand, and grabbed her favourite coffee mug with its bold black inscription, *You've Got This!* Despite the visible reminders of her success, she needed this too. A daily reminder that she could. She *was* strong enough, smart enough, good enough.

She eyed the dregs of lukewarm coffee from earlier this morning, and strode to the door, a spring in her step. She had just enough time for a fresh espresso. The door swung opened as her associate, Abby, pulled up abruptly.

"Sorry! Heading out?"

Sharon lifted her brow in query.

"You won? You won!"

Holding back her smile, she asked, "What makes you say that?"

Abby flashed a toothy grin. "You have tells. You may not be smiling, but I can read you. Your chin is up, your shoulders back, and you have that sharp gleam of victory in your eyes like an eagle."

A laugh spilled out. "I trained you well, Grasshopper."

Abby made a tiny curtsy of thanks. "Got a sec to review the Shin-Sao Foods case notes?"

"I'm meeting Meacham in ten. Perhaps afterward. Then we can go for a celebratory lunch. On me."

"All right!" Abby spun on her high heel, punched the air and returned the way she'd come, down the hushed, carpeted corridor of FSMBS. That girl would go far.

Laughing quietly, Sharon carried her mug to the sleek black and chrome staff lunchroom and lounge that was a daily reminder of the classiness of her firm, and of how far she'd come. It was occupied.

His back to the door, fellow junior partner, Dariush Shirazi, worked the high-end coffee station like a professional barista, intently focussed, the scream and groan of milk foaming emanating from his mug. He neither heard nor saw her enter.

She stood a moment in the entryway, admiring the way his bespoke windowpane check navy suit fit his shoulders like it had been painted on. He and his stylish tailoring had come from the UK a year ago to join the firm. He was a natural.

Shutting off the noise, and sensing her presence, he twitched and looked over her shoulder. Tossing her a flirty grin, he said, "Hey, Sharon." His warm, appreciative gaze swept down and up again, reminding her of the low key interest he'd continually expressed since they'd met.

With no flirty grin, she replied, "Dariush."

"Almost done here." The espresso dribbled into the cup, and she bit back a retort as he poured and stirred and sprinkled until he had arranged his fancy beverage to his fastidious liking. He was as delicious to look at as his decadent mocha caramel latte, but completely off limits. That was fine with her.

She rinsed her mug while she waited. Sharon had wasted enough of her life pining for Simon Sharpe and learned her lesson well. Success as an attorney came to her through diligence, but she was hopeless at judging the suitability of mates. Just as well it wasn't on her agenda anymore.

Earning the right to sit among the top legal brass gave her great satisfaction, though the feeling of being an imposter never ceased. Despite already having her name on the letterhead, she was impatient to enter the inner circle and control her own fate.

Stepping away at last, he leaned against the counter, waving the way for her. She hit the button for a quick double espresso, which she'd barely have time to drink now before her meeting.

"Sorry to make you wait. What are you working on?"

"Starting a new *pro-bono* case for Meacham this morning," she replied.

He nodded with a silent, *Ahh*. "My sympathies. I'm sure you'd rather be slaying dragons. Will it be very boring?"

"I'll make quick work of it." She shrugged. She'd had the same thought. She'd do anything for senior partner Arthur Meacham, even if it was boring. She wouldn't be here if not for him. He'd hired her right out of law school, despite knowing her history, knowing her father even. "Dariush, if you're as interested as I am in making full partner, you'll shift your perspective a bit. Community-outreach, and public relations are important parts of this job."

He reluctantly acknowledged the right of it with a twist of his face, taking a sip of his coffee. After a beat of silence, he cleared his throat. "Dare I broach the unpopular topic and again suggest we have dinner together? You can further enlighten me on the value of charity work."

"Ask all you like, Dariush. You know my policy. Hell would freeze over before I'd date a colleague, never mind a fellow associate partner." She would never compromise her career here at FSMBS by doing something so stupid. There were rules. This position, her eventual – dare she think imminent – full partnership, the thing she'd worked for all these years, never setting a toe out of line.

"You break my heart," he joked. Yet she didn't miss the genuine disappointment in his dark gaze.

She smiled. "I don't doubt you'll find your one true love in time. You'll just have to look elsewhere."

She glanced at the wall clock and tossed back the remains of her espresso. "Time to go." Setting her mug in the sink, she spun and stepped to the doorway, then paused and turned back, a hand on the frame, feeling a twinge of guilt. "You know, Dariush, if circumstances were different…"

One side of his handsome mouth quirked up in acknowledgement as he met her gaze.

"You're a great guy." Letting her gaze slide over his dapper form again with a smirk. "You're even my type. You'll make some woman very happy someday." She shrugged and left, her mind already jumping ahead to the meeting.

Sharon perched in front of Meacham's desk five minutes before the new client was due. She was hoping if she sat staring at the fatherly old man, he'd give her a clue about the project before they walked in the door, so she could mentally prepare herself.

Apparently, Meacham had no intention of filling her in. Instead, he calmly examined briefs while she sat stiffly across from him, observing. His eyes and cheeks were puffy, and she wondered about his health, and whether he was watching his diet. Then she frowned at the small succulent that sat on the edge of his desk, the lower leaves translucent and squishy. She'd given it to him last month, after a successful case, and tried not to read anything into its neglect.

She loved this firm and had never wanted to work anywhere else. But pleasing Meacham kept her on her toes, and lately she had the feeling she wasn't quite measuring up, though in what way she didn't quite know. Despite what she'd said to Dariush, she didn't relish what lay ahead. Meacham seemed to think if she didn't make headlines with her charity work, it didn't count. She knew PR was important, but she couldn't help being introverted. And she wanted to make a difference without getting dirty and making a scene.

It ate at her, but she kept it to herself. Whatever lay ahead, she was smart, focussed, determined. She'd figure it out. *You're a winner. You can do this!*

Thankfully, Carrie knocked and showed them in right on time.

Two people entered. A middle-aged woman strode forward. Back straight and shoulders squared, Sharon stood to greet her while her mind quickly took in pertinent details. She hadn't been expecting a corporate fancy, but this woman was down-to-earth, in an inexpensive knitted tunic over black leggings and practical grey running shoes. Her salt-and-pepper hair, cut short like a man's, framed her smooth square tawny face unadorned by makeup. She wore a pair of wire-rimmed glasses over her sharp black eyes that gave her a professorial air. Crinkled corners belied her serious manner at the moment. This was a woman with wisdom and heart.

Meacham stood, his stern old face lit up with a genuine smile.

Obviously the woman was an old friend, and that's why he'd taken on her case.

"Christine, come in!" he boomed, clasping her hand between his. "Sit down. It's good to see you."

"Hello, Arthur," she said. "It's you who's being good, as ever. Thanks for doing this."

"Anything for you, my dear. Anything to help you in your ambitious work."

"Sharon, this is my old friend Christine Watts, with the Pathway Society."

Sharon's curiosity piqued, she offered her hand to the interesting woman and introduced herself.

"I'm giving you Sharon Beckett for the duration, and I know she'll do right by you and your organization, Christine. She'll leave no stone unturned. I trust her completely, and so can you."

That was news to Sharon, but she kept her editorial thoughts to herself. She couldn't help but feel this case was some kind of unspoken test. Nevertheless, she would do what they required, and she would do it well.

Christine murmured as she sat down, meeting Sharon's gaze with a small frown, "I hope it doesn't require too much of your valuable time, Sharon," and a tiny red flag went up. This was supposed to be a quick and simple favour, *wasn't it?*

Sharon was about to take her seat again as Christine sat when she noticed a tall young urban lumberjack in a hoody step silently up behind her.

She flinched and caught her breath. "Oh! Hello!"

"This is Kent Sawyer," Christine said. "He works for me, and he's been spearheading the project. Sharon will work extensively with him when I'm busy with the kids, which is most of the time. I don't have the time to devote to the project that I would wish and still keep the operation running. But Kent is on top of everything."

Sharon stepped around Christine's chair and offered her

hand to shake, looking up, way up at his lean, broad-shouldered form, kicking the part of her sex-starved brain that heckled, *everything?* The sullen man merely inclined his head with a jerk of his bearded chin and a bare grunt of acknowledgement, not even removing the hands thrust into the front pockets of his wrinkled tan chinos. She frowned in concern and withdrew her hand. She'd be liaising with him?

He didn't look old enough to have a position of responsibility, never mind run a project. Was he some kind of student trainee? His hood shadowed his eyes, so all she could really see was his scowling mouth and scruffy brown beard. For whatever reason, he was profoundly unhappy to be here. Irritation radiated off of him in waves.

Sharon cleared her throat and slipped past him to drag a third chair over from the side of Meacham's expansive office, turning it and offering it to him. Kent. Kent Sawyer.

He mumbled his thanks, grabbing the chair from her to adjust its position before sitting, his long-fingers momentarily brushing hers before she could withdraw them from the chair's back.

His fleeting touch sent a jolt of electricity shooting up her arm, and she jerked her hand back, glowering at her knuckles in confusion, as though she'd been burnt. The jolt had not been mere static electricity, but something organic, cosmic and far more powerful, zinging through her nervous system and shaking her down to the soles of her feet.

Curious, she glanced up to catch his sharp amber eyes flickering to her face. Those striking tiger eyes flashed in recognition of the moment. He'd felt it too.

Like helpless jungle prey, her breath came fast and shallow. Her pulse raced, beating a drum in her neck. Her thoughts scattered.

She dropped her gaze, taking in his long legs to see that he wore an extremely beat-up pair of brown leather Blundstone boots. They looked like he'd worn them every day for a hundred years.

How could the mere touch of a man, an inappropriate, unattractive man at that, stir such violent excitement in her, sending hot current through her core? He wasn't in any way attractive, as different from the dapper Dariush as night from day. He wasn't wearing a designer suit, for one. In fact, his grooming was non-existent. Maybe even unclean by the look of him. He had horrible manners and no discernible communication skills. And as if all that wasn't enough, he was probably a decade younger than her. She hadn't even got a good look at his face. She'd admired many a man in her day, crushed on a few, but never had she encountered one that rendered her speechless with pure unadulterated lust.

No. Just no!

She had standards. And he didn't even come close.

Blinking, she stole another glance at his face to find his gaze still riveted on her face, staring back at her. Their eyes met, his intense golden brown eyes radiating both maturity and intelligence, and confusion and curiosity that matched her own. For a split second, his angry scowl gone. This time the zing of connection hit her through their linked gazes, sending alarm signals around her nervous system, triggering minor explosions in her throat, chest and core. In that suspended moment, Sharon thought she knew him from somewhere, he felt so familiar. But instantly the scowl returned, his Adam's apple bobbed, he nodded curtly and turned away to sit.

Well, at least he wasn't as young or as dull-witted as she'd originally thought. But who or what was he, exactly?

She sat, mentally shaking herself to bring her focus back to the meeting. Christine was already talking to Meacham and Sharon couldn't afford to miss a single nuanced detail if she was going to do this right.

Even if she had to work with *him*.

What the hell was that?

Kent sat staring at the floor between his boots, while Christine explained who they were, what they did, and what they needed.

He couldn't look up. He couldn't look at that woman. His heart was still beating too fast. He'd come here with Christine despite their strong difference of opinion about the wisdom of this course of action. He didn't expect an encounter with a woman who knocked his socks clean off. A woman who represented everything he despised.

Except – his body screamed at him – *in your bed.*

The universe was cruel.

He had to reign in his sexual fantasies and get his mind back on track. That was one fantasy that would never come true. *Focus on the job.* He'd ignore the blonde and the sparks that flew between them. She was pure establishment, everything he despised about his family's high-class world, the kind of woman he'd grown up with at the country club—ambitious, ruthless and heartless. However much she might match his dream girl in form, she was the crack cocaine of his destruction in every other way. She was off limits. One temptation to which he would never yield.

The old man sat listening while Christine went on about their inadequate temporary facilities in the downtown Eastside and the desperate need for shelter space to feed and house the youth who sometimes didn't show up for counselling or school, or even meals, because life on the street took so much out of them.

Sometimes it even killed them.

Kent scowled and peeked at the blonde he was ignoring. Despite her ice princess looks and proper, stiff demeanour, she leaned forward slightly and listened intently to what Christine was saying, still except for her big blue eyes, wide and blinking, as though she were in shock. She was beautiful, like a porcelain doll. But not sexy. No way.

"This is about property development?" she said, her voice faint, turning to question the old man with her panicked eyes. The old man's gaze flicked her way, narrowing, as they exchanged some non-verbal information.

Christine went on. "Our operating budget is small and always at risk. As long as we get excellent results, the province and the feds give us enough to get by. We have donors who top that up. But the money isn't consistent or even reliable."

As her protegé, of sorts, Kent had heard her present their mandate and mission a million times. Every time they needed licensing or funding from some bureaucratic organization or other, they had to do the same dog-and-pony show. He could recite it by heart.

"If we're able to build a dedicated facility, it will come with an operating budget which gives our school and counselling services a stable base to work from besides everything else it adds," she said.

"Construction?" the princess said, faintly, as her notebook slid off her lap. She lurched to capture it before it fell to the floor, shooting out one well turned leg. *Why is she here again?* She looked too mature to be an intern, yet she seemed flustered and insecure.

She straightened her skirt, her hands on her lap, and pulled back her shoulders, drawing his reluctant gaze to her white throat.

He was so screwed.

Not that he'd ever be stepping into Christine's shoes. She was a teacher, a counselling psychologist and a tribal healer. He was a mere social worker. But the hands-on work he did casting a wide net, working with the kids on the street, and making sure they could show up for Christine's programs was an integral part of how their organization worked. With these kids, you couldn't just hang out a shingle and expect them to saunter in the door and say, *Hey, I'd like to get off the street! Where do I sign up?*

He knew it, and she knew it too. She needed him. But that didn't mean he had the vision she had, nor her communication skills or patience with bureaucracy. He'd never been able to direct his drive and desire to make a difference until he'd found Christine and the Pathway society. This was his life's work, and the vehicle she'd created allowed him to work as hard and as long as he needed to placate the beast that drove him. To his grave, if necessary.

This work for the society was saving him as much as they were saving kids. If it weren't for Christine, who knew what he'd be doing after the disaster up North? Maybe he'd be one of the lost souls lining up at his mother's clinic, trying to numb his pain with opioids.

He shook himself to focus back on Christine's words.

On the other hand, he didn't agree with everything Christine did. Which was why this lawyer thing pissed him off. His entire career, his whole life in fact, was set up to avoid establishment power brokers. Doctors, bankers, lawyers, judges, politicians. Cops. Fathers. They had done nothing for him but fuck things up. What this project needed was community activism – something he knew something about.

The blonde seemed distracted, barely listening to Christine's explanation. She squinted at a little plant that sat on the corner of the desk in front of them, then reached out to pinch its leaves, and poked one manicured fingertip into the soil, a line forming between her pale brows.

And now the universe had sent him his nemesis dressed up in a pressed skirt suit and platinum-blonde bob. The universe had it in for him, apparently. He was fucked.

"So Arthur, Sharon," Christine was saying, "this planned facility, with its dedicated residential component, is critical for us to continue doing the work we do. It's not only about creating a safe place where we can pull in kids at risk, but will create stability and continuity for our programs well into the future."

They sat in silence for a full minute, Christine's eyes on the old man, his on the ice princess, who sat with her eyes wide and glazed.

The old guy cleared his throat. "Thoughts, Sharon?"

She dipped her chin, scowling. "If I may," she interjected, her words clipped. "If – if the Downtown Eastside is a dangerous and inhospitable environment for these kids, why build a facility there at all? Why not get them out of there? Place them in good schools, with good families – in – in the suburbs, maybe?"

Blood pounded in his ears. *Good schools. Good families. Suburbs?*

She continued, gesturing. "I mean, take this little plant of Arthur's for example. It's not thriving in this location. It needs more sun, and less water." She darted an accusatory glance at the old man, and he blinked at her.

Yeah, no kidding. Kent couldn't contain himself. He scooted to the edge of his seat and leaned in. "Because, Miss..." he couldn't call her Princess no matter how much he'd love to, but he couldn't for the life of him recall her name now.

"Beckett," she supplied, raising perfect silky brows in her beautiful bitchy face.

"Beckett," he spat. "That's where they are! They don't live in little pots that can move around. Have you completely missed the point? Have you been listening?"

She bristled, leaning back and puckering those amazing full lips. *Jesus!* He had to get out of here. He had to get away from her. For so many reasons.

"In fact I have Mr. Sawyer, very carefully." Her little nostrils flared.

"Well, you could have surprised me. You're not getting it! We're working with what *is* not some idealistic impractical paternalistic notion of how to fix this problem. You can't move them around like chess pieces. Or potted plants. We work with real kids. Where we find them. Every. Day."

Christine set her hand on his arm to calm him. He fought the urge to yank it away, jittery, his nerve endings raw. It was too late for that. It was this attitude that made him skeptical in the first place about getting lawyers involved. What they needed was to fight this at the source. This officious bureaucratic paper-pusher would be of no help to him.

"The issue, Sharon, and the reason Kent gets so worked up over this," she patted his arm again, "… is that the City Land Department has made us certain promises. And now they're reneging on those promises because a more lucrative offer has come along. At least that's what we believe. They've issued an RFP – a request for proposals – and opened the parcel up to other potential uses sidelining us. But we need evidence."

Twitching, unable to be still another moment, Kent shoved on the arms of his chair to propel himself to his feet, stalking to the rear of the office, spinning on his heel and back again.

Evidence. Evidence? He needed no more proof. They would lose their building. And waiting for a prissy lawyer to dig around trying to pull papers out of the bureaucratic quagmire would take too long. They'd get screwed. Instead, they needed immediate and decisive action.

It was just like his own mess in Fort Marian. If he hadn't followed the rules, if he hadn't waited for the cops, or a doctor's authorization to do something, if he'd used his instinct, and the knowledge and the tools he had at hand instead of following protocol, he'd still be an RN, and Joseph would still be alive. Maybe.

Maybe not.

He faced them again, palms out. "City Hall doesn't get what we're doing either. They're all a lot of crooked dealing, money-hungry Capitalists. And I know some bureaucrat at City Hall is getting their pockets lined with cash to make this happen." He pointed a finger at the trio of functionaries sitting infuriatingly sedately around the desk. "The only actual way to stop them is to expose the corruption. Go to the newspapers. Go to the streets. Go to the people."

Christine shook her head back and forth and let out a long breath. "And there's where we disagree. We can't go throwing accusations at City Council and staff without evidence just because you've got a big chip on your shoulder, Kent. We don't have a leg to stand on, and we'd discredit ourselves with the City if we behaved that way. I feel there must be a civilized and legal course for us to take to save our project. At least I very much hope so," she smiled thinly, turning to face the ice princess, who sat like a statue blinking rapidly. "That's what you need to find out."

Kent had had enough. Threw up his hands, mumbling, "I have somewhere I have to be. Excuse me," turned one final time and strode out the door.

CHAPTER 3

Sharon was rattled after the volatile and cranky Kent Sawyer had stormed out of Meacham's office, and struggled to remember what they were discussing. Thankfully, Christine was still talking, making apologies and excuses for her assistant.

Sharon could have suggested to Christine that perhaps there was someone else, someone with a calmer, more cooperative nature, with whom she might liaise. But that seemed unwise and a poor start to the case, and unprofessional. Sharon had dealt with plenty of troublesome people in her career, though none who'd melted her panties.

"I'm so thrilled that you're willing to work with us, Sharon," Christine said. "I feel that with your experience and poise, you're exactly what we need. Despite Kent's volatility, I believe you and he have complimentary skills that will help our case."

Unlikely. Sharon worked to keep a cool face on and withhold any sign of her skepticism.

It's possible she'd failed.

Christine squinted. "You know, if you think of yourself as a… a horticulturist, a gardener," she pointed at the sad little plant in front of them, "then perhaps you could see Kent as a kind of hunter-gatherer. He has natural instincts, like the *courier-du-bois* of old. Let him be your guide in the wilderness."

Sharon forced a tight smile, though baffled at the strange analogy. What had early Canadian fur traders to do with... anything?

Chagrinned, Christine said, "I want you to meet Kent in a calmer moment, and get to know him, Sharon. Can you meet us at our office tomorrow morning? I'll get Kent to show you around both our facility and the neighbourhood." Almost as an afterthought, she added, "It might be a good idea to, you know, dress more casually when you visit us. People down there are wary of authority." And with that, she had taken her leave.

At that point Sharon could have begged Meacham to release her from the case because she could in no way work with such a person, a *hunter-gatherer* that would undermine her careful methods. She did not. Meacham cared a great deal for Christine and her project and would expect Sharon to suck it up and do whatever she could to help. More than help, win.

They sat in silence for several moments before she spoke. "You are over-watering your *Crassula Muscosa*, you know. You ought to keep it on the window ledge."

His gaze flicked to the small succulent on his desk. "Why don't you take it home and nurse it back to health for me."

She narrowed her eyes at him, her back teeth grinding.

When happy, Meacham could be warm and jolly, though never effusive. At times like this, the difference between her benevolent mentor and a true father hit home. The thickening in her throat, and tightness in her chest reminded her she missed having her own father, or at least the father she'd grown up with. She hadn't had a father for a long time now.

Meacham was a man of few words. Now his stoic expression told her there would be no point in broaching the subject. His eyes got squintier, his jaw more set, like a craggy mountain face. No toe-holds there. Unclimbable.

He set down his pen and levelled his gaze at her. "Well, then. Ready?"

She released her held breath, surrendering to his authority. "I'll look over their files, start with breach of contract, see where that leads."

His head dipped in a small nod of acknowledgement. "What's wrong?"

She gnawed her lip, studying his face, hesitant to speak her mind. After last week's annual performance review, she knew something was bothering Meacham. He was both her most and least favourite colleague. Her champion and her harshest critic. The last thing she needed was to whine about difficult clients. Or uncomfortable work settings.

Her rise from articling graduate to junior partner had been meteoric because of her diligence and smarts. But then she'd plateaued, waiting for her promotion from junior to senior partner for over six years.

Meacham was the one that stood in her path. He'd been more dour with her than usual. There was something he wanted from her, yet he wouldn't ask for it. Something she was doing, or not doing, wasn't right.

"I expect I'll have to deal with staff and council at City Hall."

She could argue she was ill-equipped to deal with officials at City Hall, as he well knew, but that too seemed unwise. The nature of this test was coming clear. Perhaps it was even one he meant her to fail.

He nodded again, this time a glimmer of understanding in his eyes as they scanned her face.

"I suppose it's no accident you chose me for this case, then."

"Nothing I do is accidental, Sharon."

Was it supposed to toughen her up? Did he think to rip the bandage off?

She supposed her father would have advised just such a test. Whenever she'd complained that he was hurting his ancient jade bonsai, he'd quote the poet Rumi, saying, *"If you are irritated by every rub, how will your mirror be polished?"*

She sighed.

Suppressing the humiliating memory of her father's notorious career in municipal government was habitual for Sharon. Long ago she learned to bury the pain and move on. Few people knew the details and connected who she was now with that past self. Her mother knew. Her worst best friend from law school, Rachel Sharpe knew because over the years, they'd learned *all* each other's dirty secrets. And Meacham knew.

He'd been around back then and was one of very few people who knew her family's history. He *knew* she gave construction and property law a wide berth *just* so she didn't have to set foot in City Hall, so why was he throwing her to the wolves now? Maybe this was his way of showing her that no matter what she did, she'd never belong.

Her breath became shallow to suppress the desire to break down and cry. She blinked to keep the threat of tears at bay.

She'd begin by presuming breach of contract. It would likely be over in a few days. She could handle it.

So she opted to smile, express her enthusiasm and walk out of there with her head held high. She would hold it together. *You've got this.*

She wouldn't permit that intractable man to get in her way. And she wouldn't allow thoughts of sex to undo her focus.

CHAPTER 4

ll right, kid. You might not think you need me, but I need to know that you haven't fucked this up.

Kent grabbed his leather jacket as he raced out the door of the Pathway Society a few days later, almost crashing into his coworker Sofia and knocking her over. They steadied each other with a half hug. "Hey Sofia, have you seen Harley?"

"Oh hi, Kent, no I haven't today. Do you have time for coffee?"

"Thanks, maybe later. I just want to make sure he's OK before I start my day." He strode down the empty sidewalk along East Hastings Street, carefully examining the filthy piles of clothing and mounded tarps that kept some of the six thousand local residents warm overnight.

Where the hell was he? It had been two days already. Acid churned in his stomach as the possible explanations spun through his mind like a flickering slide show. In the Downtown Eastside of Vancouver, where Kent worked, nothing he could imagine was good. That's why he insisted Harley check in with him at least once a day. That way, no matter what he got up to, Kent could keep him from the worst trouble.

The streets were filling up. Not that many outsiders found their way into the Downtown Eastside, but a few came in search of cheap bowls of noodles, chowder at the famous Only Café, weed, or were passing through en route to Chinatown. Some had legitimate business. It was in the fringe hours that the locals dominated the streets. During the day, you had to look in the shadows to see where they lingered. Many could be found in Pidgeon and Oppenheimer Parks, which they never relinquished, and where strangers feared to tread.

Kent stopped once to peer behind a fully loaded shopping cart into the shadowy alley beyond a vacant storefront to make sure Harley hadn't curled up with old Carl again, but the old man was already up and out, probably scouring the bins for recyclables before anyone else could strip him of his day's wages.

Not everyone slept on the street. His old friend Carl in fact usually kept a room in a Union Street SRO, but there were enough of them who without shelter it made it darned hard to track people down sometimes. Moreso if they didn't care to be found.

Kent turned down Dunlevy Street and passed Oppenheimer Park and Tent City, quiet this time of day. He continued to scan the streets without luck. His long legs took him quickly along Cordova until he arrived at the door of the safe injection site on Hastings where he knew his mother would have hot coffee brewing for her clients.

Sure enough, the door was open and already she had customers, though at this time of day they were probably here for the coffee. As he turned in he met a tall hunched youth who went by the name of Fiddle for some reason he hadn't yet figured out.

"Morning, Fiddle. Did you see Harley last night?"

Instead of replying, Fiddle's bloodshot eyes widened, and his gaze darted out the door. He sped up, scuttling away. That was as good as a maybe to Kent, although if he just shot up, he may not have even registered the question. That worried Kent because he didn't like the company that Fiddle kept, and that could mean Harley was hanging out with the wrong crowd again, too.

"Good morning, darling," his mother called from behind her desk at the front of the spartan interior. "Were you up all night?"

He moved toward her, bent and kissed her cheek. "No, Mom. Just getting started early. Did you see Harley on your way in?" He walked to the coffeepot to one side of the spartan waiting area and pour himself a cup. He would need it today. He hadn't slept well, thinking of that woman and what fresh tortures the week would bring.

"Don't you have some paperwork to do?" she said, giving him the side eye.

"Always." He took another deep breath and let out a long exasperated sigh, letting go of some of the tension that rode his shoulders night and day. "You know, I just need to know he's OK."

"I know, Sweetheart. But he's not your responsibility anymore. If you wanted to do casework, you should've stayed with the ministry."

"I couldn't stand the bureaucracy, and speaking of paperwork..."

He rolled his eyes, knowing there was no need to reiterate his gripes. His mother knew what he was talking about, as he well knew. Community nurses had as much bureaucratic bullshit to deal with as social workers, as the neat pile of folders on his mother's desk attested.

"However," he added, "it turns out that project development brings its own host of administrative hassles. Christine handles most of that."

"So what's your job then?"

"Looks like I'm spearheading approvals, lobbying. Community liaison. Getting the development permits is turning out to be more complicated than we realized when we started this project. Except..."

Mom looked up, a question in her eyes.

He filled his lungs and sighed heavily. "Yeah, seems that another group has applied to the City to develop the same site. So now we're in competition and have to justify our existence." Just saying the words made his blood boil. "It's enough having to coordinate this project, work with designers, and raise the money. Now we have to fight for the right to do so." He paced the cramped waiting room. That a nonprofit group had to take the lead on a shelter for vulnerable street kids because the government wouldn't do anything was a major burr in his side. Now this.

He shook his head. He didn't even know how to explain that woman to his mother. He supposed they'd meet, eventually. "And now Christine's decided we need help, so she's got this lawyer working on the case *pro-bono* and I have to work with her."

"Oh? Is that a problem?"

"I can just tell this woman will be a handful."

She squinted at him, her sharp eyes seeing God-only-knew what. No one could see through him like Mom.

Thankfully, before she could comment further a cluster of hungry-looking clients smelling of urine, tobacco and weed, clambered noisily into his Mom's tiny clinic suddenly making conversation impossible. She was as intent on feeding them muffins and coffee as she was making safe injections available. She wasn't supposed to feed them but that didn't stop her.

Leaving her to do her own excellent work, he waved goodbye and slipped out to continue his search for Harley before he had to deal with his new nemesis.

CHAPTER 5

Here she was, between an immovable rock of a situation and a really, really hard place. She scanned the street.

Though it was only eight in the morning, a cross section of the folks who lived here, some of them just waking up in their doorways and alleys, populated the streets. This part of the city seemed to house narrow dilapidated old rooming hotels, charitable organizations and community services in second rate retail space, and either low-end cafes and shops or vacant store fronts, frequently with bars on the windows, just like the Pathway Society.

The Pathway building was a nondescript brown brick seventies storefront sandwiched between a second-hand video shop and a tattoo parlour. Across the street was a questionable-looking employment agency and a mission thrift store. It wasn't the worst part of East Hastings Street, but the walk here had put her nerves on edge, and she couldn't help but be uncomfortable about where she left her precious car, though she'd parked it several blocks away and walked. She wasn't sure which was worse.

She stepped through the Pathway Society door, searching for

Christine for her first consultation. She was hoping that if she found Christine first, she wouldn't have to meet and deal with angry Kent Sawyer. At least not yet.

Sharon didn't see what throwing herself into a lion's den of angry radicals, power-greedy politicians and disadvantaged street kids could have to do with her suitability for senior partnership, but she wasn't about to risk failing the test before she even started. She wouldn't sacrifice her career over this. She'd get through it.

Anyway, there was no certainty the case would turn into a monstrous public harangue, the way conflicts at City Hall tended to. Working her magic behind the scenes was her strength. She hated the limelight and preferred quiet, dignified work. She shuddered. Her skin crawled when she imagined the eyes of the public on her, accusing, judging, shaming. Calling out the fact that she was a fraud.

The lobby was austere, a nearly empty space with scuffed linoleum floors and cheap tables and chairs recycled from some old school. Three rough-looking teens sat in a cluster wearing layers of baggy clothing, with a healthy share of their generation's body piercings and ink. Sharon scanned the edges of the space, absorbing details. Through a window into a classroom, two casually dressed adults conversed with another group of kids sitting and standing around. There was an indistinct murmur of voices behind doors left ajar, the squeak of a rubber sole on the floor, the lingering scents of weed, body odour, and bleach.

This was a tough situation, but she'd dealt with all kinds of people before. Practicing law brought you close to the underbelly of society. But this was different. This neighbourhood was a whole concentration of people who were having a very hard life. Her heart squeezed even while her skin crawled. It was a lot more comfortable not to look at them, in all their various kinds of pain. To not think about them very much. And certainly not to walk among them.

She may not want ever to see Kent Sawyer again. But she had to admire anyone that spent his working life trying to help others. That he worked with children was even more admirable, but it didn't mean being around him would be any more tolerable. It wasn't just because of her uncomfortable jolt of unwanted attraction, which still puzzled her. That as incomprehensible as it was, was bad enough, on top of the fact that he was not in any way her type, or a man she would consider any kind of connection with. No, the worst thing of all was his volatile temper, his radical liberal politics, his complete lack of self-control.

All of those things rattled her, reminding her too painfully of her father. Her cheeks burned at the memories. Anything that reminded her of her father was not a good thing. Though she'd adored him as a young girl, and even found his over-loud voice and gregarious assertiveness comforting, that had all changed with his disgrace. Then she'd discovered what was lurking beneath all the bluster. Corruption, greed, a complete lack of ethics. By then, she'd been thirteen, and she knew enough about right and wrong to be ashamed of him.

Tackling this case by approaching and negotiating with the powerful people at City hall, informally, as her 'trusted' colleagues would be best. She'd worked hard to transform herself to be top class, respectable and perceived as a person of power and influence who was "one of them." Distancing herself from her father and his tainted reputation had been her mission. The best way to handle this case was from the inside, negotiating with the power brokers, making deals, understanding what they wanted and trading it for what she wanted. However uncomfortable that might be for her.

And this man, Kent Sawyer, and hot-blooded, sentimental fools like him, was everything she'd spent a lifetime running away from. And here he was, walking toward her, the man who would drag her kicking and screaming into her waking nightmare.

~

"I thought Christine told you to dress casually," he barked as he strode up. "You're as obvious as Mount Baker on a clear day around here. People will hassle you if you look like an outsider." She was the furthest thing from blending in that he could imagine, the last thing he needed now as he continued his search for Harley. She was so conspicuous it was laughable, and it only reinforced his belief that she was the worst lawyer he could ever have been stuck with. Just his luck. A cute, sexy, conservative, annoying lawyer with a stick up her butt. One of the kids alerted him to her arrival with his snarky, *Hey, Madonna's come to visit us. Snort!* Who else could that refer to? "And you do, Princess. Look like an outsider."

"I *did* dress… casually," she replied, glancing down at herself, pulling her shoulders back and smoothing her hands over her fancy sweater, emphasizing her curves.

He blinked to clear his mind of dirty thoughts. "Is that so?" He shook his head. Hopeless. He plucked at the expensive cashmere top and sneered at her pressed dark designer jeans and new leather boots. Hot as hell but inappropriate.

She recoiled, yanking her arm away from his inspection. "What is your problem? Have you no concept of how to behave as a mature adult? Or with professional dignity? Maybe you spend too much time on the street with the problem kids."

"Hey!" That was not okay. He got up in her face, grabbing her arm and hissing under his breath through gritted teeth, "You do *not* talk about my kids that way." If she'd been a man instead of a tiny, pretty little bird of a woman, he might have plowed her in the teeth for that.

She angled her head back, glaring at him. "Which way? Get *off* of me." She shook loose.

Fuming, he released her and stepped back, huffing in frustration.

"Come with me."

"*Ugh*. Please." Her pretty face scrunched, almost pouting. "You could at least *try* to have good manners."

He ignored her and led her to the largest classroom, where Christine was speaking to a group of about twelve kids dressed in the usual array of ripped t-shirts, hoodies and baggy pants, displaying more ink and piercings every week. Christine blended right in today with faded chinos and an ugly sweater. He gestured toward her. "That's casual." Several of the kids turned to gawk at the sparkling intruder, murmuring and sniggering behind their hands, until a sharp word from Christine brought their attention back.

Then he led her down the corridor to a small meeting room where Sofia and Van, both social workers, were drinking coffee and going over case notes. They dressed just like him, which was as much like the people who lived in the neighbourhood as possible. "That's casual."

"Hmph. Maybe if you all dressed like adults, the children would give you the respect you're due."

Give me patience. He rolled his eyes, tonguing his cheek. Then he led her to the back of the building where old Douglas swept the floor in the lunchroom. Kent waved at him and said, "Hey D." *He* wore grimy brown work pants and the ripped green parka he slept in and never, to Kent's knowledge, removed.

"This is Douglas. D, this is Sharon Beckett."

Douglas's eyes darted to her, and she nodded.

"He's one of the local residents who gets hot meals, some peace and, if he wants it, the occasional shower, in exchange for a few hours of volunteer help." Douglas came for the meals, but not the showers, as his rich aroma testified.

After Douglas moved off, lowering his voice Kent added, "That's casual." Then turned to her in her spiffy designer duds and said, as he pointed at each part of her. "This. Is. Not. Don't you own any *old*, worn out clothes? Something a little baggier, less… shiny?"

She sniffed, spun on her heel and stalked back toward the front of the building.

He groaned and followed her.

"Put this on." Shucking his plaid flannel work shirt, he tossed it at her and she caught it, eyes wide. Then he grabbed his old leather jacket off of a wall hook and pulled it on, continuing out the front door. "Come on. Let's go for a walk."

His oversized shirt swamped her, the cuffs hanging down over her little hands. She scurried to keep up. "Where are we going?"

He shrugged. "I've been looking for a friend for a couple of days. I'll show you around while we search. Put that on please." With a sniff and a folded brow, she obeyed.

And they walked, with her jogging to keep pace with his long stride. He bit his cheek hard to prevent himself from laughing at her. He pulled it back to stop her looking like a hopping chicken in her little booties.

"I assumed we would sit down with Christine today and go over the project outline."

He paused and grabbed first one arm, then the other to roll up the cuffs for her, like a little kid. He knew that she watched him, her eyes on his face, and he felt his cheeks warm under her scrutiny. Up close like this, touching her even through layers of fabric, her feminine scent, the feel of her breath, and her slight build had his libido jumping again. "Christine's busy. And you need to meet some people first. I *never* want to hear you refer to my kids as a problem again. Understand?"

He saw her swallow, peeking at him from the side of her eye as they walked. Maybe he saw a tiny nod.

"And as for your comment about dressing like adults to garner their respect, know that these kids, these people are highly suspicious and untrusting of any authority figures. That includes cops, doctors, bankers, teachers, lawyers… even parents. These kids haven't had many loving or responsible adults in their lives."

She had the decency to look chastised.

"Where's your briefcase, Ms. lawyer?"

"Pardon?"

"To take all those notes you were planning on."

She huffed and waved her giant glossy expensive smart phone in front of him.

This was why he wanted her to blend in. She was like a beacon walking around with him, and would scare away most of his usual contacts, making finding Harley even harder.

"Give me that. God, you're dense." He grabbed her phone and pocketed it, assuming she'd have nowhere to carry it in her tight little designer jeans. Jeez why did she have to be such a little sexpot? He laughed out loud.

She eyed him, as if she thought he might be one of the crazy street people. "What now?"

She didn't even know it, either. That was the crazy part. He just peered at her stern, bitchy expression, her fuckable full lips pressed together like a calling card for a prostitute, and shook his head, exasperated. This would not go well.

CHAPTER 6

To Sharon, it seemed they'd walked every inch of the Downtown Eastside in the past hour and a half. She tolerated it, supposing it would help the case if she understood the lay of the land. Research was always useful preparation.

After this introductory tour of the neighbourhood, she hoped she wouldn't need to wander about, though. Her solution to staying safe involved staying as far away from places and people like this as possible.

But he was relentless. They walked up every street and down every graffiti-scrawled, and trash strewn back alley, glanced into every doorway, and behind every dumpster. He shoved aside piles of ragged blankets and cardboard with his boot and stopped to talk to an endless stream of scary, unsavoury characters.

Those that were coherent and conscious, that is. It horrified her, the number of people who slumped in doorways, or stood like zombies, barely conscious or mumbling incoherently.

She hung back, viscerally aware now of how she stood out, even with Kent's large soft plaid shirt draping almost to her knees. When he'd first tossed it to her, his body heat enveloped

30

her, and a delicious masculine scent wafted up from the bundle in her arms, sending tingles of awareness through her pussy. She could hardly give it back, but staying wrapped in its fragrant masculine folds was doing weird things to her libido. She felt woozy and caught herself watching him with renewed interest. Without his hoodie and lumberjack shirt, he looked almost normal. Not like her legal associates, but better. He'd put on a beat up leather jacket over his faded t-shirt when he'd given her his shirt. He was probably in his thirties, like her, though she felt conservative and stuffy next to him, with his beard and messy ponytail – not quite a man bun. He didn't care enough for that.

His long lashes shielded those dangerous eyes for once, and she had a moment to admire his chiselled cheekbones, smooth and pink tinged above the scruffy lower half of his face. She swallowed, her mouth suddenly rather dry.

There was something both competent and seductively kind about the way he was with people. Where she thought he'd lacked people skills, this was where his true talents lay.

From time to time, not with everyone because some of them were hostile, he'd pull her forward and introduce her to one or another of his people. She hesitated to think of them as his friends, and yet he treated them that way, warmly and with respect and true liking.

First they encountered Marlene, who looked to be about eighty-two, with a sagging, bruised face and toothless smile.

"Hey Marlene," Kent said. "How are you today?"

"Oh Kent, sweetie. I'm okay. It's a good one." Her voice was deep and gravelly, like a man's. Or a lifelong smoker. Her sharp, deep-set eyes darted between Kent and Sharon, her curiosity clear.

Kent folded the ragged bag of bones in a big hug and squeezed and rocked her back and forth like a long-lost sister.

"You seen Harley in the last couple?" he asked.

She pulled away, shaking her head, patting his arm. "No sorry, honey."

Kent pulled a pack of cigarettes from his pocket and handed her one, then lit it with a lighter that came out of another pocket. She took a long pull and filled her lungs as though the smoke was the most delicious elixir. Maybe to her it was.

"Who's this then? One of the condo people?" Marlene asked, exhaling a stream of smoke and coughing, the rough sound like splintering wood.

Kent turned to her. "No. This is Sharon. She'll be hanging around with me for the next little while." His tone was neither skeptical, but neither was it enthusiastic. "She's on our side."

"Hi," Sharon squeaked. She hoped that was true. She wanted it to be.

"Another social worker, are you?" Marlene said, reaching up to pinch Sharon on the cheek.

She jerked at the intrusive touch, but stiffened before she could recoil, forcing a smile. What would they think of her if she acted like they repulsed her?

"I won't bite 'cha, sweetie." She chuckled, hacking again.

"Something like that," Kent answered for her, avoiding broadcasting the fact that she was a lawyer. Anything to do with the law, or institutions, would be unpopular around here. He tugged on her arm. "See you, Mar."

Marlene blew him a kiss, expelling a stream of smoke, her wrinkled lips puckering like old rope. "Bye, Baby."

Once Sharon got past the shock of seeing such a weathered, hardened face and body, the old woman's self-deprecating humour and warmth charmed her. "She's seems like a nice old lady. I'm surprised she's living down here."

"She's only forty-two." Kent's tone was flat, wooden, understanding the depth of meaning of that simple fact.

She gasped. Marlene was barely older than her! Nodding at

her shocked expression, Kent told her Marlene was a long-time resident and gentle addict, and in her better moments, a caring and well-loved member of the community, though sadly, lived with an asshole of a guy who beat the crap out of her often, leaving Sharon speechless. "She gets hospitalized a lot. Twenty-five years of drug abuse and violence will do that to a body. She hasn't got much time left."

He continued walking, making rapid turns down different side streets. He knew the area like his own backyard.

She struggled to keep up, her chest tight from the revelation about Marlene, thinking, *There but for the Grace of God...* It almost made her want to go to church. "So who's this Harley we're looking for?"

He gave no answer.

They came upon clusters of sullen and snarky young adults loitering around weed shops, soup kitchens and in graffiti-streaked Pigeon Park, where Kent told her many drug deals took place, and outsiders were definitely not welcome. The sheer numbers of young people who'd fallen through the cracks of society disturbed her.

He left her standing alone in front of a convenience shop while he wandered into the park he'd just warned her about. She couldn't hear the mumbled words exchanged from her position across the street, but she couldn't help but read body language. This was not an easy-going group of people, tense and full of suspicion when Kent sauntered up, even though they looked up, nodded and begrudgingly accepted him. Or some of them did, while others scowled and sidled away. They knew and respected him, but just tolerated his intrusion. Kent talked with one beefy, tattooed longbeard in a denim vest. He was perhaps the ringleader, or because of his maturity, less afraid.

Her chest quivered as if she sang a vibrato note, nerves fluttering through her, and she clenched her fists and glanced around her, wishing he'd hurry back. How could he stand to immerse himself in this alien and hostile environment all day every day? She wouldn't make it a week before she had a nervous breakdown.

Something flashed in her face, sending her heart to her throat, her hand flying to her face in instinctive self-defence. She let out a scream when a figure jumped in front of her, throwing herself back against the storefront in shock, trembling and unable to draw breath, certain she was about to have her throat cut.

Instead of stabbing her, the flush-faced man waved his arms about, babbling a blue streak. In her panic, she couldn't decipher his garbled words, but fragments finally penetrated her brain until she realized he made no sense, anyway. He appeared to be suffering paranoid delusions, based on the few wild things she could make out.

Biting her lip, her gaze darted across to where Kent still stood hunched by Pirate Guy. Her heart pounding, she inched away to escape the still-babbling man, and took a few steps toward the curb, hoping to catch Kent's attention. *Hurry!* She felt her pockets for her phone, worrying she'd dropped it, before recalling that he'd taken it from her.

She released a breath as his exchange ended. Kent seemed to get some useful information, because he bumped fists with Pirate Guy before crossing the street to return to her side.

Inarticulate with fear, she waved an arm toward the psychotic man behind her. Her self-control was crumbling. Nothing set off her anxieties and fears like loud, erratic behaviour, instability, unpredictability and the threat of violence. She was fifteen again and her world was falling apart.

"That's Lance. Just ignore him. He's harmless."

Good to know. She released her held breath and her pulse eased down into the normal range now that Kent was back at her side. Disturbed to catch herself thinking of him, of all people, as her protector, when he was a person she didn't trust, she decided she ought to think about taking precautions to keep *herself* safe.

She waited for him to share something else, but he led the way onward, making a sudden change of direction, presumably on the intelligence he'd just gained.

They passed a large blocky church, white layers stacked up like a wedding cake, and she thought she caught the faint hint of singing. She looked up, smiling. In this unsettling context, she found the sound comforting.

"I imagine you don't find yourself in this area, normally," he said, eyes ahead.

She huffed, though it was true. "I don't live in a bubble, you know. When I was growing up, my father moved in every circle of society, and had friends, and enemies, everywhere from the mayor's office to the unemployment lines." In fact, some people he'd trusted most were the ones she thought looked very suspect, but she'd learned to love them. He'd always taught her you had to judge your friends on their character, and their actions, and that goodness didn't always align with beauty, wealth or position.

Not even fatherhood was a guarantee of moral character.

With a grunt, Kent continued his lecture. "Ever since the government de-institutionalized mental health patients in the eighties, many of them ended up here, most of them untreated and unsupervised." Kent indicated Lance, who'd stumbled further down the street, never ceasing his inarticulate rant.

They walked in the opposite direction, his pace picking up as he rattled off disturbing statistics. "About three quarters of residents here have some mental health condition, nearly half with psychosis. Not all of them pre-existing. There's a huge overlap of substance use and mental health problems. Drugs like crack cocaine, crystal meth and fentanyl, if it doesn't kill them, can also cause psychosis."

He took her elbow and directed her across a street, ducking

between two cars that stopped. Without missing a beat, he went on.

"A large proportion of the court's repeat offenders, financing their addictions, and those who end up in hospital, are those with a combination of mental health and substance use. So much for saving the taxpayers' money, eh?"

They arrived at a small green space with a statue in its centre. On the far end was a haphazard collection of tents, tarps, and what looked like trash strewn about. A cluster of shady figures stood in the centre.

"Oppenheimer Park," he said. "You know it?" he asked.

"Yes." The growth and ongoing troubles of Tent City were in the news from time to time. Reading about it in the paper wasn't the same as walking through, though. It wasn't a place one sauntered through.

Lecture over, he grew silent and watchful.

A few solitary figures hunched on benches, but though he scanned every corner, and peeked behind every tree and tent, he didn't find what he was searching for. The mysterious Harley. Afterwards he led her into increasingly dark and dingy corners, and her alarm grew. Somehow she depended on him to stay out of trouble and keep her safe. Despite her skepticism, he seemed less sentimental-radical and more well-informed-sympathizer, both solid and trustworthy.

Kent's agitation grew by the block. She tried not to stare at him, but whenever she glanced up, his gaze bounced from place to place, his attention divided, and though he told her things about the places they passed and the people they saw, he stuttered and often lost his train of thought, interrupting himself to change the subject.

His extreme tension was rubbing off on her. Whatever he was looking for, she hoped they found it soon. Or maybe not.

From the park, he hiked back along Cordova, past Main and along yet another unnamed back alley, popping out on East

Hastings again. Then he stopped and held open the door of another nondescript storefront for her.

"My mother's a community health nurse who runs the safe injection site here," he nodded to the interior. "I'll introduce you. We can get a hot coffee."

His mother was what? Oh, my God!

This man was full of surprises.

CHAPTER 7

The place was quieter than usual. Two clients sat slumped in chairs, waiting for Mom to let them go. He stepped to the side and gestured for Sharon to enter.

Mom walked brusquely from the back with a squirt bottle in her sterile gloved hand. "Oh, it's you!"

He stepped forward to give her a kiss and hug and she jerked back. "Don't touch me, sweetheart. I've just prepped a couple booths." She turned to the sink behind her desk, stripped off her gloves and sterilized her hands. Then she came toward him. "What brings you in?" She seemed distracted.

"Busy today?"

"Not especially. We just had a minor incident an hour ago. I'm still processing it."

He nodded, understanding. "I wanted to introduce you to someone." He gestured to Sharon, standing with her fisted hands tucked tightly against her trim legs, bunching up the hem of his plaid shirt. He studied her face, which reflected both paranoia and curiosity. "Sharon?"

"Huh?" She tore her gaze from studying the clinic to blink at him. "I didn't understand what it was like in here. It's… it's more like a hospital than a…" She shrugged.

"This is my mother, Barb Sawyer. Mom, this is Sharon Beckett. She's the lawyer that's helping us with approvals."

"Ah. I see." She strode forward, offering her hand to Sharon, who tentatively unlocked a fist.

"It's ok. I'm clean now," said his mom, shaking Sharon's hand and smiling warmly. "How do you do, Sharon? Has my son been treating you properly? He can get a little edgy when he's working."

Sharon swallowed and nodded.

Kent continued to study her. She'd changed. With each passing hour, she'd lost a little more of her hard shell, and her shiny veneer. She was so accustomed to living in her safe, sterile world where she could lord it over lesser mortals – and that made him angry. He'd vowed to push her until she cracked – to force her to see the humanity of the people he loved so much, and that she didn't even value.

Guilt flashed through him briefly. He'd towed her around without so much as an orientation session, and she hadn't complained. He could admit to himself it was mean-spirited. He'd wanted to shock her, to see that varnish crack a little. To see if she had a heart under that icy shell.

But now he concluded that she did. He'd seen brief flashes of, not just discomfort and fear for herself, but compassion, empathy, sadness. He figured she had little exposure to this life before today, despite what she said about her father. He should have been easier on her.

He shook it off. If she were going to work down here, the scales had to fall from her eyes. She had to understand his world, and his mission. But she looked miserable and… strangely vulnerable. Not the same hard, officious, bossy woman he'd met yesterday.

"D'you… do you want a coffee?"

She glanced up, sniffed, and nodded. "Yes. Thanks."

He left the women making small talk while he filled two cups. "Cream and sugar?" he called back.

His mother had spoken over him. "Is development work your usual?"

"Hey, Sharon! You take your coffee sweet?"

She shook her head. Her gaze flickered up. "Just a little milk, thank you."

Figures. She could use a little sweetening up.

He brought the coffees back and handed her one. She lifted it to her lips. He watched her test its heat and flavour, run her tongue over those luscious full pink lips and then slurp a big gulp and then another. He supposed they'd been walking around a long time, and he hadn't asked if she was tired or thirsty. Despite looking ragged and maybe traumatized, she hadn't complained, and had kept pace with him while he dragged her all over for hours. Again the guilt tugged at him and he frowned at the floor.

"Can I speak with you a moment?" Mom pulled him back toward the gleaming row of stainless steel injection stations separated by privacy partitions, everything sterilized and set up for the next clients, their yellow sharps containers glowing in the low lighting like Chinese lanterns at dusk.

One stall was occupied, paraphernalia spread out, and he narrowed his eyes. "Who's that?"

She shook her head. "New one."

"Humph." He pursed his lips, then turned his attention to his mother with a tight smile. "Seen Harley?"

She sighed, dipping her chin to look up at him with infinite patience. "No." She turned to peer back toward Sharon. "What's going on here?"

"Hm?" He followed her gaze. Sharon clutched her coffee cup between both hands, sipping, her wide blue eyes scanning the clinic, noting every alien detail they encountered, her sharp mind click-click-clicking. Her short platinum blonde hair wasn't as perfect as it had been this morning, with little spikes sticking out this way and that. One strand fell across her brow, making her seem innocent. Her shiny new boots were dusty and slightly scuffed at the toes. She looked uncomfortable, overwhelmed and childlike.

"I told you. She's the lawyer Christine arranged. I'm not happy about it. But I have to work with her."

"What have you done to her? Is that your shirt? And why are you looking at her that way?"

"What way?" He leaned back.

Mom shook her head. "I'm getting a weird vibe from you. Very mixed messages. It's like you think she'll eat you, if you don't eat her first."

"Mom!"

"Well. I call it as I see it. Don't forget how well I know you, darling." She smiled wryly and looked at him from the side of her eye. "Just be careful not to blame her for someone else's wrongdoing."

His face went lax while he tried to decipher that cryptic message, which had landed low in his gut like a fist.

"Any chance you could come for dinner this week? Dad's been asking after you."

He made a sound in his throat and lifted his shoulders. *I'll bet he has.* "Right. I dunno, Mom. Not right now. I've got a lot going on. I don't need that." He sighed. "I take days to recover from dinner with Dad. You know that." He dragged a palm over his tired eyes.

She nodded. "You'd better go back to your friend."

"Heh. She's not my friend."

"Well, if you want her to fight for you, you'd better make her one."

He bent to kiss his mother's forehead, just touching her calmed and anchored his agitated nerves, and strode back to Sharon. A commotion at the door had him stopping in his tracks, jerking back. A little bundle of energy, practically spinning like a Tasmanian devil, flew in the door and catapulted himself at Kent. Kent braced himself, his heart already lifting with joy like a startled flock of pigeons.

"Kent! Kent. Kent. Kent."

"Har-ley! Buddy!"

Harley leapt into his arms and wrapped all his limbs around Kent, who likewise enveloped the boy and squeezed him tight. He blinked rapidly, panting, pushing back the burn of relieved tears that sought release. Thank fucking God.

He set Harley down and scrubbed his mop of unruly black hair. Then he lifted his pointed, smooth chin and peered hard into the boy's innocent dark eyes, searching for signs of things he fervently hoped he wouldn't find. "Where the hell have you been, little man?"

Harley bowed his head, swinging it back and forth. "Aw, shit, Kent. Sorry, I forgot to tell you. My aunt came and picked me up. I went to her house for a couple days."

Kent sighed. The aunt. Goddam it. He wished she'd either shit or get off the pot. Sure, she had her own brood of kids. But one more wouldn't matter so much. She could even use the allowance, probably. But they never seemed to be able to work it out, and Harley was still homeless, unable to stay put in foster care.

He planted his hand on Harley's shoulder and turned him on the spot to face the stunned Sharon. She'd set her empty mug on the desk to watch their big reunion.

"So you're the one we've spent all day looking for, are you?" She stuck out a hand. "I'm Sharon."

Harley had the decency to look chagrinned. "Aw, shit, Kent."

He scratched his neck. Then he shyly put his hand in Sharon's and gave it a brisk shake. "You're hot."

She tucked her chin. "Thank you?"

Kent laughed. "We had a deal, didn't we?"

Harley nodded. "Sorry."

"I'm glad you're safe." He gripped the back of Harley's neck affectionately but firmly. "You gave me a scare."

"You goin' back to the centre?"

"Yeah. I'll see you over there. Don't get lost on the way you little fucker."

Harley glanced shyly at Sharon once more before dashing out the door and disappearing down the street in a streak of denim.

"Fuck!" Kent ran his hands through his hair and leaned back, looked up to the ceiling, his muscles going limp, and had to step back suddenly to catch himself from falling. He needed to sit down. He was giddy.

"How old is he?" Sharon asked, her smile mirroring the one that stretched his cheeks.

"Twelve," Kent replied, his tone flat, his smile slipping. "As far as anyone knows."

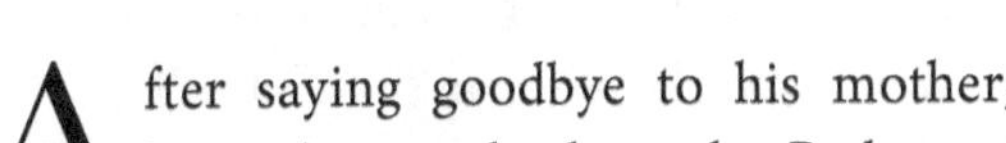

After saying goodbye to his mother, they took a more leisurely pace back to the Pathway School. The tension that had earlier propelled Kent like a madman through the neighbourhood had dissipated.

He even joked around with her and smiled a little, and she puzzled over his mercurial nature. He wasn't a bad guy, if you ignored his tendency to get wound up and snap at people. If only she could. But it was this very zealousness that reminded her of her father and freaked her out.

When she was younger, Dad had brought her with him some-times, when he met with people. He wanted her to know how people lived, and why he worked so long and selflessly to make their lives better.

They paused at a stainless steel takeout window on the way back and he bought them each a slice of pizza to go. She was getting used to the shabbiness and filth, the scattered debris and general lack of order of the Downtown Eastside. She wasn't naïve. Everyone knew what it was like down here. But she hadn't spent this kind of time here, getting familiar with the details, and she was over sensitive.

He handed her a slice which she held on the flat of her palm, the delicious aromas of tomato and herbs and melted cheese enveloping her head and releasing a flood of saliva on her tongue. She stared at it.

He turned to frown at her. "What's wrong? Eat."

"I haven't eaten street food since my early university days," she said. It was a far cry from the status-conscious white-linen prestige lunches she and Rachel shared at the University Club. She was too hungry to care but… She lifted it to her face, then stalled as the tip drooped, threatening to dump toppings on her.

He laughed, shaking his head. "Sorry, no silver spoons out here. Like this." He showed her, folding the pizza like a New Yorker, taking a huge bite. She imitated him and took her first satisfying taste, feeling the grease cling to her lips and cheek.

"There you go. Now you won't get sauce on my favourite shirt." He flashed a bright smile that made her knees go a little weak. They continued eating as they strolled back along East Hastings.

His favourite shirt?

The food revived her a bit, and as they entered the society's offices, she slipped out of his shirt and returned it to him, strangely feeling more than a loss of warmth, as if it had acted as a magical cloak that had kept her safe during their quest.

Unlike earlier in the day, the place was bustling with people, both staff and kids, teens older than Harley. Classes were in session, small groups clustered around tables in the lobby, people walking purposefully around and loitering here and there. In a back corner, a nurse in scrubs was talking to a very young-looking mother holding her baby. There was a constant hum of voices.

Again Kent focussed on locating Harley, but this time he was easy to find. He sat in the lunchroom, looking almost like an ordinary kid, his face scrubbed and his hair damp, with a half-eaten ham sandwich and a glass of milk in front of him.

Despite the enthusiastic welcome he'd given Kent at the clinic, he was cool now, and carried himself like a much older boy, one with more life experience than a typical twelve-year-old should have. He wore his baggy pants and hoody like a jaded gangster, and though his young brown face was smooth and hairless, his shiny dark hair was undercut with a long floppy top that gave him an edge.

"Did your aunt cut your hair?" Kent asked, reaching to ruffle Harley's hair.

Harley's reaction surprised her. He jerked away from Kent's touch, shoving his arm away. "Hey. Don't mess the hair."

Smiling, Kent seemed to take this change in manner in stride.

She watched Kent interact with Harley as he pulled information out of him about the past few days, and again gently chastised him for breaking his promise to check in once a day so Kent didn't worry. Kent was warm, open, loving and kind and she melted a little, watching his skill and sensitivity with the boy, despite Harley showing far less interest in him now.

While Harley was off in the toilets washing his hands, at Kent's insistence, he turned to her with a resigned half-smile. When he smiled, even a little, his harsh features softened, and he became handsome. In a Hollywood hero goes undercover kind of way.

"Is he always like this?

"Yeah. When others are around. It's not cool to be a kid. But over the years, he's let down his barriers with me a bit."

Curious, she asked, "He looks Latino. Where was he born?"

"Only partly, maybe. He's a local kid, born right here in the Downtown Eastside. That's why he refuses to leave. His aunt and mother are Heiltsuk, or some anyway. But his father could have been a john, or her pimp. No one knew, maybe not even his mother, who died." Kent poured them each coffee, setting one on the table. He sat and took a sip.

She waited, sipping her own coffee. He'd remembered to add milk, gaining another point in her book.

"Or so I read in his social work files. She was gone long before I met Harley."

Kent recounted details from Harley's ministry case file. He'd spent most of his brief life on the street amongst the only community he'd ever known, except for his mother's older sister, Delia, and a raft of cousins. But this aunt couldn't take responsibility for him despite the pleading of child welfare, because of her own five kids and borderline finances, and because he kept coming back here anyway and she couldn't control him. Nobody could. Harley seemed to feel some loyalty to his mother and not want to be far away from the place he was born.

"Back when I worked for the ministry and was Harley's case worker, multiple attempts to place him in foster care failed."

"You seem very close."

Kent nodded. "He's a great kid." A cloud of worry darkened his features and he said, "He reminds me of someone I knew once, up North." She was about to ask him, *Where up North?* but he shook off the melancholy mantle and flashed a tight smile as Harley returned.

"You going to stick around and go to class?" Kent asked him.

Harley grunted and rolled his eyes like only a twelve-year-old could.

"Yes, you are. What did RJ say to you?"

"Nothin'." Harley avoided eye contact, fiddling with something in his pocket, making a clicking sound.

"So you did talk to him."

"Never said that," Harley looked up, a righteous gleam in his dark eyes, resentful Kent had tricked him. But he couldn't hold Kent's steady gaze.

Kent said nothing, squinting at Harley, his mouth going flat. "Remember what I told you."

Watching Kent deal with Harley, making sure he ate and washed and gently keeping him engaged, warming him up, cajoling him, giving him myriad small reinforcements, but keeping it all very low key, gave Sharon a deeper insight into how he worked, his knowledge and sensitivities, and his commitment. She couldn't help but think he was a little bit awesome.

The old guy who swept the floors shuffled by on his way in, glancing at her, and she offered him a tentative smile. "Good morning, Douglas."

Christine sauntered up with the social worker beside her she'd seen earlier. He was shorter and stockier than Kent, with short buzzed hair and warm, tawny brown skin, but a similar tendency to dress like an overgrown teenager. "You want to go with Van now, Harley?"

Harley rolled his eyes at Van, but he didn't look too unhappy to go off with the man. "Mmhm," he mumbled as he slumped off, Van's hand on his shoulder, friendly but firm.

"Sharon, I'm glad you're here," Christine said. "Come with me to the small meeting room, please. I have some news. You too." She glanced over her shoulder at Kent and strode away down the hall.

Sharon sat up. The day had been so extraordinary and absorbing, she'd almost forgotten why she was in this new and challenging situation. She had a job to do, and had to remember her aim, which was to get in, get the job done, and get out so she could return to life as usual. She hadn't even found out about the transition housing project, or any of the approvals problems they were encountering. If she hadn't been so distracted during their initial meeting she might better understand what they needed from her. It's a good thing she wasn't charging them a *per diem*.

Once the three of them squeezed into the cramped meeting room, the door closed for privacy, Christine spoke.

"There's been a development at City Hall."

Kent sat down and leaned in. "What's happened?"

Christine's mouth flattened to a thin line. "What we feared. Another group has submitted a proposal. And it'll feed right into the agenda of those condo owners' associations that've been hounding us."

Sharon recalled not-so-old Marlene referring to "the condo people" when they'd met her on the street.

"Who are they? Tell me about the condo owners' association," she asked.

Christine explained that some historic warehouses along Powell Street and Alexander Street had were gentrified into high-end condominiums, as pressure on downtown land values had made it trendy and desirable to live here. She knew about those, in fact, and had even attended an open house or two when she was in the market a few years back.

"The redevelopment of the old Woodwards block made it even worse, as it brought in a significant number of new young professionals to the area."

Kent continued. "Yuppies buy down here because it's funky and cool, and the moment they move in, they freak out when they realize they're right next to the Downtown Eastside, with its own established population of unsavouries that they suddenly don't want to look at. They turn into typical middle-class home-owners bent on preserving their equity and start lobbying to clean up the area, when they were the interlopers to begin with."

Cool-friendly-guy was gone, and intense-angry-guy was

back. The suggestion of competition from an established, professional strata of society had him backed into a corner with guns blaring. She saw a pattern emerging. This guy had one massive chip on his shoulder about people with money. Or maybe it was more than that.

"So what you're telling me is that these local homeowners are lobbying the city and trying to block your project?" Sharon asked.

"Yeah. Not only that," Kent grumbled. "They march around making trouble. Call the cops every two minutes in a righteous uproar, lobby local businesses with their infernal petitions to change this and that, and even organize protests in front of Carnegie Library. They're a pain in our backside."

"Can I ask where you live?"

"What?" He glared at her. "What's that go to do with anything?"

She shrugged. "Just curious. About the neighbourhood you live in. The people there."

He shook his head and grunted. "Near Main and Sixteenth."

She smiled at him. So not a super high rent area, but gentrified, anyway. He lifted his chin, meeting her gaze steadily, as though inviting her to scrutinize him for hypocrisy and double standards. She was almost surprised he didn't live in a downtown SRO out of principle, but then, of course, he'd be too righteous and pure to take up valuable low rent space that could better go to someone in need. She nodded once, holding his fiery gaze. Turning back to Christine, she asked, "So what happened today?"

"Well, I just got a call from a friend who works at City Hall," she said. "Another group has submitted a development proposal for our site and the one next door. Apparently they have an option on that one and have offered to buy our site outright from the City instead of requesting a ninety-nine-year lease as we've done."

Sharon reached for her smart phone to take notes, finding it still missing. She blinked at Kent and flipped her hand out, palm up. "My phone, please?"

He reached into his pocket and handed it to her. She unlocked it. It wasn't like her to be without her phone for so long. He'd distracted her with his desperate hike around the streets.

"And if I recall, in the original brief, you said the City had told you the site was yours subject to building permits. Is that right?" A plan was forming in her mind. She just needed sufficient evidence to prove breach of contract.

"Yes. Our plan involves making renovations to the existing heritage building. Some of our funding is coming from Heritage, some from Social Services. Some of it from Federal and Provincial social housing and education. The combination of monies, both construction and operating, is…" her voice faltered, "… *was* how we would make this work." Christine's face flushed, and her eyes shone.

Kent stood up and stepped behind her, gripping her shoulders in an arm's length hug of support. "We'll fight them. They won't get away with this."

"He's right. Don't give up. What do you know about the competing proposal?" She directed her question at Christine, who had more details to share, though her cutting words were meant for Kent, who'd got his feathers ruffled knowing no more than she did, which was nothing.

Christine nodded. "A little. They intend to tear down both old buildings, I think, and put up a mixed-used building. Much too dense for the area. Residential over a retail base with a mix of market and social housing. The usual." She waved a hand.

Kent turned away in a huff. "A token twenty percent social housing as required by city bylaw!" He paced, his hands fisted. "This is what they did at Woodwards. A bunch more retail space to sit vacant. And everyone gets sucked in by the mandatory social housing units, citing the tre-*men*-dous unmet need, but nobody cares that the province is more interested in sterilized low income family housing than transition housing for homeless and unemployed people at risk." He turned towards her, placing both palms on the table and leaning in, his eyes dilated and chocolate brown now.

She leaned back. "I think you're jumping to conclusions."

"The people who ultimately live in those kinds of units are *never* the ones we're trying to help! Never mind the kids."

Sharon bit her tongue, watching him, willing her heart rate to slow. She faced Christine, taking refuge from his emotional intensity in the logical process of fact gathering, and it gave her some comfort. "What do you know about the party who've submitted this proposal?"

Christine shook her head. "Nothing. I was hoping you could find out."

"I'll do that." Sharon stood, eager to get away from him. "Tomorrow."

"I'll come with you."

Oh, please no. He was everything that got her rattled. The warm, affectionate, caring man she'd glimpsed, who hurt her heart with how much he reminded her of her early years, when her family had been whole and her world had been a happy and benevolent place.

But he also reminded her of the scary, intense, impassioned, unpredictable man that her father became when he was fighting for a cause. The man who'd ruined everything. These contradictory truths were always impossible for her to reconcile. She wasn't certain which she trusted less.

"I'd prefer to go alone."

His nostrils flared. "Well, I'd prefer to come with you."

Christine nodded. "It's a good idea, Sharon. Kent's familiar with our operations. He'll have information at his fingertips as you need it. And you'll need it, I think."

She squinted at Kent, relenting. "If you think you can behave yourself, you can come. But you can't be ranting and calling people names or you'll spoil our chances of success. I need time to gather the facts and analyze them before deciding on a strategy. That means keeping our cards close to our chest."

He glanced down at hers and lifted one brow.

"So to speak." She frowned, blushing.

CHAPTER 8

"Nice car." Kent wasn't surprised that she had money and spent it on luxuries. Her clothes, her hair, everything about her told him that. It shouldn't bother him so much, but he didn't want her to be one of *them*. He liked her too much. Her oblique references to her father gave him hope.

They'd planned to meet at her office mid-afternoon next day so she could drive them both across the bridge to City Hall, and a very fancy office it was, too.

She was a successful lawyer, after all. Not that he was envious of her class. That wasn't it. He'd grown up with money and luxury. And despite his modest social worker salary now, he wanted for nothing.

Having grown up with money, he also knew what often came with its privileges. And that was entitlement, arrogance, prejudice, conceit and disdain for those who had less, as though the fact of one's good fortune made you a better human being. As though chance didn't have everything to do with their lot in life.

Thanks to his politically active mother, Kent had always been aware of the less lucky. She had taught him to want to correct the imbalance. Sympathy and self-awareness were behind his decision to eschew the family business of surgery in favour of nursing, like Mom. And a twin loathing for his father's arrogance.

What motivated Sharon Beckett? Her neat profile drew his assessing gaze again and again, despite trying not to stare at her. Despite fighting his fascination and hopeless attraction.

After a rather long silence, during which he watched a string of emotions flit across her face while she negotiated busy downtown traffic, she responded.

"Why do I feel you're always judging me?"

A laugh burst out of him. "Because I am?" Perhaps too harshly. He peeked at prim and proper Sharon driving with her pointy chin in the air and wondered what her upbringing was like, and how it had influenced who she'd become. Perhaps she wasn't all those things he despised. Not completely.

She shot him a look of pure irritation and made a left turn onto the bridge. "Well, I don't appreciate it. I'm here to help."

"Reluctantly."

She did a double-take. After a moment she said, "No. Just because I'm not an excitable, bleeding-heart activist like you, doesn't mean I don't care."

Instead of raising his own hackles, her reaction relaxed him. He felt playful. She was so uptight, she was almost a caricature of herself, or of the type of woman he assumed she was trying to be. Something about the picture was off, and instead of feeling more irritated by her bossiness, her prissiness, her obvious disapproval, and her officiousness, he couldn't help be attracted, and increasingly curious. He had the urge to poke her to see what she would do. How long would it take before she let go of the tight rein she kept on herself and let her true nature show, whatever that was? There was something visible under the surface. A bubble of laughter rose again, and he held it in, his mouth quivering. Although perhaps laughing at her was just the provocation she needed.

"What?" she snapped, sending him a black look.

Ah, that pretty bitchy face again. He was getting to like it.

"Watch out!" He lurched, smacking his hands against the dash as traffic stopped abruptly on the Cambie Bridge, and she slammed on the brakes.

She pitched him another glare of annoyance. "I know how to drive."

"Okay. Okay. Sorry." He turned to gaze out the window at the Science World dome, and boats in False Creek, as they descended the bridge and swooped up into the west side of the city, giving them both some space. He wished he'd met her under other circumstances. Keeping his natural responses to her suppressed and separate from the need to maintain a professional distance, and focus on the needs of the project, were difficult already, and they'd only just begun.

"So fill me in. What's the game plan?"

"Game plan?" She darted a questioning look at him.

He shrugged.

"I don't decide strategy on the fly. First, I gather information. Research precedents. Analyze cause and effect and the human factor. Then I decide on an approach."

He nodded. Waste of time, in his opinion, but saying so would not keep the peace and facilitate their cooperation. She'd find out soon enough that following the rules and expecting everyone else to, would lead only to frustration and disappointment. He had no patience with bureaucrats. They were the least helpful, and the least objective of any breed. Everyone had a personal agenda. There were few in City Hall who cared about his agenda and that was before you factored in corruption and greed.

"Other than the name of our arch-nemesis, what do you expect to find out when we get in there?"

She shook her head. "If you decide ahead of time what you're looking for, you won't see what's there to find." They pulled into the City lot, parked and entered the echoing pink marble Art Deco lobby, and she marched to the brass elevators in a familiar manner. He, meanwhile, tilted his head back to admire the grand old building. He hadn't been here in years.

"Come on. They'll be closing soon."

Once standing at the desk in the City Land Department, he hung back and waited to see what she would do.

"Is Mr. Llewellyn here?" she asked the clerk.

Not what he'd expected her to say.

"Oh, he was just leaving for the day," the clerk replied. "Can I ask what it's concerning?"

"I know it's the end of the day, but I was in the building, and I'm an old family friend. Sharon Br-Beckett. I just wanted to say hello."

Kent frowned, puzzled. What was she playing at? Did she have an inside track? They waited.

A hunched old man shuffled down the hall and stood at the end of the desk. He already wore a light raincoat and appeared disinclined to engage.

"Mr. Llewellyn!" Her face lit up in a genuine smile, nearly knocking Kent off his feet. Wow, could she smile. Like a movie star.

The old man hesitated, peered at her. His face opened too. "Sharon? I thought she said Beckett, not Brecht."

"Yes it's me."

"Well, well, well. Little Shary Brecht." Llewellyn shook his head at her. "You're all grown up."

Brecht? Kent said nothing, the strange fact pinging around in his head like a pinball.

" I… uh, go by Beckett now."

"Ah, I see. How are you, my dear? What brings you here?" He stepped around the end of the counter and approached, and Kent watched, bewildered, as they embraced like old family.

"I had a little business in the Land Department and I was hoping you were still here. I hate to keep you late, but can you spare just a minute or two?"

"For you, my dear, of course."

"How's Mrs. Llewellyn doing?"

"Fine, fine. Looking forward to my retirement at the end of the year," he replied. "You became a lawyer, Sharon, did you not?"

She nodded.

"I haven't seen you around here before."

Her step faltered. "Um. I don't normally do construction or property development law. Mostly contracts, tax, wills, insurance. That sort of thing." She'd become agitated, her speech speeding up.

"Yes, I can see why you might avoid construction and property development, considering your father's history." He cleared his throat and his gaze skipped away. "Difficult for you and your mother, that was."

"And you," she replied. "I know he missed you, afterwards."

He cleared his throat noisily and sat back. "Yes, well. What's done is done."

Kent wasn't sure who was more embarrassed, but the air of heartache that descended could've been cut like a laser through aluminum.

Sharon reverted to her stiffest, most uptight lawyerly self, the frosty waves hitting Kent like she'd opened the door of a freezer chest. He expected to see his breath.

"How's your mother, Sharon? I haven't seen her in years."

"Yes, I know." She swallowed and straightened her spine. "She's all right. Keeps to herself these days."

"No grandkids yet?"

"Nope. No kids."

"But you're married."

"Um, no. No."

Llewellyn shook his head with a tsk. "In our day, people rode out the bumps of life and stayed married. None of this divorcing willy-nilly."

Sharon cleared her throat but said nothing. Kent's heart stuttered. Had she *been* married? Did that explain the name change? He filed away that detail as *Things to find out later.*

Llewellyn welcomed her back, and she looked over her shoulder and shot Kent an invitation, eyebrows raised.

He shot into gear and followed her down a long institutional corridor lined with small offices.

As they entered the small cubicle at the end, the old man, Llewellyn, finally acknowledged Kent. "Who's this young man?"

"Kent Sawyer," he stepped forward, hand outstretched. "With the Pathway Society, on Hastings Street?"

The hearty handshake Kent was receiving went suddenly limp. "Oh?" Llewellyn lifted his gaze to Sharon, but he was flustered now. "Sit down, please."

They shuffled around, adjusting their chairs and settling in.

"So what brings you here today, then?"

"I'm representing the Pathway Society, Mr. Llewellyn. They believe that an agreement was reached between the society and your department regarding the use of a City property. Can you tell me what you know about that?"

Llewellyn didn't physically withdraw, but Kent felt him pull back emotionally, barbs of alertness going up all over him, like the hairs of a cat defending its territory. Suddenly he wasn't having a pleasant chat with some young thing he knew as a child. He tensed, and his eyes darted back and forth between himself and Sharon as though he was trying to figure out their hidden agenda. She'd said she wanted to gather facts, including what she called the human factor. Is this what lawyers did?

Sharon asked a series of general questions about the history of the property and how it factored into the city's official plan. He also guessed that she was warming the old man up, making inferences and connecting dots.

"Erm. Sam Carter has been handling that one, Sharon, so I know very little about it. But my understanding was that there had been only preliminary enquiries made by your client."

"Sam Carter?" Sharon pulled back, her face going tight, blinking.

From his wariness, Kent could tell Llewellyn knew much more than he shared. He outlined his understanding of the decision to issue a request for proposals, with only occasional, innocent glances his way, leaving Kent free to study his body language, and hers. Sharon was good at keeping her composure. Not that Kent was any skilled poker player, but he was used to dealing with characters on the street who were hiding something, nervous and insecure. He'd gotten good at reading between the lines. When she was stressed, Sharon slowed her breathing, but blinked too much. He'd noticed it when he was dragging her around Hastings Street earlier, and the first time they'd met.

Something about that Carter guy made her uncomfortable. Mostly Llewellyn's gaze fell to the left. The old bugger! He lied through his dentures, making it sound as though Christine had made only the loosest, most tentative enquiries.

"The Pathway Society has a different recollection of what they agreed upon," Kent growled.

Kent gripped his knees behind the desk. It surprised him to feel Sharon's hand over his, squeezing, though she continued to smile and question Llewellyn in that curt, snooty way of hers. She seemed to sense that he was about to blow. Her touch had not a calming effect exactly, but a distracting one, sending that disturbing shock wave through his nervous system again. But it didn't seem to affect her at all. Ice princess indeed. How could she not feel that? Her touch set him on fire!

He glanced at her hand on his hand on his knee, and his mind lurched even as his cock twitched with a mind of its own. His imagination took his elevated heart rate and adrenaline levels and came up with a new picture. One he should *not* be seeing right now. Okay. Okay. He got the message. He took a deep breath and pulled his spiralling wrath and his spike of lust back under control, trying to be patient.

Llewellyn's version of the facts was just close enough to what Christine and he knew to be true to make it seem like a question of interpretation, subtly different in wording, and yet difficult to argue. For all he seemed like a doddering benevolent old man, he was wily and cautious.

Kent knew otherwise. They had made promises. Hands had been shaken. He felt his own blood pressure rising. He couldn't listen to any more of this bullshit.

Her cool composure irked him. His hair-trigger temper and tendency to indignation could be a problem. But Christine would be furious. And he didn't want to jeopardize the project by saying or doing the wrong thing at the wrong moment. But it mattered to him, and her detachment showed her complete lack of a stake in the outcome. If she hadn't been forced to take this case, she would probably have been just as happy, maybe happier, representing the condo owners or the developers themselves. She didn't care about anybody but herself.

He ground his teeth, biding his time.

Kent might be attracted to her like a junkie to his next bean, but he didn't trust her. Maybe she was formulating a plan, but so was he.

Sharon would get an earful the moment they stepped out of here. There was no way this project would go ahead by following rules and sitting around meeting tables, waiting politely for the City to take them to the cleaners. He'd make sure she understood this was a fight that had to be taken to the streets to be won.

CHAPTER 9

As they stepped out of Llewellyn's office, she paused at the front desk, breathing slowly to calm her nerves, waiting for her heart rate to slow to normal. That was hard. It was bad enough facing her father's old friend again for the first time after all these years, never mind that Kent had witnessed it all.

She turned to him. "I just want to make an appointment for tomorrow before we leave. Then I can drop you off somewhere."

"What do you mean? What happens next?" He faced her, hands on his hips, his thousand year-old Blundstone's planted wide on the polished terrazzo floor.

"It looks like I have to talk with Sam Carter. He'll know more about their plans for the land, and the goals of the RFP. I'm sure he'll also be familiar with the developers who are your competitors. And if there is anyone else involved." She faced the long chipped laminate counter and tapped her fingertips on its surface.

When she had impulsively gripped Kent's hand in Llewellyn's office out of fear that he would say something impulsive and rude, she'd forgotten what happened when they touched. Power emanated from his hand under hers, his muscled thigh tense and twitching. It had stolen her breath away. A long time had passed since she'd last felt like a horny schoolgirl. She'd had to exercise maximum self-control to carry on interviewing Llewelyn and not let on how it had affected her.

Now he stood there, all huffy and obnoxious, and all she could think about was how exciting it might be to kiss a man consumed with such righteous passion. In her mind, she ran her fingers through his long hair, loose from its tie, and felt a rush of primitive lust. She reminded herself for the umpteenth time that he was not her type. He wasn't even in the ballpark. She needed to get a grip on herself. Her libido was out of control.

Ideally, she could get rid of Kent and have a little heart-to-heart with Carter. Sharon would never suspect kind old Mr. Llewellyn of funny business, but she wouldn't put anything past Carter and facing him filled her with dread. She needed her wits.

"Is there something else you need, Miss Beckett?" said the clerk.

"Yes. I was hoping to meet with Sam Carter. Does he have some time available?"

"It's late today, but I could ask him if I could slip you in."

"No, no, no. Tomorrow would be better. We'll need a bit of time."

The clerk studied her departmental appointment book, frowning. "It's a busy day. He has a little time just before lunch tomorrow. Will a half an hour do?"

It was perfect, in fact. She'd study the documentation tonight, and she'd lay out her position. The less time they had, the less time there would be for something to go sideways. "Yes. Thank you."

Suddenly, Kent's face was pushing close to hers angrily. "That's it? That's all you're going to do? Have another meeting? Ask them nicely what their plans are?" He spun away, strode to the window overlooking the mall across the street. Dusk was falling and yellow streetlights glared in the blue evening shadows.

She waited, thoughts swirling, memories surfacing.

The Llewellyns had been friends with her parents. They were almost like family when she was growing up. Her father used to go trout fishing with Mr. Llewellyn.

When the shit hit the fan, and her father's dominion collapsed, she was too young and traumatized to realize how much Llewellyn would be affected by that association. Later she had time to think about the double whammy of Llewellyn's betrayal. Not only was he Daddy's friend, but his own neck had been on the line when the corruption came out. Sharon was thankful only that he'd been able to prove his innocence, but wondered if he'd contributed to her father's disgrace. At least Mrs. Llewellyn, sweet woman that she was, was spared the humiliation, and had kept her home. Unlike Sharon's mother.

Sam Carter had been the hammer that smashed her father's empire as if it were mere plaster. He's the one who had reported the original suspicious documentation that started the paper trail that led to her father. Carter had pointed the finger, and he possessed the map, so Council, and then the police, once they'd started investigating, couldn't get lost. She'd always wondered why he'd been so ruthless. It's almost like he had a vendetta against Daddy. But in fact he'd only got the ball rolling. After that there was no stopping it.

Carter might have been an officious, petty, mean-minded bulldog of a bureaucrat, but he'd been on the right side of that fiasco. She couldn't believe she had to walk into the amphitheatre of her family's disgrace, her own personal hell. Never mind face him. The only thing worse than that would be Councillor Seibold himself.

She so didn't want Kent Sawyer in the room when that played out.

His shoulders rose and fell with his agitated breath. He never seemed to dress any better. His usual boots and chinos were paired today with a brown and cream shirt under a beat-up leather jacket. At least he didn't wear his adolescent punk hoodie to City Hall. It was hard enough getting any respect around here.

She wished he weren't growing on her. Without the hood she could admire his silky straight brown hair, pulled up into a man-bun. If you'd asked her a week ago what she thought of tall lean men with beards and man-buns she would have pretend-vomited, however immature that seemed. Now, against her better judgement, she found him quite handsome. Even though he irritated the piss out of her.

As if called by her thoughts, the indignant Kent Sawyer stood beside her again, still huffing. She wished he wouldn't do that, as it made her think of other, more athletic, heavy-breathing activities. Damn it, how had she got into this mess? There wasn't another place or situation that made her feel more vulnerable and inept.

"Let's go. Where can I drop you?" she asked him, eager to put distance between them.

"Back at our offices would be great. I have a few things I'd like to say to you on the way." His long lashes lowered and flickered over the hot golden brown of his eyes, as if he were barely holding it together, not done yet, and sending a jolt of heat to her core.

She was looking at him funny when they pulled out of the parking lot. As though confused. But he was so frustrated he couldn't take the time to figure it out. He had to speak his mind.

"So is this how it goes? You have a bunch of polite meetings with a long string of bureaucrats, and then you give them what they want?"

"I told you. I'm gathering information. You needn't tag along if you're bored."

"Now I understand why lawyers' bills end up being so high. You're not exactly efficient."

"Well. If you were paying me for my services, you might have something to complain about."

He fumed and watched the car headlights as they flickered past. Bickering was pointless. It made him feel worse to pick a fight with her. But it still frustrated him like hell.

Rain had started. The days grew shorter, and the evenings cooler. He always dreaded the onset of winter. Living on the street was so much harder when it was wet and cold, even in coastal Vancouver. How many people would they lose this year?

He drew a deep breath, speaking more calmly. "It's not about the time or money. And I don't mean to insult your skill. Your methods frustrate me. You're just a freelance bureaucrat, ticking off boxes. I've seen it all before. I know what will happen."

"All right, Mr. Clairvoyant, what will happen?"

"That old guy is shady. He's keeping secrets, and it's written all over his face."

"Who? Mr. Llewellyn? He's as sweet as pie. He was like an uncle to me growing up."

He hummed. "You might be a little biased."

She scowled, her gaze darting thoughtfully.

"What's the deal there, with your Dad?" he ventured.

She gnawed her upper lip. "He was a City councillor. A very popular one. And then he wasn't. He lost his position in a corruption scandal."

Wow! Bits started falling into place. Most notably why she was so intent on doing everything by the book. Not creating a fuss.

"I'll bet that was hard for you."

"It was long ago."

"I mean going in there today."

She inhaled. "Yes. Yes, it was. I hadn't been back."

He peered at her, momentarily disarmed by the way the streetlights highlighted her silvery-blonde hair and the exquisite contours of her profile with pink and green. If he didn't look at her, he could think clearly and have a coherent conversation. But whenever he did, his brain turned to mush. He swallowed. "We'll lose our building and our project. I can feel it in my gut."

"Well, perhaps we should talk about that. When we get back to your office, I need to read all the correspondence, all the meeting minutes, everything else you have from your discussions with the City. What you need to understand is that without evidence of a contract, even a verbal contract, we don't really have a legal leg to stand on. I'll do what I can to argue that they made commitments—"

"They *did* make commitments! We told you that! Somebody at City Hall... maybe several somebodies, is up to no good. I'm telling you – "

"Stay calm. There's a procedure we have to follow. If I can piece together documentation about the series of events, and argue that your assumptions about this commitment are defensible, then at the very least we have a negotiating tool. I can file for damages resulting from a breach of contract. But I need sufficient reason."

"What will that give us? Can we force them to give us the land?"

They were back in the city centre, crawling through rush hour traffic, following a slow bus with the giant toothy smile of some realtor pasted on the back. Kent wanted to punch him in the teeth.

She drew in a long breath and sighed. "We can't really force them to do anything. They own the land. Depending on the strength of the argument, though, we'll have some leverage. In the event they insist on awarding that site to the competing development group, you'll be able to make certain demands for damages and compensation."

"If they renege on our agreement, it wrecks our entire project." His heart sank, and a knot of pain twisted in his chest. It was hopeless. He should have known. The entire project was a pipe dream, all their funding and approvals too good to be true.

"Not necessarily. Is there no other building or site that would work for your needs?"

"No! We're not like some developers with an architect in our pocket and a bank account full of cash. For a non-profit group, putting together a project like this is a complex balancing act. It's been in the works for years. We've got funding commitments from multiple government bodies. One slight change and all of those commitments are void. We'd have to start from scratch."

"Surely not. If they've all approved this project, they must like it. Why wouldn't they give you the money?"

"You can't be that naïve and call yourself a lawyer! Do you have no idea how bureaucracies work? We're lucky to have gotten this far, one building block at a time." He growled in frustration, gripping his knees.

"That might even benefit us. We'll build our case that way too," she murmured, taking the turn onto Cordova Street. "So if you don't like my box-ticking methods, what would you do?"

He scowled, shaking his head. "Petitions, protests, the press, I don't know. Drum up public support. Shame them into following through on their promises." Right at the moment, he was feeling pretty hopeless. Some days he wished he were a normal guy with a normal job. Then he might even have a girl, and life wouldn't be one big fight.

Her face tightened. "Uh-huh. The three Ps of the radical. I know them well. I'm not sure you're in the right line of work. You can't just throw a tantrum if everyone doesn't give you what you want. It's a big sandbox. Everything is a negotiation. Ev-er-y-thing. That's why I have a job. Maybe you should get yourself a nice cushy position working for the government."

"I fucking tried that! They might give you a pay-check every two weeks, but they also castrate you."

He saw her eyes flash in the reflected light of the cars in front as her gaze darted to him and back to the road.

After a beat or two of shocked silence, she asked, "Really? What did you do before?"

He would have deflected the question, but her voice had softened and lifted, as though she were genuinely interested. It was important to him she see him as more, more than just this angry and desperate social worker with no power. "When I first became a social worker, I worked for the Ministry of Child and Family Services. That's where I met Harley. I was his caseworker. Pure frustration. That's why I'm working for Christine's non-profit now. Where I can make a real difference." He swallowed, turning away to scowl out his side window. "Before that I was a nurse. Same thing. Bureaucracy incarnate."

"A nurse? Like a nurse-nurse?"

"Don't even start," he mumbled through gritted teeth. This day was going to hell. He didn't need to be ridiculed by her. Not now. "I suppose you're thinking, why not a doctor?"

"No. Didn't cross my mind, actually. I'm just surprised. So… like your mother."

He hummed his agreement. "And maybe out of… a bit of rebelliousness. My father didn't approve." Which he'd paid for with years of disdain and criticism for his choice. In fact, the contempt had been mutual. "Since I couldn't please him anyway, I'd learned early not to bother trying. It became a goal of mine to piss him off as often as possible, in as many ways as possible."

Or it had been, when he'd been a younger man. Now he didn't care. So he told himself.

"Oh? He had other plans for you?"

"Oh, yeah. Nursing was a fine career for a woman. Though

Dad doesn't understand Mom's leftist politics and community work either."

In his opinion, if she was going to be a nurse, she ought to be an O.R. nurse and work at his side, and be happy for the privilege. But nursing for his son? That he never understood or forgave.

"Then why did you *stop* nursing?"

How did he end up here? He did *not* want to talk about the end of his nursing career. Not with her, not with anyone. "It's a long story."

She pulled into a half-vacant parking lot on Cordova Street around the corner from the society offices and turned off the car. "I have time." She looked out the windows, left and right. "Do you think my car will be safe here? I want to come in and pick up some files to take home."

What could he tell her? There were no guarantees.

He laughed and chucked her under the chin. "Why don't you advertise the fact that you don't belong here and that your car contains valuables, Princess?"

Her expression was pensive as she frowned at the dash of her expensive car. "My family wasn't wealthy, you know. I've had to earn everything I have."

Huh. You couldn't tell by looking at her, all polished and prim.

"Well, mine was, and I threw it back because – " he stopped. What was he doing, talking about his family with her?

"Why are you so hard on people with money?"

"Because of the games rich people play," he whispered. It wasn't money he had a problem with. He wished everybody had enough of it to be safe and comfortable. It was the attitude. His father was the quintessence of this attitude, and his older brother the-brilliant-young-surgeon-Doctor-Aaron-Sawyer ran a close second.

"Is that why you're such a bleeding heart softie?" The words were harsh, but her tone was gentle, teasing.

"Maybe."

"Go on. I want to know why you stopped nursing."

Ugh. Why couldn't she let it go? She turned in her seat and peered at him, waiting. He sighed, surrendering.

"Once I'd finished my exams and certified as a nurse, I took a job as a community nurse in a tiny under-serviced village near Yellowknife."

"In the North?"

He nodded. "Partly because they're always looking for people, but also, I guess, to prove my worth. And partly because… I just wanted to get as far away as possible." He shrugged. "I was twenty-two. It was an especially challenging gig. I wanted to do good work, but… in hindsight, I guess I wanted to prove to my dad I was doing something important, and extra hard. Because I could. I'd talked it up, naively." He shook his head. "I was cocky. Maybe I even thought I could work some miracles."

"And you switched from nursing to social work… *why?*"

Kent closed his eyes, feeling the heavy weight of memory, of guilt and grief press down on his chest. His words, when he could push them past his tight throat, caught. "Someone died." He let out a broken breath. "A friend."

Sharon's gasp was soft, but sharp. She whispered, "I'm sorry," and lay a hand on his arm.

"Thanks." He shook himself, cleared his throat and shrugged. "Come on. Let's get those files for you."

Relenting, perhaps realizing he couldn't talk about it anymore, they got out of the car and she locked the doors, glancing around nervously as she walked around to his side. He was grateful the subject of his nursing career, and its ignoble end, had run its course.

"The police station's just a block that way. Maybe the cops'll cruise by just in time to save your precious car," he said to lighten the mood.

Her response was to scowl at him, her silky brows lowering, and he couldn't help laughing. She was so predictable, and he enjoyed pushing her buttons. But she couldn't hold on to the scowl, and he saw her lips twitch with amusement.

He shrugged, tossing her a teasing smile.

Her smile grew, and then it fell as their gazes locked, and despite their earlier conflict, the electricity that flew between them told another story. Their shared intimacy had taken them somewhere new. They understood each other.

His gaze dipped to her mouth, and she licked her lips, looking up at him, a question in her eyes.

He swallowed and leaned toward her, wavering. She drew a sudden breath of… surprise?

And then he straightened, blinking, filling his lungs with cool night air. What was he thinking? He came so close to bending his head just a little and tasting those amazing lips. And he would swear she was inviting him to do so.

She blinked, and he cleared his throat, stepping back. "Um. Right, well."

She nodded, her gaze dropping to his chest, fiddling with the strap of her bag. "We'd better hurry and get those files. I have a lot of reading to do tonight to prepare."

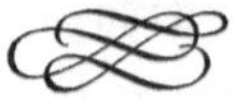

He'd almost kissed her, she was sure. Or was it that she'd wanted him to?

After learning so much about his past, she felt a new affection that shone a more sympathetic light on him.

Sharon's goal was to go over the society's files with a fine-tooth comb. Too uneasy to sleep, she stayed up late to read all the correspondence and minutes, and study their financials. This included all their proposals, all their funding agreements, their donations, everything. Some of it was boring as porridge, and much of it was repetitive, but she needed to build an argument.

She hadn't been able to focus, her thoughts wandering to their conversation in the car, and that moment afterwards in the dark.

Princess, he'd called her. Acting like he'd never been in a European car. Turning his nose up at the way she dressed. But she shouldn't be surprised, that's what people saw. It's the very image she'd worked so hard to cultivate.

Ha! If he only knew. She was the furthest thing from the privileged prima donna he seemed to think she was. She was the most ordinary of girls who'd grown up without status or wealth.

She was the girl who went unnoticed, neither popular, talented nor beautiful. A little too plump and a little too plain. Too small to be a jock. The only thing she'd really been good at was singing. Only her Daddy thought she was special and treated her so. The only princess she'd ever been was in her father's eyes.

As long as his approving and loving gaze shone its light on her, she'd been happy, and believed she was special. Yes, she'd been Daddy's girl.

It wasn't often she allowed herself to think of her father without the protective shield of resentment. If she let the sweet memories of her girlhood seep in, then the sadness snuck in with it. Her chest ached, and her throat burned when she remembered the father she'd once had.

If she couldn't negotiate a deal with Sam Carter, the next step loomed on the horizon. She'd have to approach City Council. And with City owned land, and general land planning, the most informed, involved and influential councillor was the long-seated Gus Seibold. She'd always wondered why, after all these years, he'd never run for mayor. But he was still a powerful man. She did not relish the thought of standing up before him, either in his office or in council chambers, to plead her case. Would *he* remember the fat little girl who was swept aside in the tidal wave of her father's crimes? Would he care?

Well, she'd rather not have to face him. Without even trying, he'd shred her careful disguise.

So what was she going to say to Sam Carter? What did she have to negotiate with? It was Christine's word against his. She researched Christine's life and history to build up a profile of a strong, well-educated, community leader with influential connections, who demanded respect. That part hadn't been hard. Christine's story was amazing. A Tseshaht First Nations woman who grew up in humble circumstances in Port Alberni, she'd pulled herself up by her bootstraps, got her Masters in Education and Indigenous Studies, her Ph.D. in Counselling Psychology.

She'd won awards, been recognized. But Sharon could easily imagine that the arrogant Sam Carter, and the elitist Gus Seibold, would see only the surface – a mild-mannered, humbly dressed middle-aged do-gooder. A First Nations woman, easily dismissed. Well, she'd make sure that didn't happen.

If it came to a court case, she was sure calling Christine to the stand would be very fruitful, but in the meantime she'd use all of that to shift the balance of power away from their opponents.

And she worked to pull out every letter and email and analyze the language, searching for innuendo even when intent was obscure. The oily City was accustomed to couching everything they said, even promises, in just enough ambiguity and corporate speech to leave themselves wiggle room, whether or not they intended to use it.

She'd see about that.

❧

Sharon arrived for her pre-lunch meeting with Carter in enough time to check her hair and make-up, and to calm and prepare herself, determined not to be intimidated by the city manager. She needed to make just the right impression.

"Come in, Ms. Beckett. Sit down," he said as she entered, barely glancing up from the papers on his desk. She supposed the busy bureaucrat was accustomed to fielding questions and complaints from members of the community. It's likely he wouldn't recognize or remember her. She would have been nothing to him. That was just as well.

She introduced herself and summed up her client's situation.

"I'm concerned that two things have happened here, Mr. Carter," she explained. "First, that your department has been unduly influenced by a small vocal lobby group of local condo-minium owners who don't represent the majority of long-time residents. And second, that you've opened up this request for proposals after making legally binding commitments to my client for the allocation of this property, perhaps inadvertently triggering a case for breach of contract."

Carter leaned forward, his face tightening into a smug smile. "Ms. Beckett. I'm not sure what they taught you about legally binding commitments where you studied law, but even if there was a suggestion of an agreement between us and the Pathway Society—and I'm not saying there was—it was not a contractual agreement. As we, the City, own the land, we are free to do with it what we please. And it's also our mandate and policy to do with our property that which is deemed to be in the best interest of the city and its citizens. So if additional information becomes available, we're always at liberty to consider it."

He linked his fingers and leaned back. The shit-eating bastard.

A calm clarity descended over Sharon, the tightness in her chest lifting, her chest expanding. There was nothing to fear here. Just a little man defending his turf. She lifted her chin, making direct eye contact with him.

"Which of your citizens do you suppose the competing development proposal most benefits, Mr. Carter? Would you say it constitutes the greatest good for the greatest number?"

He cleared his throat. "Well, perhaps I would, Ms. Beckett. That remains to be seen. Your client's proposal also has merit. We're still reviewing the pertinent details."

I'll bet. "Would you mind sharing those details with me? I'm very interested."

He shuffled some papers. "I'm not sure I can do that."

"Since they're a matter of public record, I'm sure you can."

His expression was wooden. "I don't have them handy at the moment, Ms. Beckett. Would you mind going through the usual channels? Making your request through the admin office? That'd be better, I think."

She nodded. His stonewalling was familiar and unremarkable, and she felt a little thrill to realize she could handle this. He stood to gain nothing from inconveniencing her but the thrill of power-tripping and delaying her slightly. She wouldn't get any more from him today. She wondered if there were any other reason stalling would benefit them.

"When does your recommendation go to Council?"

"Hmm. Let me see. Rather soon, I believe."

Yeah, she'd just bet it was soon. "But you wouldn't know off-hand, I suppose."

"No, sorry." He smiled again. "You'll have to enquire via the –"

"The usual channels. Yes, I guess I will. Good day, Mr. Carter."

She spun on her heel and walked sedately out of his office. She had more information to gather. She suspected that this matter was going before Council soon, and that the plan was to railroad it through. Which only meant one thing to her, and that was that something fishy was going on.

On her way out she asked after Mr. Llewellyn again.

"He's stepped out for an early lunch, I'm afraid," said the clerk.

Smiling, she left the building and crossed the street to the mall, making a bee-line for the A & W in the food fair. Sure enough, there sat Mr. Llewellyn, as she'd expected. He'd eaten lunch here every day for as long as she could remember. Back in the day when her father was active at the City hall, they'd come here together for their burgers and talk big fish.

"Mr. Llewellyn."

He looked up, raised his brows and swallowed the bite he had in his mouth. "Sharon? You're back so soon."

She told him about her brief but unsatisfactory meeting with Carter.

"Sit down, Sharon." He set down his half-eaten burger and wiped his mouth with a paper napkin, his movements methodical and unhurried. "What are you trying to do here? Isn't there another solution to your client's problem besides stirring up trouble at the City?"

She pondered his reaction. "How am I stirring up trouble, sir? I've only made a few enquiries. I've barely begun my due diligence."

He shook his head, lips flat, eyes down. He picked up his burger, put it down. "I can't tell you how to do your job, my dear. But trust me when I say that everyone's life would be much simpler if your clients backed down and went on their way. Found a different building." He glanced up. "Does it really matter so much?"

"Not to me, but to them it does. Are you trying to tell me something?"

"Nope. I am not. Just common sense. Why take the high road when you can take an easier path, that's all." He took a bite.

She narrowed her eyes and peered at him, trying to read between the lines. "Is there some reason you don't want me to follow through with this?"

His wiry grey brows inched up, his brow creasing. He chewed slowly and swallowed. "What would it have to do with me? I'm months from retiring. I'm hardly involved in anything anymore. It's all Carter now. He runs the show."

She wished his gaze hadn't darted over her right shoulder as he spoke. She wouldn't want to cause him any difficulties. But obviously he knew something he wasn't sharing. Something it wasn't in his interest to share. He was a good and kind man. That much she knew. But there was more to this story. Was he protecting someone?

"Tell me about the other proposal? You know I can apply for access to the documents."

He nodded with a slow blink of acknowledgment, suddenly showing all of his sixty-four-and-half years. "The applicant is S & S Developments. They've proposed an eight storey new building, apartments over retail." He shrugged. "It's an excellent project."

She frowned. "A little dense for that spot, isn't it?"

"Things are changing downtown. There's a lot of pressure to densify. Never enough housing."

"Free market housing, you mean. So condos?

He cleared his throat. "Some social too."

"Yeah. But nothing for the people on the street who already live in the neighbourhood. Nothing to help the homeless kids. How can you choose developer profit over that?"

"They want to buy the land outright. Puts more cash in the City's coffers to do other good works, programs, amenities. It comes around."

"Yes. I'll bet it comes around. Who's running this S & S?"

His restless fingers folded and unfolded the edge of his burger wrapper, and he frowned. "Seibold and Sorenson. You remember Matt Seibold?"

She nearly choked. "Gus's *son?*"

The golden boy she'd crushed on in junior high school who was everything that Sharon, as a humble and self-conscious teenager, was not: honour roll student, star basketball player, cellist in the school concert band, volunteer at local events.

So when Sharon moved to a new school after her father's disgrace, she'd started over, remodelling herself in the image of strong, confident Matthew Seibold, from designer labels, to changed speech, to his elitist attitude to raise herself up out of powerlessness. She'd even taken her mother's maiden name to distance herself from the contemptible Councillor Peter Brecht and his shameful legacy.

"Sharon?"

Her gaze focussed on Llewellyn, who had finished eating while her mind had wandered. "*He's* the developer? Matthew Seibold."

He nodded. "Him and his partners. Started up S & S a few years ago. Doing pretty well, too."

"How does that work, with old Gus on council?"

"He abstains from voting on their projects."

Does he? She nodded, pondering that fact. She couldn't even imagine a council debate without Gus being in it up to his elbows. Suddenly, Kent's skepticism, and suspicion of foul play at the City, echoed in her mind. What was going on here? Could he be right?

Keeping a neutral face, she said, "I'm sure that had nothing to do with your department's selection process. When does Carter's recommendation go before council?"

Llewellyn crumpled up his burger wrapper, his hands trembling slightly. From old age? Or something else? "Leave it be, Sharon. I don't want you to get hurt."

She nailed him with her steady gaze. "When?"

He sighed, his jaw sliding to the side, his gaze the other direction. "Monday."

CHAPTER 11

Kent sat in an early morning staff meeting with Sofia, Van, and two of the part-time teachers, Rudy and Kathy, who hadn't been part of the organization very long.

They were waiting for Christine, who always had one more thing to read, document to sign or phone call to return before joining them.

"So what's been happening with the lobby group?" asked Sofia. "It's been quiet lately. Or have I missed something?"

Van said, "I saw one of them down the block a few days ago with that petition. They just won't stop."

Kent growled. They were like mosquitos, buzzing and buzzing, chipping away at your peace.

Christine walked in. "Okay, so I just heard from Sharon. She made some inquiries at City Hall." She darted a glance in Kent's direction.

Kent's ears tingled. He hadn't seen her for two days. After their moment on the street, he got the feeling she was avoiding him. His messages inquiring about her meeting with the land office guy had gone unanswered. And now she was reporting to Christine and bypassing him completely. What did that mean?

His heart sunk with a crushing disappointment he didn't want to feel. It shouldn't matter. But it did.

Just when he thought they were forging a connection, and could work as a team, she went off on her own and shut him out. He'd have said typical for a woman like that, but she'd hinted at a far more complicated history. One he was now annoyingly curious about. He didn't want more distance between them, but apparently she did.

"It seems the question of this RFP goes before Council for preliminary decision on Monday. Sharon is still trying to get a hint of what the land office recommendation to council will be."

Kent's blood came to an instant boil. "Oh, that's a big mystery I'm sure."

"Don't jump to conclusions. She's taking care of it. This is the reason I wanted legal help."

Breathing deeply to settle his agitation, he leaned in, spoke calmly. "Christine. I know you want what's best for the Society. And I know you want this project to go ahead after all the work we've put into it. But do you really trust this woman to accomplish our goals?"

"Is there some reason we shouldn't?" asked Sofia. "She seems competent to me. I think she's nice."

"Competent?" blurted Kent. "Nice? I wouldn't use those insipid words to describe that woman." Ice princess, more like. Goddess of his nightly dreams. He pushed away the annoying thought. "Besides, we're not inviting her for tea. She needs to understand our cause and be willing to fight for it. So far all she's done is ask polite questions and shuffle papers."

"Give the woman a break, Sawyer," said Van. "She is a lawyer. What did you expect her to do?"

Kent scrubbed his face with his hands. What he wanted and what he could reasonably expect from her were miles apart. That was the problem. On so many levels. He swallowed past the thickness in his throat. "My fear is that Council will railroad this decision through before she does anything at all. If she even plans to."

Christine tapped her pen impatiently on her files. "I trust Arthur's choice implicitly and completely. He knows how important this project is to me. To *us*. He wouldn't have assigned Sharon to us if he didn't believe she could get the job done. Let's have some faith."

Faith. "I can't agree, Christine. For the record, her aloof, elitist manner is not a good fit for our project. Her discomfort and condescension towards our people was so obvious when I took her around I was afraid to leave her alone. I just don't trust her." He ignored the twinge of guilt in his gut when he said those words. Anyway, whatever her history, this is who she was now - cold, elitist. Not a good fit. He'd best remember that.

❧

Kent sat at his desk a half hour later, frustrated. He'd got nowhere trying to persuade Christine to change her mind. She remained unmoved and went on to other agenda items. She wouldn't even consider his suggestion that they rally residents and supporters to attend the Council meeting. She thought they would be too volatile and unpredictable. He thought the ice princess alone would be far too predictable and not volatile enough by half.

He'd no sooner finished the thought when there was a tap at the half-opened door. They all looked up to see Christine standing there, Sharon behind her. She wore a frown and dark sunglasses, though to the best of his memory, the day was overcast.

"Sharon's here," Christine said, turning to her. "Did you want to give the team an update?"

Sharon's expression remained stoic, but Kent had the

powerful impression she'd just closed her eyes behind those dark lenses.

"Mm. I don't want to take up everyone's time. There's nothing much to report yet," she replied, her voice oddly hoarse.

Was she whispering? Her usually clear voice was as raspy as Marlene's after a pack of her Rothman Reds.

Sofia peered curiously up at Sharon and asked, "What can you tell us about the recommendation going to Council Monday?"

Sharon slowly shook her head. Or was it carefully?

Kent pushed his chair back. "Um. Can I have a private word with Sharon?" he said, suspecting she was here to see him. "I can fill you all in later. Everyone has stuff to do."

Christine nodded. "Yes. Good. Do that. I have a class starting." And she disappeared out the door.

Kent squinted at Sofia, Van and the others sitting at their desks, some pretending to work, others staring curiously. "Um. We'll use the meeting room."

Kent led Sharon to the room they had recently vacated and gently closed the door. Giving her a flat, indulgent face to hide the smile that struggled to escape, he turned towards her. Clearing his throat, he stepped up to face her, dipping his chin to study her, then lifted the sunglasses from her face.

"Hey!" Her hand came up to block him, but he was too quick. The rapid movement caused her to wince and grit her teeth on whatever she would have said next.

He tucked the glasses into her silky hair and peered hard into her eyes. He was right.

"You are. You're hung over." Her eyes were red-rimmed and dark circled, her pale complexion greenish. He studied the tiny crow's feet at the corners of her fine blue eyes. Even hung over, she was a beautiful, elegant woman. He chuckled, touching her under the chin with his fingertip, unable to resist the compulsion to touch that soft, translucent skin. "That's what I thought." He pulled out a chair. "Take a load off. I'll get you a hot coffee."

She sank into it like chocolate melting under the sun, slumping with relief.

He snickered all the way to the kitchen and filled a mug with hot black coffee, adding a little milk.

Back in the meeting room, he sat across from Sharon, watching her sip the coffee gratefully, but still being prissy about it, her little finger cocked. Somehow this wasn't a side of this woman he'd expected to see. He tilted his head and studied her while she studiously avoided his gaze. "Something's rattled you, Princess. What's driven you to drink?"

She scowled and lifting her mug like a shield. "It's none of your business. Even if I overindulged a little last night."

"I don't get the sense you had a social evening. More like a little pity party, eh?"

She lifted her chin in defiance. "Still. Private business. No need for you to comment."

He dipped his chin in mock concern. "But I am." He paused, not sure how to broach the subject. *Just dive in.* "The other day, Llewellyn called you Brecht. What was your connection with those people? I know this has something to do with your father. And you know, I can, uh, relate. If you want someone to talk to about what you're going through."

"I don't have to explain myself to you. I'm entitled to my privacy."

This was hard for her. She was so shut down. Kent rubbed a hand over his beard and whispered, "Sure you are." Kent pulled a sad, one-sided smile. "When it doesn't directly affect your performance on my case. Don't you think the fact that just walking into City Hall has you so flustered you went on a bender, might just be my business?" He leaned closer, peering into her eyes. "How are you going to represent us on Monday in front of Council? I believe you've got some issues with that."

"This has nothing to do with any of that. That's in the past." She sniffed, lifting her pointy little chin.

He tilted his head and narrowed his eyes at her prissy pursed lips, screaming sex yet determined to shut him out. "You have heard of the internet, right?"

Her face was a frozen mask of terror, brows flat, her blue eyes darkening with fear.

"It's your choice, Princess. You walk out of here and I'm just going to look it up anyway, and you know what I'll find. You might as well tell me the complete story – Maybe you'd like to give me your spin on it? Either way, I will find out."

Her features sagged in defeat. Her eyes took on a sheen, and she pulled her gorgeous lips between her teeth and bit them, in an effort, he suspected, to control her emotions.

"Look, I know you're feeling delicate today."

She blinked away the threat of tears at his sympathy, or perhaps at the risk of her secrets getting spilled, and sniffed. "And I understand this case has a cruel twist for you personally. But if it dredges up your past and affects you, then it affects me... *us*. Our case. I ought to know the facts."

She nodded, her pupils dilated, her nostrils flaring, her fear tangible.

Kent reached across the table and took her hand in his, brushing his thumb lightly over her knuckles. He lowered his voice to a soft caress. "Well, better anyway, maybe, if you cracked that vault open now? Might make the council meeting easier, huh?"

She swallowed thickly and nodded, setting down her coffee mug. "All right, then. You leave me no choice."

He watched her squirm in her chair, her unfocussed gaze avoiding his as she began.

"This was twenty-four years ago. My father had been a popular shop steward, involved in the community. Then he was a councillor and his popularity grew. He was the champion of the little people." She gave a wan, watery smile. "Everyone loved him."

Her voice broke on the last words, and his throat ached seeing evidence of how much her father meant to her.

"Then, after a few years, suddenly, he was accused of corruption. They said he used his position on council to direct work to his friends, and to his own construction company. The land office was implicated also, suggesting that some City properties had been mis-allocated, along with funds from the Engineering department."

Her fingers twisted together, turning her knuckles white, and she spoke woodenly, as though she had to force every word out. He watched her smooth brow pulse with the effort.

Kent leaned in to cover her knotted hands with his own, stroking gently. As he scooted forward, their knees bumped, and he left his there, just brushing hers. He enjoyed touching her, and he hoped it was comforting. He appreciated how these events had shaped her, his heart squeezing in sympathy. "He was actually… guilty then?"

She shrugged, tears welling in her big blue eyes like the sky mirrored in puddles after a rain. "That's what the evidence said, despite Daddy's protests to the contrary. When it all came out, he lost his position in disgrace. The press were all over it, which was… awful." Her voice had dropped to a choked whisper.

"But it got much worse than that. Multiple parties had sued him. He lost his union post. Eventually, he even lost his company and filed for bankruptcy. We'd… Mom, and me, were raked through the mud along with him. And they vilified him in the newspapers. People were so angry. They felt betrayed." It was obvious from her anguished tone and expression that she had also felt betrayed by her father.

It seems he charmed and beguiled everyone, including his daughter. She was just an ordinary carefree kid. She'd had nothing resembling the privileged upbringing he'd originally assumed, though he gathered the financial as well as social fall had been steep. He felt sorry for her, being dragged through all that humiliation, exposed to the public eye under such negative circumstances.

He would have been only nine years old, an oblivious kid growing up in North Van, more interested in Pokémon than politics.

"How old were you?"

"Thirteen, by then. Eventually, to settle legal claims, we lost our house and moved across town."

Kent felt enormously guilty that he'd judged her so harshly without knowing her. It wasn't like him to assume the worst of someone he'd just met, but he'd been off balance by her. In a perverse way, it relieved him there was more to her than he'd thought. It meant there was a heart under that hard shell. Even though it was a wounded heart. It made her more human, and his uncontrollable attraction to her less troubling.

He tried to recall what his relationship with his own father was like when he was just thirteen. He'd still been innocent, he thought. Clueless.

"So you never were married, the way Llewellyn assumed. Sharon Brecht, eh?"

"No," she scoffed. Her head shook slightly from side to side, her gaze turned inwards. She drew a deep breath. "I just couldn't bear the name Brecht anymore. I changed my name legally. I'm not... her... anymore."

He shot her a sympathetic look, watching for her reaction. "It wasn't your fault. What was wrong with that girl, that you had to erase her, huh?"

They stared at each other through a long, tense silence. He'd offered the olive branch. It was up to her to accept it.

"I – " She shook her head, a tiny rapid jiggle, like she fought a war with herself. "I just needed distance. From all that. From my history."

The pulse in her neck fluttered like a moth's wing. If he'd wanted to breach her defences, he'd just figured out how. Somehow, though, he didn't relish that idea anymore. He squinted. "I won't tell anyone."

She pulled her lips between her teeth, and he detected a slight tremor before she pulled her shoulders back, lifted her chin and slid her dark glasses back on.

But it only proved his point that bureaucrats and politicians weren't trustworthy. As Sharon had learned the hard way, sadly. Trying to navigate that snake-pit was no way to solve problems. You could never play by their rules and win. They shouldn't be clashing over this. They should be on the same side.

Well. She may not have been born with a silver spoon in her mouth, but she'd aligned herself with her father's enemies.

"All right, then. So mingling with these bureaucrats unnerves you. I get it. What are we going to do about it?"

"I have to present to council on Monday. And Councillor Seibold will be there. And he... And I know..." She faltered.

"What?"

"The meeting with Carter was a dead end. Then I caught up with Mr. Llewellyn again."

He dipped his chin, listening, waiting.

"Well, other than the detail of Monday's presentation, I got nothing concrete out of him, either. But I am wondering. So..."

"So...?"

"I have an idea." She nodded sharply, as if to reassure herself.

"Which is?" Why was she so cold? *Come on, Princess. I know your secrets. Let's work together here.*

"That's what I came in to tell you. Even if Carter strongly favours S & S's proposal, which I think we ought to prepare for, I can buy us more time by filing a civil settlement with the City for breach of contract, demanding damages in lieu of."

He sighed. She was back to business, battlements intact. "Which will do what?"

"Once I register the file with the Court, after I present my case and table the complaint, they won't be able to approve the contract with S & S. I'll challenge Council – though I haven't got a lot of time to prepare. They can hear presentations, but not decide anything. If I speak up and oppose any rush decision, and lay out the Pathway Society's position, Council will have to take it under advisement and postpone the vote."

"What if they do it, anyway? Wouldn't it be a good idea to bring some support? Have some more vocal opposition present? Call in some press, maybe, so they can't slither away?" He lifted his brows, begging her to agree. "That'll keep them in line."

"It's unnecessary. This is enough to hold them off them for now."

"Are you sure? One hundred percent certain?"

Her lips twisted, trying to look severe, instead revealing her doubts.

He spoke slowly, through clenched teeth, trying to hang on to his patience. "It'd be safer, don't you think, to get support? What if they're all in on it together? What if they force it through? It'll be too late." Lord, she was stubborn. His jaw cramped from tension, sending pain shooting through his temples. He just couldn't get anywhere with her.

"No. I don't think so." She stood up, her chin lifted. "Don't get paranoid and start imagining conspiracies. It would be best if you let me handle this, Kent. I know what I'm doing. Don't muddy the water with your activism."

The water was already murky in his view. Kent rubbed his forehead in exasperation, not knowing what to think. Or maybe he had it all wrong. Maybe she was buddies with City staff and Council now that she'd changed brands. Maybe he really couldn't trust her, even more than he'd first thought. "I'd rather have some insurance, just the same." He stood up and followed her to the door. She sure was in a hurry to get out of here. "Wait!" There was so much he didn't yet know. "Did you talk to S & S? Do you know who they are? Are they behind the lobby groups?"

Sharon put her hand out, palm facing him, and he stopped in

his tracks, leaning back. Her face was a closed book. Fine. He got the message. She slipped out the door, stopping and turning back.

"Those questions are for after the deferral. That's exactly why I'm not rushing our challenge. We'll have time to prepare."

"It's not too late to organize a small protest." He held up his forefinger and thumb, just a centimetre apart. He flashed her a teasing grin, hoping to melt her icy stare. "I even know someone at the Sun."

"Leave it." Her full lips pursed into a frown of disapproval. "Trust me, the last thing we need is a public scandal."

"The press isn't the enemy, Sharon. Not when you're on the right side of the law." Whoops. Her sudden pallor told him he'd overstepped.

She shook her head and spun away, marching to the door without another word, her heels clicking on the floor.

His heart felt like it had shrunk along with his hope. "See you later, Princess."

Kent shoved his hands into his pockets and chewed his lip. No matter what she said, he knew the vocal NIMBY lobby group would be there in numbers. The society needed supporters of their own. They needed to make a show of strength. And, he suspected, his nervous Ice Princess might need a little support.

"Oooh, this is just what I needed," Sharon moaned, leaning her head back, closing her eyes as she sunk back into her overstuffed sofa cushions, her feet up on the coffee table.

"Me too. Enough performing for one week."

It was Saturday night, and her best friend Rachel Sharpe sat with her ankles crossed beside her, all angled elbows and shoulders and knees, somehow still gorgeous as sin despite her casual off the shoulder cotton sweater, leggings and bare but perfectly pedicured feet. Sharon was happy to be wearing her favourite flannel pyjamas and fluffy socks, her face scrubbed clean, beauty and elegance be damned.

When Rachel called to suggest they hang out tonight, casual girls' night, instead of going out for dinner and clubbing, as they sometimes did, Sharon welcomed the idea. They'd relax, have a few drinks, watch a cheesy legal thriller and have a friendly catch up.

"Margaritas. My blender," she'd quickly replied, as much because Rachel's condo was too perfectly un-lived-in and modern to be comfy as because she was too damned whacked to go out. A little down time chilling with her BFF would calm and centre her so she could be stronger for the dreaded Council meeting come Monday evening.

At the moment, she was still terrified she'd have no influence, or worse, be a laughingstock for daring to set foot in the place that had been the theatre of her family's ruin, attempting to negotiate for "the people". It was ludicrous. Her father's cause was the working class and street poor and they had shown him to be a hypocrite, liar, cheat and thief. Why would they take his daughter seriously?

"You make the best frozen margaritas," Rachel hummed, slurping back a big gulp of the treat.

"I do," Sharon agreed. "Years of practice, you know." They share a laugh. They'd been practicing this ritual for many years now, ever since law school had thrown them together and they'd found they'd had so much in common.

"Rough week, hon?" Rachel asked, eyeing her now.

She sighed. Reliving her history, having Kent discover her past, upset her far more than she let on. She really didn't want him knowing her ugly secrets. Why she cared so much she didn't know, but she felt raw and unsteady, like her very foundations were cracked.

Recent events had shaken her. More than she realized until the big confession to Kent on Friday morning. Pressure had been building up inside her, pressing down, until she was walking around ready to shatter at the slightest provocation, like a glass doll.

He'd been so sweet. So compassionate as he'd listened to her tell it, even though he'd practically brow-beaten her to get it out of her. She was angry, and somehow grateful at the same time. It made it easier to talk about it, as if letting it out had let off some pressure that had been building. He was right about that.

But it left her feeling like a deflated balloon abandoned in a hot playground.

"Yes. It's been... extraordinary. But not in the usual way."

Sharon straightened. "Meacham's got me on this *pro-bono* case, and I'm forced to fight it out at City Hall."

Rachel went still, her large hazel eyes bugging, her gaze sliding over dramatically. "On purpose?"

"I can only assume so." Sharon recalled her conversation with Meacham the first day of the case. "Yes. I have to say yes, he's trying to test me somehow."

"Are you passing?"

"Too soon to say. It doesn't feel like it right now." Her insides felt heavy and gluey, like her organs had forgotten their jobs and were all laying about in a pile at the bottom of her gut.

Other than her mother and Arthur Meacham, and now, unfortunately, Kent Sawyer, Rachel was the only person in her life that knew her past. Who else could she talk to, be herself with, that would understand what this case meant, and help her piece herself back together?

Their Netflix show paused, Sharon waited for Rachel to return from the bathroom, probably purging their delicious drinks, while Sharon was all too happy to let the tequila infiltrate her bloodstream and her brain cells. Reflecting on Friday's confession, she felt dragged out, lethargic, a little headachey, as though she were coming down with the flu. Or maybe that was the effect of the margaritas combined with a brutal week.

Rachel returned. Before they resumed the show, Sharon asked, "Anything new on the... mating front? Dating any new hot prospects?"

Rachel rolled her eyes. "I know perfectly well that you're not interested in my sex life, Sharon."

It's true. Sharon wasn't interested in Rachel's endless string of one-night stands and illicit workplace flings. She was digging for news of her daughter.

"At least you have one," Sharon quipped. "If I don't hear it from you, I have to read about it."

They laughed.

Then Rachel stiffened, pulled in her chin and made that tight face that Sharon recognized meant that she was uncomfortable.

"I saw her," she said cryptically. "The first time since I moved back to Vancouver." She hitched a thin shoulder.

Rachel never wanted to discuss her failed marriage and the daughter that now lived with her father and new step-mother Kate. It shocked Sharon that she'd taken the bait. It must bother her.

Sharon cleared her throat and took a sip of her margarita, meeting her friend's gaze gently. If there was one thing she could empathize with it was shame. "And? Something change there? You thinking of regular visits or something?"

Rachel's mouth puckered thoughtfully. "No." Rachel lifted one bony shoulder again. "Maybe. She's getting older. I don't think she needs me at all. And I feel like a fifth wheel."

A surprisingly honest admission coming from Rachel. More like a sixth wheel. Since Simon had married Kate, they'd had two children of their own to add to the family that Simon had started with Rachel ten years ago.

Sharon pondered that. "A daughter always needs her mother, and you'll always be that, no matter how great Kate is. If you don't reconnect with her now, it'll be twice as hard once she's a teenager."

Rachel pulled a face, barely creasing her smooth botoxed brow. "She seems to have enough of the hormonal thing going on already. I'm sure she despises me. She's probably better off with the ever-loving Kate anyway, you know?"

"Well, she's your daughter. You'll find a way if you want to. You're unstoppable." Sharon pushed off the sofa. "Refill?"

"You know it."

Sharon took their glasses to the kitchen and buzzed the blender to revive their iced drinks, refilling both glasses.

An image of Simon suddenly sprang to mind. She pondered all the years she'd swooned and schemed over Simon, an intelligent, philosophical and gentle man whom Sharon had always admired, and secretly lusted over. The ex-husband of her friend Rachel, Simon was everything her father was not, and therefore, exactly what she thought she wanted.

In Sharon's secret opinion, Rachel had thrown away the perfect family. Marriage to the perfect gentleman, and the elusive and befuddling question of motherhood checked off. Sharon always felt that Rachel could have juggled her career and the rest, if she'd wanted to. But she hadn't wanted to. Or couldn't. Perhaps understandably, given her own family history.

She was sad that her friend was incapable of appreciating her perfect family. She thought she would have been happy stepping into Rachel's shoes after she and Simon separated and become step-mother to sweet Madison. But even before Rachel had divorced him, he'd reconnected with his old flame from university. It was never to be. She now realized that though Simon had been her type, she was not his. Instead, he'd chosen Kate, and Sharon hadn't seriously thought about marriage ever since.

Seeming to read her mind, Rachel asked, "What about you? Succumbing to the charms of your new partner yet? What's his name?"

Sharon pulled in her chin. "Dariush. And no. I told you I will never get involved with someone who I work…" her voice trailed off as her thoughts wandered to Kent. He didn't work at her firm, but they were colleagues. Lusting after a client was even worse, wasn't it? Not as if that had ever held back Rachel, who slept with whoever she wanted, whenever she wanted to, and dusted off her hands on the way out the door.

"Sha-ron?" Rachel's voice held laughter and teasing as she egged her on. "What aren't you telling me?"

"Huh?" What had she said?

"Is there someone else at work who's got your attention?"

Sharon sucked her lips between her teeth, humming, deter-mined not to spill tea. Met with her friend's sharp, amused, all-seeing gaze, and remembering that this was a safe space, she finally admitted. "I do rather have the hots for the young social worker I just met. But it's nothing." She huffed and waved a dismissive hand, downplaying the force of attraction that had her in its sweaty grip. "I won't be going there either."

For Sharon, rules and boundaries were everything. She couldn't risk being exposed for making mistakes in correct behaviour or moral judgement. If she relaxed her vigilance, broke or bent a rule on a whim or to satisfy a fleeting urge, however potent, then she'd be just like her father. Weak. Corrupt. Shameful.

∼

Organized as usual, Sharon arrived early at Council chambers, determined to stay calm and in control. The moment she entered these familiar walls, however, she had to fight the ghosts. The sound of her father's laughter, the rhythm of debate, punctuation by the shuffling silence and murmur of bureaucracy.

She had prepared all day for the evening Council meeting. *You've got this!* Sitting near the front but not right at the front, she kept a low profile, pressing down the rising tide of panic.

She'd also filled in a speaker card for when the Property Department agenda item came up. Glancing around, she noticing the chairs had filled and people were crowding the back of the room, the whispered hum of conversation muffled by the dark-burgundy carpet and upholstered wall panels with their softly glowing recessed lighting.

She studied the spotlit faces of the councillors who sat around the long curved head table, each behind their own microphone. Mayor Taylor's seat was still vacant. Most were new people she recognized from recent municipal elections but didn't know personally. There were only a couple who had been around back then. Most notably, Gus Seibold, who was also on council with her father.

How old he looked. How could he still be sitting on council after all these years? He'd have been forty-something years old then. He should be in a retirement home.

The thought shook her. Her body tensed. Her father was a similar age. He would have been sixty-nine this year. Is that what Dad would have looked like now? Balding and jowled? Probably retired and enjoying a weekly golf game, or fishing trips with Mr. Llewellyn. She bit her lip as her mouth flooded with salty tears. This place rattled her. She had to hold it together.

Shaking off the sudden flood of emotion, she reviewed the agenda, looking for anything controversial. So many routine items went by unnoticed, it wasn't all that often there was a showdown at City Hall. Not that she'd been here lately. But some things never changed.

One never knew how quickly or painfully slowly proceedings would go. The agenda was long and they could be here for any reason. Any reason at all.

They were twelfth on the agenda, the last item for the night, assuming they got through the list without getting deferred. Breathing slowly and evenly, she waited through one dull vote after another, largely ignoring the monotonous presentations and discussions while mentally rehearsing her comments. Though the Mayor, Councillors and presenters had microphones, voices and volumes were hushed and sedate inside these panelled walls.

Suddenly there was a commotion at the back of the room.

"Leggo me!"

"Come on, let's go."

"Hey, stop that!"

Sharon turned to the back. Bodies were shoving and shuffling. A few people stood up, blocking her view. Then she saw a security guard holding onto someone. A scruffy looking older man with a long grey beard.

"What's the problem here?"

Sharon gasped at the sound of Kent's familiar voice. Her pulse kicked up. What was he doing? The discussion by the councillors had paused until security settled the disruption, so she stood up to see better. There he was in his familiar read plaid shirt. Heat flooded her body as her heartbeat pounded. She told him not to come, never mind bring his weird street people. They couldn't help, and would likely disrupt the proceedings entirely. It wasn't uncommon for delays to cause agenda items to be deferred a week or two. Had he thought about that?

Though, in this case, that wouldn't be a bad thing, would it? Alternatively, if it annoyed Council, they could curtail discussion and force the vote through.

Kent's presence irritated her, not least because he would watch to see how she coped.

She turned to see how the councillors were reacting to the fuss, peering at their faces. It amused a couple, a few seemed bored and patient – she was sure they'd seen it all before – and old Gus Seibold sitting like Jabba the Hut, his jowls quivering and his sagging skin going splotchy. He, at least, seemed to prefer no interruptions.

Kent spoke in low tones to the security guard, who at last agreed to release the old man and permit him to stay. Kent stayed behind him along the back wall. Before everyone sat down, Sharon recognized a few more rough faces from the Downtown Eastside. She laughed under her breath. He never abandoned his people.

Excusing herself as she squeezed between people, she moved to the back of the room. Sidling up alongside Kent, she hissed under her breath, "I told you I'd handle this. What do you think you're doing?"

Kent looked up slowly, his mouth pulling into a flat line

without a glimmer of humour. "You do your thing. I'll do mine. You can't stop citizens from attending council meetings. It's their right. It happens all the time, so deal with it."

"What's wrong with you? Don't you want me to help you?" she hissed.

"Humph. Sure I do. I just don't believe you'll succeed continuing the way you are." He finally looked at her, his expression softening, his eyes narrowing. "You doing okay with this?"

She lifted her chin. "Of course."

He shook his head. "The only way to fight bureaucracy and systemic corruption is to organize the people. We need the voices of supporters on the street to counter the local condo owners lobby group."

"I'm a very experienced lawyer, Kent. Your lack of faith in me is unjustified."

"We'll see if you can pull it off." Huffing through his nose, he turned away from her to speak with the old man.

"Who's that then?" Sharon asked.

He ignored her. Fine. If he was going to be like that there was nothing she could do. She'd proceed according to plan, and he could be damned. She shuffled back to the front of the room, but someone had taken her chair. With nowhere to sit, she had no choice but to return to the back of the room and stand with the others. Kent continued to ignore her, so she returned the favour. Sweat had accumulated under her arms and between her breasts.

It felt like forever, but finally their item number was called. The City Clerk stood and summarized the matter for the general public and council. Then Sam Carter stood at the staff microphone and went through the proposals. It turned out there was a third party who'd responded to the request for proposals, but there wasn't much information available, so it sounded to Sharon like it wasn't very serious. Or perhaps they were ill prepared. Maybe even just padding to deflect the fact there were two major projects vying for the property.

Sam outlined their project too, though she wasn't happy with the amount of information he provided, and then he went into considerable detail about the S & S project proposal. That he concluded by recommending the S & S project did not surprise her.

Then came the applicant presentations. After a brief and confusing presentation by the third applicant, the clerk called on the Pathway Society and Sharon stepped forward, just as Kent did the same.

They stared at each other.

"I thought I was doing this?" she murmured under her breath as they jockeyed for the podium, elbow to elbow. "Christine didn't tell me you were speaking."

"You can speak afterwards," he whispered.

"Is there a problem?" the clerk enquired.

"No sir," answered Kent. He presented the background information about the Downtown Eastside, the society and its mandate, the kids in their care and the specific challenges that led to the proposed transition housing project proposal. He also summed up the complex web of approvals and funding sources that made the project possible and finished by touching on why this building and location were critical for their project.

One councillor asked a question for clarification and Kent answered it concisely and knowledgeably.

He was impressive, articulate and persuasive, and fit a lot into the five-minute time limit. When he glanced over to her with a lift of his brow, she nodded in concession. He knew so much more about the history of the project and could speak to its significance with far more passion that she could have. Fine. She'd stick to the legal dispute then, when her turn came.

Kent returned to stand next to the old man, bending to whisper something in his ear. Next up was the representative for S & S. Sharon stood back, her stomach twisting, studying the back of the familiar man who stepped forward. He was not tall, but stocky, like an aging athlete. He wore an expensive custom suit, his golden blond hair gelled back. Until he spoke, Sharon wasn't sure it was Matthew Seibold. But there was no doubt about it. It was him.

He spoke confidently but lazily, adding little information to what Sam Carter had already outlined, speaking in developer rhetoric and dwelling on the highest and best use of the land in question, as if reporting that phrase made it true. He ended by highlighting the firm support their project had garnered with the local community, as represented by at least two resident's associations from nearby condominium projects. When he gestured to the audience, light applause broke out.

"Quiet please," the clerk demanded.

Old man Seibold cleared his throat and leaned toward his microphone. "Can you clarify for us, please, if the ratio of market to non-market housing units meets the provincial targets, Mr. Seibold?"

What a sham. Of course they did. Carter had already made that point. How ridiculous to bring it up again. So much for staying out of his son's business. It was just a play to draw attention away from the moving story that Kent had told. And what was Seibold doing questioning his own son, anyway? He should abstain from the entire discussion, not just the vote. If it came to that.

"Now which members of the public wish to speak to any of these proposals?"

Ahead of her were two or three of the condominium lobbyists, who had arrived even earlier than she had to add their names to the speaker's list.

As Matthew stepped away from the podium, he walked to the rear of the room and passed close to Sharon. She held her breath and her pulse kicked up. The likelihood that he'd recognize her was very slim. It was his father she worried about.

At the last moment, he turned his head to glance at her,

flashing an oily, flirty smile. But at the last second, his smile fell, and he peered closely at her. "Do I know you?"

As usual, her outward chill hid a racing heart and flustered emotions. Thankfully, she had a disciplined mind and had cultivated self-control. She shook her head and spoke in her coolest, most officious tone. "I don't believe so." She moved towards the podium. It was true. Though they'd once been classmates, he didn't know her. He hadn't known her as a teenager, and he certainly didn't know her now.

Once the last of the lobby group had said their piece, it was her turn.

Before she could step up, the old man with the long beard stepped up to the mic. "Excuse me," she said. "I believe I'm up next."

The clerk said, "Dr. Drummond is on the speaker's list ahead of you, Ms. Beckett."

Dr. Drummond? She stepped back, stunned, and shot a glance toward Kent, who stood politely, hands clasped in front, waiting for his friend to speak.

What happened next astonished her. And she supposed it served her right for making assumptions about people based on their appearance. She could tell the security guard who tried to toss the old man out – and everyone else in the room – were equally surprised.

Dr. Drummond started by introducing his credentials, with a summary of an illustrious medical career. His voice trembled, but he spoke eloquently. In very few words, he related his tragic family history, how he lost his family, his health and his wealth, and ended up living in an SRO on Hastings Street, struggling every day with mental health challenges and an enduring addiction to painkillers and alcohol. Then he shared his heartbreaking experiences getting to know his neighbours over the years, and how they each had a similarly sad tale to share.

The murmuring assent of voices from the rear of the room rose and fell as he made his points.

Finally, he talked about the children. How so many of them found themselves homeless, without parents or protectors, struggling to survive on the street, learning hard lessons about life from the people who were least able to guide them. How interventions to get these kids off the street and give them a fighting chance at a whole and healthy life was the best use of every dollar, and every resource our society could muster. And though he imagined the S & S developers thought they were doing good works by building a handful of low-income rental apartments, this was not what his community needed most.

When he finished, applause broke out from the back of the room, with cheers, whistles and murmurs of support. This sent Carter and the security guards into a tizzy as they reprimanded and hushed the crowd.

Sharon stood mute, processing the man's words, trying valiantly to swallow the lump in her throat, and hold back her tears.

"You're up," Kent said, stepping close.

CHAPTER 13

"Huh?"

She seemed to be in a trance. Kent gripped her arm. "I said you're up next. You'd better get up there and do your thing, Madam Counsel." He touched her hand, ever so briefly, in support. It was cold as ice, and yet he saw a gleam of perspiration on her upper lip.

After Sharon had left on Friday, he returned to his desk and conducted a little follow up research. He started by googling Vancouver City Hall and that name – Peter Brecht.

What came up was more extensive and shocking than he expected. Twenty-four years ago it was a huge news story.

Sharon strolled to the podium, waiting a beat and watching council before speaking. Councillors mumbled and whispered, their heads bent together, but it was impossible to tell if they knew her, or had a position on the property.

Her father Peter Brecht had been something of a local celebrity. Son of immigrants, owner of a large construction company that he'd built from scratch, he'd been very active in the local trade union. He'd segued that role into a position on City

Council, making it his mission to be a champion of the working poor.

There had been a real shakedown at City Hall, and in the construction industry. No wonder she didn't do construction and property law.

Then the family vanished, except for a discrete obituary for Peter Brecht, only a decade later.

There'd been no hits for Sharon Brecht, except a brief mention in some school choir concert. She'd disappeared too. Then he'd searched for Sharon Beckett, and that was a different story. This time she shone in a quiet, dignified way. Honour roll, art and music, academic scholarships, sororities, charities, volunteer positions. It all reeked of upper class privilege, an image she had cultivated out of thin air. She'd metamorphosed from a caterpillar into a butterfly.

She was like the lump of crude coal that, under immense heat and pressure, transformed into a small hard sparkling diamond. She really was an ice princess. Just not the kind of ice he'd first meant.

"Mayor Taylor, Councillors, my name is Sharon Beckett, with the legal firm Flannigan, Searle, Meacham, Beckett and Shirazi, and I'm legal counsel for the Pathway Society. You've heard a great deal of moving and persuasive information this evening regarding the project proposal before you. I'm sure there is much you'd like to discuss between you, before you put the matter to a vote, despite the strong, although I would argue, unbalanced, recommendation of Mr. Carter of the City Property Department."

Kent smiled. She was very effective, his ice princess. You'd never expect such a prissy little thing to have such a commanding presence. If he didn't know better, she might almost intimidate him.

She paused. There was more murmuring, but the general

tone, though curious and excited, didn't give any sign which way they'd go should the matter come to a vote.

"I'm here to add one more critical piece of information for your consideration, and that is that the Property Department, and Council, have on many previous occasions, made commitments to my client that make up a legally binding contractual promise. I have documentation here…" she held up a sheaf of papers, "… which traces the history of dealings between my client, the Pathway Society, and the City over the past three years regarding this exact property. I also have…" She held up a second stack of papers, "… evidence supporting the extensive damages my client would suffer should the City renege on those commitments, significantly incapacitating my client's project to the point of failure."

She paused for effect. And for breath. He couldn't tell if she was trying to railroad them or just eager to get the whole thing over with.

The fat old councillor, Gus Seibold, leaned towards his mic to speak, but stopped. He scowled and squinted at Sharon in a way that made Kent think maybe he found her familiar. Maybe he did, if he'd known her well enough back when her father was on council.

The Property guy, Sam Carter, returned to the mic, and Seibold leaned back, instead choosing to whisper into the ear of the councillor sitting next to him. "Thank you, Ms. Beckett. I would remind you, Mr. Mayor and Council, and point out for the benefit of the citizens attending, that however that may be the case, the City retains ultimate jurisdiction over the allocation and use of its properties, and is at liberty to change its mind about the best use of that property. Particularly if additional information or improved options present themselves. So even if what you have said is true, it should have no bearing on Council's vote here tonight."

She stood even taller, pushing her shoulders back. "I beg to differ, Mr. Carter. The last document I'd like to table tonight is this." She held up the document. "This is a copy, for the City's records, of a Notice of Civil Claim for breach of property contract and complaint against the City that was filed this afternoon with the Supreme Court of British Columbia on behalf of my client. Until this matter is resolved satisfactorily by the courts, the City is not, in fact, free to decide about this property. I hope this delay will provide you, Mr. Mayor and Council, adequate time to review and consider these additional factors. Thank you."

She immediately stepped away from the podium, swaying a little, and handed the paperwork to Carter. Kent stepped closer, reaching for her arm.

"Hey – "

But she turned and rushed past him, obviously in a hurry to get out of there.

Seibold looked aghast but said nothing. Kent suspected he'd rather have it out with Carter and his cronies *in camera* rather than in public. If he hadn't figured out who she was yet, he soon would.

She wasn't someone you could ignore. Faced with what he knew was stressful for her – she was formidable, determined, with nerves of steel, and a sharp intellect – and though he'd dismissed her professional efforts, obviously a highly skilled and ruthless opponent. He was very glad that despite their different methods, they were on the same team. Between them, they'd thrown a wrench into whatever crooked plans these guys had made. They made an excellent team. The only danger was that the little ball of fire and ice would walk away with his heart.

❧

Sharon rushed out of the council meeting, intent on getting as far away from Kent, his crazies, Sam Carter and the Seibold family as fast as humanly possible. She was at the end of her tether, barely holding on to her self-control, her carefully designed persona, and her emotions after that hornets' nest of a meeting.

People crowded the polished marble foyer. The golden light from the Art Déco wall sconces was glaring after the dimly lit cave of council chambers. Some citizens had already spilled out from chambers, but there were additional bodies here, milling instead of moving on. Some, perhaps, from another event, but quite a few more residents of the Downtown Eastside, by the looks of it. Perhaps they hadn't fit, or had arrived late, or maybe they weren't allowed in. There was to be no quick escape. She felt like she was trapped at a networking cocktail party from hell.

"Wait!" Kent jogged up beside her.

Damn it! She wanted to get away from him most of all. Away from all of them.

"Hey, don't run off. I want to thank you."

"What?" Not what she was expecting from Mr. Sarcastic and Cynical.

Kent tapped her lightly on the arm, and his touch was incongruously comforting. "Your presentation impressed me. It was cool to see you in action, doing your lawyer thing. You're so forceful and stylish, with a punch at the end. So… congratulations. You really knocked it to them."

She stared at him. She'd stormed out, feeling frustrated and angry with him for undermining her presentation and strategy with his antics. She wanted to tell him off, but the fury inside her waned as she studied his earnest and familiar face.

"Sharon? I said… you're really something. I didn't know you could do that."

Still unresolved in her feelings, she hesitated further, unable to speak.

Dr. Drummond sidled up to Kent's side. Kent stood several inches taller than the old, hunched man. A wave of sympathy rushed her as she recalled his tragic story. She offered him a sad smile.

"Ms. Beckett. I hope we're not imposing. I urged Kent to introduce me to you. I wanted to compliment you on your presentation. Very effective!" He smiled, his long grey beard parting to reveal a glimpse of yellowed teeth. He dressed like a professor down on his luck, with a dirty shirt, a mangled old tie that had no shape, and a tweed jacket stretched out at the elbows. All his clothes were baggy and well-worn, as though he slept in them but never washed them. She frowned. Perhaps that was true. He said he lived in a Single Room Occupancy hotel, but that was barely better than being homeless, wasn't it? Where had Kent found this conundrum of a man?

"Dr. Drummond. A pleasure," she said.

Kent looked on, smiling.

Dr. Drummond offered his hand, and determined not to insult him by hesitating or cringing, she shook it firmly. It was warm and smooth and sturdy, the way her father's broad hands had felt. Safe and self-assured. He too had been a shorter, stockier man. She looked up to catch the doctor's grin and the twinkle in his eye. "Please call me Carl. I only use Dr. Drummond when I'm trying to impress." He shot a glance back at the council chamber with a smirk.

She pulled her hand back and quickly adjusted the lapel on her coat to give herself something to look at. She swallowed, uncertain what to say next. "I appreciated your comments, too, Carl." She nodded. "You've got great insight into the heart of the community and its people."

Kent shuffled closer to her until his arm rubbed her shoulder slightly, and he turned a few degrees until she felt his body shielding her. She thought this was his deliberate way of reassuring her, touching her in a way that seemed accidental but wasn't. He set a hand lightly at the small of her back, further enclosing her in his protective force field.

"Your presentation was also very good. Excellent timing," Sharon countered. There was admiration and genuine warmth in his dark melting gaze, along with a little playful teasing. He had a way of disarming her even as he was making fun of her. Maybe that's how he was so laid back and comfortable with everybody he met. His ease and unconditional acceptance made everyone he encountered feel safe and seen.

Well, most people. Whenever he was around, she found herself flustered and on edge, both drawn to him and worried.

She nodded and attempted to smile, but she was too tense. Her face wouldn't cooperate, and it fell back into the fixed lines that formed a part of the shield she wore every day – especially days like today, that rubbed her raw and made her feel that every scary and shameful detail of her life was hanging out for the world to examine and criticize, like a long line of not-quite-clean laundry flapping in the wind.

She withdrew behind her comforting wall of stiffness and propriety. "I'm sorry to hear about your heartbreaking life story, Carl. But it was very generous of you to come out tonight and share it to help with the project."

"Ah, well, everyone in our neighbourhood has a heartbreaking story, Ms. Beckett." He set a hand on Kent's shoulder. "But like our Kent here, I take my grief and channel it into good works, to act as an advocate for those less fortunate, and less able to communicate their needs."

Grief?

She frowned, processing his words. Another reference to Kent's past that made her want to know more.

Deflecting, she said, "It turned out all right, but I much prefer to go in with a pre-planned strategy and stick to it, not get caught out with unexpected curve balls. It could have thrown me." She peered at Kent, so he understood she directed her criticism at him and not Carl. "I don't appreciate that. I feel that there was too much chaos and noise, and that may undermine the effectiveness of my approach. We'll see what kind of response we get over the next day or two. I may have prevented them from taking a vote tonight, but they still have weapons in their arsenal they can use against us."

"So do we." Kent shook his head, one side of his mouth curling up. "And just because you didn't see it coming doesn't mean I didn't plan it." He touched her under the chin with a fingertip, sending shivers racing down her neck, over her shoulders and down her ribs. She wished he'd stop doing that. Or her head did. Parts farther south got a flutter whenever he did and begged for more. "We may have different styles, Princess, but I think we make an excellent team."

Dr. Drummond – Carl – chuckled under his breath.

Sharon's face and neck tingled at Kent's stupid, insulting pet name for her. Her nostrils flared as she hissed through her teeth, "I've asked you repeatedly not to call me that. It's insulting."

This only caused Kent's beard to spread apart into a broad grin, showing his white teeth and disarming her with his good looks. "You might think so, but I know what I'm talking about. There's no need to take it as an insult. I'm complimenting you."

She huffed, pulling her shoulders back and lifting her chin. "Hardly. Ms. Beckett would sound more respectful. Especially coming from you."

Kent bent his head and smiled at Carl, to her mounting horror. "Ms. Beckett has known her share of heartbreak, too, Carl. I call her my Ice Princess, because life has hardened her into a sharp, sparkling diamond." Kent's sparkling gaze jumped to hers knowingly.

"Ah." Carl smiled and nodded.

Sharon gasped. "How dare – "

Kent squeezed her arm and wrapped his arm around her affectionately, cutting off her protest with a tiny jerk. He tipped his head toward her and peered into her eyes, calming and exciting her at once. His warm, masculine scent enveloped her. He always smelled of fresh laundry and coffee, despite always being as rumpled as his clients. Just like the first day they'd met when he'd wrapped her in his shirt, and then that intense moment on the street by her car when a powerful, overwhelming shock wave had turned her nerves inside out. It was fast becoming her favourite scent in the world.

He froze, feeling the energy between them too, and they locked eyes. She went from stiff to swooning, cold to hot in an instant, her mouth suddenly dry, her limbs weak. He swallowed, blinked, and swayed toward her, his eyes dropping to her mouth.

At that precise moment, the sneering voice of Matthew Seibold cut into their private world. "I thought I recognized you!"

She flinched, and Kent pulled back but kept his arm around her shoulders.

They both turned to stare at the slick blond man in the designer suit.

"Well, well. If it isn't little Sharon Brecht." He nodded and his lips pulled up from his large straight teeth in a grotesque imitation of a friendly smile. When she didn't respond, he kept staring, his expression pure aggressive disdain and arrogance.

"You must be mistaken," Kent said, his voice calm and low, threatening. But the idiot didn't take the hint.

Matt jiggled his head, his lip curling. "I don't think so. Maybe you aren't aware of who your little lawyer girlfriend really is." He swung his creepy gaze back to Sharon, letting it rake her from top to bottom. "This lady here is my old classmate Sharon. Aren't you, sweetheart? Look at you, all grown up. You turned out to be a regular swan, now didn't you?"

He might as well have called her an ugly duckling while he was at it. What a nasty backhanded compliment.

Although they attended the same high school, they came from very different walks of life. He was now, as then, an arrogant, entitled jerk who never gave little Sharon Brecht the time of day until the spotlight had shone its ugly light on her family.

A boy who had it all, he'd happily lorded it over her, and then gleefully tortured her with cruel words and deeds when her happy and humble world came crashing down. He hadn't changed. But she had.

"I go by Sharon Beckett now. And I am not now, nor have I ever been your sweetheart, Matthew Seibold."

He chuckled. "Well, maybe not, Sharon. But I still know who you are. And if you think you will block my project with your uppity little disguise of respectability, well, you've got another thing coming. You've got no sway with this council, and if you throw any more of your fancy legal documents around, I'll see to it you never have sway in this city again. I'll make sure everyone knows exactly what kind of low, dishonourable, cheating family you're from, sweetheart." He leaned on the last word like a mean kid in the schoolyard who maliciously points out that your mother is a hooker.

She knew what words to say, and how to deal with bullies. She'd conquered her fears and polished her skills years ago. She'd taken down meaner, smarmier and bigger tyrants than Matthew Seibold. It had been a point of pride for her to be tough enough to fight back with ease and style.

But this was different.

This was her very own personal bully. And he was poking a stick into her very own festering wound. Suddenly, she was trembling uncontrollably, cold and sweaty, hyperventilating and utterly without defences.

After briefly but firmly squeezing her arm and setting her behind him, Kent stepped into the fray. "Back off, frat boy." He stepped up close to Matt, getting right in his face. Kent was leaner but several inches taller than Matt, and he got close enough to look down on him, and he did so threateningly and unambiguously.

Matt sneered and tilted his head up, stepping back. "What the fuck? Get out of my face!"

"I'll get out of your face when you get out of Sharon's. There's nothing happening here except proper professional protocol. And Ms. Beckett, which is how I expect you to address her henceforth, is representing the society I work for and the project the City has committed the site to. So however you got yours on the agenda, we will make sure it gets right back off again." Kent poked Matthew right in the centre of his shiny silk tie, closing in again until they were nose to nose. "Because you and your greedy, profiteering partners don't have the first inkling of what it takes to deliver a housing product that meets the needs of the existing residents of the Downtown Eastside."

Matt took a step back and smoothed a hand down his tie, his gaze sliding sideways. "Well, you can't have much confidence in your chances, or you wouldn't have hired a lawyer for something so mundane. But I have to tell you, dude, you should have chosen more carefully, because Ms. Beckett, as you call her, can only bring disrepute to you and your scuzzy street friends." As he spoke, he waved his fingers and cast his narrowed gaze in an arc, taking in Carl and a few other street people who'd been hovering just behind Kent, watching the exchange.

Sharon shrank back as a crowd gathered around the confrontation. In the altercation's midst, a news team with a camera and microphone were suddenly asking frantic questions.

"Did you catch that, Sergé?" Kent said.

"What's this about, Mr. Sawyer? Has this got something to do with the controversial RFP on the coveted historic building at the corner of Hastings and Gore Avenue in the Downtown Eastside?" A young reporter pushed forward, shoving the mic towards Kent.

He turned toward the camera and addressed the journalist. "That's exactly what this is about, Sergé. The City has reneged on its prior promises to the Pathway Society to commit the property in question for a long-planned transition house to help get at-risk youth off the streets. Mr. Seibold's company, S & S Developments, has put forward a commercial mixed-use project with the merest requirement of social housing, according to the generous definitions set out by the Provincial Housing ministry. While appealing on the surface, his project is wholly inappropriate for this site. This is not what these kids need and selling the contested city property to S & S for market housing and more vacant retail space puts this much-needed transition housing project at risk."

"Hey! What is this?" Matt shoved forward, trying to get his face in front of the camera. He elbowed Kent aside. "You're not accurately representing – "

But Sharon had the impression that the entire thing was set up ahead of time, because the news team spun and kept their focus on Kent, forcing Matt to jockey his way between them to get attention. He looked ridiculous and pathetic, like he was a nobody trying to photo bomb the shot. If she weren't personally so agitated, she'd have found it funny.

Kent ignored him to answer another couple of questions from the reporter before he thanked him and backed into the crowd.

Matt surged towards them, his face red and his eyes bulging with fury. He shoved Kent in the centre of his chest. "I'll get you for this you fuckin' hipster. Nobody crosses Matthew Seibold and gets away with it!"

Kent turned his attention to Matt, his countenance serene. "Did you say your name was Matthew Seibold?" Sharon noticed the news team with their camera now pointed at Matt, chuckling as they turned away.

Matt growled and stormed off after them, his hands fisted and his shoulders pulled up to his ears. "Hey! You can't – "

Kent turned back to her. "Can I walk you out to your car? I'm giving Carl a lift home. Maybe I can buy you an Ovaltine or something afterwards?"

Sharon saw him transformed into a fierce, articulate, principled fighter, heroic and brave, and she didn't know what to make of it. He reminded her too much of her father, the way she remembered him, bleeding heart champion of the downtrodden people. Careless of his own welfare, or the rules of behaviour, or how the world saw him, as long as he was fighting for the right side and making the world better. She knew that when Kent was around, she no longer felt in control of herself or her world. Her body heated, sweat breaking out on her scalp as uncontrollable tears flooded her eyes and throat. She could barely get words out, her voice choking.

"I can't believe you orchestrated this entire thing. What is wrong with you?" She spun and stalked away.

But she didn't succeed in losing him, because the entire group of them stayed right on her heels as she stalked angrily to the parking lot outside City Hall. The group dispersed, mostly, but Carl and another person she couldn't see in the shadows lingered by Kent. She tried to ignore them and headed straight for her car.

She didn't get far.

"This'll teach you to make me look bad in front of the press, asshole!" came Matt's agitated voice, followed by an *oof* and loud smack, a grunt and a thud against the metal side of a car, accompanied by vague moving shapes in the dark. "Stay out of my way, loser!"

Sharon's pounding heart shot to her throat as she realized he'd hit someone. Her vision blurred as immediately a moaning sound came from the dark ground, and bodies scuffling in the shadows. She forgot her urgent desire to get away and raced over. Sure enough, Matt had blindsided Kent and punched him, knocking him down. She gasped. "Kent! Are you all right?" She bent and felt for his face in the semi-dark. He rolled toward her and half sat up.

"Yeah, yeah. I'm okay." He wheezed and coughed. "Knocked the wind out of me. Where is that cowardly fucker?"

She gripped his arm and helped him stand up. When they looked around, Matt was long gone. Her hand was wet and sticky.

"You're bleeding! I can't believe he did that!" Suddenly she saw Kent, really saw him, this man who selflessly devoted his life to helping others, and fought evil and corruption wherever he met it. Even if it meant getting on the wrong side of a bully like Matthew Seibold. "We have to get you to a doctor!"

"Nah. I'm fine."

"Let me see." She grabbed his sleeve and turned him sideways so a street light shone on him. It was still difficult to make out, but he had a trickle of dark blood on the side of his face. She reached into her bag to find a tissue, but he swiped at himself with his palm and wiped it on his shirt. "Does it hurt?" She gently touched him with the tissue, dabbing away the smeared blood that remained.

He faced her, dipping his head closer so she could reach. "It's much better now that you're talking to me."

"Really? Doesn't it hurt?"

"Well, maybe just…"

"What?"

He brought his face close to hers and whispered, "Maybe if you could just kiss it better?"

"Are you serious?"

"Quite serious."

His hands rested lightly on her shoulders. She still held the tissue near his face, with her other hand cradling the other side of his head to keep him steady.

"Just kiss her, Kent," suggested the stranger standing in the dark, awaiting a ride home. Carl chuckled his implicit approval.

She drew in a breath, just as he closed the distance between them. Their lips met softly, tentatively. As always, when they touched, something astonishing happened, their chemistry off the charts. His hand came up to her head, his fingers spreading to cradle the back of it as he increased the pressure of his mouth on hers. His warm tongue stroked her lips and dipped inside her mouth, reaching up to touch the roof, sending shock waves through her. An involuntary moan escaped from her throat as she abandoned all sense of where she was. His touch had that effect on her, turning off her disciplined brain, and awakening a sleeping giant of carnal desire in her blood.

He pulled back, sighing, his breath fanning her face. "Oh, Princess. I feel fine now."

She blinked as the space opened up between them, shocking her skin where the cocoon of warmth created by their embrace had shielded her from the cool night air. "Thank you," she whispered, suddenly conscious of what he'd done.

His face dipped toward her, though she couldn't see his dark eyes in the shadows. "For kissing you?"

She shook her head. "For defending me against that bully. For drawing all the attention to yourself. For deflecting what could have been an ugly scene, for me, onto yourself." She shook her head a little. "For being such a reckless fool." She dabbed his cheek with the tissue, liking the closeness. "For being a stupid radical bleeding heart liberal."

He laughed softly. "Considering the prize, the sacrifice was well worth it."

He released her and unlocked his car with a bloop. "Hop in gentlemen. Let's get you guys home. I have a date with a lady at the Ovaltine Café."

CHAPTER 14

They sat across from each other the next morning in the same cozy oak wood booth where they'd finished the previous evening.

Kent wanted to make this a regular thing. He'd introduced Sharon to the Ovaltine Café the night before, when he'd brought her here for a late night drink and debrief, and she'd decided it made a good meeting place. He like to think of it as more of a first date. He just wanted to spend more time able to gaze at her wide blue eyes, full soft pink lips, and angelic silver blonde hair. Last night, when she saw his bloody face in full light, the look of sympathy in her eyes knocked the air from his lungs. Even when she was pretending to be an icy bitch, or cross with him and telling him off, looking at her was his favourite new pastime.

Sadly, she was cross again.

Sharon shook the morning newspaper and scowled at him. "This! This is exactly what I was talking about. You think the press are your friends because of your righteousness. You think because your friend the reporter spun the story in your favour, it's neatly wrapped up." She shook the paper again, just in case he wasn't getting the message. He knew enough to suppress his urge to smile.

He'd read the news this morning on his phone and saw what the front-page article said, and what that photo on the front page showed. The local news had shown soundbites from his comments to Sergé, with Matt Seibold shoving him and blubbering like an idiot. Which was good, right?

The photo they'd chosen for maximum journalistic effect on the front page of the city news was of the two of them going at it nose-to-nose. Unfortunately, Kent looked the part of a radical lunatic, his eyes bulging and his teeth bared as he challenged the arrogant prick. Behind him, a few of his street people cheered him on. It didn't take much to make them look crazy, himself included. She had a point.

He stroked his forehead with his fingertips and lifted his coffee to his lips to hide his chagrin.

"Although I'd lined up Sergé to be there, I hadn't been expecting to have to defend a maiden in distress from a junkyard dog," he murmured in his own defence. The surge of protective macho adrenaline that had overtaken him surprised him. In the moment, all he could think was, *Get away from my woman, asshole!*

She scoffed.

He looked at her through half-lowered lids and lifted his mug of steaming coffee to his lips. When she accused him of volatility and recklessness he couldn't argue.

His way, and his plan – except for the calm and idealistic influence of Christine who believed, against all the evidence, the law was on their side, and was trustworthy – was always to rebel. Even, if necessary, to push the boundaries of lawfulness. Experience had taught him that if you wanted something accomplished, it required extraordinary measures.

True, he had a tendency to recklessness, and to take rather radical action. Christine knew and accepted this about him when she hired him. But he had his reasons and beliefs. The system, the establishment, and the Man, had never been on his side. Following rules invariably led to disaster and futile disappointment. When you'd been burned by the system, it was hard to trust that everything would work out fine if you followed the rules. The kind of tragedy he'd witnessed up north was hard to come back from.

Now he had Christine's calming influence on one side, and Sharon's proper and official methods on the other, both women reigning in his righteous anger and burning need to take action.

He knew why he heeded Christine. She was his boss, his mentor, he respected her and could learn from her. Her people, she was a member of the Nuu-chah-nulth Tribal Council, knew about rebellion, and had plenty of good cause to be angry, and yet she took the high road. Stayed calm and cool.

But what was his motive for placating Sharon, this woman who'd taken over his life like an ice storm, stopping him in his tracks, disrupting his familiar routine?

That gave him pause.

He'd always assumed they'd end up needing to protest for a hope of taking down the mercenary developers and their manipulative residents' association who wanted to steal their building from under them. It was only after he'd gotten to know her he'd seen other possibilities. She was amazing and formidable. He was falling for her. He believed in her. She could do it. His ice princess.

Her intense reaction to her personal history, her relationship with her father, made him question his own rebelliousness and tendency to seek conflict. How much of the deep well of anger he felt inside came from his own pain, rather than the injustice he saw in the world around him? How had it coloured his own lenses?

"They're not finished with you yet. Once an image and a story like this is in the public realm, your enemies can spin it round again. Get their Twitter sheep to recirculate it. City council won't take you seriously now. Matt Seibold and his influential connections – and trust me he has them in spades – can use this to discredit you, and by association Christine, the Society, and the bloody project. You fool."

He looked up, catching her gaze, allowing a small flirtatious smile to curl his lips. "Last night when you called me a fool, it sounded like a term of endearment."

"Can you be serious?"

"I'm very serious. I want to kiss you again."

She groaned and shook her head in exasperation, touching her hairline with her fingertips as she glared at the table. "What am I going to do with you?"

"I have some ideas," said Kent, grinning widely and spinning his mug around on the old scarred laminate tabletop.

Last night while they drank their Ovaltine, they'd reviewed the council meeting, admired the classic vintage diner, then talked about various local old-timers that they saw, and told stories from their childhood. The good ones. Their exchange was gentle and easy. Then when he walked her to her car to bid her good night, she rewarded him with another brain-melting kiss. Sure, maybe it was just a thank you, but he didn't see it that way.

His gaze slid to her small hand on the tabletop, still clutching the now folded newspaper, her short nails clean and pink. It took all his will to stop himself from reaching across, lifting her fingers to his mouth, tasting her. Every time they touched, it rocked his world. He didn't understand how two such very different people could connect so powerfully that it overrode every other consideration. No dating site in the world would put Sharon and him together, yet somehow it worked.

If only they could agree on a strategy to get this transition housing project approved. Then he could shift his attention to getting her approval on another project – he was already anticipating her enthusiastic *Yes! Yes!*

Sharon pursed her lips, frowning at him. He could see wheels turning behind her pretty, clever eyes, trying to figure out how to fix the mess he'd made. He still believed he could use the press and public opinion to help their cause. Time would tell. But in the meantime he knew he couldn't stop her from doing her thing, her way.

She sighed. "There's no avoiding it now. I have to suck it up and go talk to old Gus Seibold, before they use your stunt to justify giving the property to S & S. No matter what the documents say in our favour, I'll have to negotiate a deal."

He didn't know what she would negotiate with. He just hoped whatever it was, she didn't make it worse.

~

As soon as she walked in to the reception area, Seibold's secretary announced her and showed her directly into the large corner office. It may not have been the Mayor's office, but the dark polished desk and deep blue carpet spoke of seniority and status. "Well, well, well. Little Sharon Brecht. Matthew mentioned I might see you today."

"I go by Beckett now, Councillor Seibold." In all her years as the new-and-improved Sharon Beckett, she'd never faced a test like this.

Sometimes Sharon could talk big, and then immediately regret it. Coming to talk one-on-one with old man Seibold was the thing she least wanted to do in the entire universe. Chatting with Mr. Llewellyn was different. He'd been sympathetic and felt sorry for her and her mother.

"Mmm. So I heard." He wheezed, his middle jiggling with humour. "Something wrong with your old name?"

She drew in a long breath, centring and gathering her inner strength.

"Let's stick to business, shall we, Councillor?"

"Very well. Let's." The corpulent old man folded his fingers over his generous middle and leaned back in his wide leather desk chair with a creak. "I didn't think this little non-profit society would be much of a challenge. When we issued the RFP, we didn't expect them to hire a lawyer. However, it changes nothing."

She tilted her head and lifted her brows. "How so?"

He gestured to the matching chair in front of his desk, and she nodded and perched on its hard shiny leather seat, wondering how many supplicants had done likewise over the past quarter century.

"The property belongs to us. We can do as we wish with it, silly girl."

He spoke as though he were the CEO of a private corporation and not an elected representative of the people. She fought to control the curl of her lip at the feeling of disgust.

When she was young, Councillor Gus Seibold had represented everything that her father was not. Upright, dignified, refined, principled. She tried to reconcile the image before her now with that memory.

"That's not exactly true. There are two variables you seem to have forgotten."

He narrowed his eyes, inviting her to go on.

She nodded, continuing. "First, your accountability to the public... who elected you to represent their interests. Second, legal precedent. The City may own the property, but you're not above the law. If you've made legally binding promises to a party, and I have evidence that strongly suggests you did, then you're subject to civil property and contract law. And so you *will* be compelled to follow through on those promises or pay damages. And my client's records show that those damages would be considerable. How will you justify that to your constituency?"

His lower lip protruded thoughtfully. "I'm not worried about them. Your hippy boyfriend – "

What? Her heart kicked. "You refer to my client?" Why would he refer to Kent as her boyfriend? That he was aware of them at all spoke to the fact that his son, or someone, kept him in the loop.

He waved a thick hand. "Whatever. With his monkey business at the council meeting, and so diligently ensuring the press captured events truthfully, he's made sure we can keep the public on our side, whatever we decide."

"Are you saying you have yet to decide?"

"What do you think?"

"With all due respect to your personal preferences, you should be considering the merits of my client's proposal. It's not only about the commitments you and your staff have made. It's a superior project that was thoughtfully planned, is desperately needed and should be approved."

"Oh, look at you, all high and mighty. Your head's in the clouds, just like your old man."

She spoke through clenched teeth. "Leave him out of this."

He smiled, a most unpleasant smile. "Oh, but Sharon dear, he factors so beautifully into our discussion."

"How so?" An uncontrollable tremor started low in her spine, building tension and rising until her entire body was tense, and her heart racing. But she wouldn't show it, remaining perfectly still. She refused to allow him to bully her. And she wouldn't be shamed. She wasn't her father. She wasn't her father.

Sharon wasn't that cowed little girl anymore. She'd paid her dues, and paid for her father's sins, even if that mostly meant sweeping them under the proverbial mid-century shag. And she had serious skills and moxie. Enough moxie to get her through this meeting? She sure hoped so.

Foremost, Sharon considered herself a professional. She was here to represent her client, and though rehashing her family's past didn't help, she would tolerate it.

She'd chosen the law for the intellectual challenge of its precision, its influence and prestige, and for the opportunity to help people and further the public good. Precisely so she could avoid the low-brow circus of street fighting and deal-making that had been her father's way of solving problems.

Whether out of carelessness, greed, or because that very tussle had compelled him to make deals and decisions that were not defensible in the light of day, she swore that would never happen to her.

However, the law didn't really protect her from morally grey areas. Lawyers defended people they knew were guilty. Deals were made every day. But she was an excellent lawyer, smart, experienced and tough. She could do this in her sleep. As Bentham had famously said, *The power of the lawyer is in the uncertainty of the law.*

Seibold laughed, low and slow, mocking. "I remember you, Sharon Brecht," he drawled. "Always at your father's side, looking up to him with those innocent adoring eyes."

She sat silently. And why wouldn't a young girl look up to her father, especially when he was such a respected, principled and dynamic man? Seibold was trying to manipulate her, trying to deflect the conversation away from the facts. She suspected that Kent was right, and council had already made some kind of deal with S & S.

How would she find out?

"It looks kind of suspect, doesn't it, that council not only favours, but is making special concessions to a project proposal put forward by your own son's company?"

Seibold waved that away too, so confident in his position. "I don't have to vote. I hardly have to speak. They do as I wish, the lot of them. Or the majority. And that's all that matters, isn't it?"

"Including the mayor?"

"Even Mayor Taylor, who is young and always grateful for my seasoned input on important matters, given my seniority on council."

She peered at him, so smug and entitled, wondering how

Mayor Taylor would feel if he knew the nature of this conversation. "Yes, you've been in power a rather long time."

His smirk widened, and he ran a dimpled hand down his silk tie.

She suppressed the urge to shudder with disgust. How had he maintained his popularity with the electorate when he was such a thoroughly unpleasant man? Was her perception so skewed she didn't remember, or had not perceived that fact? He was repulsive, and another involuntary shiver gripped her spine as she recalled how, as a girl, she'd cower when he spoke to her father, thinking he was so commanding. Maybe on some level, her instinct was trying to tell her something.

Especially during the scandal. He'd been the one who laid the shame on with a shovel, holier than thou. Making hay to advance his own political career, Gus Seibold had set the tone for that camp, making sure everyone knew of her father's sins, and punished him, regardless of the collateral damage. It was from him that his son Matt had taken his cue.

Was the whole scandal an elaborate charade?

"I still have the law on my side. And I wouldn't count on the public's support so confidently. That vote is still to be determined. It wouldn't take much to dethrone you, sir. As you well know, any hint of favouritism or corruption by an elected official is enough to bring your tower of power crashing down."

His lips curled. "Are you threatening me, young lady?"

She laughed. "I'm not so young anymore, Councillor. And I'm not inexperienced or without my own friends in high places. But no, I wouldn't deign to threaten you, I'm simply observing there's a great deal I could do to shine a light on your record here. I mean..." She paused and peered out the window at the bright blue fall sky, tilting her head.

It was becoming increasingly clear that Gus Seibold was not the upright citizen and representative of the people he claimed to be.

"... isn't it rather remarkable for a man to hold the same elected position for twenty... four years? It looks kind of suspicious to me. Was it Abraham Lincoln who once said, *Nearly all men can stand adversity, but if you want to test a man's character, give him power?*"

Gus Seibold had been a newly elected councillor back when her father had been disgraced for his alleged corrupt business dealings. She, along with everyone else, had assumed Seibold was full of idealism and righteousness. The venom and vigilantism of his attack on her father suggested it.

Her father had always maintained his innocence. Even now, years after his death, her mother continued to argue that he'd been scapegoated for someone else's corrupt dealings, and was framed. Sharon had never bought it, assuming that he'd only made those claims to save face at home, and to spare her and her mother's feelings, and their belief in him. And she'd told him so.

She turned back to meet Seibold's gaze head on. "As a responsible citizen, I'd say it bears closer examination. It would be terrible for the City's *public* image to be seen doing deals behind the scenes." She disarmed his obvious retort by owning her history. "As I know from personal experience."

She had no intention of going public with her claims. Creating a sensational news story was not her style. She believed a quick resolution was possible, quietly, behind closed doors. As long as she achieved her ends for her client.

"You make a valid point, my dear. It's true I remain very popular with my supporters. I always have their best interests at heart."

Her skin crawled at his tone. She was sure he'd held on to his position all these years precisely because he was such a good deal-maker. But what kind of deals was he making all these years? She'd soon discover. She smiled, though. Because they were getting to the crux of the conversation.

"What would be the extent of the damages suffered by your client, should they lose this property? Roughly."

She drew a breath and let it out slowly. He obviously hadn't bothered to review the documents she'd filed. Now they were getting to the money talk. "According to my review of their files, they would be subject to losses in the range of one point three million." If you factored in the potential loss of an ongoing operating budget, it could be a higher number. But she'd hold that fact in reserve for a strategic moment.

He whistled silently through pursed lips, his meaty pink forehead folded into sausages. "So much? Indeed, that could cost the City a lot, couldn't it?"

"It's possible, yes. It would be my duty to look out for my client's best interest and ensure that number was maximized. There's all the time and trouble and inconvenience caused to them by the City's sudden change of plans. I'd want to ensure they were compensated for that as well."

"Is that so?" A slow jaundiced smile crept across his jowled face.

She nodded.

"That's a great deal of work for you, isn't it?"

She lifted a shoulder, taking it slow, playing it cool. "Just doing my job."

"I'm sure you have many other worthy, and profitable... projects you'd prefer to work on. A lawyer's career must be a very busy one. Perhaps you would prefer to redirect your efforts elsewhere."

What? This wasn't what she was expecting. She gently drew her brows together, tilting her head, feigning innocence. "What do you mean, precisely?"

"Without getting into details, what I mean is, it might be better for your career in the long run to turn your attention toward your other projects, and let this one unfold naturally."

"Naturally." She hummed her agreement. "And why would I do that, Councillor Seibold?"

"Why? Well, I can't imagine there are any big bonuses that result from *pro bono* cases. If you focus your attention on other projects, you could sooner afford that renovation to your condominium, or that new Mercedes, or that vacation to the Caribbean you've been dreaming about, my dear. That's why." His lips pulled back, reminding her of his son's creepy and threatening manner the other night. "Or you might receive incentives…" he tapered off.

She sat for a moment, processing his words. Was that a bribe? He was coy enough about it. Unbelievable. She wished she had a recording of it. He'd deny ever saying those words or what they meant. But maybe, maybe it was in her best interest to play along.

"Do you really think that's what kind of lawyer I am?"

"I know what you are. The apple doesn't fall that far from the tree." His lips pulled back in a forced grin.

The accusation caused Sharon's insides to clench like a fist in protest. He meant her father. That if they could corrupt him, then she was fallible too. Maybe that's how things worked in his family, but she'd made it her mission to be as different from her father as she could. She wanted to scream at Seibold. He may have known her father but he didn't know her.

Sharon wondered about apples and trees. Neither old Gus nor his son Matthew struck her as honest or honourable in their character and dealings.

With her new perspective, and the benefit of a legal education and career under her belt, she wondered if there was more to her father's story than they had led her to believe as a young girl.

She stood in front of the broad desk, studying his jowled, pink-tinged face, twisted in scorn, and his corpulent figure over-filling his large leather office chair. His posture suggested supreme confidence, arrogance and disdain. Few people had crossed this man in the last twenty-odd years, and he'd grown accustomed to his power, and very comfortable. Maybe even sloppy.

But considering his long, uninterrupted reign of power, and the blatant bribe he'd just offered her to bugger off and let his son's development company win this proposal call, she had to wonder whether there had ever been a grain of honest selflessness in this man's makeup.

She needed a new strategy. She needed to buy some more time.

"I already have a rather nice car, thanks." She dipped her chin and smiled. "But you know I couldn't accept gifts, offered by you or by anyone. Whatever you believe my father guilty of, I am not him. I am an honest and law-abiding citizen, and a member of the bar. I know the difference between right and wrong, sir. And that would be wrong."

He nodded. "I was afraid you'd say that, foolish girl."

"But…" She paused, allowing her gaze to drift out the window as though an idea was just now forming. She counted the seconds until an electric trolley bus pulled away from the curb. "… perhaps we could negotiate a way to compensate my client by being a little more creative? That wouldn't be dishonest. The City owns other properties, does it not?"

He nodded, pulling on his lower lip in interest.

"Surely there are alternate locations that wouldn't offend the neighbourhood lobby group that's been so persistent in their complaints about my client's project. I'm wondering if there might be another option that would benefit everyone involved."

"You're missing the point, I think. The alternative for you is not pretty."

Threats, now? "And that is?"

"How do I know you'll honour the agreement?"

"You mean you're looking for leverage? Why would I lie?" What was he getting at now?

"You've done a good job with the smoke and mirrors, I'll give you that. I'll bet there's nobody left that even remembers where you came from, eh? Maybe no one knows your actual name, never mind your dirty family secrets. No one would ever associate your proper upright image with the dirtiest corruption scandal in the city's history, would they? That wouldn't look good on your resume."

The lock down on her nerves threatened to crumble as a tremble of panic raced through her chest and her limbs like an earthquake, setting her gut roiling. Sharon tightened her grip on her briefcase, willing herself to keep her cool. *Hold it together. You've got this.* Slowly, she filled her lungs and exhaled, trying to stay calm. She could feel her face heat, however, and knew her pale complexion would give away her stress. "I'm unclear. Have you changed tactics, Councillor?"

He observed her through narrowed eyes, the corners of his mouth twitching with satisfaction. "How would your stellar legal career hold up after we had exposed you for the fraud that you are? Especially now, wheeling and dealing in city properties and developments, following in your daddy's footsteps, eh?"

Who was wheeling and dealing? Was he trying to set her up? Is this how he lured people in and tangled them in his web of power and corruption? Tempt them with something they needed, find a vulnerability, trick or bully them into making deals, and then sucking the life out of them?

Was that what happened with her father?

Had Seibold manoeuvred him into a corner somehow? Had he been trying to get rid of him, like he was trying to get rid of her now?

In a flash, the memories Seibold meant her to relive raced through her mind like a jagged, broken film, each frame dredging up confusion, pain and shame. Her father's volatile emotions as his enemies circled and his friends turned on him, his protests of innocence. The day he was dismissed from office. Press crowded around their car and on their front lawn. Police at their door. Whispered meetings with lawyers. Her mother's painful shock from attacks at the supermarket by neighbourhood women she thought were her friends. Sharon's own humiliation when kids at school took up the cudgels, echoing their parents' outrage by painting her entire family with a tainted brush, Seibold's son righteously leading the pack of her tormentors. Then the financial collapse, first the business, then more lawyers, then the house and her school. Everything she'd ever known, her entire world, ripped up by the roots.

These were memories she preferred to forget, as the old man knew. What child would swim in the murk of her worst nightmare, reliving the trauma that defined her as an adult, given the choice?

Strangely, though, as she sat in her habitual stoic pose, expression serene, spine straight, in absolute control of herself – so unlike her hot-tempered, passionate, troublesome father – an outward illusion of icy cool she had worked long and hard to refine, and which defined her very identity, she felt a change flood through her veins. Instead of a hard, icy shell to protect her, she felt something warm, serene and life-giving flowing inside.

A deep calm rooted in self-knowledge and confidence filled her from the inside out, soothing the violent tremble of fear and rage that threatened to crumble her facade. She didn't need to give in to that wild, frantic force, and neither did she need to remain in such tight control of herself. Her calm came from knowledge, skill and experience. Because she knew what to do, and who she was.

Sharon surprised herself. Instead of being cowed by his threats, the way he wanted her to be, her strategic legal mind went to work like an obsessive teenager with a Rubik's Cube, sliding coloured squares around, searching for patterns. She could be wrong. But her gut told her that her hunch was worth investigating.

Sharon had done nothing illegal or untoward. Maybe her father hadn't either. But she wondered if that was true for the fat cat sitting across from her.

For the moment, it was in her interest to let him believe that he intimidated her. Was she intimidated? Why would revisiting the worst trauma of her life have that effect? If he spun her family history into the threat of a fresh scandal, and went public with it, it would be ugly and uncomfortable for her. It played right into all her insecurities and fears. That was true, and it would be a rough storm to weather. But she had broken no laws, and she would not. He couldn't really hurt her, only intimidate.

And she refused to be intimidated.

Sharon was a different person now. And if weathering that storm meant she could help Christine's society have their well-deserved and worthy project, help those kids, and potentially expose a bloated and corrupt city official… it would be worth it. She'd take that risk.

She knew she'd done no wrong. Sharon was far too careful to let that happen. She knew herself well, and the guilt and shame she carried for her family made her extra cautious. It may have made her unpopular, but whether in school or on her way up the corporate ladder to her current position as a junior partner at one of the most prestigious firms in the city, she had *never* put a foot wrong. If she did her homework and managed this carefully, there would be no need to air her dirty family laundry.

She widened her eyes and hunched her shoulders slightly, the opposite of her accustomed mask of fearlessness and power. An entitled, power-blind old man should fall for that, right?

"I see you've come around to my way of thinking, my dear."

She knew what cowed looked like. For good measure, she sniffed, licked her lips and blinked rapidly, as though fighting off tears.

She dipped her chin and let her head bob minutely. She needed to make it seem that she'd caved reluctantly to his threats without doing so. "I… I might speak with my client. The optics are bad if I do nothing more for them, despite the fruitlessness of this RFP. I wonder if I might take an offer back for their consideration. To save face, you understand. It might not work out. It might not be a suitable property. But I have to offer them something. It would look better for both of us if I could."

He nodded. "I see your point."

"Well, can we leave it there for today? I have another appointment, and much to think about." She stood up. "And I'm sure you'd like to speak to Mr. Carter and get back to me?" She had a great deal to research and to plan.

CHAPTER 15

Harley was missing. Again. Goddam it! He wished the kid wasn't so inclined to bugger off and do his own thing. Then Kent could tell the difference between when he'd forgotten to come to class versus when he was in trouble. Real trouble.

Dark clouds hung low over the rooftops, rain imminent. It would be miserable out there today. Kent pulled on his leather jacket and tugged up the collar against the damp air as he headed out. As Kent stormed out the door to make some strategic enquiries, he crashed into Sharon on her way in.

He paused, grabbing her arms to steady them both. "Hey. Hi." He'd expected to see her earlier, but he hadn't yet wondered where she was.

She frowned, her gaze combing his face in concern. "What's the matter?" Could she read him that well? In the same moment he had that thought, he read the signs on her own face. Stress at the edges of her blue eyes – that had hardened again – her full lips tight, pulled in, her posture stiff and battle ready.

He didn't have time to talk to her, but the least he could do was check-in. "Do you have news? Did you get anywhere?"

Her gaze dropped, avoiding his, then scanned the foyer

behind him. But his preoccupation meant he'd have to pursue that question later. "I talked to him. But – "

Impatient, he took her by the arm. "Walk with me. What happened?" He turned her and they set off down the street. He could kill two birds with one stone. The streets were busy with the early lunch crowd from surrounding offices and the university.

She shivered, pulling her coat closer, and shook her head, stepping alongside him. "It's not looking good, Kent. He's a very stubborn, entitled old man used to doing as he pleases. He won't give in. There are some ideas on the table and I'm waiting to hear from his staff."

This skin on the back of his neck prickled in warning. "What ideas?"

She stalled, staring across the street at a kerfuffle between a man, a woman and a shopping cart that had come to a stalemate, leaving them in a grim vignette like a painting.

"Sharon? What are you not telling me?" Why was she avoiding looking at him?

"It's just a negotiating tactic, you understand. I'm sorry, Kent. I won't give up, but I thought it was prudent to leverage what they're doing to you guys to at least get some other properties on the table. The City owns – "

"What the fuck?" He stopped and turned to face her, getting in her face so she had to meet his gaze. "I told you most of our funding is tied to this specific building, didn't I?"

"Yes, yes, you did. I tried. And I will keep trying." She glanced away, then back, lifting her chin, nostrils flaring. Was she trembling?

Something was way off. He started walking again, and she scrambled to keep pace with his long strides. "No. You can't give up that easily. I won't quit! And we won't negotiate. I told you these guys were corrupt. They're only interested in what's good for them and their careers. What about these papers you filed? I thought you could stop them?"

She said nothing, her eyes flickering, watching the people they passed as they strode down the sidewalk, darting and dodging. "I have stopped them from approving anything. For now." She reached to tuck stray strands of hair behind her ear.

"He got to you somehow, didn't he? Did he threaten you? What's happening? Talk to me!"

"No!" Her gaze darted across the street. "I explained about the damages. He's very bullish that they can justify their choice. I'm sorry. The chances of our winning by council vote are slim. I'm trying to do what's best for you by leveraging some options. Just in case."

"Yeah. Right." Kent glared at his boots for a moment, his gut tight. He grabbed her arm, stopping and spinning her towards him. "Are you getting something out of this?"

She pulled back, gasping. "How dare you! Don't you know me better than that?"

He scowled, his jaw ticking. *I don't know! I don't know if I do.* He flung her arm down. "I can't deal with this right now. I have to find Harley. Just come with me and we'll talk later."

She faltered. "No, I can meet you – "

"I said come with me!" He growled in frustration. He didn't mean to sound threatening, but her blue eyes flared, lips pressed together, and she resumed walking beside him, subdued. Jesus, he was feeling like he was a lunatic. Please, just let Harley be okay and then he'd focus on her and sort this out.

There had to be another way. He hadn't even rallied the troops yet. He hadn't expected her to drop the ball with so little effort – even though he'd told himself to – he'd even warned Christine about this. It didn't seem right.

There's Lenny. He jerked to a halt. "Hey Lenny. You seen Harley today? Or last night?"

Lenny, an addict typically too out of it to answer a question like that, shifted from foot to foot, his fingers twitching, which meant he was still on a quest for his daily bean. His head whipped towards Kent, his eyes conveying the typical paranoia of a junkie. "Nah, I ain't. Hey Kent, Kent, where's RJ? You know where I can find RJ?" His manic eyes flickered up and down the street.

"RJ's back?" Kent grabbed Lenny's sleeve and gave him a tug to get his attention back. "Lenny! You saw RJ?"

"Yeah, but I can't find him." He yanked his arm away and careened down the sidewalk away from them.

"What was that about? Who's RJ?" Sharon said, falling in beside him as he resumed his crusade.

She was getting used to his ways. And she was getting used to the Downtown Eastside. Kent studied her out of the corner of his eye. She wore narrow dark pants with a thin grey-blue parka that matched her eyes under the cloudy sky overhead, and low heeled short boots. More discrete, but still... She looked privileged and put together and hot, as always, and his blood heated. From the moment he'd first met her, she stunned him, but he hadn't let himself look past his distrust and dislike of her profession.

Now that he knew her, knew about her past, and had experienced the bone-melting impact of her kisses, he could no longer ignore the fact that he wanted her something fierce. No matter what she did for a living. He pushed those thoughts away. For now.

She might be petite, but she was energetic and powerful. It looked like she could walk all day. But he was a foot taller than she was and knew it was challenging for her to keep pace with him. Today he didn't care. He couldn't afford to care.

The part of his brain that was free from obsessing over finding Harley was pissed with her, so he'd make her walk. He was punishing her. It was childish, but he couldn't process his anger any other way at the moment. He'd keep her with him until he could have it out with her. And if she saw some ugly truth of life on the street, all the better. Maybe it would inspire her to fight harder.

Meantime, he marched her from street to street, park to park, alley to alley in search of Harley. The last time he'd seen him was two days ago. All the business with City Hall, and to be honest, his preoccupation with the woman beside him, had disrupted his routine, stolen his concentration and his vigilance. One teacher at the society had said they'd glimpsed Harley on the street yesterday midday, but he hadn't come to class and he didn't show up this morning to check in with Kent. Damn it! He blamed himself for looking away. Harley was always at risk, too fearless for his age, too ballsy to know that he was out of his league most of the time.

Especially if predators like RJ were roaming around.

They circled round to Pigeon Park again, and this time he saw him. At last!

"RJ!" God, just the sight of him made Kent's skin crawl. He was the worst kind of criminal, utterly without principles. He wore the usual combination of luxury dress wear and overpriced outdoor gear. Today it was low riding black suit pants with Italian leather slides, a bright orange Arcteryx anorak, open at the front to show off his brand name bling. Kent's gaze swung over him, noting the obnoxious array of Gucci shades, Hermes branded cap, Rolex watch, long thick gold chain and leather belt with its conspicuous Luis Vuitton diamond encrusted buckle. It made him want to puke. He was as used to seeing these luxury brands on his father's cronies and their wives. The conspicuous consumption disgusted him. They were all the same, wearing their power and privilege like a badge of honour.

Stealing another glance at Sharon, he decided she wasn't so terrible for wanting tasteful design and quality fabrics. He stepped up to RJ, Sharon standing stock still behind him.

"Where's Harley, RJ?"

The slime ball turned toward Kent and sneered. Then Sharon caught his attention, and his brow lifted in interest, his lips parting with a glint of teeth. Kent took hold of Sharon's arm, nudging her behind him. RJ's greedy gaze slid up and down, and Kent felt her stiffen and pull up closer to him. She had a good instinct for evil. RJ Kovak wasn't just a drug dealer. He was a pimp, a pusher and a predator. Kids like Harley were his candy. If he could charm them, lure them into using, and secure their dependency, then he could coerce them to do anything for him, enlarging his army of sex workers and errand boys. This was the reason Kent was so determined to get kids like Harley safely sheltered and off the street forever. Once the likes of RJ got their hooks into them, there was little hope of turning back.

RJ continued his unsavoury perusal of Sharon. "Who's the sexy benjamin you brung wit' you today, lumberjack," he said with his Eastern European accent mangled with street slang. "I'd like me a piece a that." He lifted his upper lip and reached toward Sharon's face with his gold and diamond be-ringed hand, and she recoiled just as Kent hauled her further out of his reach.

"Hands off, RJ. Answer my question."

"Heh. She's your box, da?" He cackled, showing an unholy number of gold-capped teeth. Then, as Kent continued to glare at him wordlessly, he pulled his mouth down at the corners, in a pantomime of thinking. "Yeah, maybe I saw the kid yesterday. I don't exactly recall at the moment."

"I warned you to leave Harley alone! Where the fuck is he?" Kent got up in his face, and maybe he remembered how much trouble Kent could make for him when he wanted it. Maybe it wasn't worth the hassle. Or maybe Kent was just stupid.

RJ mumbled something that sounded like Balmoral. Kent growled and grabbed Sharon's arm, marching off.

CHAPTER 16

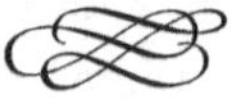

"What is it? Something bad?" She jogged along, trying to keep up with his long and angry strides, but he couldn't slow down for her. Not now.

He led her to the seediest old SRO hotel on Hastings, its infamous name screaming in black and white paint on the side wall, peeling and fading from the signature serpentine sign bracketed to its face. The worst of the lot. He wished the City's many attempts to close it down had succeeded. They entered past panels of rusty construction fencing barricading broken windows and doors, through the nondescript opening in the grimy yellow brick facade.

The dirtbag proprietor of the Balmoral stood among loitering residents in the lobby, his scowl revealing crooked and missing teeth. "Fuck you, Rick!" Kent barged in past them. "Why didn't you let me know?" Turning to Sharon he said, "Wait here," and stomped up the stairs two at a time, not knowing what horrors he would find. His gut clenched like a rock, his limbs trembling and his heart racing with adrenaline.

Sharon dashed up the scuffed wood stairs behind him, breathless, her little boots thumping like a snare drum. "Don't leave me down there alone," she hissed, holding her hands up, palm out, to keep them away from the dirt and graffiti-sprayed walls. She caught up. "What's going on?"

She squeaked as they topped the landing, stepping around a crying junkie in a heap on the top step, his syringes and gear scattered around him, and marched down the hall. Stinking garbage spilled out of one gaping doorway, a filthy toilet in another doorless room. The next revealed a stack of stinking, stained mattresses sagging against the wall.

When he came to a closed door covered in sprayed green script, a yellowed eviction notice hanging from a tack, he crashed through the door. He quickly scanned the tiny cluttered room, making a mental inventory: crumbling drywall covered in marker scrawl, plastic milk crates piled with trash, a broken television on its side, plastic tarps taped over the broken window. A messy bed.

He dashed to the bed, shoved aside pillows and piled up sleeping bags to reveal a tiny, half-dressed brown-skinned boy, curled up in a fetal position, limp, unconscious. He was barely recognizable. Kent's worst nightmare.

"Fuck! Harley!" His hands flew over the limp body, checking his weak pulse, lifting his eyelids, listening to his shallow breath to confirm his fears. "Jesus! He's still alive."

Sharon gasped. "Oh, my God. Is that Harley?"

Kent nodded and turned. She stared at the scene, frozen to the spot, her mouth open.

Kent scooped up the thin figure, light and limp as a rag, scanning the room. Drug paraphernalia scattered everywhere, on top of a cardboard box standing in for a coffee table, on the filthy linoleum. He roared in rage. As he spun to carry the boy out, his tiny arm flung out and bounced, so that no one could miss his blue-tinged fingernails, or the sores, bruises and track marks that marred his smooth young skin.

"Call 9-1-1," he barked as he charged back down the stairs.

"What? I – " she followed on his heels, her breath coming fast and sharp in his ears.

They pounded down the narrow dim stairway and catapulted out onto the sidewalk. He stopped, curling the boy closer as he murmured words into his ear. "Harley, buddy. Can you hear me? Harley."

From the corner of his eye he saw her fumble with her phone, fingers trembling, dialling 9-1-1 while Kent held Harley's limp body, continuing to talk to him, urging him to consciousness. Praying.

"Hurry, please, God." His heart squeezed into his throat, anguish in his voice, and as he met Sharon's frightened gaze, tears burned his eyes.

When the dispatcher answered she shoved the phone toward Kent's face.

"Ambulance to the Balmoral, East Hastings, 10-58, juvie!"

After that, there was nothing to do but stand, tears streaming, pulse pounding, praying. He coddled and jostled and cooed to Harley, urging him to wake up. Finally he stirred, and whimpered, and Kent hugged him, his eyes wet with tears. "You'll be okay, buddy. The ambulance is coming for you. Hang in there, Harley."

The cops arrived first, two women getting out of the cruiser and approaching. It was Jenna and Ashley who stopped beside them.

"Is that Harley?" Ashley asked.

Kent nodded and murmured. "RJ's back."

They stood by, hands on their belts, waiting with them for the ambulance, one of them murmuring into her radio, the other exchanging quiet words with Sharon, who gestured back towards the gaping door of the Balmoral, explaining.

At last, with a single *whoop* of its siren, the ambulance pulled up alongside the curb and paramedics hopped out and took over, whisking the tiny figure out of his arms. Harley's small hand gripped Kent's weakly as they pulled him away.

"I'm coming to the hospital, Harley. I'll be right there, buddy. Hang on."

Kent stood back, hooking his arm around Sharon's shoulders, curling it to pull her close for comfort. Despite his desperation and determination in searching for Harley, because he'd known in his gut something was wrong, he was now calm as they watched the ambulance pull away, sirens blaring, lights flashing. His worst nightmare realized. There was nothing more that he could do, for the moment. Harley was in the hands of the experts now.

But under the calm surface, black oily fear coiled low in his gut, tendrils of horrific memories wending their way thorough his veins, bringing to life the pain, the grief, the shame of his past. He couldn't lose Harley. He wouldn't survive another loss like that.

She turned to him, resting her forehead against his chest, and he wrapped his arms around her, sighing. He didn't know if he was comforting her or himself, but he was glad not to be alone this time.

Ashley squeezed his shoulder before they left. "We'll get him, Kent. Hang in there."

He nodded. He prayed they would. "Come on. Let's get my car."

He drove to the hospital in stern silence, the heaviness of his mood filling the car. She didn't know what to say, but she wished she could lessen his pain. Despite the horrors of the day, Sharon marvelled that Kent maintained a calm presence of mind, and bold, proprietary manner, as though he were personally responsible for everybody in the entire neighbourhood, like a jaded, weary mother with a large unruly brood of children. His caring oversight lent an air of humanity to the unimaginable and shocking.

She felt emotionally drained, an ache in her throat, and could only imagine how he felt. She touched his arm, and when he glanced her way, she sent a sad smile of support. "So. This is what you do," she finally said, her voice soft.

In response, his face tightened, his shoulders hitching slightly, as if to say, yes, but. It was more than his job. It was his calling. Though she almost had the sense that he was punishing himself for everything that went wrong in the world.

"You okay?"

Sitting by his side, Sharon felt a tingling warmth in her limbs, a fullness in her chest. In the short time she'd known him, the entire place and everyone in it had shifted in her perspective just a little, and her admiration for him grew. If he weren't with her, she'd have fallen apart long ago. The fact he'd given up his nursing career filled her with a heavy sadness.

What a loss to the health care professions. He was exactly the calm, caring, competent person you wanted with you when your life was in shambles or you were in pain. He had a unique talent for nurturing.

She'd had a tight chest all day. Added to the stress of events, she carried the guilt over keeping the details of her meeting with Seibold, and her suspicions about him, a secret from Kent. He didn't deserve to be deceived. The other day, after he'd pressed for details of her personal history with City Hall – more than pressed, threatened to dig them up himself – she'd had no choice but to capitulate. Then he'd started advocating to bring in the press and the public.

How could she trust him with the full truth now, knowing how he felt?

"Can you wait here?" he asked when they arrived at the hospital.

"Yes," she said, settling into a hard plastic chair, watching him from a distance, and realizing she could see the tension in his high shoulders, in his taut face. At first glance, he appeared relaxed, cool, and as handsome as ever in his careless way, but she saw the price he paid. Kent had to make phone calls, show his identification and fill out forms to get permission to visit Harley, since he wasn't next of kin, and he hadn't yet been able to reach the aunt. Since Harley was technically a ward of the state, there were special protocols to follow. It was a tedious bureaucratic process, and after checking her messages and emails, she had plenty of time to think.

She carried inside her at all times an innate mistrust of radicals, activists, politicians and the press.

Her father had taken his bellicose charm and articulate, outspoken compassion for his fellow man well beyond letters to the editor, the voting booth, petitions and protests, to the extreme of running for public office himself because he believed in walking his talk and taking action to push for change where he could. He was always on the television, or being interviewed for local radio. She had grown up fully indoctrinated in his socio-economic and political worldview and still, despite everything, shared those values. Mostly.

Her father's methods and the lifestyle it imposed on them had always been uncomfortable for a shy girl, but something she tolerated and assumed was necessary to achieve his honourable ends.

Only now, she understood how change really happened. It happened in the back hallways and corner offices of power, whether political or corporate. And more often than not, those with power operated in their own self-interest. Far from the best interests of the common man, let alone those disenfranchised souls relegated to society's fringes. Elected representatives, she'd long ago decided, were too close to the power to resist its allure, and were soon sucked into the evil vortex of corruption. If her once idealistic father could succumb to its temptations, anyone could. In her mind, the roles were inseparable.

She no longer trusted politicians. But she didn't trust social activists either. They were two ends of the same continuum in her book. The only reliable, honourable and effective route to lawful social change was the law itself. And that's the path she'd chosen, to the extreme of avoiding contact with both politicians and radicals at all times.

Until now.

If Kent knew of the tentative deal she'd brokered with Seibold, he wouldn't give her a chance to explain how it was part of her larger investigation. The way this day was going, she expected his fuse was shorter than usual, his sense of outrage fully primed. She couldn't bear to be on the receiving end of that righteous indignation.

As the evening unfolded, her sense of guilt grew. But even if she wanted to tell him, when had she had the chance? It had been one thing after another all day, and it wasn't over yet.

At last they were in Harley's room. Sharon hung back as Kent went to him, a tiny brown face in the large white space. The boy was still groggy, but had somewhat recovered after having Naloxone administered. He also was getting fluids via IV.

"Hey, Harley, buddy," Kent said as he went forward, taking the boy's limp hand and leaning on the edge of his hospital bed. He rubbed his thin arm above the IV, and Sharon's heart squeezed. Harley's tough exterior had vanished, and he was just a skinny, sick little boy, all alone in the world. Except for Kent.

Harley didn't speak, but his large dark eyes looked up at Kent's and filled with tears. His dry lips moved a little, and Kent bent over him to hear what whispered words he spoke.

"It's not your fault, Har. RJ's a monster."

Harley nodded, a tear sliding down his cheek, and Sharon could only imagine what threats or bribes the creepy dealer had used on him.

"I warned you about him last time. You can't outsmart a devil like him. Just stay close to me. That's all I ask. I'll watch out for you."

Harley's heavy eyelids drifted closed, and Kent sat and gently stroked the mop of black hair back from his brow again and again, soothing him. Just watching them soothed Sharon, too.

A blue-scrubs-clad doctor strode into the room, gripping a chart. "I thought I'd find you here. This one of yours?"

Kent looked up slowly, his face wooden, devoid of expression. Not the reaction Sharon would have expected to a doctor's attentions.

"Aaron." Kent's voice was flat, and his eyes narrowed before he turned back to Harley and seemed to ignore the doctor.

The tall, dark-haired man hadn't noticed her, standing by the wall beside the door, and she hesitated to step forward and talk to him. "I don't know why you keep getting attached to them. There's nothing you can do for them. You'll just disappoint yourself again and again."

"Don't you have an appendix to remove or something?"

What? Why were they both being so rude?

The doctor stiffened. "Don't be like that. I'm just looking out for you, little brother."

Brother? Sharon gasped, blinking in disbelief.

"Sure you are." Finally Kent looked up and met the doctor's gaze. Sharon had never seen such an expression of disdain on Kent's face. Except, she realized, at the moment they'd first met. Just before they'd touched for the first time, and he'd rocked her world. For a split second, she'd been the recipient of that baleful glare. "Don't bullshit me, Aaron. You'd never miss an opportunity to ride my butt, and you couldn't pass up this one, could you?"

The doctor, Kent's brother Aaron, apparently, was silent for a moment. "Not true, Kent. I only came by because Dad asked me to deliver a message. He wants you to stop by his office before you leave."

Sharon's stomach dropped. Their father was here at the hospital, too? Her head was reeling with new information that didn't fit her image of Kent and his family. Somehow, she'd filled in the blanks and assumed it was just him and his mom, the community nurse.

"Yeah, I'll bet." Kent glanced up briefly. "Thanks for the message, monkey-boy." His dislike mingled with a begrudging fondness.

Aaron turned to leave and flinched when he noticed Sharon, his chin lifting as the corners of his mouth turned down. "Hello."

She swallowed and nodded, unsure how to greet this arrogant man who Kent scorned without an introduction. Her gaze scanned his face, his form, searching for a family resemblance. There was a little, but she'd have never guessed. "Hello."

Kent turned toward her, his voice thick with irony. "Sharon. Allow me to introduce my big brother, the-brilliant-young-surgeon-Doctor-Aaron-Sawyer." He pulled his mouth wide and tight in a parody of a smile. "Aaron, Sharon Beckett. Attorney at law."

"Oh!" Aaron's brows lifted in a surprised smile. "I assumed you were one of the street... I mean social workers."

She straightened her shoulders and lifted her chin. If she were a social worker, he would have insulted her with just his tone of voice.

"Right then. Must go. Cases to check on. A pleasure, Ms. Beckett."

She had an inkling, suddenly, of what inspired Kent's disdain for the brilliant-young-surgeon-Doctor-Aaron-Sawyer. She deigned to nod briefly, her gaze following him as he strode out the door.

After leaving Harley's room, Kent led her to the elevator and then down a labyrinth of hospital corridors. He seemed to know his way extremely well, and she wondered how much time he'd spent here. "Your brother is a surgeon. What's your father?"

"Also a surgeon. And hospital administrator."

"Administrator of this hospital?" St. Paul's was one of the biggest, busiest hospitals in the metro area.

He gestured to a row of waiting room chairs. "You don't have to come in with me. It won't be pleasant." He gestured to a row of waiting room chairs.

She looked up and realized they'd arrived at the hospital administration offices. She frowned. She would not let him go in there alone. "I want to."

"Suit yourself. My father's no more agreeable than my brother."

They entered his office, only to stand for several minutes in front of the silver-haired man's big mahogany desk and wait for him to finish a phone call, then wait for him to read and type something on his computer screen, before he looked up to acknowledge them. He was a handsome middle-aged man in an expensive suit, who, Sharon could see now, had more in common with his elder son Aaron, than with Kent, who shared more with his mother.

"Son." His gaze swung to take her in. "And who's this?"

"Sharon Beckett, solicitor with..." he hesitated, gesturing toward her to fill in.

Surprised, she stumbled. "Um... Flannigan, Searle, Meacham, Beckett and Shirazi. How do you do?" She thrust out a hand to shake.

He pursed his lips while studying her hand. "Your father's a partner?"

She frowned in confusion before understanding the question. "No, Dr. Sawyer. I am."

His expression morphed into one of quiet assessment and curiosity. Apparently deciding she was interesting, he half stood from his desk chair and took her hand softly, the briefest of greetings. "Ms. Beckett." Apparently, he was curious to know why she was here with his son.

"We came to visit a patient. We're working together on his project," she offered to fill the silence and satisfy his curiosity, which Kent had no intention of doing, and received a subtle eye roll for her efforts.

Dr. Sawyer scowled, as though he didn't quite know to which project she referred. "I see." He continued to peer at her, his gaze jumping back and forth from her to Kent and back again.

After an awkward silence, Kent cleared his throat. "You beckoned, sir?" He stood stiffly, unnaturally, Sharon realized, with none of his accustomed serene confidence, approachability and grace.

Dr. Sawyer the elder scowled at Kent's tone. "I heard a kid came in from your area. I just wanted to know what happened. If it involved you."

Kent filled his lungs, paused and let it out before speaking. "I would have thought your legion of staff could do a better job of that than me."

The elder Sawyer tilted his chin down to his chest, frowning. He made a vague growling noise in his throat. "Don't be like that, Kent. Can't I ask to see my own son?"

"You know where I both live and work, Father. And yet..." He left his sentence unfinished with a note of expectation and a lift of his chin, and Sharon inferred that his father didn't inconvenience himself to stay involved in his son's life.

Dr. Sawyer sat upright abruptly, rearranging a few papers on his desk. "I thought you could tell me something about what happened to the boy. However, I see that you're not in the mood." He cleared his throat. "Your mother would like you to join us for dinner on Sunday. Can you manage that for a change?"

Kent stared at the surface of his father's desk, his lips moving with tension, seemingly torn between pleasing his mother and avoiding his father.

In the gap of fraught silence Dr. Sawyer added, "Why don't you join us, Ms. Beckett? I assume you've met Kent's mother?"

She nodded, uncertain how to answer the invitation. She glanced at Kent, who filled his lungs and sighed heavily, his jaw ticking. He glanced at her, a question in his gaze, and she answered with her eyes.

Kent shook his head with a twitch of irritation. "Fine. We'll be there."

CHAPTER 17

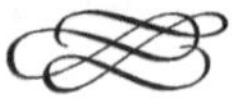

Kent couldn't get out of there fast enough. His head pounded from the aftermath, his jaw aching from tension that he couldn't shake loose. No encounter with his father left him without emotional turmoil – a sickening mix of rage and loathing and shame and sadness that sat in his stomach like a tumour, eroding his peace of mind. That, on top of his grief about Harley.

But this time his father had spread his high and mighty judgement over Sharon, stirring in Kent a protective fury that nearly had him leaping over his father's pretentious desk to strangle the old bastard.

And to make matters worse, he'd used Sharon to leverage a commitment to Sunday dinner, a weekly ritual that Kent avoided as often as possible. If it weren't for his mother, he would never go. Though they kept in touch and saw each other often, he knew it was important to her to have her family all together, however strained the atmosphere. But as if exposed to some toxic substance, it took Kent days to recover from the painful and draining events. He dreaded them.

Kent needed cleansing now, as a matter of fact. Restless and punchy, he knew he'd pick a fight with someone before long if he didn't turn his mood around. God forbid it was Sharon, who'd been nothing but patient and supportive as he dragged her through the murk and turmoil of his life.

"You got a little more time? I want to take you somewhere," he said as they drove back downtown.

Glancing at her watch, she shrugged. "Sure, okay. The day's over, anyway." Her tone was gentle, as if sensing that he'd come away from the hospital wounded and fragile. She reached over to touch his arm lightly, and he flinched, tense, forcing himself not to jerk away, because that's how raw he felt. Her hand slid away, and he felt a wave of regret. She was only trying to comfort him.

They left his car at International Village and walked down to the corner of Hastings and Main. He led her inside the grand Victorian-era Carnegie Library and downstairs to the community spaces. A few people sat around. Carl was here, which he'd expected, and he was glad. Carl always provided a comforting counterpoint to his own father's chilling influence. Since he'd lost his own family, Carl appreciated human connection, and Kent always valued his quiet wisdom. He had a soft spot for the lost souls in this community. Sometimes Kent was one of them.

He went to him, and they gripped each other's hands and arms warmly, holding on for an extra beat or two. Sensing some distress in Kent, Carl held on, wrapping one hand around his shoulder in a gesture of comfort, his eye contact steady, compassionate and wise.

"I heard about Harley," Carl murmured. Word travelled fast. There was little that went on in the Downtown Eastside that Carl wasn't aware of. He cared deeply about his adopted family and community. "How you holding up, son?" Kent nodded, swallowing a sudden thickness in his throat, and tried to pull his tense lips into a small smile of reassurance.

Sharon stepped toward them, her face lit up with a smile.

"Sharon, nice to see you." They hugged. Kent felt his brow slide up.

Kent moved around, greeting the others he knew, getting introduced to the few he didn't. Marlene was here, with fresh marks on her face, and he took a moment to talk to her and give her a big comforting hug. Her Philippine girlfriend Carla was with her, a sometimes sex worker, though Kent knew she didn't want to be, and had tried to find and keep other work with little success. She couldn't make enough to support herself and her kid, who ended up living with her mother more often than not. This made her sad and hopeless, as she wanted more stability for her child.

Two First Nations teens sat together with an older, pony-tailed guy he didn't recognize, strumming a guitar. They talked as he illustrated chords. Kent noticed a few regular volunteers, including Hedi who helped with tutoring in the learning centre. Just being here was a comfort to him.

"You want a coffee?" he asked Sharon, who still chatted with Carl, who'd introduced her to Louis and Walter, old-timers who were neighbours. Kent knew they came down here for company, and to do Tai Chi classes together, watch films, and stay warm and dry. Today they seemed to have abandoned a game of chess.

"Sure, thanks. Just a little – "

"Milk. I know," he said and went to fetch it. That made him smile and wonder at himself. Since when did he memorize how a woman liked her coffee and finish her sentences? There were few details about Sharon Beckett he didn't notice. Fixing the coffees at the self-serve bar, he glanced over his shoulder at her. She still had that air about her, of being a little removed, and always put together as though she were going into battle. Never a hair out of place. But just the same, he sensed she was relaxing a little, and starting to know and care about these people. It pleased him to see she was open, curious and non-judgmental.

She felt him looking at her and glanced up, returning his smile, her cheeks flushing a little pink.

He brought the coffees back and handed her one, standing and listening to Hedi explain their adult literacy program to Sharon.

The louder strum of a guitar caught their attention, and everyone looked up to see the stranger tuning his guitar, while the two teens moved chairs around into a circle.

"What's happening?" he asked Hedi.

"We have a sing-a-long planned. Iñigo is visiting from Spain, and he offered to play some Flamenco music, and then lead us in some folk songs."

"Wow." He and Sharon moved to some chairs and sat down, sipping their coffees in silence. Someone dimmed the overhead lights, and they waited while the newcomer, Iñigo, said hello and introduced himself. He spoke in heavily accented English, explaining that he lived in the Basque region, and telling a little about his culture. Then he started strumming and picking some soft, beautiful traditional guitar melodies.

After a few instrumental tunes, he played traditional folk songs. At first he sang in Spanish, including *Hasta Siempre*, or what Kent thought of as the Che Guevara song from Cuba. Then Iñigo switched to English songs, starting with a moving, senti-mental version of Dark Eyed Molly, and though he sang English lyrics, Kent deduced Iñigo, with his shining eyes, was thinking of a singular dark-eyed girl back home in Spain.

Kent glanced at Sharon as she became engrossed in the music, eyes closed, humming. *Huh.* Who knew she'd be a fan of folk music. The thought he was breaching her hard exterior shell brought a smile to his face, and he thrilled at the prospect of getting to know her even better. He reached over and set his hand over hers, feeling the instant warmth coil between them like he'd plugged in a heater, and watched her kissable lips tuck in and curl up at the corners as she felt it too.

He had to reel his mind back from some breath-stealing images involving those lips that shot way out ahead of where they were at, his pulse kicking up. But he had a vivid imagination, and the wild chemistry that played out whenever they touched inspired rather dirty thoughts.

People hummed, and then sang along when Iñigo began Waltzing Matilda, and This Land and other familiar tunes. One of Carl's friends pulled out a mouth harp and introduced some beautiful harmonies. One of the teens kept up a beat by drumming on a plastic chair.

Kent did his best to keep up, even when he didn't remember the lyrics well enough. He discerned one voice that rose above all the others, a perfect, delicate soprano to complement the rich tenor of their Spanish accompanist. He didn't need to look to know it was Sharon singing How Great Thou Art. He could feel the air vibrate, and the poignant energy coming off of her, her hand under his gone utterly still.

But he did look. And then he couldn't look away. She kept her eyes closed, and he wondered if she'd forgotten where she was. Rocking with the rhythm, her head tilted slightly back as she lost herself in the song. The others' voices faded back as Sharon's voice soared. Kent scanned the room, and his gaze caught on Carl's. They exchanged a knowing smile.

Kent's attention fixed on Sharon, who was still lost in the song. For the moment her cool, detached ice princess persona had melted and he could see the tender-hearted girl that hid beneath. He yearned to get past that protective facade. If she would let him, he wanted to know her better.

~

After the sing-a-long, Sharon remained subdued. While he felt closer to her, she'd gone somewhere inside herself, walled off again. Was she embarrassed? Or had the music altered her mood? Either way, she seemed lost in thought as they left the community centre, evading his gaze, and his heart thrummed with concern.

Waving goodbye to the others, he said, "Where'd you park?"

"I took the bus. I was tired of worrying about my precious car on these streets." A hint of self-deprecating humour coloured her tone, though she kept her face neutral.

"I'll drive you home then."

It turned out she lived in a restored heritage brick building on Fairview slopes, overlooking False Creek. He found a spot on Spruce Street and he walked her slowly to her townhome, keeping his strides small to match hers, their arms and the backs of their hands brushing lightly as they moved in sync down the narrow sloping sidewalk, sending sparks of electricity shooting up his arm, literal torment.

Her street was quiet at this late hour, but the occasional hum of traffic drifted up from Sixth Avenue and the Cambie Bridge traffic. He scanned the sparkling city lights with the globe of Science World, and the glowing golden line of bridge over water.

"Nice view of the city from up here," he murmured, wanting to keep the connection alive.

She paused at her front stoop flanked by neat shrubbery and turned to face him. He sensed in her a matching hesitation to end this day that they'd shared, so full of emotion and turmoil.

"You okay?" he whispered, testing the water.

She hummed ambiguously in reply. Unlocking her front door, she turned back, her blue eyes seeking his face. The street light on the corner highlighted her bright hair, and the beautiful angles and curves of her cheek and jaw, robbing him of breath.

Watch yourself, Sawyer. He didn't want to do the wrong thing. Make a move that would cause her to push him away again. He held himself at a distance, unsure where they stood after a day that seemed to have left them both raw and vulnerable.

Her retreat on the project with City Hall still annoyed him, but he couldn't deny she'd come a long way toward connecting with and caring about the residents of the Downtown Eastside. That meant a lot to him. The entire experience of finding Harley today, and meeting Kent's family at the hospital, was enough to scare anyone away. Yet she'd stuck with him, supportive and comforting through it all, and he felt his chest expand with gratitude as a tingling warmth coursed through his limbs. Maybe there was still some hope of persuading her to fight harder and even take their fight public. He so wanted them to be on the same team.

His own nerves felt frayed and numb. What he wanted was a stiff drink and a good night's sleep. At least, that's what he'd settle for, since he couldn't have his first wish, which was to take hold of her curvy body, and cover her sweet, plump mouth with his, sinking into her softness. A much more pleasant kind of forgetfulness.

Or could he?

Their eyes met and held, flashing with heightened awareness, and hers were hooded as she slowly blinked and glanced away, sending instant tightness to his groin. Her sudden shyness drew a slow smile from him and straightened his spine with a surge of primal male want.

When he'd first met her, he'd wanted her instantly, like a firestorm, despite being angry and intimidated by her cold facade, convinced she'd try to crush him under her heel. Now, her gaze made him feel taller. She looked at him like a man she admired, and a trusted friend, causing his blood to roar in his veins.

He wanted more. More of her. He still felt bruised and vulnerable from the day, but being with her soothed him. Yet he wouldn't make a move without knowing what she wanted. The magnetic pull was powerful. Despite her softening, and the compelling sensitivity of her singing, he waited for an invitation from her. Perhaps he signalled his desire with his eyes.

"Would you like a cup of tea?" she whispered.

Hell, yes, he'd like a cup of tea. He'd drink swamp water from the moat if it meant crossing the ramparts of her fortress. He nodded mutely and followed her inside, a wave of relief surging through his veins, his pulse pounding joyfully like a kid promised ice cream.

"Make yourself comfortable." She kicked off her shoes and gestured to her sofa, a slouchy denim thing far more casual than she herself, and took his jacket, carrying it away and disappearing into the kitchen. He could see her moving around through an old-fashioned pass-through, putting a kettle on and messing about in the cupboards. A slow melody by Adele started playing, and she hummed along softly with a blues-y grit different from what he'd heard at the centre tonight.

"This is cozy," he said.

Her laughter tinkled. "I know what you're thinking."

Did she? He'd pictured her in a sleek, modern, luxury apartment, all white and hard edges. But though she was in a trendy area, her condo was funky, cluttered and comfortable. She was a woman full of contradictions, and he thought about the soft centre she protected with her icy shell.

She returned with mugs of tea. Black, the way he liked it. He smiled up at her. "Thanks for coming with me tonight. I needed – "

"I know. I knew that." She lowered onto the sofa beside him, not too close, but not so very far away, and his heart kicked again with wild hope. "But thank you for taking me along. That was a lovely event."

He hesitated a beat, unsure if she was self-conscious about it. He flicked a glance her way. "I didn't know you sang. I mean really sang."

She flashed a quick smile of acknowledgement and hid behind her mug of tea, eyes cast down, her lashes brushing her cheeks, steam rising. The lamp beside her cast a golden glow over her smooth ivory skin, and he fought to keep his gaze there when it longed to wander, pulling his attention down the column of her neck, past the elegant line of her clavicle to the soft mounds of her cleavage just barely visible at her open neckline, rising and falling with each breath. His cock lurched in sync with the surge of his heart, and he swallowed. *Patience.*

"I sing in a choir at church." She took a sip. "A few, actually."

At his puzzled frown, she expanded.

"I grew up going to church, but I quit after the – " She shrugged. He assumed she referred to her father's scandal, and their forced retreat from society, and so he reached across to take her hand, risking further distraction but unable to keep his distance. He stroked the top of her soft hand with his thumb, and her gaze flicked to his as she inhaled. "I got out of the habit of going while at university. But I missed the music. And I do love to sing. So now I only go for the choir."

He smiled and shook his head. "You're an enigma, Princess." He released her hand and sipped his tea, letting silence settle around them.

"Tell me about your father." She sobered. "Why are you at odds?"

He leaned back, stroking his beard. "I'm not the son he wished for, I guess."

Her eyes crinkled as she smiled softly, her gaze raking his features as she returned the favour by reaching out and slipping her hand into his on the sofa between them, this time threading her fingers between his, sending a jolt of heat straight to his heart. "That can't be true." She met his gaze head on. "You're honest and selfless, passionate and caring." Her fingers squeezed his. "The world needs people like you more than anything. Who wouldn't be proud to have you as their son?"

His heart gave a flip at her kindness, and her touch, and he turned to look at her straight on. "Thank you. But I think it's more that I don't idolize him as he thinks I should. His ego won't accept that."

"I know a thing or two about rebellion. It's hard to…" she hesitated.

"Fight your inherent nature?" He blurted, and her eyes widened, making him instantly regret his words. "I'm sorry. That's the rebel in me talking. You had good reasons. You wouldn't be as successful as you are if it were true."

She pursed her lips, suddenly vulnerable, and he had to fight to keep his attention on her words as his skin tingled with the urge to touch her. To take her in his arms and really touch her.

"I was very young and I may have… over-reacted." A sheen of tears turned her eyes into mirrors before they spilled over her lashes. "I know," she swallowed, looking down, "that I wish I had my father back. I can't undo the past, but I miss him. And I wish I'd been more…" She shrugged. "Tolerant. Loyal, maybe. He was a great dad," she whispered.

"You did your best." He cupped her chin and peered into her glassy eyes. "But I see more than the woman you forged. I respect that, but I'm drawn to the other parts of you. The parts you hide, maybe."

"I don't let my guard down with many people."

"I'm glad you trusted me," he whispered.

She pulled her lips between her teeth, nodding, and he reflected that maybe he hadn't given her much choice. Something bigger had swept them up into its embrace.

"You know, you don't have to come to dinner. Don't let my father intimidate you."

"I wasn't intimidated. I want to come. I like your mom, and I'm curious to know where you came from."

He grimaced, skeptical. "You sure about that?" He never would invite someone he'd just started seeing to a family dinner. It infuriated him that his conniving father had finagled this invitation with no warning, blind-siding him, trapping Sharon.

She nodded without hesitation.

He took a deep breath, sighing. It would be humiliating, undoubtedly. "I dread the dinners. No matter how hard I try, he provokes me. And then I hate myself afterwards." He scoffed. "I… it…" He exhaled. "It won't be… I mean, it usually ends badly. More of a train wreck, really."

She raised a brow, pressing her lips together in amusement. "Really. I couldn't have guessed."

He flashed a grin. Lord, he wanted to kiss those lips so badly. "So basically you're just coming to rubberneck."

"No. I want to help." She smiled up at him, her gaze flicking from his eyes to his mouth and back again.

Suddenly there wasn't enough air in the room. Were they still talking about dinner? Clearing his suddenly tight throat, he said, "If you really want to."

"I really do," she whispered, her double entendre unmistakable in the breathy tone of her voice. Her cheeks pinked. Her gaze heated, enlarged dark pupils chasing some pale blue into the night shadows.

Oh. Lord. His dream come true.

She set down her mug and rotated slightly to face him, lifting one knee onto the sofa, tucking her foot under the other.

His tentative smile faltered at her open posture, his gaze skipping from her sparkling eyes to her full smiling lips down her white neck to the soft mounds of her breasts, rising and falling rapidly. He swallowed, his throat dry.

She leaned ever so slightly closer, searching his eyes. Nodding, her full lips stretched into a gentle, alluring smile. His gaze flicked to her mouth, back to her sparkling blue eyes, back to her mouth. She stole his breath, and he felt his nostrils flare in hungry need. A separate conversation was happening between the lines as he realized they'd moved closer. She was radiating intent that rocked him and sent his blood racing.

His gaze swept her features. She was so beautiful. Excitement rolled in his stomach as he scanned her lips, her cheeks, her beautiful blue eyes that gazed back at him, his fingertips tingling with the need to touch. The way she looked at him, so open and inviting, was new and thrilling.

He registered the message in her body language, her direct sultry eye contact. Blood rushed from his head to his groin with a roar as a jagged white flash of pure lust shot up his spine. A sense of weightlessness filled his chest and emanated outward, lifting him up until he was floating, in his body but also above it, on the edge of ecstasy. "Sharon?" His whispered voice broken.

"Yes, Kent." Her whispered voice shook. She'd trembled, with fear or with desire, he didn't know.

"Is this a good idea?" Please say yes, his throbbing cock begged. He'd give her one more chance to back out, but all it would take was one flick of her wrist and he was a goner.

"It's a terrible idea." She knew it. Her lawyer's mind was busy arguing both sides of the case, but something else had taken over. The wild chemistry that had made their interactions fraught with desire from the first moment had reached its boiling point.

She pushed up onto both knees, sitting on her heels to face him, her heart racing. She leaned a little closer. "It's so wrong. So completely wrong. But... but I maybe..." She chewed her lip, thinking.

Sharon was in trouble. She'd been trying to tamp down the surge of desire she'd been feeling for him all evening. Her heart, already softened by events earlier in the day, gave in. She wanted this. She wanted him.

Her pulse raced at her dangerous thoughts. This went against every rule in her book. "We're adults." She tried. "We can manage this, right? It doesn't have to affect our work, and we can be discrete."

"Stop," Kent shook his head, his eyes darkening, sending her pulse hammering behind her ribcage. *Stop?* "I see you, Princess. You don't have to manage this. Let it be. This thing between us is huge and we can't control it. The only thing we need to do is give in to it."

Her stomach quivered, sending a shiver racing over her skin.

"Relax," he whispered, stretching his arm towards her, touching the side of her neck with his fingertips, sending a shock wave of desire through her. The place his fingers touched her skin seemed to zing with an electrical charge. "This. Is. Inevitable." With a flick of one eyebrow, he rasped. "I'm in charge now."

The hair on the back of her neck lifted at his sudden bossiness. It was unexpected. He would not let her keep her guard up, and the thought both terrified her and lit her on fire.

Her chest rose with a deep shuddering breath, and fell again, drawing his gaze to her breasts with a dangerous flash of hunger. Her nipples drew tight, tingling, and she knew he noticed, and craved his touch more than anything. "But – "

"Nuh-uh." He stopped her words with a fingertip over her lips and lifted his sexy mouth on one side in a smirk. With a fierce glint in his eye, his head shook a little, and she shut up, releasing a smothered sigh as her heart pounded at the promise of his passion released, aimed at her.

He was just as much a cocky alpha male as his father and his brother, but his heart was ten times bigger. Part of his intensity was how he focussed his attention on the things, and the people, he cared about, and that made her knees go weak with desire.

He groaned and closed the distance between them, stopping when their lips were but millimetres apart. The charge hit her instantly, pulling them closer like magnets. Yes, it was inevitable. There was no denying the irresistible chemistry between them.

"I've been wanting alone time with you for quite a while now. Once I let go, I don't know if I'll be able to stop."

"I don't want you to stop," she squeaked, her voice cracking as the truth broke free.

Kent covered her mouth with his then, giving her everything

he had, and everything that had been building up since they'd first met, first touched and the heavens had opened. Their first kisses only intensified her awareness of how much she wanted him, chaste as if they were standing on a street corner.

Now, unrestrained, he reached for her, slipping his long fingers gently behind her neck, opening his soft, insistent mouth over hers, sweeping into her with his demanding tongue. His ravenous kisses carried her to a whole new level of fearlessness, and she let go of every last cautionary argument that was buzzing around her head, surrendering to this magical thing happening between them. There would be consequences, was the last coherent voice she heard. His other hand slid languorously over her shoulder, gliding down her ribs to her hip, pressing his fingertips into her flesh possessively.

The anticipation of touching was nothing compared to reality. With every contact, the powerful current ran between them, firing electrical currents like a Tesla coil, jolting her, speeding her heart rate. She didn't know her skin could be so sensitive as she trembled under his skimming, worshipful hands.

His lips and tongue explored her mouth, his muscles growing rigid with desire as he leaned in to her. She opened to his plundering tongue and let him dive deep, indulging their pent up desire and discovering where this incredible, mutual attraction would lead.

Sharon met his desire head on, unhesitatingly, and the effect was explosive. He lay her back, following her down with his beard chafing softly as he explored her ear and neck and the open vee of her top and she wrapped a leg around his hips, pulling him closer, pressing her burning core to meet him, her body rushing hot with a wild hunger.

He moaned as he came down on top of her, pressing his hardened need into her softness.

She thrilled at the weight of him holding her down. Was that needy sound coming from her own throat? It fanned the flame of his want, and instantly he'd hooked a hand behind her knee, straightened her body and covered it with his own, needing full contact as much as she did.

Unable to stop herself, she lifted her hips off the sofa to meet him, demanding more, raking her hands through his hair, loosening its tie. Explosive heat radiated from his body. This was moving so fast!

She gasped, and they broke apart, panting. He lifted his gaze to her eyes, touching foreheads, long strands of his golden brown hair falling forward in a curtain, gasping for air, their open mouths still touching. His darkened gaze locked on hers with certainty and want. He kissed her again and pulled back, sitting up, tugging her with him, slowing his breathing.

"Princess, I want you so badly. I've dreamt of this since the first time I set eyes on you. Since our first touch." He shook his head, tugging his hair back and clenching a handful in a tight fist. "We have to slow down or I won't be able to..." He glanced up with a tiny laugh. "Do all the things to you that I've been dreaming of."

She swallowed thickly and nodded, her gaze darting to her bedroom. He growled and rose, lifting her with him, spanning her ribs with his hands as her arms wrapped around his neck, sweeping her into another consuming kiss, shifting her weight up to wrap around his hips in a full body embrace at the same moment.

He carried her to her bedroom door, their mouths fused hungrily.

She pointed, and he followed her direction. In seconds they stood by her bed, face to face, heat waves bending the air between them. Fingering the edge of his shirt, she delved beneath, grazing his smooth stomach with cool fingertips that sent visible shocks through him, his mouth opening in a grimace, and an awed fascination rippling through her at her power over him.

She tugged, wanting to see all of him. Touch all of him. He lifted his arms and stripped off his t-shirt, revealing his contoured pecs and acres of smooth skin, turning his attention to peeling away the layers of her clothes. His fingers shook with anticipation, and her breasts tingled, heavy and hot as he unhooked and peeled away her bra and paused just inches away, staring at her breasts, his breath catching.

Her hands came up to graze his smooth chest, trailing her fingertips over his hard chest to his rippled abs, down the trail of dark hair to caress the lines of his abdomen, tracing the waistband of his pants with the back of a fingernail where his erection pressed insistently against the fabric of his fly, making him jerk and tremble.

His voice rasped as he encircled her wrists and pulled them from his body. "I need a moment." He lifted one of her palms and tilted his head, pressing his face into it, inhaling deeply, kissing it, his tongue darting out to taste her. The heat of his tongue on her sensitive palm sent shivers over her exposed skin, and her knees wobbled, threatening to give way.

He dragged his tongue down to her wrist, up to the inside of her elbow, turned to lower her to the bed, and she let herself swing back as he watched her succumb to his attentions.

She watched his dark head bow over her arm. In the dark room, her white limbs were all that was visible in the borrowed light that streamed in from the window and the living room. She wanted to see him. She pointed to the lamp beside the bed, and he bent to turn it on, casting a warm glow over them both, highlighting her pale skin on the dark bedcover. Then he stood over her, worshiping her with his dark gaze.

"Look at you, my Princess. Tiny, curving sweetness, blue-tinged and precious like a diamond. My ice princess."

He grazed his fingertips over her silhouette, pausing to gaze at her arms, her breasts, and her belly as he passed them. A tremor shook her. She was a puddle of desire now, utterly melted under the heat of his touch.

"My god, I want you." Hooking two fingers under her panties, he slid them down her thighs and over her feet, tossing them aside. In seconds he dispensed with his own pants and stood, letting her look at him in her turn. And she did, raking his beautiful, lean, muscled form and proud cock with her hungry gaze. She'd never seen a more exquisite man, his strength and vitality visible in every pore and bulge and lean muscle.

With his hands on the bed flanking her, he bent over to place a kiss on her ribs beneath her breasts, sliding his mouth onto her belly, gently pressing her thighs apart to make space for himself. Slowly he dropped to the floor on his knees, dragging his thumbs and his mouth over the bumps of her ribs, from the curves of her belly, past her navel and lower, to the inside of her thighs, trailing over each inch of her hot skin with his tongue. Her ribs lifted from the bed of their own accord, eager to meet him halfway, and his hands slipped up the sides of her burning breasts, and over their crests, circling lightly over her erect nipples, and then pinching them, drawing a cry of need from her lips. A profusion of sensations swept over her in quick succession as his mouth and hands explored her curves and crevices. Kent was so very skilled at this. His sensitivity and empathy made him an attentive and generous lover.

She held her breath, shuddering at Kent's mouth against her most private places. Every point of contact, every sense was on high alert. She'd never felt such intense desire. He turned her on like sun, every cell glowing and vibrating with energy as he kissed and licked his way closer to her hot centre.

She brought her hands to his head, threading through the tangled strands of his loose silky hair as he explored her wet folds with his tongue.

His hair fell forward, brushing her thighs as he dragged his beard against her smoothness, and she gasped as she lost herself in her senses.

"I like this sooo much," she hummed. "I didn't know how hot long hair and a beard could be."

His lips at her clit, sucking softly, he hummed with laughter, and she vibrated with sheer sensual pleasure, moaning.

When the powerful trembling in her legs brought her close to breaking, he stood up and bent to capture her mouth again, pushing his tongue hard into her mouth, gripping her butt cheeks with his hands, lifting her tightly against his hard cock with a primal grunt. A shudder shook both of them, and she knew they couldn't wait a moment longer.

He groaned. "Sweetheart. Your soft heat is driving me mad with need. I have to have you now. I need to bury myself in you."

She let out a shuddering sigh. Then she moaned softly, gasping, "Condom?"

"Hell, yes," he shot back. He scrambled for his pants and in seconds sheathed his cock and was hovered over her, a wicked grin on his sweet face, eyes gleaming with passion.

Sharon sank back on the bed, eager to have his body on her, and in her, filling her. As his eyes caressed her, she stroked his shoulders, his chest, and slid down his abs until she wrapped her fingers around his hard cock. He groaned, his eyes rolling back, and followed her guiding hand until he could sink deep into her hot wet core with a drawn-out groan and a sigh.

"Oh, fuck, yes. Yes!" He laughed. "I'm so happy. God, yes."

She laughed, too, enjoying his delight, gasping. "I'm glad… to be able… to cheer you up."

"Princess, you have no idea. You're a miracle worker." He withdrew and sank deeper, seating himself firmly against her throbbing clit, sending incredible sensations shooting through her.

He slowed then, pulling up her knee. He shifted his weight and slid back and again gliding in, the friction of their contact so exquisite. Sobering, as they gazed into each other's eyes in wonder, his flashing, intense and earnest like flame, he whispered, "You really are an angel."

After that, passion consumed them. He cupped her breasts between his firm hands, pinching one nipple, then the other. Her head tilted back, mouth open, lifting her ribs as shock waves rippled through her. Open and vulnerable, she trembled and shuddered and whimpered. Lacing their fingers together either side of her head, he responded like a storm, his hips rocking, driving slowly into her again and again as she rose to meet him. Their mouths reunited, tongues slick and sensual, every nerve ending on fire, their gazes locked in wonderment.

A rhythmic spasm gripped the base of her spine and ripped her open with a keening cry. Kent's moan echoed as she floated up in a flash of blinding, sparkling white. He buried his face against her neck and slipped both hands beneath her hips, pulling them tightly together with a jerk, releasing a long slow breath into her neck with a groan and a shudder of pleasure.

She convulsed with a sudden release of tears, softly, openly, gasping, and he lifted his head to press his nose and mouth to her wet cheek, whispering, "All right, my love?"

She nodded, smiling at him through her tears. "Oh yes. It was glorious." She couldn't believe that had just happened, and she didn't believe she'd survived thirty-seven years without it.

Kent kissed her cheek then, and then her lips, softly, and she tasted the salt of her own tears and purred like a kitten.

CHAPTER 19

Sharon started the day with an upset stomach, unable to eat breakfast. It might have been last night's heated gymnastics, which made her feel rather faint. But more likely it was the guilt that grew and gnawed at her. Keeping the truth from Kent would be much harder now. He was sensitive and in tune with her moods. But it was still necessary. In fact, she was convinced it was the only way to win this war.

Kent was too invested, too passionate, too volatile to trust with this information, so she had to keep him in the dark – for a little longer.

If she went head on against Seibold and the City on the society's project alone, she'd lose. They'd *all* lose. The inauspicious writing was on the wall. But if her suspicions were right, there was more ammunition to find. Much more.

Her task now was to find it. Even if it meant keeping secrets from her new lover.

As she stepped onto the elevator at her office building, she glimpsed her own reflection in its mirrored interior. She reached to push an errant strand of hair back into place. Her pale complexion glowed with rosy colour, her light blue eyes sparkled, and there was an unfamiliar languorousness to her movements as she set her palm to her heated cheek. She had to pause and shake her head.

New lover!

She hadn't seen that coming. Yes, sure, there had been an instant attraction between them from the moment they'd met. A nine-point-oh earth-shattering attraction. Or the moment they'd touched, despite their initial and mutual dislike – or perhaps distrust was a better word. All her warning signals had clanged like a clarion bell the moment she saw him, all the red flags waving. He was the sort of man who meant trouble. And she avoided trouble.

Yet she couldn't stop herself.

A tremor raced over her skin as the visceral memories of his touch flashed in her mind. She could feel him and smell him.

Never in her wildest dreams did she see herself involved with a man, a younger man no less, who was a rough-edged and angry social worker committed to helping people on the fringes of society. On the remote Siberian steppes of her own carefully curated life.

By design.

Until Kent, who had drawn her back into the circle of civic politics where she oh-so-desperately did not want to be. In fact, she'd found herself surrounded by all nine circles of Dante's hell, including Lust.

Kent.

Yes, he was gorgeous with panty-melting cognac eyes and a sexy, firm body. But she didn't act on every lustful urge. She wasn't a horny young girl anymore.

She squirmed, feeling herself tingle and grow moist between the legs just thinking about him.

No, it turned out she was a horny mature woman now! The age gap wasn't significant enough to earn her the title of cougar, but she felt almost as naughty. A shudder gripped the back of her neck and shook down her spine as memories of his magical electrical tender touches flashed in her mind and echoed through her nerve endings. His scruffed face against her smooth skin. His silky hair that he used to render her liquid with need. Nobody had shaken her world like this, ever. All while she felt a tender admiration for the man inside the desirable package.

Kent was nothing like the shiny young legal associates on their way up the corporate ladder she admired. Like Dariush. Like Simon. Even he'd lost his sheen. In hindsight, he seemed too tame, too refined, too calm.

Kent, who took control and gave her exactly what she needed. His big heart fueled his restless energy, his drive, his mercurial nature. When focussed on her pleasure, it was just right.

If she'd been mistaken about Kent, what else had she got wrong?

Another shudder raised gooseflesh on her arms, and a jolt of heat caused her insides to clench at the memory of their love-making last night. How could she have known she was missing out on the physical passion that came with the volatile nature? Or that she had such an appetite for it?

Maybe she should have gone against her better judgement long ago. Now she knew what dark delights she'd been missing. For all her determination never to step over the line, Kent seemed just as determined to break every rule and expectation. Now her straight and rule-abiding world had been good and properly rocked.

But it wasn't just letting loose with any sexy, rough-edged younger man that did it for her, as though it were the novelty that turned her on. No. There was so much more to Kent. More under the surface that intrigued her curious lawyer's mind, and if she told the truth, warmed her secret hidden heart. His incongruous upper crust medical family rife with resentment and conflict. His unconventional caring career that came with sweet, touching relationships with sad old men, weary weathered women and lost boys. His selfless, passionate commitment to get involved in their lives, protect them and help them driven by what? A painful secret in his past. Some dark force pushed Kent to do what he did. She felt it. She just didn't understand it.

But it made her want to know more about him. It made her want him more.

Right now, though, she had work to do. And she needed the help of her people to get it done quickly and discretely. She took her swelling heart and tucked it away to take out and examine later, but the warm feeling stayed with her.

She prayed he'd forgive her once they'd won, for not trusting him with her own secrets.

"Ms. Beckett! Good morning."

"Good morning, Carrie." Sharon greeted the earnest young woman who answered the phones, so keen to prove herself to her father, senior partner, Arthur Meacham. As Sharon also was, in her own way.

"Here are your messages." Carrie trailed her down the corridor. "You haven't been in lately, Ms. Beckett."

"It's this *pro-bono* case. It's been keeping me busy." Sharon continued to her office. "Can you gather Tim, Ella and Abby please? I need to get them working on something."

Sharon flipped through her messages, jotting names and notes for her team so she could delegate most of them. She froze, staring at one pink slip, her jaw going slack, her stomach clenching.

Important Message:
    FOR Sharon Brecht
DATE Yesterday
FROM Uncle Gus
√ Telephoned
So good to catch up with you at the family reunion other

day. What an accomplished young woman you've become. So lucky your family is here to support your career.

*W*hat the what? Was he serious?

Fifteen minutes later, a fresh coffee in hand, Sharon sat with her three best associates briefing them on her needs, filing away what she could only construe as a veiled threat to the back of her mind, for the time being.

Newly alerted to the risks, she gave her team instructions to be as discrete as possible, and use the cover of other projects to shield their enquiries from curious City employees as she sent them off to research every land and development deal, every staff hiring and firing, every major money transfer that had taken place during the long tenure of Gus Seibold. She also asked them to look into municipal elections since he was first elected City councillor twenty-three years ago, and his personal relationship with every elected mayor. Follow the money, she instructed them. She didn't even warn them away from her own family's sordid history. Let them find whatever there was to find.

Very few people knew her as Sharon Brecht. She preferred it that way. But now, with the taste of vindication and revenge on her tongue, she was prepared to take the risk. She trusted her team. It wasn't as if they'd blab it to clients or the world at large.

"Also, Sharon," said Tim. "We found out that S & S Developments has retained their own legal counsel to prepare for our challenges."

Interesting. If Seibold was confident in his threats and bribes, he – or they, same difference in her figuring – wouldn't bother hiring lawyers, would they? But he wouldn't have gotten where he was without covering every base. Maybe he worried just enough about Sharon's own stellar legal reputation to make sure he left no vulnerabilities exposed. Little did he know the ace she held up her sleeve.

"Who did they hire?"

All three of them looked away, busied themselves straightening papers, scribbling notes.

"Who?"

Abby looked up, her face suffused in blush. "Um. It's Ms. Sharpe?"

"Rachel?" Her best friend? "Are you sure?"

Abby nodded, and the others confirmed it with their sheepish expressions.

Huh. He must have done it on purpose, thinking she couldn't oppose her best friend in a genuine conflict. He'd researched her, the devil. Well, he didn't know her at all, did he? He didn't know either of them. Long ago, when they were still students thrown onto project teams and mock trials, she and Rachel had vowed never to let their friendship interfere with their careers, or vice versa.

Sharon stepped into the hall and hit speed dial on her phone. Rachel picked up after two rings.

"Hey, Rach."

"Hey, yourself. You all set for lunch today?"

Taken aback, Sharon realized she'd been so caught up with Kent and his world and the City, she'd forgotten her regular date with her friend. "Oh. No. I've been so busy I forgot what day it was. I'm sorry, hon. I can't do today."

"Maybe another girls' night then? On the weekend?"

She hesitated, reluctant to commit. Right now she didn't know what the next twenty-four hours would bring. "Can I get back to you?"

"Sure." Rachel's tone of voice carried implicit questions.

Finally Sharon asked, "Why didn't you mention you were working for the opposition?"

"I would have if we'd had lunch. I only found out two days ago."

"You didn't have to accept the job, Rach."

"I accepted it before I knew it involved you, Shar."

"Fine," Sharon huffed, frustrated. Another secret to keep. She wanted to warn her friend that more than a minor civic property squabble lurked in the offing. That things were about to get really big and really ugly and that she was on the wrong side of history. But she couldn't. She couldn't risk giving away even a hint of her plans. Not even to her best friend.

"Well, it's been awhile since we've been opposing, but I guess it's inevitable. Maybe text me a warning next time so I don't hear it from my associates, okay?"

Over the sound of shuffling papers, Rachel said, "Sorry. I was getting around to it. I know you've got baggage with the City, hon. I'll be gentle, I promise."

Sharon chuckled, though she felt anything but amused at her friend's condescension. "As gentle as I'll be." They both laughed. "Don't worry. I can handle it."

"I know you can. I'll still love you in the morning, sweetie."

"I hope so. Bye." She really hoped so.

"Sharon."

She stopped in her tracks and turned at the gruff sound of Arthur Meacham's voice. He stood in the open doorway of his office, arms folded across his barrel chest.

"Sir?"

"You seem very busy. Is everything going well with the Pathway project?"

"Yes. Everything's under control."

His eyes narrowed, and his lips thinned, his chin dipping in a nod of acknowledgement.

She cleared her throat. "Well. It might not be going as smoothly as we'd expected, but I have a strategy."

"Oh? You were you expecting it to be simple?"

She opened her mouth to reply and realized she had nothing to say. She frowned at the suggestion that he knew something she did not.

With a sharp nod he turned and walked away.

Then she headed home. She had her own research to do. And this part she had to do herself, alone. She needed to make a stop somewhere on memory lane.

~

In the afternoon, Sharon stopped to check in at the society office to speak with Kent. Despite keeping secrets from him, she still wanted to touch base after their night together. Whether from the visceral echo of their shared passion, or grinding guilt, he was on her mind.

Sharon entered the Pathway lobby, glancing left and right, hoping to find Kent standing around, but she couldn't see him anywhere.

"Hi Sharon."

Sharon spun to face Sophia, one of the other social workers who worked there. "Hi, Sophia. How are you?"

"Can I help you with something? You looking for Kent? Or Christine?"

"Oh, Kent, thanks. Is he here today?"

"He's around somewhere. I think he's gone out on a walkabout. But he's due back in less than an hour for a staff meeting scheduled for this afternoon. Do you want to wait for him? You can sit in the staff lounge."

She was far too pent up and restless to sit and wait. "Thanks. I'll head out and walk around a few blocks near here. Maybe I'll bump into him. It's no big deal." The Downtown Eastside wasn't that large, just a dozen blocks.

Instead of heading for the safe injection site – she had a gut feeling he would not be there – she went in the opposite direction. She took Main to Cordova, veering nearer to Oppenheimer Park, but reluctant to go all the way there, and praying Kent would just appear in front of her, making the search unnecessary.

Walking alone in the neighbourhood still gave her a sense of unease, but she was toughening up. Getting to know a few of the individuals diminished the sense of discomfort. She was coming to understand that it was a living neighbourhood, one where, despite their difficult circumstances, or sometimes because of them, people chose to live. It was a community. The housing, such as it was, was cheap, awful and insufficient. But more than that, it was a place they could escape judgement, a place they could find friends and the support and understanding they lacked from the rest of society. A place, for them, of relative safety. She had nothing to fear.

As if to throw that thought back in her face, her phone dinged with a text. Glancing at it, half expecting it to be Kent, the message from an unknown number sent her heart to her throat and her stomach to her shoes.

You know it's not safe for you to wander these streets alone, Ms. Brecht.

What? Brecht again. From an unknown number. Who was this from? An associate of Seibold? The hair on her neck lifted, sending a shiver down her arms and over her scalp. She peeked left, right, across the street. Was someone watching her? She saw nothing out of the ordinary. One or two people walking past, minding their own business. A few individuals sitting in a row, slumped on a brick window ledge, blankets over their shoulders, heads bent. Just passing the time. She studied them discretely. Nobody even glanced her way. She may as well be invisible.

But not to everyone, apparently.

Before she could decide what to do, her phone dinged again.

Where is your boyfriend today, Sharon? Does he know you're out alone?

She stopped walking, staring down at her phone. Again with the boyfriend innuendos. Another shiver gripped her shoulders and neck.

She and Kent had been spending a lot of time together. Was someone who'd seen them together trying to wind her up? But it gave off a more threatening vibe than that, somehow. Who would have her number?

Just then the faint lilting sound of singing reached her ears. She turned around, tuning in to the angelic melody. A choir? Her heart skipped a beat at the familiar hymn that drifted out. Half a block ahead of where she stood squatted the enormous white stucco Saint James Anglican Church on the corner. She'd noted it before, on walks with Kent, like a giant Art Deco wedding cake amid all the heritage brick buildings and urban squalor of the Downtown Eastside. It called to her in more ways than one.

The collective voices rose in volume as she stepped inside the chancel. Entering the gloomy interior, scented, as churches always were, with furniture oil, candle wax, dust and must, she felt safer. Whatever was happening out on the street, a church with its door open offered a haven.

She'd been here once before, though the choirs she regularly attended were closer to downtown. She was an actual bona fide member at the Holy Rosary Cathedral, as much for its neo-French Gothic architecture, with its delicate, beautiful blue interior with red marble columns and stained glass, as for the quality of the music and companionship. And sometimes she practiced at St. Andrew's Wesley United, where they were more experimental, and less traditional, in their musical selections.

She followed the singing to the far end of the nave. Unlike the Catholic Cathedral's choir loft over the chancel, this modern church had its choir at the very front, tucked behind the altar. She approached, waiting until they finished the hymn, and when the choir director welcomed her with an open hand, she stepped to the end of a row of singers. A thin, bald man passed her a spare hymn book, and when the organist started the next hymn, she joined in. Though she tried, she always tried, to sing softly, it was never long before those who stood near her singled out her clear soprano voice. She nodded in acknowledgement, but lifted her chin and closed her eyes, focussed on the music. Everything fell away when she sang - her worries and fears, her regrets and loneliness, her ambition and her guilt. Even her sense of self gave way to something larger and more diffuse. Time passed unmeasured, healing all wounds.

Afterwards, she felt much better. She stood at the choir railing studying the bright, cavernous interior of the church, settling back into her body with a sigh. Other than the choir members themselves, who filed out in twos and threes, murmuring between themselves, people rarely came to listen on a weekday. A solitary man rose from a pew at the back and slipped between the retreating singers, trying to blend in. Her heart kicked her ribs. Attuned as she was to the lanky body of that man, and his effortless grace, however, every detail called out to her, familiar and dear. What was Kent doing sitting in the back of this church? Did he know she was here? Didn't he want to talk to her?

He disappeared into the crowd, squeezing out through the double door. She jogged down the aisle to catch up with him as he slipped through the front foyer and onto the tall front steps of the church.

"Kent?"

He stopped, then turned around, a sheepish expression on his face. A blush rose to his cheeks.

"Hey, you. Were you spying on me?" She stepped close, and his smile faded as he tipped his head down to gaze into her face, his pupils dilating, darkening his eyes from amber to whisky. His nostrils flared just as she registered the familiar scent of him, weakening her knees.

He clicked his tongue against his teeth, the corner of his mouth quirking up into a self-conscious smile. "Hello, Princess."

"Well? Why are you sneaking away?" Her voice was breathy,

flirtatious, her heart racing the moment they stood face to face. Memories of last night surged in her veins.

His smile flashed. "The singing was beautiful. I'm not religious, but I love the sound of your voice. I recognized it above the others."

She felt her face flood with heat. "You listened to the whole thing?"

"Most of it. I'm sorry." His cheeks pinked too. "I'm not stalking you." He laughed and shook his head, lifting a hand to caress her arm, his talented fingers sliding down to circle her wrist, sending fluttering sensations through her. "I didn't want to intrude. Sophia told me I'd just missed you and then I saw you ahead and was trying to catch up." He pointed over his shoulder with his thumb. "Then you went in here and I didn't want to interrupt so I just waited."

"You're not bothering me. We're finished."

"I had to see your beautiful face today," he whispered, recreating the intimate bubble they'd built last night, his gaze locking on hers, sharing remembered heat and carnal knowledge, triggering an instant throbbing pulse between her legs. "I didn't know if you wanted…" He shrugged.

She dipped her chin, nodding in acknowledgement. "I missed you all morning." She felt shy now. Despite their shared night of passion, their newfound intimacy cowered in the light of day.

"Me too."

"Hey, did you get a new number?"

He frowned. "No, why?"

"Did you text me? Before?"

He shook his head, suggesting that they walk together back to the office, and she fell in stride.

"What have you been up to?"

"I had to work at my office today. Papers, you know. It's our stock in trade, we lawyerly types."

A silent beat passed as they walked side by side.

"I hope you're not regretting last night. I could barely tear myself away this morning." His voice was hoarse, but he sounded like he was smiling. She sympathized. After last night, all she wanted was to stay in bed forever. With him.

She sighed, her breath catching on an internal tremble, causing muscles to clench involuntarily in secret places. "No regrets. Your voice is doing weird things to me. I might get more work done away from you."

He harrumphed. "Work? What's work? All I can think about is your creamy – "

"How's Harley doing?" That ought to distract him from his naughty thoughts.

"Umm. Right. I visited the hospital this morning. They'll let him out after a day or two of observation. Because he's so fucking young, they don't know what the drugs have done to his body."

Her distraction worked too well. He was sober again, preoccupied. "I'm sorry. That's exactly what you were worried about wasn't it?"

He hummed.

"You okay?"

"Yeah. This is what I do. It comes with difficulties."

After a pause she repeated, "I'm sorry."

"It's not your fault. It's that creep RJ."

"I know. I'm just sorry for Harley. What are you doing about RJ?"

"Hmm. Not my jurisdiction. I have to file a report with the cops. Share info with the Ministry. I help however I can... eyes on the street, you know."

"Well, it's probably best I'm not around to distract you then."

"Right. Well. We've both got work to do, I guess."

Suddenly their very different approaches to their joint problem resurfaced, along with yesterday's tension. He hadn't forgotten that she'd taken what he deemed the cowardly bureaucratic route and felt disappointment in her, again. Knowing what she kept from him made her nervous and withdrawn. How could she tell him now? What would he do? She hated lying, though it was often necessary in her job. It was probably best to keep her distance while she completed her research. At this rate, she'd be spilling all her secrets before long.

They paused in front of the Pathway Society's front doors, facing each other in silence.

"I guess I'll head off then. I've got some research to do."

His brow came down. He whispered, "You okay?"

"Yup. Yes. Just have to get on with my work day. I'm falling behind. I only wanted to… you know." She glanced up, blinking. Because of the weird texts, because of her secret work, she felt awkward around him now. She drew her lip between her teeth, wishing all this didn't have to come between them at such a delicate time. Maybe last night was a bad idea. They should have waited before acting on their crazy desire. Her heart rate stuttered, emotions pulling her this way and that. This is why she didn't do relationships, always over thinking things. She was terrible at intimacy, always retreating just when she ought to trust and connect.

He searched her eyes, his own betraying his uncertainty. "You still coming with me to dinner Sunday?"

Oh! She'd forgotten. She recovered, smiling. "Of course."

His voice warmed, speaking past a wry smile. "Your coming almost makes me look forward to it. You know it will be dreadful, right?" He linked a finger with hers, letting go after a moment, and her chest swelled, flooding with warmth. This was Kent. They'd be all right.

"Whatever happens, I promise to comfort you afterwards."

"Bring it on."

They laughed and turned their separate ways, each to their own problems to solve.

CHAPTER 20

"What's the matter?"

Sharon smiled. "Can't I visit my mother?"

She couldn't really call this her childhood home. It was the far lesser abode they'd moved into after the scandal, much further to the East. A modest bungalow between Fraser and Knight Street where she never felt she belonged. Nothing like the grand if informal West Side Craftsman bungalow she'd grown up in, walking distance from her top end school. She'd been thirteen. She'd spent her teen years here, but those were the hard years. The years of shame and reinvention.

Mom crossed her arms over her ample chest and pursed her lips. "It's eleven in the morning on a weekday, Sharon. I'm always happy to see my only daughter, but I wasn't born yesterday."

Sharon couldn't blame Mom for being skeptical. She had been a rather inattentive daughter, what with law school, her busy career, and the general disinclination to remember where she came from. She relented. "Fine. I need to find something. I have to search through Dad's old City files."

Without a word, Mom's chin went down and her brows slid up. She stepped back, opening the door wider in invitation.

Without uttering a word, a lot of history passed between them. That her father insisted on keeping every shred of paper from his working life, though there was scarcely room in the small house. And that, after he died, when Sharon wanted to burn it all in a fit of bittersweet revenge and reluctant grief, Mom informed her that Dad had made her promise to never throw it away. Not until they vindicated him. *As if.* The futility and arrogance of it had angered Sharon. She'd been in law school by the time he died. Did he really expect that she would one day clear his name?

Looks like you knew something I didn't, Dad. It was time to find out what he hid here.

"It's nice to see you too," Sharon offered.

"Would you like a coffee?"

"That'd be wonderful. Thanks, Mom." She shed her jacket and tossed it and her bag on the old chintz armchair across from the sofa. Then, reconsidering, she fished her phone out of her bag and tucked it into her back pocket, just in case she got a call. She didn't need her mother answering it for her. That would be unprofessional and weird. And, she silently acknowledged, she'd prefer nobody knew where she was or what she was doing until she found what she was looking for. Especially after those disturbing texts and messages this morning. And then, if she did find what she was looking for she would decide what to do about it.

"How've you been? Arthritis bothering you much?"

Mom *tsked*. "Depends on the weather. Coming into the damp season now."

"Would you like me to book you a getaway? Somewhere hot and dry?" She asked her every winter, and every year she declined, preferring her routine, even if she was uncomfortable.

Mom hummed, waffling.

"You can take a friend. I'll pay."

"I'll think about it," she replied, handing Sharon a mug.

Carrying her coffee and notebook to the cramped back bedroom, she sighed as she scanned the stacks of neatly labeled file boxes that lined the walls, the only vestiges of her father's long and infamous career as City councillor. *Where do I start?*

The choices were overwhelming, her mind flooding with specific images from all those years ago as she scanned her memory banks. There were two potential events that would likely lead to questions, if not answers. And questions were a good start.

One was the enormous scandal that got her father kicked out of office, sued and shamed so he could no longer get clients for his construction firm, pay his loans, or even find a decent job afterwards. Once the dust settled, he was a social, political and professional pariah.

Sharon's predominant memories of that time were visceral. It's no wonder she avoided thinking about it, never mind opening the wound and digging around, reawakening the pain, shock, and shame of her father's downfall.

It began and ended with her father's rage. She could still see, smell, and feel the day her father stormed in from the office, red-faced and swearing. Pouring himself a whisky. Making calls. Men coming to the house. She could still smell the whisky, the onions her mother had been frying, taste the raisin studded cookie she'd been eating after school, hear her mother's soap opera muffled in the background – everything about that moment frozen in time.

At first, the uproar had disoriented and confused her. Then the shock of seeing her father, along with Gus Seibold and then Mayor Weston on the local news channel. Listening to her father's alleged crimes enumerated, and looking at him, his scowling face. Feeling nauseous, on the verge of tears, trying to piece it together in her mind.

Then the shame of the police coming to search their home, though they never found sufficient evidence to press charges.

Yet the damage was done.

Suddenly the noise was intolerable. So many people, mostly loud, angry men, crowding her world. Politicians, pressmen, business associates, constituents, neighbours. Shouting, cursing, accusing. And the lights. Lights and camera lenses invading her life. Terrifying her, encroaching on her innocence, her privacy and calm routine.

Her parents, more Mom since Dad was more than occupied, insisted she give up swimming, dance, choir, and even friends to stay home where she was safe. Away from prying eyes and overt hostility. They even stopped going to church on Sundays in the flurry of negative attention that swarmed around them like hornets.

None of them could go anywhere. Even the grocery store exposed them to two or three bitter neighbours, former friends or constituents lashing out with hurtful words, and even physical violence. At home, on the street, in church, at school, even at the supermarket. Even if that physical violence was often overripe produce or garbage. That was almost worse, salt in their wounds.

People were so angry with her father, at his perceived hypocrisy. The very people her father had championed lashed back in outrage. That's what people said, what they held him accountable for. It wasn't only corruption, but the sense of betrayal.

And her deepest shame was that she agreed.

She still felt bruised from the intensity of hostile emotions that poisoned her existence for months and months until they could withdraw from the public eye. That sequence of events was almost too huge to pick apart. And too close. Perhaps it was a better task for her staff. However, there were documents here she needed to find.

Was it possible her father had been a victim and not a villain?

If that were true, then not only had they stolen her idealism and her youth, but they'd stolen her father from her. She shook herself free of the taint of those memories and donned the mantle of a professional attorney at law. Now was not the time to wallow in self-pity, as she had done a million times before, she pushed the painful emotions aside and bent to her work. *You can do this!*

Sharon had always sought approval as a path to find redemption for her father's sins. A flutter of hope, like a tiny moth's wings, stirred in the cage of her ribs. The relentless burden she'd placed upon herself as a young girl to build an identity and career without reproach, strong, successful and prestigious enough to smother – no to obliterate – the roar of shame that ran in her veins like tainted blood. That young girl still lived. Lived and hoped for just a taste of the self-love, freedom and joy she'd known.

Could she free herself from the bounds she'd placed on her young self all those years ago? Was it possible? Did she dare hope?

She shifted boxes, checking dates. The second, smaller event that niggled at her brain was the new deck and fence that Dad had had built behind their old house. Though it happened a few years earlier, they dredged it up during the shakedown, somehow linking it. His accusers had said he'd accepted kickbacks from various tradesmen and suppliers, though he'd managed the general construction himself. They said those kickbacks related to the City contracts he'd allegedly influenced over the years.

Strangely, not unlike what Seibold was doing now. Claiming to be hands off and objective, he was anything but, sitting back and pulling strings like a puppet master. Was the same true of her father? Was corruption endemic in the halls of municipal politics? Or was there something more insidious going on?

A bubble of hope appeared in her gut. It fizzed, rising, expanding, pushing on her heart, stretching the hard protective shell she'd worn, driving hairline cracks in her armour. Dare she let hope grow? Could it be? Could Dad's claims of innocence and conspiracy be true?

It was a simple enough paper trail to track down. She took a long swig of coffee, sharpened her metaphorical pencil and dug in for what she knew would be a research undertaking unrivalled since her articling days.

She took no calls while she worked, except to coordinate and receive reports from her team. Kent didn't text or call, seeming to understand that she was busy with work. If he knew what she was up to, he'd cause an uproar. The only texts that threw her were the series from Rachel. First she'd left a message insisting they get together this weekend. Then she'd texted several times. Apparently she wanted to talk about something important. Something about the case? Sharon didn't reply. It would wait.

Three hours later, when she came up for air and a bit of the late lunch Mom had prepared, she had questions enough.

She'd rebuilt the deck, piece by piece, chasing every trail of crumbs until it petered out or led to a hard fact. But there were some things she couldn't explain and wanted her mother's take on.

While she nibbled on her chicken salad sandwich, she queried her.

"It was Uncle Nick that painted the fence and surfaced the deck on that project, wasn't it? I remember him and his son Phil working on it, spreading that goop around. Am I right?" Nick was one of those family friends who'd always been part of her life growing up, a constant fixture. Someone she'd implicitly trusted whose reputation and honour were tarred with the same black brush that brought her father so low.

"Mhm," Mom nodded, chewing.

"But I can't find an invoice or a receipt for the work. And Dad was meticulous in his record keeping. Do you know why?"

Mom nodded again, her gaze distant. "Because it was a gift. Dad didn't pay him cash for it."

Uh-oh. The bubble of hope quivered, its walls unstable, warning of collapse like chewing gum that had failed, threatening to burst. Sharon narrowed her eyes and asked the question she wasn't sure she wanted answered. "Why? That must have been worth several thousand. Why would he do that?" Her pseudo-uncle Nick, a close friend of Dad's, was a notorious tightwad. She couldn't see him doing it out of the goodness of his heart.

"It was for the fish."

Sharon screwed up her face, her chewing gum image dissolving into thin air. "What?"

"Dad took them out fishing that time, up the coast. He won that fishing trip to that luxury place… what was it called?"

Sharon scowled, her gaze scanning the familiar knickknacks around her mother's kitchen. She locked onto a tacky ceramic cookie jar shaped like a giant beer stein that jogged her memory. "Do you mean Painter's?"

"Yes, that's it. Dad won that all-inclusive trip to Painter's at the Mayor's charity ball the year before. And it was expiring or something, because Leroy couldn't get away. Anyway, he invited Nick and his boys, and Stu, too, if I recall."

"And…?"

"They did really well! Caught tons of salmon and halibut. Enough to feed us all for a year. Nick was ecstatic. You remember how cheap he was."

Sharon chuckled. She also remembered eating fish, baked, boiled and fried, almost every day until she wanted to run away from home. "So Nick did the decking to repay him for *that*? The trip and the fish?"

"That's right." Mom took a sip of her tea, her gaze wandering to a half-done crossword at her elbow. "It was a trade."

Humph. Such a simple explanation. And exactly the kind of thing her father would do. If he had a character fault, it was to err on the side of being too generous. That's why she'd felt so betrayed, as if he'd spent half her life teaching her a set of values that he then knocked down in one reckless wave of his hand like a stack of dominoes. She felt like her entire childhood had been one giant lie. The bubble of hope got a kick of carbonation and grew another size or two, fuelling her continued research.

Could she piece together enough evidence of that transaction to begin to dismantle the case against her father? If she could find a money trail that linked Seibold and those "favours" they accused her father of, wouldn't that be interesting...

She pushed her plate away. "Back to work. Thanks for lunch, Mom."

"But you didn't finish your sand – "

"Lost my appetite." How could she eat when so much was at stake?

Did Mom understand the implications of these details? At the time, she'd seemed as stunned by it all as Sharon felt. Though what did she know of conversations that happened behind closed doors? Afterwards, Mom stoically and silently stood by Dad, never questioning his innocence as he ranted about corruption and conspiracy, and then sank into the drinking binge and depression that ultimately killed him. Through it all, she'd been constant and faithful.

Unlike their daughter.

Mom either knew the truth in her heart, or loved Dad so much she didn't care. Either way, Sharon determined to find the truth at last. If there was the slimmest chance she could redeem her father's honour and restore her family's name, she wouldn't stop until she succeeded. It wasn't only her own family that was harmed and lost everything. How many people had Seibold stepped on or scapegoated over his twenty-four-year tenure in power? How many mayors did he blackmail or bamboozle to do his bidding? How many murky deals did he make to secure his seat? How many taxpayers' dollars were fraudulently rerouted to line his own pockets?

Before the close of the workday Friday, she called an old law classmate who now worked for Crown Council. When Patty returned her call, she laid out her theory and requested a "hypothetical" consultation of the evidence on Monday when she'd gathered it all together. If all went well, she'd be ready to submit evidence by late Tuesday. Before signing off she asked, "Who do you know in the Vancouver Police Investigative Services Unit?"

Sharon kept at it for three endless days, poring over boxes and boxes of files. She even slept over at her mom's one night out of sheer exhaustion. On Sunday morning, bleary-eyed but pleased with her findings, she loaded the most important papers into her car and called her team to tell them the news.

She had found what she was looking for. Not just to prosecute the Civil case on behalf of her client, but also a solid Criminal suit. They needed to compare her notes with their findings and put a case together. But that was for next week. Now she planned to have a very long shower, dress for dinner with Kent's family, and emotionally prepare herself for another kind of battle.

CHAPTER 21

Kent picked her up at her condo in his older model Subaru and drove south to his parents' house in near silence, the tension radiating off of him. Her chest tightened in sympathy, and she reached across to give his thigh a squeeze, a comforting gesture that seemed strange for her. But everything about Kent made her want to be different. Warmer, kinder, sweeter, and more herself. With him, she felt safe.

Oh, how she wished she could confide in him. She felt like a complete shit for lying. He could help her. He was well-connected, and could, perhaps, advise her who she could, and could not trust in the police department. And then she wouldn't feel so alone.

Sharon watched the buildings on Oak Street crawl by. Traffic was terrible. After grumbling for several blocks, Kent turned west on Twelfth, trying to find space to move. Evening fell quickly in October and it was nearing dark.

Now that she'd seen the depth of Seibold's wrongdoing, her biggest worry was that his corrupt influence was powerful enough to slip the noose around her neck, just like it had with her father. Or at least make it impossible for her to expose him.

197

Besides real estate, planning, zoning and development officials and staff, she wondered who else was in his pocket.

Her mind even touched on the remote possibility of her friend Rachel, but rejected that notion. Rachel was ruthless, but not without ethics.

Seibold's tentacles, however, likely stretched deep into the business community. Where did his influence end?

Kent would surely run to his journalist friends to expose Seibold's corruption to the world in a storm of righteous anger, without first formulating a strategy or having a solid legal foot to stand on.

The slightest hint of what she had planned would undoubtedly set off a flurry of defensive manoeuvres and destruction of evidence that would harm her case. She would hold her tongue and gather intelligence.

When pretending to be cowed by Seibold's bribes and threats, she'd been vague enough. She hoped. In truth, confronting him had rattled her.

"Are you tired?" Kent said, covering her hand with his and squeezing.

"Mhm." She nodded, her stomach roiling again. "Long week." The past three days of sifting through tedious paperwork had ground her down. She'd showered, dressed and put on a smiling face, but she was exhausted, her mind foggy, spinning. Worries that she'd missed something critical chewed away at her attention.

She prayed she hadn't made a mistake. Her entire adult life – her career that she'd so carefully built, the reputation she'd cultivated – could come crashing down like a case built on circumstantial evidence. If he had some public humiliation planned, it would devastate her. She would go down in flames and never recover. Not this time.

Keeping secrets was hard and she had to proceed cautiously.

It wasn't every day that one case entailed a Criminal and a Civil suit. She wished her father were still alive. Not only to witness her, hopefully, triumphant retribution and takedown of a career criminal, but also so she could have pursued a slander case too. That would be the ultimate revenge, but without him, she didn't have grounds.

For now, she couldn't allow any of her plan to slip out. If Seibold or his cronies got a whiff of what she was doing, he'd prepare his defence, scuttling back into the dark like the cockroach he was.

It was important to her plan that everyone continue to believe that she had made a quiet deal with Seibold so that his son's development project moved forward. She not only wanted to expose past wrongs, but to catch them red-handed and save the society's project. If she timed it right, she could kill three birds with one stone.

The small screaming voice in her head demanding justice had to be tamped down. Swallowing the indignation and the hurt, she had to remain rational and use her well-honed skills and the power of the law to take Seibold down.

She pressed a hand to her churning stomach. As her nerve endings crackled and buzzed with anticipation and dread, she regretted not going to her regular choir practice yesterday, which calmed and centred her. How would she play nice and eat dinner wound this tightly?

Anyway, she'd been through worse. *You've got this.*

Glancing again at Kent's stoic profile, she drew a deep breath and let it out, trying to dispel some of her anxiety. He seemed more worried than she was.

"Are you always this tense before a family dinner?" She kept the teasing out of her voice, as this was no laughing matter for him.

He grunted, shooting a wry smile at her with a twitch of his cheek. "It's never fun. But it's worse today. I'm introducing my new girl."

A bark of laughter flew out of her, tossing her head back. "Right. Are you worried they'll disapprove of me?"

"No. They've all met you. But..." He turned away to scowl out the side window, leaving his answer unfinished.

She swivelled to face him, studying his face in silhouette, the streetlights sharpening his profile, the elegant straight line of his nose, the crisp angle of his jaw showing through his short beard. A ripple of desire flared in her belly, sending a shiver through her limbs, but she set it aside. There would be time for that later. Tonight she was here to support him. "What?"

"I should warn you that once my father gets going and Aaron jumps on the bandwagon, they can come down hard on me. It gets ugly. Fast."

"So..."

He sighed, his shoulders rounding, then shot a wary glance her way, his jaw jutting. "I guess I don't want anything to change the way you see me."

She smiled and then let her face sober for her next words. "It won't. I promise."

She drew her bottom lip between her teeth and stroked one finger along her collarbone. "Your mom is such a loving person. Won't they consider her feelings?" Considering her line of work, and her usual clientele, Barb Sawyer was probably a take-no-prisoners kind of woman.

He grunted. "I wish."

Hopefully Sharon could provide some vague moral support for Kent without getting involved. She suspected it was his personality and socially-minded line of work that provided the focal point for whatever unpleasantness arose. She'd see soon enough.

Maybe as an outsider, she could play a useful role in keeping the peace.

Sharon took pride in being unflappable. People assumed she was a cold bitch, and she was alright with that. She excelled at keeping her cool in tense, conflict-filled situations. She excelled at keeping secrets, too, even when she was bursting to share them, like she was tonight. These skills helped make her a successful lawyer.

Having dinner with the tension and conflict-filled family of her brand new lover was just like that. Wasn't it?

Kent glanced over, his tight expression softening in a half smile, and she met his gaze, smiling back. They'd get through this together.

"You know my first impression of you wasn't – "

Her purse emitted a special trilling tone that meant Rachel was calling. She pulled her phone out, hesitating. "Sorry. I'll make this quick. It's my friend Rachel calling, and I forgot to tell her I was out tonight." She answered the call. "Hi, Rach."

"Hey, stranger," Rachel replied. "Where are you? Are we getting together or not? Want to grab a drink?"

"Oh. Sorry. I'm on my way out for dinner."

"Dinner out on Sunday night? Hm. What's that about?"

"I'll explain… another time, okay?"

"You're not alo-one?" Sharon tried not to feel insulted by Rachel's tone of disbelief. It's not like Sharon never dated. Just maybe not as much as her gorgeous friend.

"Maybe." Sharon chuckled, glancing at Kent, whose eyebrows slid up in query, blinking at her assessing gaze, his sexy mouth pulling to one side in a half smirk.

"Ooh. Dying for details. What's been happening with you?"

"I'm sorry I didn't call you this week. It's been busy. I was staying at my Mom's."

A beat of silence passed, and Sharon's gut twisted with worry. She shouldn't have said that.

"Your Mom's?" Rachel's tone shifted from teasing to suspicion. She knew too much about Sharon's past. They'd shared too many drunken confessions during their uni days, and later, as suffering articling juniors. She knew Sharon rarely visited her mother, let alone stayed overnight. And she had a frightfully clever mind.

"Mhm. Yeah. She wasn't feeling well, so I wanted to make sure she was okay." She caught Kent's frowning enquiry and shook her head with a reassuring smile. It was even more important that she convince Rachel, though.

Rachel seemed to accept that explanation. "Look. The reason I wanted to talk to you… it's work related."

Uh-oh.

"My client mentioned that you'd negotiated a property swap with the City on behalf of that society pro-bono case you're working on. I just wanted to say, I'm glad. I'm relieved, actually. It's the right approach. These guys are determined to put that condo project in the heritage block. It makes a big difference to their marketing." She cleared her throat. "And I wasn't looking forward to fighting it out with you."

"Right. Well, I'm not dealing directly with the developers, so I wouldn't know. It's Council that seems intent to do the switch, and I…" she paused, her gaze darting at Kent, "… it wasn't advantageous to start a war with them. I'm sure we'll find a suitable alternative."

"No. You wouldn't want to start a war with *them*." Sharon's nerve endings jangled in warning at Rachel's intonation, sending a shiver up her spine. Them, who? That sounded like a veiled warning. What did Rachel know about Seibold's plans?

"Have you worked for this team before?"

Rachel's response came slowly. "Once or twice."

"So they're good clients? You like them?"

"Development work is easy money, Shar. So I can spend more time on my criminal cases. It's business. You're a partner now. You understand."

"Junior partner." Sharon's jaw ticked. She wasn't jealous of

Rachel's rapid rise to full partner, exactly. She just wanted the same for herself. Maybe it was Rachel's polish and people skills that helped her get ahead. But she began to wonder why some people seemed to find success with so little struggle.

"You're almost there. I'll let you go, hon. Let's talk tomorrow, okay?"

Sharon put her phone away, lost in thought. Doubts swirled in her gut like a stew of noxious chemicals while she gnawed on her lip. There was something about that exchange that didn't feel right. She gave her head a shake. Ridiculous. Her paranoia was making her suspect her best friend of criminal dealings.

"So that's it, is it?"

What? Her head whipped around at Kent's agitated voice. "Pardon?"

"It wasn't advantageous to fight?" His chin jutted as he quoted her. "You're sure we'll find a suitable alternative."

"No." Ooh-kay. This was bad. "I didn't mean that, Kent. I just needed to – "

"I understand. You're not getting paid for this job, so you can't be bothered to make an effort to fight them. It's fine. I don't know why I expected more from you. I've been a complete fucking idiot." Rage rolled off of him in waves, his shoulders tensed around his ears, his jaw tight, his knuckles white as he jerked the steering wheel, pulling off of King Edward into a quiet treed street.

Sodium street lamps bled yellow-orange pools of light onto the manicured lawns, trimmed shrubbery and curving sidewalks. The serene setting contrasted with his suddenly violent mood. The abrupt change in his manner flooded her veins with panic.

"Please don't think that. I really fought them on this. I'm... I'm not finished fighting. I've got..." damn it. She couldn't tell him a damned thing. Look how he'd reacted to the mere hint of her plan. "I'm not done yet, Kent. I've got more ideas. Truly."

"Sure you do, babe." His voice dripped with icy disdain, his flashing eyes raking her with contempt.

Her stomach hard, a tremor working its way through her limbs, Sharon silently stared at large and stately manor houses ostentatiously lit, one after the other. Holy shit! She felt her eyes widen in surprise, holding back her gasp of wonder. His family home was in Shaughnessy? The oldest and most prestigious neighbourhood in Vancouver? But now was not the time to comment. She'd process that later.

She huffed. "Rachel's representing S & S Developments. I had to deflect her. Reassure her so they think they've won. It's part of the game!"

"They have won!" He slammed his hand down on the steering wheel, then gripped it and cranked sharply into a grand curving driveway between tall hedges. "It is just a game to you, isn't it? You really don't care who wins and loses, even if it means innocent people go to jail, and criminals walk the streets. I know all about you. Your type is never willing to risk or sacrifice anything for someone else. It's all about number one. You walk away unscathed and leave a trail of wreckage behind."

"No! It's not true. That's not what I meant. It's just… the law!"

"The law," he spat. "The law is about power games and manipulation. It's about self-interest and greed. All the worst qualities of mankind."

Her face heated, her eyes burning with tears. She bit her lips between her teeth to stop them trembling until they hurt. She couldn't make him understand unless she put her entire plan at risk. He already hated the establishment. Now he hated her too. And she had to suck it up.

He pulled up outside a grand Neo-Tudor manor house, three storeys tall, with a timber-framed front porch at the head of the curving drive, and shut off the car. They sat in silence listening to the ping of the engine cooling, breathing heavily while she fought tears.

Her gaze scanned the large manor, not sure what brand of house she'd expected from the administrator of a hospital and a community nurse. The house itself disarmed her. If she thought the commodious old Craftsman bungalow she grew up in was special, this was in another league altogether.

Kent drew a breath and huffed. "Let's go."

"We don't have to do this."

"We're here now. Might as well get it over with." Grunting, he jerked and jumped out of the car as though by sheer force of will, rounding the car to open her door. She stood, stepping close to him so she could feel him, trying to regain some warmth, standing on her tiptoes to brush a kiss lightly against his lips.

He pulled away, shaking his head, sending her heart plummeting to the soles of her shoes, fresh tears surfacing. He led her to the front door and rang the bell, which they could hear faintly chiming from inside. He waited with his hands in his pockets while she wondered why he didn't feel enough at home to walk right in.

Without turning to her, he said, "I'm extremely frustrated at your deal. And…" his gaze lifted and scanned the dark beams holding up the porch, his jaw working. "I'm disappointed in you, Sharon. I thought you cared."

She gasped. He'd never used her name before, always using his teasing pet name. That one distancing gesture stabbed her heart like a knife. "I do! I'm on your side. I'm taking this case very seriously. As seriously as any work I've ever done. Believe me. Kent." She lay her hand on his sleeve, and his gaze dropped to it. He didn't pull away, but he swallowed loudly and spoke.

"It's only fair to warn you, I've been talking to members of the community, some people I work with, and I've had regular discussions with Sergé and some of his friends in the press. We've laid the groundwork for a pubic rally at City Hall. We'll be expediting the plan now." At the sound of footsteps, he turned towards the door, withdrawing his arm from her touch.

Sharon let her hand fall to her side, pulling with it her gaze, which slid down to the weathered red brick stoop. She swore her heart lay there on the brick pavers, crushed. He'd completely lost faith in her. But how could she blame him? She'd given him nothing.

It was Aaron who answered the door.

"Kent. Sharon. Welcome," he boomed, his tone amused. Stepping back, he opened the door wider.

"Oh look, it's the brilliant-young-surgeon-Doctor-Aaron-Sawyer," deadpanned Kent as he strode past his brother without looking directly at him, leaving Sharon to enter alone.

Awkwardly, she hesitated in the doorway. "Good evening, Aaron. Nice to see you again."

"At least your girlfriend has manners," Aaron said, smirking at her. "May I take your coat, Sharon?"

She slipped it off, Aaron stepping closer to help her, as Kent sloughed off his own and shoved it at his brother, scowling.

The three of them stood in silence, Aaron astutely picking up the waves of distress coming off of them both. "Humph. Trouble in paradise?"

"Come on," Kent gestured to her to precede him through a doorway to the left of the entry hall.

She hesitated, wishing she could escape. Her muscles were tense, she was flushed and hot, and in no condition to face his parents. "Is there a powder room I can use to freshen up?" She addressed Aaron.

He pasted on a gracious, conciliatory expression and dipped his chin. "Right this way." As she followed him, she glanced at Kent, who stood with his eyes closed, his head shaking minutely. Then he appeared to brace himself and disappeared through the arch.

～

"It's just there," Aaron gestured to a dark alcove and disappeared with their coats. "Take your time."

She needed to pull herself together and fast. Fighting back tears that prickled her eyes, she ducked through a doorway and felt for the light switch in the dark, finding one of those old-fashioned push button types from a hundred years ago. At first, the light didn't come on. Then, with a delayed flicker, the room where Aaron had directed her revealed itself in all its splendour.

Her head tilted back, jaw dropping as she took in the space.

This was no ordinary powder room. Good grief! The plaster ceiling medallion floated some ten feet above her. The flickering chandelier projected jagged prisms of silvery light down into the grand powder room and onto her. Shoulder height ivory-painted wainscotting gave the room gravitas, while richly coloured dark floral wallpaper stretched up to the thick crown mouldings. Miles of spotted honeycomb floor tiles stretched between her, a wide pedestal sink on spindly brass legs, and the awkward antique toilet with matching brass fittings at the far end. She shivered, feeling weirdly small, like Alice in Wonderland. If this was their bathroom, what did the rest of this house hold in store?

The room was as cold as a morgue, and her gaze found the leaded glass window on the end wall leaking an icy draft that coiled around her legs, arms, neck, raising gooseflesh. Her intestines roiled in complaint. Now she was supposed to bare her bottom?

Gathering her strength, she used the inhospitable toilet, fumbling to figure out the antiquated flushing lever. It flopped and clanked, but no water flowed from the narrow tank behind. Adrenaline flooded her body with panic, her body blooming with cold sweat. She tried to flush again and again, to no avail, while she stared with dread down into the bowl. *This can't be happening!*

Giving the old toilet a moment to regroup, Sharon went to

the sink to do the same. She turned the brass and porcelain taps and a tiny trickle of cold water dribbled onto her hands. "What the hell, sink?" *Was this for real?*

The water was paltry, even colder than the air, or the uninviting toilet seat she'd just vacated. She fiddled with the taps, turning them this way and that, trying to find the best flow of water, and any temperature other than ice cold. It gurgled with a hollow sound, then spurted, splattering her silk blouse with dark wet spots. *Shit!* Slowing her breathing, still fighting tears, she grabbed the stiff hand towel and dabbed herself, backing away from the demon sink.

Unbelievable! This house was out to get her.

Could tonight get any worse?

She understood why Kent was so furious with her. If he were not she'd be disappointed in him. But it hurt that he believed her capable of cold selfishness. Their relationship was brand new. She got that. They barely knew each other.

"All right, you." She went back to the toilet and tried flushing again, and this time, thankfully, a half-hearted, slow-motion swirl of water dragged the waste away. It felt like an hour had passed, her panic rising with each minute. Instead of calming herself, she became increasingly agitated, sweating, shivering, her face heating with shame and frustration. How could they keep a room like this, so out of date it barely worked? Was the rest of the house like this? All ostentatious show and no comfort?

She waited for her blouse to dry a little, dabbing sweat from her brow and between her breasts, thinking about the room she was in, this house. Did Kent grow up here? Is this the house that the lovely, warm-hearted Barbara oversaw? Sharon shook her head, pulling herself together. *You've got this,* she said to her image in the mirror. *Just another hurdle you can handle.* She could sort out her misunderstanding with Kent another day. Tonight, she was here for him. She was not so fickle in her affections.

You've got this, she repeated until the reflection in the ornate bevelled wall mirror looking back at her was calm, contained and in control. The ice princess was back.

After another labourious attempt to clean her hands, she finally escaped the Victorian torture chamber and went in search of the family who called this place home.

CHAPTER 22

Following the muffled sound of bickering voices, Sharon found the entire Sawyer family in the centre of an oak panelled dining room. They sat around a long white linen-covered table glittering with silver and crystal. The demon powder room paled compared to this imposing room, with its wood-beamed ceiling and magnificent tiled fireplace at one end.

Conversation came to a dead stop as she entered, and all four faces turned toward her.

"There you are, Sharon, dear. We thought you'd gotten lost!" Barbara said, standing.

"Oh. No. I'm sorry." She smoothed a palm down the front of her blouse. "I had a little trouble with the… plumbing, but it's all right now."

Aaron snickered. "Did you use the mausoleum?" His laughter grew into guffaws.

Barbara shot her elder son a withering glare. "Oh, that's dreadful. The new powder room is across the hall from it. We keep that one in its original state. For the heritage tours, you know."

What? That was the wrong room? She shot a glance to Aaron, who worked to turn his expression of glee into one of conciliatory apology with little success. Had he meant to be vague with his directions?

"It's fine. I'm fine," she said.

Kent kept his gaze down, glaring at the gleaming brass candlestick in front of his plate, his jaw ticking. "You're such an ass," she thought he murmured, presumably to his brother, though she wondered if he secretly thought she deserved the moniker. He took a big gulp from his glass. She noticed he was drinking some golden liquid rather than the wine everyone else drank, and wondered if he was trying to numb himself.

"I'm so glad you could join us, Sharon. Please sit down." Barbara stood and gestured along the table, gripping her hand as she passed, smiling. Her warmth and candour helped to calm Sharon's frazzled nerves. "We so rarely drag Kent away from his work commitments these days."

The three men rose from their chairs as she entered, and despite his scowl and downcast gaze, Kent stepped to pull out her chair and settle her in place.

Kent didn't look at her as he returned to his own seat, and she forced a smile onto her shell-shocked face. So she was on her own. "You have such a beautiful home, Mrs. Sawyer. Dr. Sawyer. Have you lived here long?"

"Eighteen years now. We couldn't believe our good fortune when it came on the market. It's one of the early twentieth century industrialist mansions, designed to show off the rapidly accumulating wealth of the age. I'm a bit of a heritage buff – " Aaron punctuated this admission with another rude snort. " – and I'd admired it for years." She sent a scolding look to her elder son.

"Aaron," Dr. Sawyer Senior barked. "My apologies, Sharon. Both our sons are behaving like children tonight. Although we never could repress Aaron's mischievous spirit," he added with an approving grin at his older son. As if his behaviour was appropriate to a man in his mid-thirties. Kent, apparently, was invisible to him, as Sharon was to Kent.

This family is unbelievable. Aaron behaved like an unruly teenager, not at all like a prominent surgeon. People really did revert to their childhood selves when thrown into the cauldron of family. She reminded herself that she was here to smooth the waters, and support Kent with his family. She'd set aside thoughts of his disappointment in her, would rise above, take the higher ground. Soon enough he'd find out what she was doing, how principled she was, how much she cared. She cared a great deal, she realized, clasping her shaking hands in her lap.

If she'd been wearing a mask, these past twenty-four years to survive the battlegrounds of university and law and business, she could damn-well keep wearing that mask for another day or two. Even if it meant being dishonest to Kent, with whom she wished she could share her thoughts, her fears, her hopes. She was strong, and she knew what she needed to do. *You've got this.*

Sharon gazed up at the frosted glass bowl of the elegant light fixture hanging over the long oak dining table, wishing she could sail away on it like a magic carpet, out of this uncomfortable situation. "This is such a beautiful room. Tell me more about your house, Mrs. Sawyer."

"Please, I insist you call me Barb." Kent's mother smiled warmly and Sharon wondered whether she was as oblivious to the undercurrents of conflict among her men as she seemed, or inured to them. "They built it in 1921. One of a series of elegant Banker's Tudor mansions designed by Bernard Palmer that coincided with the economic boom between the wars." She sipped her wine. "The crown jewel of his portfolio."

"You've made it a hobby, I gather."

"Mm-hmm. With my line of work, I need to immerse myself in beauty to remind myself that the world is not all doom and gloom."

Sharon smiled and nodded. An understandable sentiment,

but a rather costly distraction from the harsh realities of the world. Sharon never could bring herself to spend her handsome salary ostentatiously. Except perhaps her lovely little car. But even then, she'd only allowed herself the indulgence because it was a fantastic deal. She could never forget how little they had to live on after the scandal. There'd been nothing but debt in those days. And shame. And powerlessness.

A woman in black came in to set the salad course in front of them, and the conversation continued to flow around this interruption, Sharon encouraging Barbara to wax poetic about her beloved heritage house, with its beveled glass, oak panelling and ten tiled fireplaces, which had apparently been on the City heritage tour twice. If the Sawyer's money was not old, this house made it appear so.

"So you were still in school when you moved in here, Kent?" she tried, sending him a pleading, steadying glance.

But it went to waste. He didn't even lift his head from his salad to look at her, merely murmuring his agreement. Disconcertingly, hot tears pricked at her eyes, forcing her to blink rapidly to dispel them.

"Oh, yes. Aaron was just off to university, and Kent had another year of high school when we moved. I don't think you appreciated being uprooted, did you, honey?"

Kent looked up then, his expression long-suffering. "That's right, Mom. I had to change schools and make all new friends in grade twelve. It was great fun." He was apparently unwilling to play nice, since the only stranger among them was Sharon herself, and he'd written her off. Her heart pinched at his disdain. She missed the way his golden brown gaze melted her insides when he looked into her eyes affectionately, with humour, or with heat, the subtle teasing warmth of his half smile. She hadn't felt this way about a man since her long, unrequited crush on Simon. And though she'd admired him very much, they'd never had a relationship at all. In fact, this was the first time she actually liked someone she'd allowed herself to get physically close with. Usually, she found it best to keep affairs of the heart separate from her physical dalliances. Kent was different. Kent was… important to her.

Through a series of strategic questions, she kept the conversation going until the main course had replaced the salad plates, and wine glasses were refilled.

Apparently Dr. Sawyer had been waiting for this moment to pounce.

"So. You're a lawyer, Ms. Beckett," Dr. Sawyer said, tipping his wine glass back in a thoughtful pose, peering at her over the rim.

She nodded, perking up. "Yes, that's right." She quickly lifted a forkful of potato to her mouth to prevent the need to elaborate.

"Interesting. It's difficult enough to persuade Kent to join us for Sunday dinners. This is the first time he's brought a guest."

Before Sharon could reply, Kent broke in with a snarky, "You made sure of that, Father, didn't you?"

Dr Sawyer chuckled. "Well. Perhaps I did." He sent a cryptic look along the table to his wife. "I admit I was curious. You're not the usual calibre of citizen our son fraternizes with. A cut above, I'd say."

Sharon squeezed out a polite smile, wondering if he'd ever in fact met any of Kent's friends from the Downtown Eastside, or merely heard rumour of them from his wife. Also, whether Kent allowed himself any other society. "It turns out we make a good team."

If she was hoping to stimulate fond memories of their meeting, or remind Kent of the tender moments they'd recently shared, she'd been mistaken. The look Kent flashed at her was hard and resentful, as though she'd deliberately set out to deceive him and lure him into her web through seduction, like some kind of evil witch. It was too much to hope they could be a team tonight. The cold distance between them squeezed her heart, pushing the conversation into the background. Salty tears pooled in the back of her throat. How she wished they could get away from here and be alone. Alone together, they had a special magic. She wanted that feeling back. She hadn't felt love like this for –

"What's your opinion of this business my son's involved in, Sharon? I can't see this is a productive use of his time, wandering the streets at night chasing after delinquent orphans."

She loved him!

Pulling her attention back, Sharon cleared her throat.

"I don't think his efforts are wasted. Someone has to be there and know the people to understand their needs and know what's going on day to day. Just last week, Kent saved a young boy from an overdose death, as you know. And only because he knew where to look for him." She kept her eyes down, focused on another forkful of beef, hoping if she were busy chewing, Dr. Sawyer would move on. Her heart pounded in her chest at the realization. She loved him.

"That's all very well in theory, but how much good does it actually do? We literally save hundreds of lives at the hospital every day! Kent's time would be better spent in work that could make a larger impact than just one kid."

Sharon swallowed, keeping a tight rein on her own rising emotions. How could he so belittle what Kent was doing?

"It's time you stopped wallowing in your guilt and quit this nonsense. Go back to school and do it right this time," Dr. Sawyer grumbled.

There was nothing worse than a loud bully, or an angry man, in her books. It triggered her like nothing else did, and she fought the tremor of nerves that fluttered through her body. She pulled her shoulders back and lifted her chin in defiance. "There is more than one way to save a life. Not everyone needs to practice medicine. Kent is responding to a different calling. And he helps many people every day."

"Those people are a lost cause. If the boy's inclined to do drugs, he'll just go back to it until he self-destructs. My wife sees these addicts every day at her clinic." Dr. Sawyer's face grew redder as his speech continued.

With a surreptitious glance at Kent's frowning concentration on his plate, Sharon realized there would be no one to challenge Dr. Sawyer. Kent looked like he would love to say something, and she supposed he might have, but was tamping down his anger because she was here. Her throat ached with sympathy at his suffering. And yet she had to tread carefully. It was not her place to tear his father and his arguments to shreds in his own home. This was no courtroom. And although adversarial, he wasn't her opponent. That would help no one. Knocking him down a notch would accomplish nothing. If Kent was important to her, and he was, then she wanted to help him mend his family, not intensify their woes.

She cleared her throat. "I agree that changes should be implemented at a systemic level, and the political will has to be there. That will never happen without education and advocacy, so the people who elect our officials can choose the representative who will do the job." The doctors perked up at her words, and she continued. "That's one reason I studied the law, Dr. Sawyer. Because I believe the system can improve our lives. All of our lives, though there are many who fall through the cracks at present."

Dr. Sawyer nodded, his well-groomed brows twitching up on one side. "Well said, Sharon. Well said." He appeared to be thinking something through as he surgically cut his food into small pieces. "Have you considered an elevated career in politics? It sounds like your legal training would qualify you as a candidate."

"Oh! No, no, never. Not me." Sharon recoiled, the very thought sending a cocktail of anxiety racing through her veins. "I loath the limelight. I prefer to work behind the scenes, thank you. All I've ever wanted is to make full partner at Flannigan, Searle and Meacham and continue winning cases. Perhaps make judge one day. That's the extent of my ambition, thank you."

"An ambitious woman. I like it." He grinned. "Well, your skills and your charm are wasted in back rooms and courtrooms, if you ask my opinion." He was happy enough to offer it unsolicited. "You'd be an asset in politics, perhaps working on someone else's campaign if not your own." His eyes slid over to his eldest son, and the brilliant-young-surgeon Dr. Aaron Sawyer nearly choked on his food he sat up so abruptly. His brows came down in a slash, his appalled glance cutting to his father in question.

There was a collective indrawn breath around the table.

"You've got to be kidding me!" Kent shot out of his chair and went to the bar cart under the mullioned window to refill his glass with whiskey, Sharon warily eyeing the level in his glass. "Since when do surgeons run for political office? Is there no limit to your scheming?"

"Sit down, Kent, honey, please," Barbara murmured.

"I thought being a doctor was the be-all-and-end-all to you, Father. Now you want politicians for sons. Wonderful!" Kent's tone was confrontational, his expression grim, his jaw jutting, and Sharon feared he was looking for a fight now. He'd have to have the patience of a saint to withstand this, and she knew he did not. She cringed. No wonder he avoided family dinners.

Her heart thumped in her chest. There was nothing worse than angry, shouting men. Her pulse throbbed in her throat, choking off her breathing. She hated this. It painfully reminded her of the terrible time around her father's scandal, when there were people around all the time for months on end and nowhere to hide. People didn't hesitate to stop any member of the family and express their outrage in the strongest language. There was nothing worse than a corrupt politician.

With all that going on, there were many harsh words spoken in her young life. More than she could bear.

Once they had forced her to move both school and house, leaving friends behind, she had found a few harsh words for her father, too. However betrayed other people felt by his dishonesty, it didn't compare to the sense of betrayal Sharon felt. None of his claims to innocence convinced her. She'd suffered too much, and she made sure he knew it.

Her idolized father had mutated from a hero to a villain, from a king to a pauper in her eyes. Worse, he was a charlatan and a snake in the grass. He'd stolen her very faith in human nature and broken her heart.

She could hardly look at him, let alone sit at the dinner table and have a normal conversation. His attempts to restore their close relationship made it worse. The arguments left her drained and they lived in tense, heartbroken silence until she could escape. Looking back now, she wondered what had done her father more harm. Rejection from his colleagues, or of his only daughter.

Something in her face must have let Barbara know it had to stop.

Barbara stood up. "Come with me to the terrace, Kent, please."

He scowled at her.

"Come on, honey. You need some air. It'll do you good." She stood next to him, her expression firm, until he huffed and relented, following her through a doorway, Sharon's gaze following them. *Don't leave me alone in here!*

CHAPTER 23

He smacked his hand against the top of the railing. "I'm sorry, Mom. I'm doing my best." Kent tried to let go of his clenched jaw, tried to draw a deep breath as he gazed into the pools of light cast over the landscaped side yard.

She stood behind him. He felt her hands on his arms, rubbing up and down, trying to sooth him. But he was beyond being soothed by her touch.

"This is why I don't come here anymore. He never changes. And I can't pretend. I don't know how you stand it, and..." He turned to face her. "I'm feeling angry with you, too."

Her gaze was unwavering. "He's a good and loving husband and father, honey."

He gave his head a shake. "You should be able to respect and admire your spouse."

"I respect your father. And admire him. He's brilliant and strong and wise."

"Well. Like then. You ought to *like* your husband. And don't tell me you like that asshole in there." He jabbed a pointed finger at the French doors from which they'd come.

"Perhaps not at the moment." Her small smile was wry. "But

usually I do. He's witty and charming. He's kind, and affectionate. I don't like how he treats you, but I understand the sentiment
behind it. He only wants what's best for you. I'm afraid you see
the worst of it. He's just – "

"What about love? Do you still love him? Because I can't!"

Mom's chin wobbled, but then she turned it into a watery
smile. "Oh, Kent. Of course I love him. " She paused, her gaze
turning inward. "Relationships are challenging. There will always
be trials in marriage. We've been a family for decades. It's woven
together our lives. We were kids together, students together,
parents together. I'll always love him." She patted Kent's chest.
"And you do too. If you didn't love him, you wouldn't care so
much. And neither would he."

Kent growled and returned his gaze to the darkened trees
beyond the terrace where they stood. The air was cold tonight.
Fall would soon turn to winter, the hardest part of the year for
people who lived on the street. The people who lived in tents in
Oppenheimer park, or under layers of cardboard and old blankets behind dumpsters in back alleys. He huffed a sigh. This
winter, like every winter, he'd lose friends.

Turning back, he saw his mother shivering in her light dress.
He wrapped her in his arms, squeezing tight, and tried to warm
her. Thank God for her. "I'm sorry, Mom. I wish I could make it
stop. But I can't seem to get through to him."

"He's hurting, too, in his way, Kent. I know he acts like he
favours Aaron, but it was you he had high hopes for. He always
believed you'd be the doctor, the better doctor. You have the
bigger heart. He thinks you're not living up to your potential,
and that frustrates him. That's all."

He released her and leaned back. "If he believed that, he'd get
what I'm doing. He'd stop belittling and provoking me."

"He pokes at you hoping to dislodge you from your stubborn-
ness. You're young yet. He still hangs onto his dream you'll go
back to medical school."

"Well, I won't. You know that. I've never wanted to be a doctor. If he values my intelligence and my heart, he'd understand I'm doing what *I* have to do. He'd trust me."

"Are you though? Don't you wish you'd stayed in nursing?"

Kent chewed his lip, scowling. "I'm not sure. I haven't quite figured out how to make an impact, but I believe what I'm doing is important work. It's what I have to do right now."

She nodded. "I thought so. And I know you'll figure it out."

"Will he though?"

"I just know he loves you, and maybe when you're happy, he'll be happy for you."

~

Dr. Sawyer carried on unperturbed, waving a hand. "I'm speaking in generalities. Medicine is the most honourable of professions. But politics..." He raised one finger, nodding towards Aaron, "... is the way to elevate your position in society like nothing else. You'd be a great asset Sharon." Dr. Sawyer chuckled. "Your temperaments are better matched, as are your interests."

"Dad. Stop," Aaron pleaded, but the elder Dr. Sawyer carried on.

"With respect, Dr. Sawyer, I don't think you know me well enough to say such a thing. And surely if Aaron has political ambitions, he'd want to choose his own campaign... manager."

Dr. Sawyer barked with laughter. "Campaign manager? I was thinking of a political wife! Every ambitious man needs a smart and well-spoken woman at his side."

Of all the gall. Her heart hammered behind her ribs like a judge's gavel. If only there were someone with authority here to put an end to this man's grandstanding.

"I'm glad we got to know you this evening, Sharon. But I can't for the life of me understand what you see in my wastrel of a younger son. Now that I think about it, politics or not, I believe you'd make a far better match for Aaron than Kent. It would be a great pleasure to have you as a member of this family."

"Oh, my god!" moaned Aaron, lifting his glass and gulping back his wine.

Screaming inside, Sharon tamped down the urge to run after Kent and his mother or, better yet, cower under the table. At this moment, she'd much prefer a time out in the evil mausoleum of a powder room than this torment. A bathroom break right now would relieve the acid stew of adrenaline that swirled in her gut, pinching her painfully and making her break out in a cold sweat. But there was no escape. She drew herself together as she had a million times when called upon to perform under pressure, whether in depositions or in front of judge or jury.

"Thank you for that vote of confidence, Dr. Sawyer. But, sadly, I'm not the marrying type. In fact, I'm a committed career woman." She gathered her courage. "I practice law because I want to and need to have my own career and be my own person. I have never hoped to marry, and I likely never will. I think I'd make a perfectly dreadful wife, political or otherwise." Her face felt as tight as lacquer when she smiled, trying to lighten the delivery of her contrary opinion.

"There, you see?" Aaron gasped. "Your matchmaking efforts are for nothing, Dad. What a joker you are."

Nice try, Aaron. She gave him a tiny smile of thanks. Perhaps he wasn't as awful as he at first appeared. And Kent was perfectly lovely, though his passion and hair-trigger temper still terrified her. "I think you do Kent a great disservice. He works very hard, and he's very committed to accomplishing great things in his own arena – "

"Pah! I don't buy it. Guilt drives Kent, plain and simple."

Sharon's pulse raced, her heart pounding at his ominous words. "Guilt? For what? He's the most selfless man I've ever met."

Aaron snorted.

"I wish that were true, my dear. But I'm afraid Kent is as driven by his own demons and ghosts as he is by his liberal views."

Driven by ghosts? "What do you mean?"

Dr. Sawyer's face fell, his gaze turning inwards. "As doctors, we can't save everyone. We've all lost patients. Even Aaron, who's so new at this. The problem with Kent is, he's not trained to understand and accept this reality. He still believes he's a knight on a white horse who can swoop in and save everyone." He looked up, meeting Sharon's gaze, his eyes glistening with tears.

At her puzzled frown, he continued.

"He hasn't told you."

"With good reason, Dad!"

"No, Aaron. She should know what motivates him if they're involved."

"He wouldn't want – "

"There was another child," he interrupted. "A little too much like this Harley he obsesses about."

"In the Downtown Eastside?" Sharon asked.

"No. In Yellowknife, up north. A few years ago." Dr. Sawyer stood up and moved to the bar cart, meticulously pouring himself an inch of Scotch, carefully adding two ice cubes with a quiet clink-clink. He swirled them around, tossed the entire thing back in one swallow. His chest rose and fell. "He was a community nurse in a tiny First Nations village. A reckless thing to take on in the first place, but that's our Kent, always taking on impossible challenges. I thought he was just burning off some youthful idealism and rage. We thought he'd go back to school, become a doctor. But there were challenges beyond his power to remedy. When everything went badly he withdrew, throwing himself into this futile job he does now."

"Dad, don't – " Aaron tried again, but he plowed on, determined.

"It would upset anybody. A boy who died on his watch. In his very arms, in fact. A boy who could have been saved, if he'd had more medical training." Kent's father turned back to her, his cheeks red. "That's why he's so relentless with this social work. That's why he won't let go. He still seeks atonement for a death that was preventable."

"Is that why he quit nursing?" Sharon's thoughts flew back to that time they talked in his car. He'd evaded the question. Was this it?

"Yes. He was heartbroken. He came to me, trying to understand. So I told him the truth. The boy could have been saved, in other circumstances. But there was no local doctor in that remote location. Kent didn't have the knowledge nor the drugs or tools he needed to save the boy's life. He was in over his head."

Sharon gasped as understanding landed. "So... what? You made him feel even worse that he never studied medicine? He's already punishing himself. How was that helpful?"

"That's not the point." Dr. Sawyer barked, slumping back into his seat, glaring at his empty plate. It was the point, in Sharon's view. He jabbed at the air with his pointer finger. "If he'd studied medicine like I wanted him to, he'd never have been there. He wouldn't have suffered that tragedy. And he wouldn't now be working this scuzzy job with addicts and homeless bums on skid row, trying to find redemption. Who knows if he'll ever recover from his great self-pitying wallow."

Aaron groaned, leaning his head on his hands.

Sharon gripped her hands together on her lap, fighting to maintain control of her temper. The urge to jump up, scream and shout rattled her to her bones, but she held it together. *You've got this.* He was no better or worse than a temperamental client, or a cranky judge. She'd managed people like him before.

"Kent's not wallowing. He's doing something meaningful. What happened up there may have hurt and frustrated him. But he wouldn't have gone there in the first place if he didn't want to make a difference in people's lives. He's just doing it a different way now. Can't you see that?"

"I don't buy it, young lady. If he had more confidence, he'd be able to go back to school. He could do something meaningful by righting his wrongs. He could join us saving lives at the hospital every day!" Dr. Sawyer's face flushed with his agitation.

"Kent is saving lives now. More than just Harley's life. He's part of that community. He understands people and knows what they need. There are other ways to save lives than cutting them open. He doesn't have to go back to school to be what you think he should be."

He huffed and shook his head. "He'll get nowhere this way. It makes me immeasurably sad."

"You shouldn't be sad, Dr. Sawyer." Sharon's chin quivered as she fought off tears. "You should be proud. You have an amazing son, and he's doing monumental work. He deserves your admiration, not your scorn and b-bullying."

The corners of Dr. Sawyer's mouth pulled down sardonically, his sharp gaze assessing her. "I still think you're possibly the best thing that's happened to him in a long time, Sharon. You've got fire in you. He needs a wake up call."

The truth landed in her gut like a block of granite. She hadn't happened to him. He'd happened to her. He was the fire from which she shied and yet needed. He'd woken her up, made her feel, allowed her to see that she'd been hiding behind a cowardly shield of propriety, safety and security, denying her own values and her legacy. He'd forced her to fight for what was right and given her the incentive to lift the burden that had held her down all her adult life.

Mom's words weighed heavily on him. Kent's jaw jutted in frustration as he gripped the railing. True happiness had eluded him for years. A week or so ago, he'd been bordering on happy. Content anyway. He enjoyed his challenging job. The project he'd committed himself to seemed to be moving in a promising direction. He had faith in Sharon's ability to help them get past the obstacles. And he'd also discovered an unanticipated joy in her blue eyes, in her sweet voice, in her passionate arms.

"Are you falling for her?"

"Huh?" He turned back to Mom. How did she do that? "What are you talking about?"

Mom jerked her head towards the patio doors they'd left ajar, the muffled sound of conversation between his father, his brother and his lover drifting out to them.

He let out a cynical cough of laughter. "Oh, my God. I left her alone with them." He ground the heels of his hands into his eyes, trying to push away his anguish and find some clear thinking.

He'd been worried about her lack of commitment to the project. But his attraction to her clouded his judgement, and perhaps he expected more from her than was fair. It's just that there was something about Sharon that, from the moment their eyes first met, he'd simply wanted. He should focus on the project, pushing her to do more. But it was *pro bono* and he hadn't had high expectations to begin with, had he? He knew what they were up against. They might not win.

He wished he didn't feel a bitter satisfaction that she was being punished for her… betrayal? Was he going to think that? Really? She'd warmed, delighting him in ways he hadn't expected. Her singing was a secret gift of tenderness and light she hid inside her hard shell. In bed, she was more fire than ice, so much of her passionate heart hidden away, buried beneath that icy facade. Maybe under that rigid shell she wasn't so tough. He admired and liked her, and respected her, even if they didn't succeed. Maybe she wasn't the formidable Amazon he'd first thought.

"What's going on with you and Sharon tonight?"

He studied his shoes, his jaw ticking, his chest tight, recalling their argument in the car. He'd behaved like an ass, even if he didn't like what he heard, or what she was doing. Her compromising methods felt like they were giving up. "I don't know. We argued. But it's more than that. I don't... I'm not sure she's what I... I'd hoped she was."

Mom chuckled softly. "What if she's just what she is?"

His throat thickened. Was he being too hard on her? Did she betray him or was he being unrealistic? His idealism often made him a harsh judge of others. He knew that about himself. His sense of guilt fought with his anger. "We'd better get back."

As they passed through the tiled sunroom, the conversation in the adjacent dining room became clearer. Kent came up short, putting a hand up to stall his mother, and listened with mounting horror.

CHAPTER 24

"He's the most woke man I've ever met."

Dr. Sawyer grunted, leaning his head into his hand. "What about this project you're working on together. Why do they need a lawyer involved? Why does he always have to take on these impossible challenges?"

She shook her head. "It's complicated. There's a dispute over who gets to use the building in question, so we have to challenge the City Land Department. The competing developer is the son of Councillor Seibold."

Before she could think of another thing to say to calm him down, his father jumped in again. "Councillor Seibold? Is that who you're dealing with?"

Her head shot up, eyes widening in dread.

"Gus is an old friend of mine." His chest puffed out like a rooster. "He made several generous donations to the hospital. And we've golfed together for years. If you're having some trouble at City Hall, I can put a word in."

"No! Please." Sharon almost swallowed her tongue in shock. "I-I mean, I've got everything under control there, thanks. Councillor Seibold and I have come to an understanding. Everything will be fine."

Dr. Sawyer drew a breath to argue.

Sharon straightened her spine, pulling her shoulders back. The last thing they needed was his father meddling. He could ruin everything with one well-intentioned phone call. Her thoughts scrambled. If he was close to Seibold, anything she said now could hurt her plan. She had to stop him. "There's no need to – "

"That's just perfect!" Kent snapped as he re-entered the dining room. He pointed at his father. "You stay out of my business, if you don't mind!"

Sharon jerked at the sound of Kent's choked voice. Her heart lurched in her chest at the sight of him. He stood in the doorway, his mother hovering behind. Her gaze jumped from Kent to his father and back again.

"How touching, Princess."

Kent's jaw clenched, the tendons in his neck taut. He glared at his father with potent hatred, then turned his dark accusing gaze her way, eyes like dark gemstone, glittering with vitriol. What had he heard?

"Kent! I – I – Wait. What – ?" she squawked. Her heartbeat raced, thumping in her chest as a loud buzzing took up residence in her head. Her thoughts scattered like the chipped rainbows of light fractured by the crystal chandelier over the crisp white tablecloth.

"Kent?"

Slipping into the room to stand behind Aaron, Barbara took the measure of her sons and husband, peering intently at Sharon. Concern in her eyes, she rested her hands on Aaron's shoulders. "What's going on?" she asked.

Kent ignored her and turned to face Sharon, his hands on his hips. "It seems you're working the wrong side of this case. You should represent the Seibolds, since you're doing everything to give them what they want."

"What?" she squeaked. Tremors had taken over her body, and a hot flush had swept her from her neck to the backs of her knees, which threatened to buckle. "I'm not… he… he… he won't win. I promise. I'll make sure of it."

"If you feel that way, why aren't you trying harder to help Pathway win our case? Why are you allowing Seibold to intimidate you?"

"You know why." Her voice faltered, weakening. "But I'm fighting him, anyway."

"All you're doing is laying down and giving in to Seibold and his son," he spat. "It's not good enough. If you planned to fight them, I think I'd have noticed it by now."

"There's no need for all this," interrupted Dr. Sawyer. "Gus is a reasonable man. I'm sure if I – "

"No!" Kent barked at him.

"I haven't given up." She heard her own voice trembling, choked off by panic and the tears that coursed down her cheeks. " I told you. I have a plan. You just have to give me time."

He sneered, shaking his head, defeated. "What for? I've watched you work. We've been at this for weeks. I've given you time." He paced the length of the dining room, clenching his fists.

Sharon, her head down, twisted her fingers together, agonizing over the secrets she kept. What a mess! Her heart drummed rapidly, pushing against her clavicle, trying to leap right out of her throat. "I can't… I can't explain it right now. Trust me, Kent."

"Trust you? Trust you?" He scoffed. "What reason could I possibly have to trust you?"

Please don't fight. Please don't shout. Her stomach felt like it was on fire, tension radiating through her limbs, her entire body shaking. She pinched her lips between her teeth and shook her head. How could she make him understand? Horrified that she'd lost control here in front of his entire family, she pressed her fist to her mouth to stop her trembling lips. She fought the tears that burned at her eyes and throat. *Come on! Pull yourself together. You've got this!*

Not alone in her anguish, she saw that tears had left pale streaks in Barbara's makeup. She swiped at her face and bent forward, burying it in Aaron's hair, her hands on either side of his face while he sat frozen, a look of distress on his face. How many of these horrible quarrels had this family endured? Instead of smoothing the water, Sharon's presence had made it so much worse.

They had to get out of here before this situation got any further out of control. She stood up. "I appreciate your offer to help, Dr. Sawyer," she reverted to her most proper tone, holding herself tightly together. "But as I explained to Kent, I have a plan in the works. We have to stick to formal negotiations and legal actions. Your interference could compromise our position further. I'm sure you appreciate that."

Sharon backed towards the door, stepping around the table, trying to get closer to Kent. If she could get him to leave, maybe she could give him some facts. Just enough to help him under-stand there was still hope. Quite a lot of hope, if she wasn't mistaken. If she didn't screw this up. She had to get Kent alone, to calm him down.

He trusted her so little; she knew there was no hope for them, and that broke her heart. But even so, she couldn't bear his contempt. She had to explain.

Kent suddenly noticed her approach and turned toward her. "Don't." He thrust out a hand. "Stay away from me. I'm done with you and your lies and secret deals."

"But..."

"Kent, honey – " his mother tried.

"We don't need your help anymore, Sharon. I followed the

rules, and it didn't work. I'm sick and tired of playing the game established by a power elite to serve their own interests. The system that you love is broken. I told you what I'm going to do. So never mind *his* interference. Get ready for mine." He thumped his own chest, then stalked to the entry hall.

"Kent, no, please. Public protests accomplish nothing. All they do is rile emotions. You'll make yourself and the society look foolish and… and desperate. We have to ta – "

But there was no time to finish her thought. In a flash, Kent had spun on his heel and stormed out, the boom of the heavy front door echoing through the massive house, rattling the windows.

She ran out after him, shooting onto the porch to see him yanking open the door of his car.

"Wait! Kent," she pleaded, her heart breaking for what she knew was coming. "Wait for me. Aren't we… What about us?"

"There is no us, Sharon. Maybe you *should* hook up with my brother." The look he tossed her way sliced her heart in pieces. "You'd be very happy together. Maybe Seibold can help him get elected to council!" The sneer on his face crushed her, bringing a flood of fresh tears to her eyes. He slammed the door and his car roared to life, pulling out of the drive.

"Oh." He'd left her alone here with his family.

CHAPTER 25

Furious with himself as much as with everyone else, Kent parked his car near the society office and walked.

He scowled at the darkened Pathway windows as he passed, then continued wandering the streets. He could grab something to wear if he had his keys, but he did not. A shiver wracked him and he dug his hands deeper into his pockets. In his hurry to leave his parents' house, he'd forgotten his jacket. Few stars were visible in the purple haze of the city's lights in the sky above him. Gathering rain clouds did nothing to warm the night. He might have had a few too many whiskies. *What an idiot!*

Walking the streets had become a balm to his battered soul, if not an addiction. Even though he knew he was doing little good, it comforted him to move among the shadow people who lived here. When everything in his life seemed out of control, it felt like here at least, he could serve a purpose.

When no one seemed to have his back, and nothing was going his way, he found comfort here among others who life had shafted. Contrary to many people's perception, these people were trustworthy. No pretensions. No lies. They were solid, grounded, honest and loyal.

His throat thickened, and he punched his thighs to release his pent up frustration, growling. Shoving his chilly hands in his pockets and hunching his shoulders, shame filled him to think he came to *them* for comfort.

He approached Oppenheimer Park, where most people who didn't have a room or a bed would settle in at this hour. The cooling autumn weather made those that weren't out of their mind more inclined to huddle and stay warm. A low, congenial murmur of voices rose from the messy conglomeration of tents, tarps, cardboard, and scattered garbage.

He knew his heartache and discontent weren't in the same league as their troubles, though there was plenty of heartache here too. He'd had a privileged life, with every opportunity. He had a job, a home, his health and safety. He had friends. His situation didn't compare.

But he felt at home here. These people hadn't asked for a shitty deal. They didn't ask for favours either. They were surviving anyway. He took strength from that.

"Hey Kent," a junkie he'd met at his mother's clinic a few times, and chatted with over a cup of coffee, called out in greeting as he ventured onto the damp trampled grass. "What you doing down here?" Ryan, he thought. A homeless guy from Ontario who drifted west for the warmer weather. He'd find winter was winter even in the Pacific Northwest, and a helluva lot wetter, and he'd soon wish he had a roof over his head. Kent lifted a hand in greeting and shrugged. He didn't have a good answer.

The night grew colder by the minute, and the fog of alcohol was wearing off, leaving him shivering and feeling stupid.

His thoughts swirled. A part of him recognized that he was too emotional to think straight at all, and that it was a terrible idea to wander alone around the Downtown Eastside in this mood. He needed to be sharp to be here at night. Despite his familiarity, there were always dangers.

Kent waded further into Tent City, scanning right and left in the limited light, taking it slow. He didn't want to look like a madman on the hunt, but he also didn't want to miss a detail. He had no idea what he was looking for. Trouble, maybe? People were less likely to stop and chat if he looked agitated or on a mission. But still he always kept a sharp eye out for Harley, or any of the other underage kids who he knew spent all, or part of their time down here.

There was one now. A heavily pierced fifteen-year-old named Fatima. He stopped a few feet away. "Hey Fatima."

She eyed him warily.

"You remember me. Kent. From Pathway."

"Yeah. What you doin' here so late?"

"Just chillin'. Came down to see how everyone's making out with the colder temps tonight." He scrutinized her face and body for signs of drugs or abuse, but she seemed to be okay tonight, bundled in a hoodie with a ratty blanket draped over her shoulders. She was one who came to the Pathway Society off and on, when it suited her. He thought she'd go for the housing option when their project was ready. When she showed up for classes or counselling, she had a solid head on her shoulders. So many of these kids were sensible survivors, who, when you knew their story, chose life on the street over less palatable alternatives.

"Whatcha gonna do about it if we're freezin' our tits off, eh?" She snorted.

He obligingly laughed. At least she still had her sense of humour. "Well, not much, I guess. You see Harley?"

She hummed and shook her head. "Nah." She turned away, took a long drag on her cigarette, blew a cloud of smoke slowly up into the night air. He glanced up at the cloudy sky. The blue-grey dome of light cast by the city began to drop light rain on the transient community, the descent of individual raindrops visible. He pulled up the collar of his shirt, though it offered little protection.

What the hell was he doing down here tonight, but wallowing in self-pity?

He couldn't believe what he'd overheard as he returned to the dining room. He was so angry, yet he didn't even know why he cared anymore. Why had she looked at him that way? With regret in her sad blue eyes? He knew exactly what Dad had told her. His chest squeezed with melancholy, the hope of love slipping through his grip like mist. Whatever he thought they had, he'd been a fool to think it. How relieved she must be to discover his weakness before she got too involved.

His father was one thing. Dad had been ripping him to shreds for years. He expected nothing else from him anymore. It had hardened him. But Kent's gut burned thinking of Sharon's betrayal. Sitting there, back straight in her hypocritical prim and proper lawyer mode, like the day he first saw her, chatting away with his father as though everything was just fine. As if Kent was just another problem for them to manage from their high-and-mighty chairs. That hurt.

He'd thought they were a team – him and Sharon – but he'd been wrong. He'd had the idea he had to protect Sharon from his father, and instead she'd rejected his solidarity and confided her deal with Seibold to him as if it were no big deal. Just business as usual. The little schemer. She'd lied! How foolish he was to think because they'd had sex – once! – there were any feelings involved?

He let out a bark of cynical laughter. He was pathetic. It was just a passing moment for her. A bit of slumming. She didn't want him. A woman like her wouldn't want a genuine relationship with a man like him. Dad saw it. Aaron saw it. Why was Kent suddenly blind?

How could he forget that he couldn't trust those kinds of people? They were all looking out for number one, judging those deemed lesser. Patients to count. Cases to win. Feathers in their caps.

He'd lost his perspective because of her beauty and brains and let the fact that he wanted her cloud his judgment.

He belonged down here, in the shadows, as far from the bright, shining elite world his father and brother inhabited as possible, as far from the likes of lawyers like Sharon and power brokers like the Seibolds. The people down here on the street made sense to him. They got him, too. This was his true home.

He spotted Marlene and Wheeler, her brute of an old man, and deduced that they'd lost their SRO hotel room again. That would be hard on her. Strolling up, he pulled her into a bear hug when she saw him and grinned.

"Hey, there, Kent, baby." She tipped her head back.

"Hi, Mar. You get evicted or something?"

"Don't you know it." She stepped back. "Douchebag here spent the rent money on a bottle again."

Wheeler barked, staggering, "Shaddup, y'old cow," and she ignored him.

"I'm sorry. It's getting cold, eh? Did you check the shelters for space?"

"No room. I'll be fine, darlin'." She belied her words with a hacking cough that had her bent in half for a full minute. She righted herself. "Why you got no jacket on, eh? You look like you're freezing, honey. S'pose you're looking for your kid."

"Seen him?"

"No, but I seen that devil RJ down here tonight." She peered up at Kent with her sunken, racoon eyes narrowed.

"He causing trouble?"

"The usual. Cock-a-doodle-doo." She tucked her palmed cigarette between her withered lips and took a pull. "Buildin' his empire."

"What about Carl?"

"Carl's gone to his room a while ago." She waved a hand toward Union Street. Thank God for that. He worried about the old guy, too.

"Right. Thanks, Mar. Take care, huh?"

Damn it, if JR wasn't hanging around the neighbourhood still causing trouble. He was a wild hare, and Kent would like nothing better to be rid of him. But Kent knew, when RJ had moved on to some other city, another low-life would move in to take his place. Except the next creep might not target Harley so maliciously.

Kent hadn't seen Harley since Friday. Or Carl. He ought to have stopped in at Carnegie yesterday, but he'd been so preoccupied.

With Sharon.

He couldn't let down his guard for a moment. The need to check in with them played in his mind on a loop, and he reluctantly acknowledged that his father had a point. His quest for atonement had become a kind of sick obsession.

He continued weaving between the tents and huddled people, with no sign of Harley anywhere, until at last he came upon RJ with two of his thugs. RJ sat tipped back in a plastic lawn chair, gnawing on a stick of beef jerky like he owned the whole damned park and everything in it. Kent strode up and halted, hands on his hips, his narrowed gaze focussed on RJ's ugly, laughing face, his arrogant swagger, his flashy gold bling.

Frustration, rage and pure hatred boiled up in him, filling his chest with red heat and his gut with sour bile. Kent's vision narrowed until all he could see was RJ's gold teeth caps, the hideous expression of evil that this loathsome prick represented in the world.

"Hey, if it ain't the lumberjack. Da angry little social worker out for a nighttime stroll. What can I do for ya on dis fine night, Sawyer?"

Kent said nothing, eyeing his nemesis with a scowl, then assessing his two thugs who stood at his shoulders like surly bulldogs, bulky and dull-witted young Russian kids he'd picked up on his travels. Kent clenched his fists, his arms and hands tingling with a twitchy energy clamouring for an outlet. It would be the height of foolishness to challenge these professional criminals, but he didn't care. "This isn't your shop, Kovac. It's not your place to welcome me. It's you that don't belong here."

RJ laughed and laughed, tossing his head back, his derision a blatant insult that pushed Kent past his civilized limit. "Where's dat sweet blonde benjamin tonight? Yep, I'd sure like me a piece o' dat."

Kent scowled at him, ignoring his question, pushing the uncomfortable reminder of Sharon out of his mind. His pulse hammered in his temples and neck, his breath quickening. He had to do something. There had to be some way to stop this petty crime lord from victimizing his friends.

RJ ripped off another chunk of jerky and rolled it into his cheek like tobacco, gnawing with his mouth open, his gold teeth gnashing. His lips curled into a sneer of disdain. "But it too late for dat, lumberjack. Dat boy mi-ine already. Waste a your time. "

Something snapped in Kent's head, his vision flooding with red. A storm of blood surged through Kent's body, lifting his tense shoulders to his ears, making his head pound like a war drum. He kept his voice to a low growl, afraid he'd scream if he let himself go.

"Where. The. Hell. Is. He?"

"Don't fuss. He just havin' a nap now." RJ grinned, his dark eyes glinting with malice.

"What? Where?" Kent's head whipped around? "Right here? In Tent City?" He strode forward. "What the fuck are you talking about?"

RJ laughed maniacally, exposing his half-chewed meat.

"You son-of-a – " Kent lunged at him, kicking out the legs of his plastic chair and sending him tumbling to his ass on the damp grass. He scrambled, his lackeys pulling him upright, brushing him off, setting him to his feet. His face twisted into an angry sneer, his eyes like black holes in his face. Black as a junkie, high on power. Lurching toward Kent, he got up in his face, screaming.

"You little shit! Nobody touch RJ Kovac."

Kent's stomach turned at the stench of salty smoked meat over a potent stew of halitosis, sweat and burning plastic. He gagged and stepped back, turning his face away.

One thug shot out an arm to grab a fistful of Kent's shirt.

RJ scoffed, flicking a hand in their direction. "Never mind. Leave it. Is dogshit on my shoe." But then he quickly spun and jabbed one ringed finger hard into Kent's chest. "The fuck. Why you don't visit your little friend? See if he even know you tonight, eh?" He cackled and with the flat of his hand, shoved Kent back so hard he stumbled to catch his balance, falling into the Russian.

The bruiser grabbed Kent by the arms, pulling them hard behind his back with a stab of hot pain and dragged him to another tent nearby. He yanked back the entrance flap and tossed Kent in head first.

With a grunt, he fell hard to his elbows and knees, knives of pain jarring his bones. The interior was pitch black, the weak light from streetlights dully illuminating Tent City making no impression in here. Kent scrabbled around among fetid piles of damp sleeping bags, blankets or clothing, he couldn't tell. Wetness seeped into the knees of his jeans. The stench of burned plastic and sweat was stronger here. Was there someone in here with him?

"Hello?" He croaked. "Hey is someone in here?"

Sharon's hands shook as she paid the taxi driver and stepped out onto the dark, empty street across from the Pathway offices, her pulse racing. The night couldn't end like this, on such a disastrous note. What did he think of her? She had to find him.

She shivered in the chilly night air, pulling her coat tighter around herself. It felt like rain. She wasn't dressed for a walk, but if Kent were here, and she could explain, maybe tonight wouldn't be a complete disaster. Another day couldn't pass knowing he despised her. That he'd so utterly lost faith in her. Heat flooded her face, her eyes burning. He had it so wrong. Was she naïve to think he should know her well enough to give her the benefit of the doubt without evidence? They hadn't known each other long at all.

After Kent's abrupt departure, his parents and Aaron were subdued. No one knew quite what to do. Sharon included.

"Can I give you a ride home?" Aaron had asked in desperation.

She firmly rejected his offer with a hard look. "I'll get a cab, thanks."

Dr. Sawyer summoned one for her, eager to bid her good-night. Aaron brought her coat, and Barbara stood in the entryway with her, waiting, while the two men retreated to another room.

"I'm so sorry, Sharon. I don't know what's going on with you and Kent. He said you argued. But this... *this* wasn't about you. I promise. I'm sorry you had to witness it."

"It's all right, Mrs. Sawyer. Kent prepared me." She thought he had. But this had escalated to another level, uglier and darker than she'd imagined. She'd thought she and Kent would have faced this together, as a team, not as... adversaries. But they weren't enemies. They were still on the same side. He just didn't know it yet. "I thought my being here could make it easier. Bett –" Her voice broke as a sob of anguish wracked her.

Mrs. Sawyer rubbed her arm. "It's not all right. There's nothing about this that's right."

Sharon shook her head. She agreed, but it wasn't her business. She would carry on with her plan, but there was nothing she could do about Kent's family. Not right now.

"He's very upset right now. Please give him another chance."

Sharon sighed heavily, blinked at her haggard, red-eyed image in a gilt-framed hall mirror, pressing her tired eyes with her fingertips, and sighed. "I think it's him that has to give me another chance."

Another shudder brought her back to her surroundings. Where was Kent? Where would he run off to? She had to find him. She had to make it right.

CHAPTER 26

A faint mewling rose up from a corner of the dark tent.

"Hey. Harley? Harley!" Kent lunged closer, feeling his way until his hand landed on a shallow form beneath the blankets. With both hands, he felt up and down until he found the shape of the boy, thin and limp.

"Harley, Harley." Tossing back the cover, Kent found his thin face. His hair was damp with sweat and plastered to his scalp. He couldn't see whether his eyes were open, so he felt gently the surface of his face, touching his cheeks, his nose, his brow with trembling fingertips, one hand pressing for a pulse at his neck. He leaned closer listening for breathing.

The boy whimpered again, a thin, feral sound so feeble he was barely there. "Jesus, Harley, Jesus. Why, kid? Why do you do this to yourself?" But he knew, it wasn't Harley's fault. A fist of black rage rose up his gut. His jaw tensed. That scum Kovacs took pleasure in bending those weaker than himself to his will, manipulating them until they had no choice but to do his bidding. God knew what horrid things he's already coerced Harley to do when his body came down from the drugs and demanded more. He would do anything then, if he was even conscious enough to resist.

He picked him up and dragged him, crawling, out the tent opening. A roar of outrage ripped from his throat, aimed at RJ as he elbowed his thug out of the way. Holding Harley up, he tugged his phone from his pocket and speed-dialed 911 again. Then carried Harley to Powell Street to meet the paramedics, running top speed, gasping for breath.

In moments they arrived with a flash of red light and *whoop whoop* of the siren. At least one ambulance always stood by in this area at night, and was invariably needed. With practiced efficiency, the paramedics had Harley on the stretcher in the back, checked his vitals, set up an IV, oxygen and administered emergency medicine.

"You want to ride back with him Kent?"

Kent hesitated. He should. He wanted to, but rage coiled around him like a coat of barbed wire, pricking him, goading him. He couldn't just leave. Not yet. He had unfinished business. "RJ did this. Again. He's trying to kill him."

Marco, the paramedic, shook his head sadly and shrugged. He'd seen it all. "You coming with us or not?"

Choked with fury, Kent's thoughts clouded by a savage desire to smash RJ and stop him for good. He shook his head, suddenly overcome with a calm determination. "There's something I've got to do first. I – I've got my car. I'll meet you at the hospital."

Leaving Marco peering warily after him, he loped back to the area where RJ and his minders had been, panting, his vision swimming with red. But they were gone.

Fuck! Fuck! This was the final straw. His fingers curled into futile fists at his sides. He wanted to kill RJ. He saw himself pounding his face to pulp. Choking the life from his skinny neck. But he was gone. Again. Slipped away, seemingly beyond the reach of justice or the law, like the evil snake he was. His grimy plastic lawn chair sat there, vacant, taunting Kent like an empty throne.

Lunging and grabbing the stupid chair, Kent swung it, flinging it as far as he could over the tops of the tents, into the darkness of the park beyond with a roar. "Aaarrrgghh!"

This act of futility did nothing to diffuse his anger, only firing his veins with adrenaline. His heart rate accelerated, his muscles twitching with the need to crush something. Or someone.

RJ.

He had to find that bastard. Enough was enough. If nobody else would stop RJ from spreading his evil and hurting innocent kids, Kent would do it himself. He would not stand by and let this continue. He would not be a passive bystander while people were being harmed. While children died. Not anymore. Not this time.

~

Sharon stood on the sidewalk, staring. The Pathway Society windows stared bleakly back, vacant and black, the door securely locked, as many businesses in this area were, behind a steel grill. Nobody answered when she banged, as she knew they would not. Then, with a gasp, she spotted Kent's Subaru parked a block down, confirming her instincts.

She shivered, clenching her teeth. The weight of this moment pressed heavily on her chest, strangling her breath, her heart thudding with the knowledge of where he'd gone. Where she would find him? Where else might he go? She knew he'd come here for comfort. Why would he go to the school when he could walk down any street or alley and find a friend? Someone who accepted him without criticism? People he could trust who wouldn't lie to him, or betray him.

Her heart squeezed with the realization that she was not one of them. Instead of treating him with respect, and trusting that he would keep her secret and cooperate with her once he knew her plan, she'd withheld the critical information. She'd treated him like a child, just as his father did.

With a knot of tension lodged in her throat, she knew she deserved his anger and derision.

The smart thing to do would be to phone him, but she also knew, in his current state of mind and emotional turmoil, he wouldn't answer.

She had to find him. Talk to him.

Maybe he'd gone looking for Harley again. She could head towards the Balmoral, just in case. Dare she go there alone? If she could find him, it was worth the risk. Kent was worth it.

Hesitant, terrified of what she was about to do, and yet knowing she would do it anyway, she strode down Hastings Street, trying to keep her steps confident, suppressing the trepidation that raced through her veins. Further into the dark underworld of the Downtown Eastside, a place she wouldn't have, just a month or two ago, ventured alone even in broad daylight.

Shoulders tight, her breaths coming fast and shallow, she held her trembling arms and ribs together in a tight wrap. She'd lost her mind. She was an idiot.

An idiot in love. An idiot whose heart was breaking.

Her breathing came in shallow bursts, her neck and shoulders knotted. She wore heels and a skirt, carrying her purse, and it felt like she wore a glowing target on her back. A beacon screaming Vulnerable Woman Alone at Night!

Swallowing, she got her keys out of her purse and threaded them between her fingers, tightening her fist until her knuckles glowed white under the streetlights. Blood pounded in her ears, drowning out the *shush* of distant tires, the lonely click of her own heels on the pavement.

She'd ruined everything with Kent. Even if her strategy to save the project went well – and it was compromised by his disregard for her as well as his determination to pursue his plan to stage a rally at City Hall – even then, she'd thrown away her first real shot at true love.

Kent knew her. He saw past her cool facade, her tight control, her fearful armour and knew her for who she really was. And she'd thought that maybe he could love her. That maybe they could have made something together on the foundation of their fragile trust.

But she'd broken that trust.

The dark streets were nearly vacant at this late hour. She jumped at every muffled voice or scuffling sound from the deep shadows she passed.

Maybe in the years since her world came crashing in, and she'd been living like a hermit crab, hiding inside a hard shell to protect her soft and vulnerable centre, she'd begun to calcify. Maybe she'd absorbed the ways and beliefs of the people among whom she'd hidden and become like them. Cold and calculating. Enough that people like Kent really couldn't trust her.

Not with his wounded heart.

Was she too entrenched in her belief that she had to follow rules and keep her head down to survive? For the first time in years, doubt wove around her like a tangle of threads, threatening to trip her and bring her to a standstill.

She pulled her coat collar up, tucking her bright hair inside it as much as she could. Tugging the coat tighter around her, she crossed her arms and hunched her shoulders, leaning into her stride, trying to walk with confidence, though each block eroded what little she had left.

Her plan had worked for her so far. But despite considerable career success, it felt like a slow slog over endless obstacles, with little joy along the way. At thirty-seven, she was still alone and struggling. She felt like an automaton, a slave to her own ambition. Sure, she had success, but she had neither the glamorous career Rachel had, nor had she found love the way Simon had with Kate. She had a fragile relationship with her mother. She'd broken her father's heart and would never get him back. Never be able to apologize for losing faith in him or make it up to him now that he was dead.

And she was still at a loss as to what Meacham and the other senior partners wanted from her to cross that last barrier to the inner circle of full partnership at the firm. Now all she felt was doubt. Was that even the validation she wanted? Needed? She didn't know anymore. Not if it meant continuing to compromise her core values. Not if it meant living a solitary, joyless existence.

Was Kent right about her? Had she really become the lawyer – the person – she wanted to be? Or one that she despised? Maybe the right thing to do was fight for what you believed in, regardless of the consequences, like Kent. Like her father.

What did it really matter if you had a certain salary, or a particular title painted on your office door, if you didn't respect who you'd become? What really mattered?

And yet, she still didn't believe Kent's methods would accomplish the job. She wanted to show him, to prove to him she could do this, her way. And more than that, to vindicate her father. Somehow. No public protest could accomplish that. Only hard evidence would clear his name, and free her from this cage of lies.

If she could find Kent and explain, at least enough to make him understand, then maybe he'd forgive her. Maybe he'd give her another chance.

Head down, she walked on.

CHAPTER 27

"Where's RJ?" Kent ran up to one person after another, grabbing them, shaking them. "Have you seen where RJ went?"

Someone scowled at him. "Don't man. There's nothing you can do."

Grinding his teeth, Kent glared back and forged on through the maze of Tent City. He had to be here. He couldn't have gotten far.

He came upon Ryan again. He squatted on a blanket on the ground with two other young guys, a tiny blue flame flickering between them. They were cooking drugs, focussed on their task.

Kent bent and shook Ryan's shoulder. "Ryan! Ryan, did you see where RJ went?"

Ryan lifted his head, as though it were a great lumbering melon that his neck couldn't support. His eyes were unfocussed, his lids half shut. Kent sighed. He was gone, lights out for the night. He wouldn't notice a freight train if it roared right past him.

Kent turned to go, continuing his search.

In dull, laboured speech, Ryan's reply caught up with him as he stepped away. "You. Shoun' be. Here. Dude. The slow delivery of his warning sucked at Kent, as though, standing here in the dark, he sank into a vat of quicksand. Violence tore at his limbs, demanding release. He yanked himself from the hypnotic stupor and strode on.

Wheeler stepped in front of Kent, his beefy inked arms spread out from his torn denim vest, immune to the cold, blocking his path. "Get outta here before you regret it. RJ's outta control tonight."

Kent shook his head and stepped around him. If tough guys like Wheeler were giving RJ wide berth, he was out of control. As Kent moved through the crowd, asking person after person, he found no one willing to tell him what he wanted to know. Yet the warnings grew more dire. As though everyone was trying to keep him from RJ. Trying to keep him safe.

"He-eey. Lumberjack."

Kent spun at the voice, the Russian accent giving its bearer away as one of RJ's bullies. He stood there squinting with his shaved head, neck tattoo and cheap windbreaker, crooking his finger at Kent.

It looked like he'd found RJ, for better or worse. He steeled himself for the latter, his senses on high alert, his muscles taut, pumped, ready for action, whether for fight or flight he didn't know. He followed the bruiser further towards the darkened fringe of Tent City, though now he could make out objects in the dark. His hearing, too, elevated the minute midnight sounds of people milling around, murmured conversations, faint music and moans.

The faint shape of RJ in his familiar bright orange Arcteryx anorak standing at the edge of the tents came into focus as they drew nearer. Kent found he was no longer shivering with cold, either, yet his arms and legs vibrated with some kind of electrical pulse.

RJ began clapping his hands in slow motion. *Clap. Clap. Clap.* The flash of his rings, his Rolex, his gold teeth lighting up with his movement as he laughed, as though a current ran through him.

"You are not a pansy after all, lumberjack. I'm impressed."

As if impatient to provide him with the answer to fight or flight, Kent's body shot forward without his conscious thought, lunging at RJ, his hands reaching for his neck, grabbing at the lapels of his jacket.

"Hey, hey. Not so fast."

The Russian thugs plucked Kent off of their boss so fast his feet momentarily left the ground. They backed him up and set him down with a thud that nearly buckled his knees, but he twisted out of their lazy grip and shot at RJ again with fists flying, catching the edge of RJ's chin with a glancing blow. Kent was no fighter, but he was young and fit and strong, and all the strength he had was channeled right now into his burning desire for vengeance. He let it all out, punching, kicking, fuming with rage let loose at long last. "You son-of-a-bitch!"

"Get yuppy lumberjack outta my hair. I'm sicka his ranting."

The Russian who beckoned him body checked him, grabbing him by the arms from behind and yanking his shoulder joints so hard Kent shouted with pain, sure they'd been dislocated. He let out a growl of mixed pain and fury.

Uuughhh! A sudden blow to his gut doubled him over with a grunt as his breath left him in a rush of agony. He'd barely seen the other Russian come at him, materializing out of the dark like a mad anglerfish, teeth bared, protruding eyes glinting in the faint light.

Kent stayed down, sucking air, gasping. *Is that it? I'm done already?* Some avenging knight he was. What had he honestly thought to accomplish with this stupid move?

Just when he could draw breath, the Russian who held him grabbed him by the ponytail and yanked his head back, pulling him upright. He screamed, his scalp on fire, just in time to feel the crunch of the other's fist against the side of his head. Strangely he felt no pain, only heard the solid, jarring THUNK in his skull, solid and bony. His teeth crashed together on the rebound with an echoing CRACK.

Dark spots flashed before his eyes, his ears ringing.

Before he pondered this new experience, he'd received another brutal fist to the gut that dropped him to his knees, a blunt kick to the thigh that would have landed on his junk had he not twisted at the right moment. He registered that, faintly, through the roaring noise of rushing blood in his head, buzzing like a cloud of bees. The dark world spun out of focus, and tilted, the grass at his feet rushing toward him, just as a final blunt WHUMP to the back of his head sent him face first into the black earth.

~

As Sharon advanced down the dark empty street, her tension rose. Her hands were clammy with sweat despite the chilly night air, yet she couldn't move them from their tight grip around her ribs. She would surely come apart if she let go.

A sudden crash had her squealing, jumping into a crab pose like some kind of cartoon martial arts black belt, lurching away from a dark alcove where the clanging noise had come from. Her keys dropped to the pavement with a clatter. With racing pulse and panting breath, she froze in her tracks, waiting for information to settle into her brain, or something to counter her primitive reflexes.

Evidently she was a mouse, a mouse that dealt with danger by becoming immobilized, passively awaiting death.

Another scuffling noise and it was gone. It was nothing. A cat or something knocking over a garbage can. She released a shaky breath.

How many times could you die?

What did it matter if you hadn't lived?

She bent to retrieve her keys, repositioned them between her cold knuckles and carried on, determined to find him. The sudden fright released her tension, giving her a shot of adrenaline, and she strode on, feeling bolder, more confident, less fearful. She swiped at the tears that streaked her cold cheeks, wiping them away. *You've got this.*

It was all starting to make sense. Her need for safety and control led her to make the same mistakes again and again. Sometimes you didn't have it all figured out. Sometimes you couldn't do it alone. Sometimes you had to trust.

Love and trust went hand in hand. If you loved someone, you had to trust them. You had to believe in them. Hadn't she learned that lesson the hard way? She ought to know better by now. You couldn't always use empirical evidence to prove innocence or guilt.

Sometimes it was a matter of faith.

When – if – she found Kent, she would tell him everything. She had to apologize for not trusting him. They needed to work together, not at odds. They wanted the same thing. But perhaps it was too late. Maybe he wouldn't hear her. Maybe he couldn't forgive her.

The same passion and volatility that made him who she loved might keep him from trusting her.

Her chin quivered, her vision blurring, and she gasped at the truth. She had to tell him she'd fallen in love with him.

She passed a few solitary people on the street, but kept her head down, wanting to pass unnoticed. It drizzled, and she questioned the wisdom of venturing out in the middle of the night. But she pressed on, determined.

Very little traffic punctuated life on the street at this hour. The swish of tires on the wet road occasionally interrupted the eery quiet, an irritable outburst, a shout, a clattering bottle on the pavement, or an argument that echoed in the empty lanes. She continued straight along Hastings Street, sticking to the pools cast by the streetlights, afraid to venture down any of the darker side streets.

What if she got to the Balmoral and he wasn't there? Kent knew this neighbourhood like his own backyard. He didn't hesitate to walk down any street or lane, or talk to anyone.

The old brick facades loomed, closing in on her, their dark windows streaked with rain, following her progress like a jungle cat in a tree. Her heart thudded behind her ribs. Her rising panic brought her to a standstill, uncertain whether to go on. What was the point? She'd never find him in this labyrinth.

A dark-coloured Mercedes sedan, gleaming wet, slowed and stopped beside her. She took a half step away from the curb, confused. The rain streaked passenger window silently slid down, and she stared at it, listening to the rhythmic thud of windshield wipers. Nobody sat in the passenger seat. She tilted her head, peering in. Was someone from out-of-town lost and looking for directions? The silhouette of the driver, male, showed a shadowy face leaning towards her, the flash of a smile.

She frowned. "Are you lost?"

"I'm lost without you, darling. Can I give you a ride home?"

"What? Excuse me?" What a jerk! Was he trying to pick her up?

"How about I buy you a drink and we'll go from there?"

"Uuhh… oh, crap." The penny dropped. Oh, Lord. "No, thank you." Thank you? Seriously? She was suddenly mortified to be bent over in her elegant clothes and heels having a conversation with a John in his car on Hastings Street in the middle of the night. Was she freaking born yesterday? She stood up stiffly and backed away from the car, shaking her head. "I'm not… not what you think. You've misunderstood."

"Come on, gorgeous. I'll be good to you."

Sharon turned away from him and marched on again as fast as she could manage in her heels. Her ankles were wet and cold as water splashed up with each step. She couldn't get away fast enough. Oh, God! Without thinking, she turned the next corner and hurried into a side street.

"Hey! Hey, you." A woman called after her.

Sharon hesitated, turning to see who it was.

"You new here? You can't just move in on my space."

Sharon spun away and continued walking, her heart racing.

"Hey! Come'ere. I wanna talk to you."

"No, no. I'm not! He... I... it's not what you think!"

The woman leapt at her and grabbed her by the arm, her claw-like fingernails digging into Sharon's flesh right through the damp fabric of her coat. She yanked her arm away, but the woman's grip was hard and she wouldn't let go.

Sharon raised her gaze to take in the woman's appearance, her skin-tight sleeveless dress and sky high platform heels. Ok, wow. Now that was a prostitute. The john in the car probably couldn't believe his luck, getting a fresh one. He'd pulled his car to the corner and sat there, waiting. For her to change her mind? Change professions? "I'm not working here. And he's waiting." She pointed over the woman's shoulder toward the john in the car. "If you want that one."

The hooker glanced over her shoulder. She looked older than Sharon by about ten years, but given what she knew about Kent's friend Marilyn, that meant nothing out here. Up close, she had on heavy makeup, set into creases, especially around her sad dark eyes.

Suddenly Sharon stopped feeling fear, relaxing into the woman's grip, her chest filling with softness. She was only trying to make a living. More vulnerable and at risk than Sharon would ever be. She wished Kent were with her now.

"What's your name?" she asked softly.

The woman squinted at her, sneering slightly. "What's yours?"

"Sharon. Do you live down here? In this area?"

"What's it to ya?" Finally she released Sharon's arm, flinging it away.

Sharon shrugged. "Sorry. Not prying. I just wondered if you knew my friend, Kent?"

The woman said nothing, scowling.

"I'm looking for him. That's why I'm here."

"Kent?" At Sharon's nod, she spat, "Nah. Never heard of him." With a last suspicious eyeball, she glanced over her shoulder.

In the minutes they'd spoken, another hooker had moved in on the john in the Mercedes. She leaned into the open car window, her tightly wrapped behind elevated above tall heels under the edge of a dark umbrella.

"Hey, get lost! That's my trick, you bitch." The first hooker took off like a giraffe on the run, all gangly hips and knees.

Sharon sighed and continued walking, even though she didn't know the name of the street she was on. What did it matter? She'd never find Kent like this.

A half block further, she stopped walking, her legs too heavy to go on. Her breath hitched, her throat, her chest, her stomach tightening with hopelessness. She wiped rainwater from her face, pushing back her ragged hair. What should she do? Where was Kent?

A group of several men and women suddenly poured noisily out of a doorway, weaving and chattering, a residue of music trailing them until the doorway slammed shut. They stumbled by her, shoving her to the side, closer to the dark facade of a building. They disappeared around a corner, their voices fading into the night.

A dark figure lurched out of the shadows, and she squealed and leapt ahead to get away, remembering how matter-of-factly Kent dealt with every irregularity, calmly explaining who everyone was.

That didn't mean there wasn't danger here, nor that everyone she met meant her no harm. She paused, blinking. This was going nowhere.

Her phone trilled, and she jumped in surprise.

Fishing it out of her purse, she realized it was a text. Lighting up her phone, she saw a short, cryptic message from Rachel.

What the hell did you start?! she read. *What?*

What was she doing texting at… after one in the morning?

Sharon bent to reply, thumb-typing her query, **What are you doing…** when another dark car, parked across the street, slid into motion with a swish of tires and move purposefully toward her. *Shit!* Not another stupid john on the hunt for some action.

She ducked into a narrow lane, hoping the car would pass by and leave her alone. She stepped a few yards into the lane where spectacular, multi-coloured graffiti scrawling indecipherable names and slogans in spiky script sprayed the brick side walls of the old buildings, glowing neon in the dark, reflecting streetlight. To escape the errant john, she continued past overflowing dumpsters and garbage bins, toward a skanky mattress and a pile of wet clothing smashed into the rough dirty pavement. Her nostrils filled with the rank odour of stale urine and rotting garbage roiling her stomach.

Hunched over her phone in the dark lane, trying to respond to Rachel and find out what she meant, and why she needed to text her in the middle of the night, she was unprepared for what happened next.

In a blur she couldn't disentangle, a car – – the same dark car? – – screeched into the lane, its engine revving, and sped up with a squeal of tires directly towards her. In the same moment, a black-clad figure dove at her from behind a dumpster, grabbing handfuls of her coat and yanking her so hard she stumbled, losing her footing on the tangle of wet rags underfoot.

The car clipped her, sending a shock wave of bone-jarring pain through her skeleton, knocking her flying. She landed partially on the discarded mattress, partly on the hard brick pavers, bouncing and scraping at the same time like a batter sliding home. Her balled up form spun and rolled and crashed into the brick side wall with a THUD, her breath gushing out of her in a rush, and everything went dark.

CHAPTER 28

He wasn't dead.

Either that, or he was dead, and Hell was Tent City for all eternity.

As the shock and adrenaline ebbed, a tsunami of throbbing pain flooded in to take its place, and he became aware most viscerally that he was still alive, though suddenly freezing and wet. Without warning, his body heaved, and he lifted his head just in time to vomit on the grass beside him. Doing so caused explosions of sharp pain to ignite in his head, shooting agony through every part of him. His left leg failed to respond to his command to lift his body, instead throbbing and shaking like a useless fish. His stomach convulsed again, and he lay his head back on the cold wet grass, letting the rain fall on his face, moments later opening his eyes a slit to get his bearings.

Sounds finally surfaced through his mental fog. The distant rapid *weeah-weeah-weeah* of an approaching police car rose on the night air, punctuated by fragmented noises of people scuffling, bodies crashing, grunts, thuds and shouts. His fuzzy brain worked to process the melée at the edge of his field of vision, like a slow motion underwater ballet.

Some shadowy figure grabbed RJ's orange arm, twisted it and tore some blunt object from his ringed grip. Kent saw the object swing through the air in a blur and smash into RJ's face with a meaty crunch. There came a thunderous roar and what sounded like cursing in a guttural language. A broad figure shot past. Bodies crashed into tents, which collapsed. Glass shattered. Arms flailing, a many-headed creature lumbered, tumbling to the ground in a heap, screaming. The scene went out of focus as pain continued to pulse in Kent's head, and waves of nausea overwhelmed him again and again.

When he opened his eyes a second time, RJ crouched in a mound of orange Gortex, his hands a screen over his face, black blood streaking the backs of his knuckles, the whites of his eyes flashing through the cracks. Agitated voices lifted in a frenzied debate from the cluster of people who had disentangled themselves from the mass.

One of the Russians stood up, shaking off his attackers like dolls, looking around.

People scattered.

"Who done that?"

"Not me. I ain't gotta blade!"

"Get outta here! Get lost."

More scuffling. A few bodies pulled away and scrambled off into the night. Kent recognized Marilyn and Wheeler, heads bent together, looking intent. Then they vanished into the darkness. A few outlines passed through his view as he faded in and out of consciousness.

The dull *hronk-hronk* of an emergency vehicle in the distance roused him.

After a time, the crowd thinned and disappeared, and he lay there, watching it all from a great distance. Heavier rain continued to fall, obscuring visibility. Kent saw only RJ's jacket, a bright blurry patch of orange stumbling around, and one of the Russian kids hunched over near the ground. A desperate wail came from his heaving shape at odds with his bulk – – a high pitched keening, gurgling noise. Then, "Stop Georgi! Georgi, nooo!"

RJ stood up, spit, stumbled closer, sputtering obscenities. He bent over, then threw his shoulders back and howled, his face smeared with blood. "Who done dis! I'm gonna kill you. I find you and kill you!" Then he spun and swung out a foot, kicking the other thug in the chest, shoving him back. He stumbled, stood up and stopped, shoulders shaking.

Kent got an unobstructed view then of an enormous form flat on the ground, head twisted to the side, his glassy dead eyes in line with Kent's angle of view. *I see you, fucker.* Thick black blood gushed from a slash on his neck like a geyser of tar. The other Russian thug bent again, pushing his hand against the flow.

The ringing in Kent's ears returned, and his vision narrowed, flashing black and bright spots floating in front of the scene. Dully, his rational brain questioned what he saw. Jesus, what happened here? How many people were involved in the brawl? Who had pulled a knife?

"Georgi! Who done this to my Georgi?" RJ stood up. He stepped closer to the other one and in a rage kicked his shin and slapped him hard across his face. "You stupid fucker, Aleks! Your brother was worth ten of you. What we gonna do now?" RJ stumbled back.

Everything faded to black.

He wasn't sure how long he was out. Some time later, maybe it was only a minute, two cops in dark anoraks showed up and milled around asking questions. Then paramedics appeared and took away Georgi's body. They took a few others that were still bickering and scuffling into custody. He couldn't see RJ anymore. The paramedics treated a few people for minor injuries on the spot. Then a flash of yellow vest hovered over him.

"Kent? Ashley! It's Kent."

He recognized Mark. "Jesus, man. What the hell are you doing in the middle of this mess?"

He coughed up some blood, spat and groaned. "I think I started it."

Ashley suddenly appeared beside Mark and the other paramedic. "Kent? That you? Did I hear right?"

He groaned his affirmative, slowly sitting up, head in hands.

Jenna stepped up beside her. "We'll need your statement." She turned to Mark. "You guys taking him to St. Paul's?"

Still confused, disoriented, feeling numb, he asked the paramedics, "Hey, did you hear about Harley? I never made it to the hospital. Is he okay?"

"Nope. No news. Busy night."

"Really guys. I can drive myself. My car's… over… there." A shiver shook his entire body and his stomach heaved again.

Mark nudged him towards the stretcher. "Uh, yeah. No. Have you seen yourself?"

He surrendered, too weak to choose, and they nodded and helped him up, strapped him to a stretcher board despite his protests he was fine. Before they carried him away, Jenna said, "We'll see you over there," shaking her head. "Don't go anywhere. I get the sense you'll be able to shed some light on this clusterfuck."

They took him to the emergency entrance of the hospital, poking and prodding him en route. Kent was still stunned, dizzy, his cumulative aches and pains overwhelming his focus now that the skirmish was over. He kept his eyes closed against the glare of light, stilling the spinning room.

He was an idiot to challenge RJ. It's a miracle he was still alive. It could have been him instead of Georgi laying dead on the grass with his neck slit open. But more than anything, more than reeling from his own stupidity, he was shocked that so many people came to his defence.

Sure, they may all have been sick of RJ moving into the neighbourhood and causing everyone grief. But they didn't have to do what they did. People put themselves at risk for him. And someone, God knew who, had killed Georgi. Probably they would never know. He was glad he'd blacked out and missed it. It would be the ultimate act of betrayal if he had to turn someone in.

At the hospital, Kent enquired about Harley, but they wouldn't tell him much, saying they didn't know yet. Ashley and Jenna spent twenty minutes asking for his version of events in the park, and he did his best to recall, at least those parts he was conscious for, and signed some forms.

Medical staff ushered him into a stretcher bay and did a battery of tests, including, after a long wait, a CAT scan. He attempted to get up and push them away, saying he had to see Harley first, but they insisted and he finally surrendered to their ministrations. His only relief was learning his brother was not on duty. That was one final aggravation he could not have born.

Hours passed, and he was frustrated, miserable and then exhausted, though they wouldn't let him sleep until they'd cleared him of concussion. Thoughts of Sharon drifted across his mind. The way he'd abandoned her at his parents' place in a moment of overwhelm, the tortured expression of disgust and hurt and pity on her face that he could no longer bear. All he'd known was that he had to get away, and as usual he acted first without thinking.

It was his grief at losing her that drove him to the Downtown Eastside to begin with, seeking solace or escape, or ultimately, catharsis.

What would she think now, to discover what mayhem he'd caused with his rash action and uncontrolled emotional outburst? No doubt she would be even more critical of him.

Some machine beeped beside him, and an attending nurse stepped up, pushed a few buttons and left again. His longing for Sharon persisted, his remembrance of her steady cool gaze, her challenging banter and her tender sympathy softening his determination to sever their connection, and drawing him into a dreamscape of more hopeful possibilities. He would like nothing more than to set his head in her lap and go to sleep.

Staff shook him awake when he nodded off, and then he'd chastise himself for sleeping at all when he still had heard nothing of Harley.

After a tedious amount of waiting, they cleared him to leave at two-thirty in the morning, having determined that he had no significant internal or head injuries. He limped away with only a few stitched lacerations and several bandages, but bruising all over.

"Get some sleep, will you?" the doctor said as Kent hobbled out.

"Sure, I will. As soon as I know that Harley will be okay."

He turned the corner and returned to the triage nurse at the desk in emergency. He knew the ropes and filled out the forms to access information. Finally he talked to the Paediatric doctor on duty and get a report. The news wasn't great.

"I can't let you see him yet, Kent. His vitals are weak."

Kent rubbed his face and raked his hands into his hair, encountering his bandage with a wince. He'd been here so long, he was parched with thirst, and he licked his lips and swallowed before he could speak. "I won't disturb him," he croaked.

"It's not that." The doctor hesitated, then squeezed Kent's arm in sympathy. "It's his youth. Because he's gone into crisis so many times, we're concerned about brain damage, and permanent damage to his heart. We need to do some tests once his vitals stabilize and he wakes up. Test his memory, his perception, coordination and such. We'll keep him here for observation this time to make sure."

And what if he wasn't okay this time? Had persistent abuse disabled him? What would happen to him then, in a system full of holes as big as moon craters that people routinely fell through? What future would he have? RJ would have won.

For the first time since he'd met young Harley, four years back when he was first assigned Harley's case, and hoped to place him in a stable family, Kent felt hopelessness descend on him like a heavy fall of snow. The kind of snow that buried everything in sight, muffling him, blurring the shape of his dreams. Just like the snow up north, so oppressive as to vanquish even a sense of your own will. For all his careful oversight and diligent guidance, maybe the unfortunate circumstances of Harley's birth pre-determined his destiny.

"Have they notified his aunt?"

The doctor shrugged. "I assume they called, if she's next of kin. But it is the middle of the night. Let's wait for morning."

Kent nodded slowly. He knew they'd given him drugs to dull his superficial pain, yet numbness permeated his chest, weighing down his heart under layers and years of defeat and frustrated hopes.

It was foolish to invest so heavily in one unlucky kid, when there were so many that needed his help. But the moment he'd met Harley, he'd been painfully reminded of Joseph in Fort Marian up north.

He and Joseph had forged a special bond in that tiny remote community, and he'd fallen in love with the child's resilient spirit and kind heart. Kent was convinced he could make a difference, that he mattered. And yet neither Joseph's spirit nor Kent's diligence and caring had spared him his dreadful fate.

"Go home and rest. We have your number if he wakes up, or we have news." The doctor squeezed his shoulder, turned and moved on to his next patient.

Kent stood motionless for a few moments in the corridor, watching the doctor walk away and disappear through a door.

Exhaustion so overwhelmed him, he could've slid down onto the floor and fallen asleep on the spot.

His father's waiting room probably had a soft place to lie down, to find a little privacy and to sleep. Instead, he meandered back to the main waiting area by the emergency doors where they knew his name. He ought to go home, yet he knew he couldn't leave. Not until he knew. He sank down into one of a dozen empty molded grey plastic chairs and dropped his bandaged head into his hands.

Instead of his usual determination and stubborn hope, despair swallowed him, as though he'd sunk to the bottom of the sea, cut off from the world, from everyone, all sound, colour and life muffled by the weight of water. The bright promise of Sharon was gone, leaving an aching loneliness in the centre of his chest. Harley dangled like a weak lifeline, a faint reminder of his purpose fading from view. If Harley slipped away, Kent would disappear.

CHAPTER 29

"**H**ey! Wake up!"

A high-speed train exploded inside Sharon's head, the rumble and roar sending a shock wave through her that reverberated outward and inward at once, kicking her heart with a bang that triggered a wild drum beat.

"Hey there, girl. Are you injured? Where does it hurt? Can you sit up?"

With a gasp Sharon sat upright, staring blankly, her gaze unfocussed, at a graffiti-covered brick wall across from where she sat. She tilted her head to the side, and her head seemed to float, as if it were full of sloshing water, or helium.

He came closer, squinting. "Sharon? Sharon! Oh, damn it. What are you doing here, sweetheart?" He turned away and rummaged.

It was pretty, with swirling curlicues in neon green, black, white and hot pink that came in and out of focus. She studied it, uncomprehending, trying to read that word, squinting. Did those twisted backwards-leaning pink words say TRIPLE? TOPPLE? PEOPLE? Was that a name? The artists were very talented, anyway.

She realized her seat was wet and cold. She lifted a hand and looked down at it, covered in dirt and embedded with fine grit, streaked with bloody scratches. It was shaking, as if she was standing on that train as it rattled over tracks. She blinked and blinked again.

The man in black turned back, wrestling a pair of wire-framed glasses onto his face. "You're so pale. Can you stand? Sharon, do you know where you are? Do you recognize me"

She lifted her gaze to take in the concerned face of the older man who spoke. In his dark overcoat, he seemed vaguely familiar. "What street is this?" Her voice shook too. Her breath was shallow and rapid, her mouth slack, dry. "I'm thirsty."

The man placed his arm around her shoulders and shifted her to the side. Pain jolted up her ribs, flashing hot.

"Ow!" She lifted her shaking hands, patted her mouth, her hair, her coat.

"We should call the police. Do you have a cell phone with you?"

Phone? "In my purse." She looked around in the dark, seeing nothing. Making sense of nothing. "Where's my purse? I just had it. Do you see it?" She leaned forward onto her hands and knees, her palms burning as if the wet pavement were on fire, and crawled, searching.

"Oh, hold on now. Take it slow. You're in shock." The man pulled her back, sat her down again. "I don't see it. Never mind the purse. I'll go flag them down. They're never far. Stay here." He patted her arm and lurched away, the tails of his dark coat flying like the cape of some mysterious superhero.

When he disappeared around the corner into the brighter street beyond, she tried to get up and swayed, her legs wobbly. She plopped down again onto the dirty old mattress. Where would she go? Although that bright street looked more inviting than this dark place. What was she doing here?

Her feet were bare. She looked down at herself, her fine skirt and blouse dirty and ripped. What happened to her shoes?

She thought about the old man, his shoulders hunched, but his bearing proud. Slight and squat, but fine-boned. A kind face, like a kindly professor. He was nice, trying to help her.

Silhouetted against the streetlights beyond the alley, the man limped back toward her. He seemed very familiar. "They're coming."

"I know you," she croaked.

"It's Carl. Kent's friend. We met at Carnegie. And at City Hall. You remember? Did you hit your head?" He bent down and reached for her head, rubbing his calloused fingers over her messy hair, gently searching for bumps and cuts.

"Carl! Where am I? What happened? There was a woman. There was a…"

A visceral shock jolted through Sharon, an image flashing in her mind of the quickly approaching dark car ballooning in her view, the panic flooding her veins, the blur of the man, the shock of impact, then – – She flinched, as if it were happening again.

"Oh! I remember. Did I pass out?" She looked around, saw the trash, the mattress, the dumpsters. She grabbed his shoulders. "Did the car hit you? Are you okay?"

"I'm fine. It didn't hit me, I hit it to get them to swerve. It's you I'm worried about. It knocked you pretty hard into the wall. I heard a crack."

"Who were those idiots? Didn't they see us? Were they speeding?"

She looks around at the narrow alley. It's so narrow here. What were they thinking? There's hardly room to drive…

Their gazes met, her eyes going wide at his stern expression.

"They were trying to hurt… to kill us?"

He shook his head. "Not us. No one cares about me." He studied her face. "It's just damned lucky I was here. I was walking around a bit, on my way home to bed. I saw you."

Details flooded back. The full meaning of Carl's words hit

her, her mind spinning with the implications. "Me? They deliberately hit me?"

Carl nodded slowly, his kind eyes holding her steady, scanning her face.

"I'm looking for… Kent. I couldn't find him."

The full picture came into focus. Would they try to hurt Kent, too? Heat flooded her head, her stinging eyes letting go, tears blurring her vision. Carl wrapped his arm around her. She let go then, the shock and fear overtaking her as she mewled, babbling about the terrible dinner, the fight, her secret, his rally. Everything was ruined. She had to find him to explain.

"One thing at a time, Sharon." He glanced up at the sound of approaching footsteps.

"Carl? Miss… Sharon, is it? Can you tell us what happened?"

The cops escorted her to their cruiser, wrapped her in a blanket and bundled her into the back seat. Carl seemed familiar with the two cops, and after a murmured conversation on the sidewalk, he climbed in after her.

To the thumping chorus of the windshield wipers, they asked for her name and address, and asked what she remembered, as if she could explain what just happened.

The blanket warmed her cold limbs, and she felt a wave of gratitude toward the old man. She wasn't sure if the cops hassled him for being out on the street, or were watching out for him. They seemed to treat him with respect. It was hard to see him as a street person, when he carried himself with such an air of benevolence and dignity. The urge to repay him swept over her in a flood of tears. "Carl saved me! He… he jumped out and…" she looked at Carl, confused.

He shrugged. "I banged on the hood, made a big noise, hoping they'd swerve away. They did."

She gripped his cold, damp hand in hers. "You saved my life, Carl. They would have hit me full on and left me to die!"

The police asked if either of them could identify the vehicle, or saw the plates by any chance.

"No. It was too dark," Sharon replied. "I thought it was another john."

Carl shrugged, his thin grey brows lifting. "Maybe it was, and I startled him."

"I don't... Thank you, Carl. For being there, for helping me afterwards."

"We look out for our own. Kent is one of us... and you're his girl."

She cast her gaze down, recalled her babbling confession when the shock had hit her system. "I don't think I am anymore. He's furious with me."

"He'll come around. The boy needs to learn patience."

She was sure the hit and run was not an accident, but she didn't want to get into her theories with Carl, or with the police. Unless he could shed some light on the event. "Do you think anyone would do that on purpose?"

He replied, "Only you know the answer to that, girlie. Trust your instincts." His tone implied that she knew. "Leave Kent. He'll show up. You stay out of trouble now. It's not safe for you around here alone."

She nodded, fear tightening her stomach. What Pandora's box had she opened? How many people were part of Seibold's crime syndicate? Were some of them living in this very under-world she was now a part of?

One cop cleared his throat, eager to get moving. They dropped Carl off at his hotel. He smiled, gave her hand a gentle squeeze and got out of the police cruiser, hunched into the rain as he shuffled off into the night.

"Now. Can you tell us what you were doing in the neighbour-hood before the car approached?"

The tone was accusatory. Sharon looked down at what remained of her expensive clothes. "Do I look like a... I don't know? A prostitute? A drug dealer? A criminal?"

The officer sucked his cheek between his teeth. "All right then. Who did you see? Did you talk to anyone?"

She told them about the encounter with the john and the hooker just before. "Maybe one of those girls will find my shoes and purse." She looked up and met his gaze with a wry smile. "They match."

The cop reached below his seat, grabbed something and handed over her purse, wet and bedraggled. She took it, frowning. She opened it, searching for her wallet, her phone and other personal things. Everything seemed to be there except her keys.

"Oh! I had my keys in my hand. Did you find them?"

"No. We'll have another look around."

The officer asked her if she had any reason to think someone would want to harm her. What could she say? Could she even trust the police? They seemed honest, professional and caring. But who could say they weren't part of a larger network of corruption. That wasn't unheard of. The Chief of Police would be a colleague of Seibold's. Who knew where their loyalty lay? It wasn't safe to tell them anything, not until she'd done her legal work, so she said no. She'd only been looking for her friend.

"Down here? At this hour of the night?"

She nodded and frowned. How many hours had passed since she left the Sawyers? "He works here sometimes. He knows people."

The cop gave her a look, lifting brows, with a side smile, as if to suggest he could be up to no good, and that made her suspicious by association.

"He's a social worker. With the Pathway Society?"

Their eyes widened, and they darted at each other in a loaded silence. "You mean Kent Sawyer."

She squinted at them, puzzled. "Yes, that's right. You know

him?"

"Oh, yeah. Everyone knows Kent."

They accepted her answer, dropped the subject and drove her to the hospital. On the way, the events swirled in her head. Even Carl seemed to know more than he was saying.

It had to be deliberate. Why else would – whoever it was – follow her into the lane? Definitely deliberate.

The police officers left her in the emergency entrance of the hospital, signed some forms and nodded to her on their way out. She hobbled to the reception desk, not sure she needed medical attention, despite a constellation of aches and pains. She was wet, dirty and tired. An attendant in green patterned scrubs approached her and asked her to follow him to a curtained bed. He handed her a form on a clipboard, handed her a thin flannel sheet and pulled the curtain closed around her, leaving her alone.

Sharon absent-mindedly filled in the blanks, pondering.

But how did anyone know she would be there, in the Downtown Eastside? Nobody knew she would be there. She'd only decided once she got into the taxi. How did they know it was Sharon and not some... another one of those hookers she was talking to?

It was terrifying to think someone, anyone, had those kinds of eyes on the street. On her! That they could track your movements if you were a person of interest. She wondered about the taxi driver who dropped her off. About Kent's father, with his avowed friendship with Seibold. Who could she trust?

This had to be a scare tactic to intimidate her, to back off her investigation and pressure on the City. A deadly one. This was a bigger and more worthy fight and she couldn't hold back. Kent was right. They had to use all the ammunition they had, and all the tools at their disposal – which meant they had to go public with the corruption, any way they could. Though it was late, and exhaustion overtook her, she was still determined to find Kent and make sure he had all the facts before another day dawned.

CHAPTER 30

S haron staggered out of the ambulatory area of the emergency ward between rows of curtained stretcher bays where inpatients awaited attention or assessment, back toward the triage intake desk. She was dead on her feet, so exhausted she could barely keep her eyes open another minute. Yet she couldn't rest until she found Kent, however unlikely that was at this point.

Perhaps in the time she'd been wandering the Downtown Eastside and getting hit by a car, interrogated by the police and examined at the hospital, he'd made his way home and was now asleep in his bed. She scoffed. *You think?*

She checked the time – almost three am. If only she knew where he lived.

There wasn't anyone she could ask at this hour. Unless...

She stepped up to the admission counter. "Excuse me." When the nurse attendant looked up, she asked, "Is there any chance Dr. Aaron Sawyer is working tonight, or on call?"

The nurse blinked at her. "I can't tell you that. I'm sorry. Why do you want to know?"

Sharon shook her head with a sigh. It was a long shot. "I'm a friend of his family." That was a stretch, after the fiasco of tonight's dinner. "I was hoping he could tell me where I might find his brother."

The flat look of detached boredom reminded Sharon how many hysterical and irrational people the staff encountered in a single night shift at this desk. The nurse's voice was deadpan when she clarified, "His brother."

"Kent Sawyer. He's often in here with various people from… the street." She rubbed her temples. She wasn't thinking. This was hopeless. She was out of ideas and out of options. "Never m — "

"Kent Sawyer?" The nurse frowned at Sharon, blinked, glanced over Sharon's shoulder, her face twisting in confusion. "The social worker. You lost him?"

Sharon tilted her head, her attention caught by the curious tone in her voice. "Yes! You know him? I'm trying to find him."

The nurse's eyebrows lifted to tuck behind her bangs. She inclined her head, pointing with her chin at Sharon, or… behind Sharon? Understanding dawning, she glanced behind her, suddenly wide awake, her jaw dropping.

She turned to face the wall of dark windows, scanning the rows of mostly empty grey plastic chairs. One solitary figure in a blue oxford shirt, just like the shirt Kent wore to dinner, sat with his back to her. Except the shirt was now wrinkled, wet and stained with dirt, grass and blood. Instead of a scruffy messy man-bun, a giant bandage swathed his head. Her pulse skittered, shooting sparks of fire and ice down her arms and legs, while her stomach dropped to her shoes.

Oh, my God.

"Kent?" She stepped closer.

Kent hunched over in the chair, his bandaged head resting in his hands, his elbows on his grass-stained dirty knees. She staggered forward, her heart thundering.

"Kent?"

His head jerked up, his face screwed up, blinking at the light. His eyes were red-rimmed, his face wet, and he scrubbed quickly at the tears on his cheeks with the heels of his hands. The confused blinking continued, as though he couldn't process what he saw.

She sank into the chair beside him, turning to face him. "I can't believe you're here. What happened?"

His intense gaze traced the outline of her face and hair, dropped to take in the disarray of her dress and coat. Attempts to right herself in the bathroom had accomplished very little. When his gaze reached her bare dirty feet, his eyes bulged.

His voice emerged cracked and hoarse, distressed. "Oh, God. Why are you here?" He lifted his hands to cup her face, continuing to study her. His thumb gently traced the scratches and scrapes, the bandaged cut on her forehead.

His eyes went wide with fright. Jerking back, he dropped his hands. "You weren't at the fucking park, were you?"

She frowned. What park? "I don't understand. Where did you go? What happened to you?"

His breath rushed out of him, and he slumped back in his chair with a groan. "There was a brawl in Tent City."

"Is that why you're all..." She gestured to his bandaged head, his scrapes and cuts, and his blood spattered jeans.

His gaze flickered to the left, his gaze wavering, as if replaying a movie in his head. A muscle ticked in his cheek when he ground his teeth.

"I went down there..." he shook his head. "Looking for Harley, or that's what I told myself. Just to wallow, check in with people, feel... I don't know." He shrugged.

"You got caught up in it?"

His voice was hoarse as though he had to drag the words out across gravel. "I got up in RJ's face. I wasn't thinking straight. I provoked him, and then he let me see Harley... passed out in a tent." He sighed heavily.

Not again! Sharon's chest squeezed in sympathy, and she reached out to set her hand on Kent's arm. "Is he all right?"

"He's here. In critical condition."

Her eyes heated and prickled at the thought, her chest tightening. "That's horrible!"

Kent nodded morosely. "The doctor's waiting for him to wake up. They want to test him for…" his mouth quivered, tightening to regain control, "… permanent damage."

She slid her hand down and took his, squeezing and stroking. "What about you?" She scanned him for injuries. Aside from an obvious head wound, he looked like someone had worked him over. "Were you attacked?"

His mouth curled in disgust. "I should have ridden in with Harley, but I was so fucking angry. I went back, looking for RJ, out of my mind. RJ sicked his thugs on me. I didn't have a chance." He exhaled, blowing air out slowly through pursed lips. "But… I'm lucky. I got knocked out, so I don't know what happened. But when I came to there was a huge brawl, all kinds of people fighting. And one of RJ's guys went down, his neck slashed open."

She gasped, her heart jumping. "He died!"

Kent nodded, his complexion darkening with the memory. "It could have been me. It should have been me. But those guys…" His head tilted to the side. "They came to my rescue. They saved my ass." His eyes filled with tears again, his mouth pulling into a grimace, and Sharon reached to stroke and massage the back of his neck. "I got a guy killed tonight. Not a nice guy. But even a young thug has some hope of redemption, I guess. And that brawl… that was definitely because of me."

She frowned. "RJ is evil. I'm sure there is plenty of resentment and anger toward him."

"Those folks, they're in survival mode. They don't pick fights. They don't stick their neck out unless they have to. I still can't quite believe what happened."

"I guess they felt they had to."

~

Kent tried so hard to contain his pain, but his chin wobbled, his lips curling with the effort. He hated that she watched him struggle as first one tear and then another traced down his cheeks and disappeared into his beard.

She reached for him, wrapping him in her arms, and he clung to her, burying his face in her shoulder, inhaling her sweet comforting scent. "I don't deserve it," he murmured.

He'd gladly put his life in danger again if it meant he could have this. Have Sharon close again, tender and sweet. But he couldn't rejoice in what he'd done.

After a long moment, he released a long breath and sat upright. "It feels so good to hold you. I thought I never would again." He wanted to say more, but daren't. Not now.

"It's you that left," she whispered. Her steady gaze probed his, her teeth gnawing on her bottom lip, as if she were afraid to tell him something, and his gut twisted with guilt.

I'm such an ass. He nodded, silently acknowledging what she was saying. He'd started this. "I'm not angry with you," he whispered, dipping his chin, looking up at her. "I was just… angry in my usual way. I'm sorry I left you at the house with my horrible family. That was shitty. I shouldn't have done that."

She swallowed, her eyes tearing up, as if she just remembered that part of their night. "It was shitty." Her voice was watery.

She looked down, her hand curling around his, and remorse overcame him. Her hands were scraped, the skin raw.

He lifted the back of her hand to his lips, pressing them against it, holding it a moment, like an embrace, asking forgiveness. What he wanted was to take her in his arms and hold her tight, breathe her in, reassure her with kisses.

"Tell me what happened to you tonight. Where are your

shoes? You're a mess, and..." he reached up and lightly touched the bandage on her forehead. He could see antiseptic and the edges of butterfly stitches peeking out. His gut clenched in guilt and terror. He prayed this had nothing to do with him, but instinct told him that wasn't true, and he would not like what she said. "You're hurt, too."

"A car hit me." She shrugged, as if to say, what can you do? Life sucks.

She might as well have doused him in ice water. He jerked back, blinking, his jaw dropping. "What?!" Did he hear right? "What happened? Tell me." He'd been thinking only of himself, and meanwhile he could have lost her!

She nodded, closing her eyes. "I was trying to find you, maybe at the Balmoral. After I left your parent's house."

Each new piece of information landed like he was in an elevator in freefall, jerking down, down, down. He couldn't ask where. He just had to wait for her to finish, cringing as she revealed each detail. He did this. He was responsible for this, too.

"I didn't get very far. It's so easy to get lost. I didn't know where to look. And this car just..." she halted abruptly.

What the hell? Was she on the road? Crossing a road?

She briefly recounted the story about the John and the prostitute, and her momentary confusion about the second car. Then how it followed her into the lane and sped up. How Carl, of all people, had shot out of the shadows from behind a dumpster and saved her.

He couldn't believe his ears. A cold heaviness settled over him, his chest hard and tight. He couldn't make sense of it. "Why? I don't understand why? It sounds like it wasn't an accident. As if the driver was trying to hit you."

"I think that was his intention. I believe I might have died if it weren't for Carl. Or been seriously injured." She reached up to touch her forehead. "I got off lightly."

"Who would want to hurt you? Who even knew you would be there?"

"That is what I've been asking myself. I have a good idea who, and why, but not how. I decided in the taxi after I left your parents' house. Nobody knew. Unless maybe they followed me?"

He still couldn't process the disparate elements of her story.

"You say you know who?" He leaned closer, suddenly conscious of others overhearing their conversation. It felt very cloak and dagger, as if the walls could hear them, danger lurking in the shadows. He glanced around to see if anyone nearby looked suspicious, eavesdropping or looking at them. He shook his head to clear the paranoid thoughts. But what else could he think?

Turning back to Sharon, their gazes met, and hers widened in concern, as if this thought just occurred to her. "Can we go somewhere private to talk?"

"I'm waiting to hear about Harley. But we can go... somewhere." He led her to the far end of the Emergency waiting room, away from the triage desks where the nurses wouldn't overhear. Tugging her down to sit in a chair beside him, he kept her hand in his, nestling it gently. Whispering, he asked, "Who would try to run you down? I'm not getting this."

After a beat she said, "I haven't told you everything I've been doing. It's... I feel terrible that I didn't trust you with the information. I worried you'd get so upset, you'd do something rash."

He scowled, his demeanour relaxing in defeat. He deserved that. "I guess you were right."

She shook her head. "No. I should have told you from the beginning what I found out. And I will. I'll tell you everything. But the bottom line is, it's Seibold. I think he's the one trying to get rid of me, or at least intimidate me, so I shut up."

"The developer? S and S?"

"Mm. I don't know, but probably they're involved. But no, I mean the old man. Councillor Seibold. I discovered things he would not want anyone to know – – in my Dad's files." She raised her eyes to meet his meaningfully, and his heart thumped in his chest like a fist, his mind whirling as pieces fell into place.

He'd known something was off at City Hall. People dismissed his rants, but he knew it. "This is all too much. I'm overwhelmed with trying to make sense of it. Slow down and tell me facts."

She did, starting with her bluff to Seibold, her suspicion, and how she kept it secret, which was so hard to keep from him, from Christine, from everyone, that she'd made a deal to trade their building for another site. A deal that had no chance of going through. She'd known that. It had been part of her strategy to allow him to intimidate her – – or appear to. "I tried to tell you."

How angry he'd been! He'd lost faith in her ability and her commitment. He'd underestimated her cleverness. And he'd been so rude, so cold and angry towards her these past days. And she took it standing up, never once giving her secrets away. He cupped her cheek in his palm, shaking his head, his chest tight with remorse.

"Oh, Princess." His voice choked with guilt. "Now you've had to deal with this, and I wasn't there for you."

He tried to be honest with himself. Would he have gone along with her silent behind-the-scenes work to gather evidence? Or would he, as she feared, have gone off half-cocked and raised a storm of protest. Which he'd done, anyway.

"I may have messed up your plans," he said, grimacing, lifting a hand to grip the back of his neck. "We haven't much time before all hell breaks loose."

She nodded. "I figured. I want to know everything you've done."

His breath rushed out in a long sigh. "I'm such an idiot. I was upset, feeling betrayed, lonely..." he let his gaze take her in, her silvery blonde hair hanging limp on either side of her face, her wounds and the filth and rips on her clothing. Her bare feet. This was his girl, who never had a hair out of place. He'd let her down. "I thought I'd lost you."

She shook her head minutely, her blue eyes intent on his, moist with tears. She pressed her face to his suddenly, her luscious lips gently touching his bruised and cut ones, cool and dry, and his heart burst with sheer relief. Unbelievably, he was getting another shot at this.

Kent dropped his forehead to hers, feeling like he'd found a haven for the first time all week, the feeling of warmth filling him up on the inside, chasing away the cold. His ice princess. How wrong he'd been. "I missed you so much."

She turned her face and tucked it against his cheek. "I'm sorry I shut you out. I missed you too. So much. I thought you'd never speak to me again."

He wrapped his arms around her, pulling her closer. Her hands came to slide against his chest, but she drew air between her teeth, tensed and pulled away.

"Poor baby. I'm so sorry." He pressed her hands together and wrapped them softly in his own, kissing her knuckles. "I should have trusted you. I should have been there to protect you. You'd never have been there alone if I weren't such an ass."

"It's not your fault Seibold sent someone after me. That's on me. I'm the one who's a threat to him. Maybe they would have got to me no matter where I was."

If they were following her, then that might be true. But if he and Sharon weren't fighting, he'd have been with her. He sighed, wrapping her in his arms, holding tight, rocking her gently. If anything worse had happened to her, he'd never forgive himself.

She did this for him. She put herself at risk for his project. Meanwhile, he was being selfish and short-sighted as usual. He'd abandoned her, mistrusted her, and dismissed her without a second thought. He always judged others harshly, always ready to assume the worst. What a rude wake up call. An education in humility. While he raced around trying to save the world, he'd abandoned his responsibility for the ones closest to him he loved best.

Touching her chin, tilting her face towards his, he leaned in, their lips just brushing when a throat clearing beside them had them jumping back.

A doctor in blue scrubs and a white coat stood two feet away, his hands in his pockets.

Kent shot out of his chair. "Doc! How is he?"

CHAPTER 31

The doctor nodded, his mouth firm. "He's out of the water. And he's awake. Why don't you come and see him now so everyone can get some sleep?"

Kent flung his arms around him, hooting at the good news.

Sharon stood up and Kent spun and grabbed her, lifting her off the floor. "Let's go up."

She yelped as her various injuries flared.

"Settle down," the doctor said, though he hid a smile as they walked together to the elevator. "We still have tests to run. It'll take a day or two to figure it all out."

Kent angled his head at the man, narrowing his eyes in question.

"It looks good, Kent. It looks like he will be all right." He cleared his throat. "You both look like you could stand to go home and rest. Get cleaned up. You've had quite a night, apparently."

They glanced at each other. In their emotional state, they'd hardly registered how filthy and bedraggled they both looked. Kent's lips twitched, and his dark caramel eyes twinkled with humour.

She sniffed. "You are a bit ripe, now that I stop to notice."

He guffawed. "And I've seen you looking better, Princess."

Moments later, they stood on either side of Harley's hospital bed. In this setting, he always looked most vulnerable, just a little boy who had no parents, no home.

"Kent," he croaked as Kent took his hand. They made it up to his room just in time to see his faint smile as he drifted back to sleep.

"We ought to go," Kent whispered. Faint grey light pressed through the blinds on the window. The sun would come up soon. It had been quite a night, and she was bone tired. She could see he couldn't tear himself away just yet.

"Let's sit for a few minutes. Watch him sleep," Sharon suggested.

His smile was grateful. They sat for a while, too tired to speak, content to be together again.

"My plan..." She huffed a small laugh. "My plan was to support you during dinner. I would be your rescuer. I thought together we could handle your father."

Kent scoffed.

"He's quite... uh, *well!* More than I expected," she said.

His mouth pulled into a sardonic line as he nodded his agreement. "We didn't end up as allies, did we?"

She lay her hand on top of his forearm, stroking down to the top of his veined hand, threading her fingers between his, relishing the fact his calm solidity had been restored. His presence was like a warm fire in the heart, strong and nurturing. He withdrew his fingers and scooped her hand gently into his palm, bringing his other hand over it, holding her in a soft embrace that sent a shudder through her body, suddenly remembering his physical strength, but also his gentle attentions.

"Was he always so hard on you? Growing up?" she asked.

"He was strict and demanding, but supportive. Until he found out I had no intention of following in his footsteps. He was always about making Aaron and I into two little clones of himself. Aaron was good enough to oblige." He shook his head, his jaw jutting, and she imagined him as a stubborn, willful teenager, pushing against the rigid expectations placed on him. Her heart swelled with love for him.

She had been the opposite, wanting nothing but to be as similar to her wonderful father as possible, even if it went against her more introverted nature. Until she was thirteen, anyway.

Kent continued, pensive. "By the time I was fourteen or fifteen, I'd seen enough of his life, and was critical enough of him, that it's the last thing I would do."

"So you followed your Mom instead."

"You don't grow up in a house full of medical practitioners without acquiring an interest in it. And I didn't set out to do what Mom does, exactly. I just always wanted to be out in the community. But that's where I ended up… until…"

She twisted toward him, angling her legs so her knee pressed up against his lean thigh, craving more contact. She remembered the things his father had said during dinner. "Explain that. What happened up north?"

"When I finished school, I was very idealistic."

"Might I point out that you still are?" She smiled, gently she hoped, teasingly. Affectionately.

His mouth quirked. He blinked, dropping his gaze to her mouth, his tongue tracing the arc of his bottom teeth. "I sought the most remote, challenging community I could find to work in, hoping to help… and maybe to make a point to the old man."

"And?"

"And I did. For a while. I thought I did." His shoulders twitched and slumped. Sharon rubbed the centre of his back in small circles, saying nothing. "That was before the diamond industry, when there was nothing but poverty and boredom and trouble up there. It's better now, in some parts." He rubbed a hand across his bearded chin. "But then, I was trying to create a place for the community to come together. Not just for their physical well-being, but emotional, spiritual. It wasn't my mandate, exactly, or my business, but I cared. I thought, if the community centre was a place where the kids and elders could connect..."

Sharon sensed that, despite his disappointments, he still felt passionately about this work. She kept up with the back rub, encouraging.

"It was helping. But I think I maybe got a little cocky. Supposing I could fix all their problems." He rolled his eyes, acknowledging his youthful arrogance. "Joseph..."

She waited. That was the name of the boy who had died.

Kent's breathing slowed, then hitched. Shadows darkened his warm caramel gaze as he spoke, warily. "He was a great kid. He trusted me, and we were great buddies. But I couldn't save him."

"He got into drugs?"

"No. That's the thing. He was fine. A great kid. Smart. Good-natured. It was his..." Kent struggled to speak, his mouth quivering, and he pressed his lips together. Sharon listened to his laboured breaths, her own throat thickening in sympathy. After a moment he continued. "He had a brother, a much older half-brother. Like, nine or ten years older I think. He was messed up."

Sharon bent her head, listening, her gaze caressing his tense face. His grief and guilt ate him up, and her chest tightened with pain. She lifted her free hand to press the base of her neck, tasting salty tears at the back of her throat, suppressing the urge to cry.

"The cheques used to come to the grandmother. She managed the household, doled out allowances. The parents had died years back, in a car accident. The older grandson was the addict, and there was no one to help him. No mental health practitioners who could have reached out."

"So... he'd used up whatever drugs he'd got in Yellowknife

and was in withdrawal. He demanded money from the grand-mother. She refused. He got increasingly angry, threw stuff, broke stuff, and I think probably hit her. Harley…" He stopped speaking suddenly, his eyes squeezing tightly closed. He cleared his throat. "I mean Joseph." He swallowed. "Joseph tried to inter-vene, to help his grandmother. Then the older brother locked the trailer door, so nobody…" His voice cracked. "There was no way in. I banged. I shouted. I couldn't help. After the brother left we found Joseph. He must have been knocked into the table or something."

The image of him, locked out, unable to do anything to help, listening to sounds of violence, crushed her. She sat with him, matching her breathing to his, tuned in to his emotions.

Kent sat for several minutes, reliving his nightmare, his breathing laboured. Sharon waited, trying to imagine his frustra-tion and futile rage, the weight of it pressing down on her.

"No police?"

"RCMP up there. I called them, but no. They had a large area to patrol and were far away."

"So how did Joseph die? This doesn't add up."

"A massive head injury on an eleven-year-old – " He shook his head. "There was no local doctor, which is normal for that remote region. A locum drove in once a month to see patients. And the Medi-Vac couldn't get near us that night, because of winter weather. I would have done anything, but there was nothing I could do but hold him while he… faded away."

Sharon wrapped her arms around him again.

He continued. "The closest doctor or emergency ward was in Yellowknife, about an hour and a half drive on a terrible road in decent weather. So, I was it. I had more medical knowledge than anyone else in the village and I did a lot of things that year. Deliver babies. Stitch up wounds. Even counsel. When I needed help, I called it in and the doctor diagnosed, walked me through it the best he could. But still I was in over my head. Even if I had the training, and the confidence, I didn't have the tools or the drugs I needed."

She leaned her forehead onto his shoulder, whispering, "Nothing about that horrible situation was your fault, Kent. At least you were there. You were doing everything you could to help them."

She lifted her head, peering into his pain-filled eyes, so dark with shadows they were almost black. "Why does your father make it sound like it was your fault? What does he think you could have done?"

"In his mind, if I'd been a doctor, I could have saved Joseph. But it's not true. He needed cranial surgery. And if I were a doctor, I would have been the locum several villages away, not the community nurse with his hands tied."

"So…" Understanding failed her. How could his father criticize him for any part of that? "It wasn't your fault. It wasn't even your responsibility. You know that, right? Kent?"

Kent sucked the inside of his cheek and nodded slowly. "Not my fault, maybe. But I felt it was my responsibility. I knew the older brother was using and didn't…" he shrugged, as if he knew there was little he could have done. "I couldn't stand it. I left. And quit nursing."

"Nobody could predict that constellation of events. The family, the weather, the fact there was no-one to help you." She reached to take his face between her palms and turned him to face her straight on. "You are the most caring, selfless, responsible person I have ever met. You can't control every person and event, even in your little circle. Kent, you can't keep everyone alive and well. You'll drive yourself mad."

"Not even that young guy tonight? That brawl wouldn't have happened at all if not for me. Now he's dead too. And Harley – " He cringed and dropped his head.

"You just can't. So much is beyond your control – and the work you do is the most valuable contribution you can make.

You have nothing to feel guilty for. So many people say they care but do nothing. You live your entire life on the line for the people society has discarded and forgotten."

He deflated, the breath rushing out of him in a whoosh. "I know you're right, Princess. I get pretty caught up in the details, though."

"I understand why Harley and this community, and the Pathway Society's work, and our project, are so important to you. I get it. But you have to have some boundaries or you're no use to them at all."

He lifted his soft brown eyes, his brows kinked, seeking reassurance, melting her heart. Setting his jaw, he gave a slow nod, gazing at the floor.

"You are doing outstanding work. Important, noble work, and you should never, ever listen to your nasty narcissistic father. You have nothing to prove to him. You're a hero in my eyes. You're ten times the man he is and you have nothing to be ashamed of." She tried to lift his face. "Look at me. Look at me, Kent." He did, meeting her gaze. He needed to hear what she was saying. He needed validation so much after all he'd been through. "I admire you so much. Your courage. Your passion and commitment. Your big, stupid bleeding heart." She inclined her head. "I think I love you."

A question flitted across his expression, a shadow of doubt and insecurity.

"Yes, I love you. I realized it tonight, at dinner, when I saw what you dealt with, and how steadfast you are in your principles." She smiled faintly. "I wanted to jump up and shout it out, to you, to your family. And I sat there, tormented by your disdain, praying we'd get another chance."

The tight lines of tension inscribed in his face loosened, lightened, and his expression filled with hope. "You amaze me, Princess."

"I don't know if I've ever known a man I respected more, and that's saying a lot. My father was a lot to measure up to, an icon, but he pales compared to you."

"I think I'm bad for your career." His mouth quirked.

She gave a soft laugh. "I don't care."

"Kiss me, Princess."

They both angled their heads instinctively fitting together, their eyes falling shut as their mouths came together in a kiss that filled her up. Her body clung to his, ecstatic that she'd found her home again, her nerve endings reaching out to connect with him.

He slipped his hands into her hair, holding her head, tilting it just right so he could get closer, sweeping inside with his tongue. Her mouth flooded with tingling sensations that raced through her body, pooling between her legs, pulsing with need. She had to stop herself from wrapping her leg around his and crawling into his lap.

She whimpered and returned the passion that rose in him, her tongue meeting and tangling with his, losing herself in his touch, memories of their time together flashing in her mind and sending jolts of desire flaring through her. All his passion and energy directed to her, into her. She wanted that again. A low groan emitted from his throat, and he took her hand and pressed it to the swelling heat of his groin, letting her know he wanted her too.

"Princess?"

"Mmm?"

He leaned back so he could look into her eyes. He gently stroked the side of her face with his fingertips, tucking her hair behind her ear. "You know I love you, too."

She blinked slowly several times. No one had ever said that to her before. Not since she was a little girl. But this was different. She realized how much she craved it, needed it. The knowledge that Kent loved her filling her with such overwhelming joy she shuddered with it. It soothed all the raw and ragged edges and broken bits inside her.

When he dragged a fingertip to her swollen, well-kissed mouth, she pouted in thought before smiling her pleasure. She made her voice low and seductive. "Do you love me enough to put me up for the night? I lost the keys to my condo in the alley. I think I'm homeless tonight."

He smirked. "You're not disgusted by the idea of squatting at my slummy apartment?"

She shook her head, her small smile stretching wider at the thought. "Not in the least."

CHAPTER 32

Back at his apartment after a short taxi ride, Kent poured them each a warming shot of whiskey while he watched Sharon meander thoughtfully around his living room in her bare feet.

"So... you live on trendy boho South Main," she teased. "I knew you wouldn't live in a dump. You were coy enough the first time I asked. Defensive. After I saw your parents' house, I thought... he can be as rebellious as he likes, but you can't erase the spoiled rich kid – "

"Excuse me!" He chuckled, feeling his face warm as he saw his home through her eyes. It was sparse and modern, but he knew he had expensive taste. The building was new, his apartment on the ninth floor, with a pleasant view over the highrises and construction cranes of the downtown core and North Shore mountains. Although they hadn't yet slept, glittering orange sunlight shot obliquely into his floor-to-ceiling windows as the sun asserted its presence on the new day, sending strongly contrasting highlights and shadows angling across his leather and chrome furniture.

It wasn't fancy, but when he'd exhausted himself on the grimy pavement and in the cramped squalor of the Downtown East-side, and filled himself up with sadness, desperation and hopelessness, he needed respite. "I'm not, despite appearances, a complete martyr," he replied wryly. His possessions weren't showy, but they were sturdy, comfortable and stylish. It's true he bought good quality things when he bothered at all. But his tastes were simple.

"Has your father been here?"

"No, actually, he hasn't."

"He might not feel so sorry for you if he saw how you live."

"You think he feels sorry for me?" She made a good point. He hadn't completely given up on the pleasures life offered. He let his gaze dance over her sweet, rumpled curves, her angelic face. Not at all.

The gentle tinkle of her teasing laughter stirred him, hardened him, but he was patient, just happy to have her back where he wanted her now, on his turf, warm and willing. He wasn't in a hurry. They had a lifetime now to explore and enjoy this chemical attraction that had thrown them together like a mad experiment, with all its inherent magnetism, vibrations and explosions, like something destined and essential and life-changing. And maybe it was. What did he know of the workings of the universe? It was accurate enough that in order for something to be created, something else had to be destroyed. And Sharon coming into his life disrupted old patterns, breaking down the prison he'd built for himself.

"What do you do when you're not working?"

He lifted one shoulder with a jerk, recoiling from the sharp reminder of his new bruises and pulled muscles. "See friends. Work out. Listen to music. Read. Normal stuff." Not all that much lately, he realized.

"Oh. You have friends?" She said over her shoulder. He caught her teasing glance and replied with a smile. She turned her attention back to the sunrise, and her prowl around his space.

Along with the morning sun, it dawned on him that his dogged commitment to his job, the Downtown Eastside and its residents had become an unhealthy obsession. It galled him to admit his father might have been right. A little bit right, anyway, even if his complaint came from his egotistical nature. Mom would say it was only because he cared that Kent be well and happy and live up to his potential. But to Kent it was more about how his life reflected on the successful, powerful man's legacy. He'd always felt like a line item on his father's resumé.

Eldest son, the brilliant young surgeon, Dr. Aaron Sawyer.

And below the fold, somewhat shameful second son, the troubled, bleeding heart weakling, failed nurse and obscure social worker, Kent Sawyer.

His very existence tarnished Dad's record.

Which was not why he'd chosen this path – – although he couldn't honestly say it didn't give him some pleasure when his life choices irritated the old man, or that he didn't relish proving him wrong.

The residents and transients of skid row needed and deserved a champion, and he was happy to fulfill that role. But Sharon was right, too. He was not responsible for everyone's safety and well-being. How arrogant would that make him?

Despite his shortcomings and even his mistakes, he might be worthy of love too. And he might have to risk loving someone else to find it. Even a shy, fearful girl who was running from her own past.

He stepped up close to her, towering over her compact frame, her pale blond head bent to receive and take a small sip from the glass of whisky he passed to her. She was a foot shorter than he was, he guessed, without her shiny little boots or pointy heeled shoes. Not that he was some kind of macho alpha male, but he liked it. Her stature came from her poise, her style, and intimidating no-nonsense manner. But this way, stripped of her armour, she was soft, sexy and cuddly. Feminine.

He took a leisurely sip of his whiskey, savouring the heat on his lips, his tongue, burning a path through his throat, pooling in his belly, spreading its warmth through his battered body. Tension released its relentless grip on him, and he felt it slip away like the last of the night shadows.

Even though he had been no kind of victor last night, there was something strangely satisfying about the fact that he'd behaved like a primitive male, behaviour he rarely, if ever, indulged in, priding himself on his, if not self-control, at least his intellect, responsibility and civility. She'd unwittingly, and unintentionally, brought out a side of him she thought she despised. He wondered if that was true.

Quiet laughter bubbled up from deep in his belly.

Her gaze flicked up to his. "What's so amusing?" she murmured.

"When we first met, you disliked my… rough edges." He lifted a hand and stroked the side of her head. "You, with your tidy pale hair, and your buttoned up designer clothes and pointy heels, were afraid of my anger, my passion and my bluntness."

She dropped her gaze, blushing, and her head tilted back and forth, conceding his point.

He smirked, angling his head to the side to peer into her eyes, remembering their shared passion. She seemed to like it very much when he took control. "But you like it, don't you?"

Here, in private, he could be the powerful one. Though they'd been together just one time, it had been a shocking revelation to him. The promise of their first touch, their first glance, realized in a storm of mutual desire. That her mere proximity could drive him into a passionate, primal frenzy until he hardly knew himself. That she went soft and quivering, submitting to him, melting into his hardness, only excited him more.

He tilted her pointed chin up so he could look at her fine smooth face, her unfocussed baby blue eyes, and zero in on her full, soft pink mouth. Her nostrils flared when he locked his gaze on hers, reading his mind, sharing his hungry thoughts. Heat shot through him like a torch, desire gathering in his groin, his gut tensing. A different tension. A kind he'd not indulged in lately, and welcomed.

He bent to cover her lips with his own, hungrily. He tasted the fire of the whiskey on her tongue, but also the heat inside her, melting, inhaling the womanly scent of her, knowing she was his now.

He'd always been driven to sacrifice himself and his own needs to help others, and he didn't want to change. That's who he was. But for the first time, he felt the desire to serve one person more than any other. And not out of a misplaced sense of guilt. This service would bring him immeasurable joy and contentment, fulfilling him as a man. From the well of his devotion, he would draw even more strength with which to care for the world.

As long as he had her.

She filled him up.

And he would fill her.

He angled her head, deepening the kiss, plundering her soft mouth with his tongue as his wanting built.

Together they would be stronger and could do more than either of them alone.

He wasn't responsible for every terrible thing that happened to the people in his sphere. But he was responsible for the choices he made, the good he did, the service and support he provided. And he was responsible for giving this woman pleasure, protecting her with his body, and loving her with all his heart.

That heart was a fist now, thumping on the wall of his chest, *ba-dum, ba-dum*, rising to the expectation, the anticipation of what would come. But despite his desire, fatigue pulled at his aching limbs. He knew they were both exhausted, tender, stiff, redolent of street and park and hospital. Not scents he wanted to encode this night.

"I know what we need." To the question in her lifted gaze he replied, "Come with me."

Taking her fingers in his hand, he guided her to his bathroom, where he set down his glass and started running a bath in his large soaker tub. He walked past her, his half smile small and mischievous, to dim the lights low. He strode out to the kitchen, returning quickly with supplies. Two lit pillar candles, which he positioned on the vanity, and a tiny bottle of blended essential oils he had for cuts and bruises. He added handfuls of Epsom salts and several drops of the oils into the filling tub, swirling it with his hand, releasing the slightly astringent plant aromas into the steamy air.

"We can't get our stitches wet, but this will help all the minor scrapes and bruises."

She stepped closer. "It smells divine. What is it?"

"Lavender, cypress, frankincense, and… something else."

She stood inhaling the healing, soothing scent, blinking. "I'm going to like dating a former nurse."

He grinned and faced her, took her drink and set it down next to his. His healing knowledge came in handy, but he picked this combination of remedies up from the people he'd cared for, up north, and elsewhere along the way. His voice was a quiet growl when he replied, "I think we're doing more than dating, Princess."

The soft sound of her indrawn breath stirred him again, drying his mouth, and tightening his stomach. He bent to kiss her gently at the corner of her sweet mouth, then trailed kisses along her cheek and jaw, behind her ear, down her neck. As she set her hands on his chest, he reached around her, found the tiny pull on the zipper of her fitted skirt, and slowly peeled it from her hips, dragging it down. Then he crossed his wrists with hers and undid the row of tiny pearl buttons down the front of her blouse, one of which had gone missing overnight, slipping that from her shoulders. He pressed feather light kisses along her porcelain skin in the wake of the retreating silk.

A fist of desire formed at the base of his spine, his want for her suddenly so complete and fierce. His hands shook, and he clenched his jaw.

"You are so beautiful," he groaned.

Her head tilted to the side, her expression skeptical. "I recall you saying I'd looked better."

"You have never looked better to me than you do at this moment." He stroked her jaw with his fingertips, gently setting strands of her mussed hair behind her ear. "I adore you."

Her translucent skin couldn't hide the blush that rose delicately on her breasts, neck and cheeks, even in the dim light. She was exquisite.

To lighten the mood he said, "Even more without the dirty, ripped clothing." He raised a critical eyebrow at the pile of clothing on the floor. He would lovingly tend to her scrapes and scratches later. "Come."

Holding her hand, he steadied her as she carefully lowered herself into the swirling warm water. She winced and sucked air through her closed teeth as the water came into contact with her wounds. Then he quickly rid himself of his soiled clothing and prepared himself for a similar shock as he followed her in to soak and stroke away the stink of their ordeal.

The effect of the water, the aroma, the salts, was immediately relaxing. Not to mention the exquisite softness of the curvy woman beside him. He slid behind her, lifting her over him, wrapping his arms gently around her ribs and sinking down until they were both covered in the healing bath, their legs entwined. Scented steam rose from the surface. They remembered nothing of the pain now, and they both sighed and moaned in relief, laughing. He raked his fingers through her hair, and skimmed his own at the edges of his bandage, keeping the water from his crown and her forehead where they both had sutures. His insistent desire ebbed under the effect of the soothing soak, and they lay together, tangled but loose-limbed, letting the residue and damage from their terrible night subside.

"Kent."

He jerked awake with a small splash. "Hunnh? Sorry! Sorry."

Her soft chuckle tickled the side of his neck. "The water's starting to cool. I think we should get out."

He'd dozed off. "How long have we been in here?"

Her shoulder twitched. "Maybe half an hour?"

"I must have passed out instantly. M'sorry."

"I don't blame you. You had an exhausting night, and it's wonderful. What a lovely idea. Thank you."

"Mm." He took a deep breath and braced himself, hauling his exhausted body, water streaming from his arms and legs, his abs and his cock. He watched her gaze trace the lines of his body, following the path of the sluicing water from top to bottom. In response, his cock twitched to life and stood up. His micro nap seemed to have restored his power. "I'm waking up."

"I see that," she murmured, her attention fixed on his blooming erection. Her legs stretched out, then she pulled her knees up again, squirming and rocking from side to side, sliding a hand between her legs. "I think I am too."

He met her darkening gaze and swallowed, his desire roaring fully to life. Nothing, not the chaos and violence outside, not cuts and bruises, nor exhaustion, would prevent him from loving her this day. He reached down to pull her silken body from the water, leaning in to fuse their mouths, his hot tongue sliding over her wet face, her scented lips, her seeking mouth. The way she gave herself to him, all the rigidity going out of her as she moulded her curves to his body, filled him with wild primal energy, heat and power flooding his limbs. In his mind's eye, he ran naked and fierce through a forest, climbed mountains, fought beasts. He grabbed a large towel and wrapped her in it, bent to lift her, carrying her through the doorways to his bed, and lay her gently down, lowering himself over her.

"I need you."

She opened her thighs, welcoming him.

No words were necessary now. They looked into each other's eyes, silent and sober, nothing between them now as he slipped inside her heated centre, joining them together as one. Everything was right with the world again.

Warmth from the midday sun woke them sweaty and tangled in his sheets. After gently, carefully losing themselves in restrained union, they'd both fallen instantly asleep despite the rising sun.

Yesterday's injuries made themselves known anew.

"I need more nursing," Sharon mumbled, unable to move her stiff, aching limbs.

His head nodded slightly as he groaned. "My head's killing me. I'll get us some meds." Slowly he withdrew from her, allowing air to cool her hot skin. She tentatively stretched out in his bed, making a mental inventory of her injuries. The abraded surface of her palms was already drying and scabbing, less raw than last night. The tub soak had helped. She tentatively touched her forehead, still swollen and tender around her bandaged stitches. Lifting her arm sent pain shooting through her ribcage as sprains and bruises announced themselves. Her left hip and back throbbed with heat where she'd come into abrupt contact with the brick wall in the lane.

Fragments of images and sensations flashed through her mind as she relived the moment the dark car had assaulted her, the violence of impact, the blur of flying, bouncing, landing hard. She flinched at the visceral memory. Again she marvelled that the discarded old mattress had broken her fall. And that her head had not smashed like a melon against the wall. She was blessed.

Kent returned, shuffling carefully, lowered himself to the edge of the bed and held out pills and a glass of water. She shimmied up to take them, swallowing. He crawled over her, wrapping himself around her in the still warm bed, planting his face into his pillow, both of them waiting for the painkillers to kick in so they could move without agony.

"I can't believe you put yourself in so much danger just to chase me down." The pillow muffled his voice.

"I must really love you." She gave his arm a squeeze.

He lifted his face and kissed her, pressing his lips gently but firmly against hers, and staying for a sighing breath, as though soaking her in, a silent acknowledgment of his feelings.

When he pulled away, she said, "It's not like I knew someone would run me down, though, did I? How about you? You're always putting yourself at risk for your clients, and for your principles. Why is that okay? What if you got killed last night? How would your family feel? Or me? Do you think about that?" She paused for a breath, staring into his eyes. "That you need to take reasonable care of yourself for the people who love you to, so they won't lose you?"

He stared at her face for a long, thoughtful moment, his gaze tracing her features. "I never thought of myself as worthy of love. I feel like I've always had to prove myself, to earn it, and still was never enough to deserve it."

She pulled back to frown into his shadowed eyes, determined to help free him from his demons. "I see that young boy who was criticized and rejected. I see that young man who felt guilty and inadequate. But you know that's not true. You do, right?"

After a pause, he nodded slightly, his gaze wavering.

"Look at me, Kent. Look in my eyes. I'm telling you the truth. Other people's expectation and judgements don't have to be yours. You decide who you are, and what you want to do, and why. Don't compromise yourself to please others, or to avoid – "

Abruptly, she stopped talking, clarity dropping with a bang like a judge's gavel, reverberating into her consciousness.

"What?"

"I did it too," she said, her voice suddenly small instead of strong.

"Did what?"

She shook her head, swallowed. Drew a full breath.

"I… internalized the betrayal and the shame my father's tragedy made me feel. And… I reshaped myself as someone else to escape the shame. Someone who would be as different from him as possible. Someone who would be above reproach. Someone who could never be guilty of wrong-doing or shamed for it." Her face buckled, her eyes filling and spilling tears as the magnitude of her betrayal of her father's constant love hit home, crushing her heart.

Kent dragged a fingertip down her cheek, tracing the path of her tears, whispering, "But that wasn't your fault at all."

"Neither was what happened to you."

They lay in silence for several long moments, each alone with their thoughts, yet sharing their melancholy.

He cleared his throat. "I guess we're both just too damned good for our own good, huh?"

She laughed softly, lifting her eyes to meet his again. His golden whisky gaze was becoming her favourite sight. He reached up to wipe the tears from her cheek. Despite his teasing smile, his deep amber eyes, with their dark brown rings, carried a world of sadness. Her smile fell. "It's wrong. We have to stop."

His mouth pulled into a flat smile of agreement.

"Trying to be better than my father, or more powerful than the competition could never make me happy or undo the past," she continued. "Rather than competing, or worrying about judgement, I have to follow my heart. Be true to myself, and passionate about my beliefs and the people I care about so I can feel good about being me."

"You're right, Princess. That's all that matters, isn't it?"

She smiled. "And maybe it doesn't hurt if we each have one huge fan, who thinks we're awesome no matter what fool thing we do."

He pressed his lips together, containing the quiver that suddenly overtook them. She lifted her eyes to see that his had become suddenly wet. He blinked away his tears, and no more came. Instead, his eyes darkened with intense emotion that fanned the fire in her chest. It flared and crackled, filling her with power and energy, light and heat. She knew they would be all right now. They had found each other.

"I love you," she whispered. And she meant it. With Kent by her side, she would never be afraid again. She would never cower and hide her true self. She would stand tall and proud, courageous and honest, and do what she knew needed to be done.

Reality flooded back. She moaned. Today would be hard. She forced herself up to a seated position, wishing the painkillers to work faster.

"The last thing I want to think about right now is the case. But I have to file the lawsuit and get my team to submit the evidence we've collected to the police so they can apply to the courts for the search warrants. There's a lot to do." She glanced over her shoulder.

"Do you believe me now?" Kent said and elaborated. "That not all problems can be solved with back room deals and handshakes and paperwork?"

She nodded. "It's complicated. I don't think we can take down Seibold without the law behind us. The information I found in my father's records is crucial to depose him from his tainted throne. But…"

He waited, his eyes scanning her face.

"After last night, I concede that the law is not enough to take down this vile, corrupt man and his network. He's manipulated and intimidated people for so long, I can see him worming his way out of having to pay for all he's done." She lifted his hand. "I know what to do. My plans have to go ahead, but if we work together, we can squeeze him out from both ends."

"What have you orchestrated? How much time do I have?"

He inhaled and pulled his shoulders back with a grimace and sucked his teeth. "Can you do with two days? I'll call Sergé to hold off as long as possible. And put the word out that we're working on something complicated and need a bit of time to pull it together. It'll give us a chance to gather a larger force. But not long. I'm afraid I've poked the hornets' nest."

"I hope the search warrant comes through quickly." She swung her legs to the floor. "I'd better get to the office. But I need something clean to wear."

Kent stood and opened a dresser drawer, then another, pulling out items. "There's nothing here that won't swamp you, but try these. We'll get you home to change at least."

"I still don't have my keys."

"Hm. Let me call someone." While she showered and dressed, she heard him on the phone.

Not twenty minutes later, as they drank coffee at his table, a buzzer sounded. Kent used his phone to answer it with an enigmatic smile. A moment later a knock sounded at his door, and he rose to answer it. When he opened the door, it shocked her to recognize one of the women cops who'd helped with Harley in the past. They exchanged a few murmured words, and then she followed him in.

"Hello," Sharon said, smoothing her hands self-consciously down his oversized shirt. She hadn't seen this cop or her partner last night, but Kent seemed to know them well. "Everything all right?"

He shrugged. "You remember Ashley? From the beat?" Kent said.

"Hi, Sharon," Ashley said.

"I remember you." Sharon nodded and shook her hand lightly, avoiding pressure on her palm, sending a quizzical look to Kent. "Is this about last night?"

Ashley jiggled her head, glancing at Kent. "Except for this." She held up Sharon's key ring, and Sharon gasped in delight.

"You found them!" She reached out and took them.

"Constable Liu and Murray did. In the alley where you were run down."

"Oh, thank you so much. What a relief."

"My pleasure." She winked at Kent and took her leave.

Sharon thanked him with a hug and returned to her coffee. "*Now* we can get started."

CHAPTER 33

Tuesday was the final prep day. Nervous energy fizzed in Sharon's belly, but she knew her stuff, and she was confident everything would fall into place. Well, she knew the legal business, but the fact that there would be a public – very public – component to her scheme turned her to jelly. But she couldn't change it now, so she put it from her mind. Time was of the essence.

She strode into the large boardroom where all the boxes and piles of evidence files were being assembled for submission. She'd sent Tim over to her mother's house yesterday to retrieve the files there, all eleven boxes of them, neatly organized and labeled.

She'd called Mom this morning to explain, minimally, what was happening. For now, she kept the rally under wraps and let her mother draw her own conclusions about her plans for Dad's records. Tomorrow, if all went to schedule, she might consider suggesting Mom attend the rally. Maybe.

Her chest suffused with warmth at the thought of her father's redemption in the public eye. It would never make up for all that their family had suffered. It wouldn't bring her father back, nor mend the rift that broke both their hearts and kept them apart until it was too late, but it was something. Something that would be meaningful to her mother and to herself.

Meanwhile, Ella and Abby sorted the evidence they'd discretely gathered from City Hall, and NDA-secured depositions with City Hall staffers and others in the community who'd had dealings with Seibold and the Building and Land Departments over the past twenty years. They'd also stacked the correspondence, the forms and legal documents to be filed with the police shortly.

They lay piles of paper out in neat rows, fringes of coloured sticky tags everywhere Sharon needed to review or sign. Every detail had to be finalized and organized so they left nothing to chance.

Her heart pounded a fast steady beat, and all that she dreaded and hoped for swooped and swarmed in her empty stomach like an entire flock of starlings.

She'd chosen her team of interns and aids for their sound record of diligence and detail orientation because she knew there'd be a mountain of paper before they were through. She was attempting to prove two decades' worth of corruption. She'd also selected them based on loyalty and discretion. Meacham had nodded his approval without asking for details, but she wondered what he'd think when this all came down.

The element of surprise was a critical component of their plan.

The incident with the car had made her paranoid. Having her whereabouts and activity tracked like that gave every wall eyes and made everyone around her suspect. She still could hardly believe that Seibold maintained such a network of spies and hoodlums, nor that her own actions had warranted surveillance. He must have suspected something. Or he knew he had a lot to hide. It smelled a little like desperation to her, and she wondered whether Seibold had half expected the ghost of Peter Brecht to rise one day.

She knew with fair certainty that his fears were speculative. There was no way anyone outside of her team could imagine the scope and severity of the attack she had planned. She trusted them implicitly. The press, not so much. However, combined with Kent's public relations onslaught, Seibold would go down. He simply had to. If Sharon failed, she shuddered to think of the consequences.

Abby, Tim and Ella whirled in a frenzy of activity, shuttling paper back and forth. A convoy of dollies parked in the corridor awaited their mass exodus later today. Sharon bounced from one to the next to the next answering questions, checking every detail, and confirming the location of every document.

It comforted her know that Kent was out there, working out the details of his part of the plan. No matter what happened, they would have each other, to celebrate, to commiserate, to watch each other's back. She pulled out her phone to check for text messages.

Like her, he must be run off his feet. A simple throbbing heart emoji sat on her screen since the last time they'd taken a moment to talk. At least he was thinking of her too.

She texted back an answering heart and a question: *How's it going? Are you nervous?*

A moment later her phone rang. She stepped out into the corridor for a little privacy.

"Hi." At her breathy tone, her assistants stopped what they were doing and looked up, three inquisitive pairs of eyes blinking at her through the glass conference room wall. Shaking her head, she pulled a tight mind-your-own-business smile and jutted her chin at them, sending them instantly back to work, though she caught the edges of their smiles. She felt their nerve endings stretched towards her in their rubbernecking curiosity.

"Hey, Princess. What are you nervous about?"

"Who said *I* was?"

He laughed softly. "Don't worry. We have all the bases covered. It will go brilliantly."

"I wish I had your confidence. But I'm glad you have it, anyway."

"I have enough for both of us, mostly because I know how awesome you are."

"Mhm." She chuckled. His tone of voice suggested that she was awesome at something other than being a kick-ass lawyer. "You're not so bad yourself."

"Are we meeting up later?"

"Of course," she purred, shimmery waves of pleasure ribboned through her core as the picture bloomed in her mind. "Bring food to my place?"

"Will do." They signed off. They'd be spending most of tomorrow together when everything started moving, but would have scant opportunity to talk. And no one knew how their plans would unfold. Tonight she wanted only to lie in his arms and feel understood, safe and desired.

"Everything okay?" said Dariush, approaching from the direction of his office, eying the dollies in the corridor, and the mad dashing of her assistants in and out of the boardroom.

"Yes!" Heat climbed her cheeks, as though he could read her thoughts. Had he overheard something? Had she said anything unprofessional, or merely thought the thoughts?

"Need a hand with all this?" Dariush asked with a warm smile, his sharp dark gaze sweeping her undoubtedly pink face, gesturing at the boxes with an open hand. "I'm happy to help."

"Got it all under control. Thanks, though." She smiled, wondering if he could read from her body language how a few moments on the phone with Kent melted her panties and warmed her skin. Now she wondered if the kind of man that heated her blood and made her knees weak shocked him.

But those thoughts had to wait.

She blew a breath out through pursed lips to cool herself down. "You're welcome to come to City Hall tomorrow, if you want to rub shoulders with the rabble, though," she offered in consolation, as much as to distract them both.

Late tomorrow, or the next morning, when she had the assurances she needed from the judge that the search warrants and everything else was in order, she would give Kent the go-ahead.

Not that he could delay his end for long. He'd already met with his Sergé at the local news station and stirred him up. But today he was letting him in on the bigger picture, hoping that with fuller understanding he could push back his publication and broadcast deadlines. When he understood the implications, she was sure the story would make headlines.

After Sharon filed her documents with the police, they would submit their affidavit to the judge for search warrants for Seibold's files at City Hall and at his home. Once approved, based on a substantial likelihood of conviction, and in the public interest, the police could recommend that charges be laid. A shiver of excitement rattled through her.

The rally would have to be timed perfectly so that the public realized this domino series of events at just the right moment, and not a moment too soon. When they got wind of the police's plans for making the arrest, they could speed up the public relations efforts. Though she knew it was necessary, this part filled her with dread.

Kent's friends and their friends, all regulars and residents of the Downtown Eastside, were on notice, Carl running interference on the ground. Christine, the Pathway staff and Kent's other colleagues had been informed, and were busy rounding up support from their professional and social networks, to maximize the number of bodies that would be present to strengthen their cause. Sergé, and all of them, she supposed, had their various contact lists and social media channels to drum up more awareness.

Not only to maximize the impact of what they were doing, but to bear witness to the events. Though the very thought of this public rally terrified Sharon, she understood that the citizens, the residents, the community that cared had to be a part of the solution. Her stomach clenched at the magnitude and significance of what she was about to do. She really ought to tell Mom.

Many deals were made behind closed doors that benefited only those power brokers party to it. And consequently because of power politics, the effects of these deals could reverse in a nanosecond. She knew that this was precisely how Seibold had escaped the law or exposure for so many years. Surely there had been close calls, honourable folk who suspected or discovered his nefarious activities, and would have exposed him. But with so many tentacles reaching out through the municipal bureaucracy, and into the community, Seibold could always step in, and influence these people in his favour.

But his time had run out.

When everything was ready, and the dollies were piled high with carefully labeled boxes ready to go to the police, they prepared to leave.

Arthur Meacham stood with Dariush in the doorway of his office, his favourite perch to oversee the activity of the firm and touch base with associates. As her helpers bundled out with their loads, she fell back to speak with him.

"Arthur. A word?"

"Certainly, Sharon." He turned to Dariush. "Excuse us?"

"Of course." He stepped away.

"I'm sorry about all this," she said to Arthur. "I'm afraid this little *pro-bono* case has ballooned into something rather massive. I'm sure it's not what you were expecting. If all goes well, I'll be back to my regular schedule soon."

His knowing smile planted doubts in her mind.

"I knew you'd do whatever had to be done, Sharon. That's why I trusted you with this case. Only a barrister as strong, determined and principled, and dare I say motivated, as you would have known what to do with it, and been able to follow through."

She pulled back, studying him. The implication was clear.

"You knew?"

"I've been around a very long time, Sharon. I knew your father. I knew Seibold when he was a young man. Many people either knew or had suspicions. But he's a slippery son-of-a-bitch. And ruthless. People that might have been useful had a tendency to disappear."

Her eyes widened, and her heart punched her ribs, thinking of her near miss in the alley. If only he knew. "Not…"

"I wouldn't say so, not directly. My theory is that he compromised people, so they shut up out of self-preservation."

She gasped, an idea popping into her head. "Like Llewellyn?"

"Like Llewellyn. He's a good and smart man, a loyal civil servant all his life, and he was a good friend of your Dad's. He's no pawn of Seibold's, but he was castrated years ago. Nothing he could do without causing his own family harm, I expect."

She nodded. "Yes, I see how it's done. Seibold's made a fine art of it."

"Well done. Well done." Meacham extended his hand, and she took it, feeling its promise. He covered her hand with his and squeezed affectionately. "Best of luck tomorrow."

"Thank you." She blew a nervous breath through pursed lips. "We'll need it."

CHAPTER 34

Sharon scanned the growing crowd milling at the base of the broad City Hall steps on Thursday afternoon. The hum of their conversation built in frequency as the minutes ticked by. She was a tightly wound ball of anxiety, twitching and jumping at every movement in her peripheral vision. More people joined, and soon passers-by loitered at the edges to find out what the fuss was about, not wanting to miss out on something interesting.

She fidgeted, stomping from foot to foot. Sweat clung to her despite the cold air. The fall day had dawned clear and crisp, the sky so blue it hurt your heart to look at it. She prayed it was a sign of good things to come – a city government purged of corruption, a case won, a father vindicated. A fresh beginning.

She glanced over at Kent. He strategized with Sergé a few feet away, their heads bent together, their voices an indistinct murmur. The stitches on his head were healing, and he no longer needed a bandage, so he pulled his hair back in his usual messy style, leaving no obvious evidence of their recent descent to the city's underworld. She reached up to touch her own small bandage, a concrete reminder.

In his rib-knit dark sweater, his favourite lumberjack shirt and warm denim jacket, he appeared at ease. With his usual relaxed posture, he sipped his Starbucks coffee, just as if this were another ordinary day on the street. She envied him and longed one day to be as comfortable in her skin as he seemed in his. Trying to dislodge the tension this situation awoke in her, she inhaled slowly, filling her lungs with cool air, feeling stronger when she saw him there, just steps away. Her partner, in this and, she hoped, when all the dust settled, in many things.

One of Sergé's guys set up Kent with a wireless headset mic and fiddled with a small black box on the ground beside him. She imagined this was a modern, high-tech version of a megaphone, a device with which she had no familiarity nor expected to befriend in this lifetime.

Sensing her gaze on him, he glanced up, his eyes crinkling when he saw her, melting her heart with his tender regard. In the cold air, his cheeks had pinked above his trimmed beard, and his eyes sparkled with excitement and anticipation. He was in his element.

Christine, Sofia, and Van from the Pathway Society hovered in a knot nearby on the top of the steps. She also saw a few of their students hanging around, including Harley, thin and pale, who stayed with his aunt for now. According to Constable Ashley, they assumed RJ Kovacs had skipped town, though Sharon knew concern for Harley's safety never disappeared from Kent's mind.

She wished she could relax. She had done everything *she* could do. Yesterday afternoon, she and her team had transported all the evidence and documentation to the Investigative Services Division of the Vancouver Police Station for filing. They had notified the police superintendent who oversaw both financial fraud and organized crime, as well as the provincial Crown Council and the mayor's office. The starting flag came down on

Kent's team to put the rally in motion. There was no turning back now.

She checked her phone for the hundredth time. She knew the police were inside the building. Their task was to arrest Seibold and secure the building so no one could remove or destroy records. Then, with the search warrants they'd secured this morning, additional materials could be identified and added to the case file.

She had stationed Tim inside City Hall over an hour ago, waiting for some sign that the police had arrested Seibold. Ella and Abby stood together with Dariush a few feet behind Sharon. Dariush surprised her by turning up to support her, too, and she exchanged polite smiles with him. If he'd had a mind to ask her out again, seeing her with Kent should have quit him of the notion. She made eye contact with Abby and wordlessly asked if they'd heard from Tim. No, not yet, she signaled. The two young women looked as nervous and excited as Sharon felt, jiggling and talking.

My God, this had better work. Her stomach churned, the muscles that wrapped around her middle quivering with tension, her breath rapid and shallow. This was the most high-profile case she'd ever worked on, and it felt like all the eyes of the world were on her, judging her.

She jumped when someone squeezed her arm from behind. Turning, she felt her eyes widen to discover her mother standing behind her bundled in a scarf, against the cold autumn air.

"Mom! You came." Sharon had called her late last night, explaining all.

"How could I miss this?"

"I hope we're not all deeply disappointed," Sharon murmured.

Kent strode toward them, his long legs eating up the distance. Those beat up old boots, she thought with a fond kick of her heart, watching as he sidled up beside her, bending his long body to look into her eyes, his expression affectionate and teasing. Her internal quivering settling down at his nearness like a trained animal. They looked into each other's eyes for a long moment.

"My mom came," she said, her stomach fluttering again.

He turned to her, cool as ever. "Nice to meet you, Mom of Sharon. Is it Mrs. Brecht?"

Mom nodded, smiling and looking up at him with a sparkle in her eyes, and Sharon felt her chest expand with the delight that these two people who were so important to her, were meeting and smiling at each other.

Mom replied, "You can call me Sandy, I think." She smiled some more. "I'll be over here with your friends. Good luck."

He rubbed Sharon's arms, steadying her. "Ready?" he whispered.

"As ready for this dreaded event as I'll ever be." She shuffled her feet and jammed her fists harder into the pockets of her warm overcoat.

"C'mere." Kent wrapped his arms around her, pulling her in close to his body, squeezing until there was no space left for a single shiver, or a single sliver of doubt. "You'll be fine. Are you positive you don't want to give the statement?"

She scoffed. "Are you kidding me?" The very thought of cameras recording today's events made her knees watery and her stomach turn over. Thankfully, Kent happily embraced his role as spokesperson on behalf of the Pathway Society and the community. This size of gathering, the heightened emotion, the cameras and press, she could not handle.

"All right, all right. Just giving you one last chance. This is your baby, you know. You ought to be the one on the six o'clock news."

"Over my dead body." She faux swooned in his arms, knowing he'd hold her up, and they both chuckled. She sobered. "Thank you. You make this easier."

He bent his head to capture her mouth in a possessive and heartfelt kiss that drained her of willpower, her fears forgotten in a pool of desire and contentment. "I love you, Princess. Just remember that."

"I love you, too," Sharon replied as he stepped backward from her, returning to Sergé, her smile filling him with a feeling of connection and belonging. The feeling stayed with him as he resumed his scanning of the growing crowd, pondering his new reality. She actually loved him. The thrill of that fact sizzled in his gut, sending arrows of heat out in every direction, making his chest swell with it. He couldn't wait until all of this was finally over and the two of them could mellow into a genuine couple. He wanted to spend every moment with her, getting to know all those things they hadn't had time for.

Kent half listened to Sergé, watching beside him as large groups of people began arriving, vehicles and buses stopping at the curb, and offloading a steady stream of citizens. Senior citizens, students, people in jeans and people in business attire, families with kids in tow. He marvelled at the breadth of support his friends had summoned in such a short time, the sketchiest of information spread by word of mouth alone. But it had done the trick. Nothing like a whiff of political corruption to stir the masses to action.

In the gathering throng, Kent recognized familiar faces. He waved at Carl who stood at the bottom of the steps with his cronies from the Carnegie Centre, and when he scanned the faces near him, he saw Marilyn with several other residents of the Downtown Eastside, former clients, and even the old homeless guy Douglas who swept the floors at the society. He noticed someone waving at him from the middle of the crowd and looked up to see his mother. He raised a hand to wave back. She blew him a kiss, smiling as a warm feeling spread in his chest. It quickly faded back, however, as the inevitable undercurrent of melancholy about his absent father filtered in to poison it. But he shook it off. Sharon was right, it didn't matter. Kent was doing what mattered to him, and he was effective and authentic. What his materialistic, status conscious father thought was immaterial.

Sergé's camera crew were set up off to one side of where they stood. Other press reporters and photographers gathered, making small talk, presumably still very speculative at this point since he'd given details only to Sergé with strict orders not to share.

Once Sergé's sound tech guy gave him the okay, Kent flicked a switch on his headset and cleared his throat, testing the sound, which amplified out into the plaza. The technician squatted to adjust the volume.

With one last glance at Sharon, he inhaled deeply. Show time.

"Hold on, hold on, patience everyone. We'll answer as many of your questions as we can. But first, let me give you a quick overview of what's going on here today at City Hall."

The buzz and hum of conversation rose from the crowd as people talked among themselves, then settled down into an expectant silence, punctuated only by the whining of a child. He waved to the crowd.

"Thank you. All right. Good afternoon, everyone. Thanks for coming out today to support our cause. My name is Kent Sawyer, and I represent the Pathway Society and School." He gave a brief description of the society's mission and mandate, and background on the new building project and its purpose. "With this project, we'll have the resources to provide more counselling, more preventive health care, more education and vocational training. We can provide short-term accommodation for kids from the street who need to be safe, to get clean, to have their babies and get the step up they need to create a life for themselves in the absence of family support." He paused while that information soaked in.

"We retained legal council to advise us when we became concerned that local lobby groups, aligned with competing development interests, were unduly influencing City officials and staff, and commitments were at risk of reversal. That's when Flannigan, Searle, Meacham, Beckett & Shirazi became involved, represented by our solicitor Sharon Beckett." He gestured her way, locking gazes with her for a split second before hers skittered away.

He eyed Sharon's tense smile as she nodded at the gathered throng. Glancing left and right, she pulled at the lapels and belt of her coat, straightening the already straight folds of fabric with hands that trembled nervously.

Her gaze shot back to Kent, seeking reassurance, and he met her distressed gaze steadily, sending her a warm smile that seemed to settle her rising panic. With a tiny nod, he took back the crowd's attention by speaking again.

"As you will all discover when the details of the charges laid are in the news tonight and tomorrow, long-standing City councillor Gus Seibold had just been taken into custody. The alleged crimes are serious. They include: misuse of power of an elected official, buying contracts, peddling influence, extorting colleagues, embezzling and misappropriation of municipal funds, blackmail, defamation, money laundering, and nepotism, continuously in a systematic shady underworld of business dealings over the past twenty…four…years. Of elected office."

The press noticed it first, all of them pivoting to the double doors of the building behind them. The reporters standing beside him jostled one another as they turned their attention away. A sudden roar of murmuring voices gathered momentum as the crowd caught on, punctuated by the odd shout. The mass of faces turned in a wave toward the flurry of activity at the doors, where a group of people emerged. Shouts of outrage rose above the sweeping din of the crowd.

Kent turned to look.

CHAPTER 35

Sharon gasped as Tim dashed out and darted towards them. Behind him, several uniformed police officers appeared, forming a defensive barrier. Just behind, two police led a red-faced, handcuffed Gus Seibold, his beige trench coat flapping open as a gust of wind blew up the steps. The press rushed him, crowding around, barking questions.

"What are the charges, Councillor Seibold?"

"Who has filed against you, Sir?"

And Sergé, with his advance knowledge, "Councillor Seibold. Is it true you're accused of peddling influence, buying contracts, extorting colleagues and embezzling municipal funds for over twenty years?"

"This is all a terrible mistake," Seibold growled, flustered and angry at being hauled away in handcuffs. "I've done nothing wrong. This is mischief-making. You'll see."

Then as suddenly, Rachel shoved in front of Seibold elbowing Sergé and the other reporters away. "Councillor Seibold has no comment. This misunderstanding will become clear in due course." She looked up, scanning the crowd of people gathered at the top of the stairs, her gaze locking on Sharon like a laser beam.

Sharon swallowed. Tingling swept up her neck and cheeks, becoming a buzzing in her ears as her head went foggy, as though it would separate from her neck and float away. Rachel was furious, surprised obviously, along with everyone else, as Sharon had planned. Sharon hoped she'd get over her personal frustrations and be able to look at these events with professional objectivity. Maybe even compliment Sharon's work. But not today. Today she hated her best friend. Sharon could see her fury burning in her green eyes.

And if she saw shock and frustration in her friend's eyes, the look in Seibold's as he discovered her in the crowd was one of pure hatred, so cold and black it filled her with terror.

She had made a certain enemy there. If these charges didn't stick, she'd be in a world of trouble.

A roar surged behind her from the crowd, causing her to jump and glance over her shoulder, her pulse speeding up, as if she were the object of their rising outrage. But she saw, in fact, that Seibold's fate was set in the minds of the populace, eager to paint him as a villain.

The police led a protesting Seibold away, escorting him into a waiting police car. She let out a breath of relief. It was over in moments.

A few curious City staff trailed outside as the police dragged Seibold away, among them Sharon recognized first one and then a couple more of the other City councillors. Later she noticed the mayor standing among them behind her team, his expression grave.

With no further information to gain from the accused or his counsel, the press swarmed over to Kent, Sharon and their compatriots. This was the quarter where they would get answers. Sharon took two steps back, closer to her team, as people crowded closer to Kent, clamouring to hear. Agitated citizens suddenly surrounded them. Questions flew at them left and right.

"Why did they take away Councillor Seibold?"

"What's this about influence peddling and embezzlement?"

"I never trusted that bastard!"

"What did he do? Tell us!"

K ent squared his shoulders and addressed the angry, questioning faces that circled him. He understood their wrath. It mirrored his own roiling emotions these past few years and months. Now he was confident that, together with Sharon, they were taking action to make meaningful change. He breathed easily, feeling a lightness in his chest, his muscles relaxed.

"We all put our trust in those elected by the people to represent our interests at all levels of government, rightly or wrongly. We also hope that these individuals are worthy of that trust. With Councillor Gus Seibold, we were wrong."

More crowds' roar rose into the crisp fall air.

Kent's voice was clear and powerful, resonating over the din of the crowd. "Why does this matter?"

Why indeed? For as long as Kent could remember, the injustice, greed and corruption he saw in the world disturbed him, and he had to act on it. This was something his mother understood, but his father and brother... just didn't.

How ironic that he'd been born into this privileged family, all of them smart, strong and ambitious, and yet so dichotomous in their worldview. He'd often wondered if his father had drawn Kent's mother to him as an idealistic younger man. Had a sense of his own greatness seduced and lulled him? Kent knew his father believed what he was doing was the highest and best use of his abilities to help people. And it was important work, no question.

That just wasn't for him. He was sure of that now. This was his work. If his father couldn't see it, and didn't understand it, and never valued the way he lived his life, well, then it didn't matter. It was his life to live.

He let his gaze rest on Sharon, whose very presence settled him, focussing all the swirling rage and frustration and even the guilt and futility into a clear and strong sense of himself and his worthy purpose.

"Why do we care?" He waited a beat, letting expectation settle over the audience. "I'll tell you why." He softened his tone to a stage whisper, inspiring his listeners to quieten to hear him and tune to his emotional state.

The reporters stood by, recording his speech, finding no reason to either interrupt him or prompt him with questions. He glanced at Sharon whose wide eyes and high colour boosted his confidence further. Her gaze glittered with emotion and love, filling him up, redeeming him. She loved him just the way he was, without qualification or expectation. Despite her own wounds and fears. He realized that they'd changed each other in the past weeks, healing and learning to depend on and appreciate the other's strengths.

Maybe he couldn't save every child, but he could be an instrument of change for a better society, for a better, more humane future for all children, no matter the circumstances of their birth or situation.

Then he told the story of a child. It might have been Harley's story, or it might have been the story of a thousand kids who lived on the street with no home, no family, no protector, making it on their own, or not, with the smarts that came from experience and survival. His audience fell quiet, letting him weave his magic web around their hearts with his narrative.

"Don't you think these kids deserve a chance to have a better life than fate has given them?" He stopped talking, just nodding his head, for a moment moved beyond speech. "I do too." He sighed. "But this…" He gestured to the City Hall behind him as though the drama of Seibold's arrest were still unfolding.

"This is about more than just our project, and these kids." He swept a hand to include some students from Pathway below him. "This is about every citizen, and every taxpayer's dollar. In our efforts to put together a case against the City to hang on to our new school project, our lawyer, Sharon Beckett, unearthed the most shocking evidence."

He paused for a beat, two beats, three, to allow the murmured reaction of the crowd to rise and fall again like a wave. In the gap, he let his gaze sweep the crowd to measure people's reactions to his words. In the distance, he noticed a dark sedan pull up to the curb, and a couple more men step out to join the rally.

"We have discovered that one man is behind a broad network of criminal activity within City Hall, abusing the power with which we, the unsuspecting voting citizens of Vancouver, entrusted him. Councillor Gus Seibold, who has, by manipulating, bribing, blackmailing and defaming honourable and hard-working City staff, elected officials and citizens, has maintained his privileged position for twenty-four years!"

Another discontented grumble rolled through the assembly, punctuated by angry muffled shouts, which roiled as the newcomers shoved their way through.

"Ms. Beckett's firm filed a significant amount of evidence at the Courthouse yesterday, and hundreds more files were sealed and secured within City Hall today so that the investigation can cont – What the…?"

"Stop! Stop these outrageous slanderous lies!" shouted a light-haired man in a dark trench coat bursting from the throng and surging up the steps two at a time.

"Hey!" Kent faced the intruder. He was just hitting his stride.

The guy was at the top, lunging for him before Kent realized it was Matt Seibold. In every respect, his adversary.

Kent's head jerked back, mid-sentence, mouth ajar. Blinking

in confusion, he tried to go on, "Er… continu… uh…" and stuttered to a halt as Matt elbowed his way up and aggressively reached toward his head. Kent's arm came up to block his face, half expecting another fist to his eye from the guy who'd jumped him in the parking lot recently. "Hey! Get off me, man!"

Matt ripped the headset off of Kent's head with a crackle and squawk, catching his hair with it, and ripping it loose from its tie, pulling his long hair across his face. A collective exclamation rose from the crowd.

Sharon gasped and lunged toward them, grabbing Matt's arm and shouting, "Don't hurt him!" getting hauled off her feet as she stumbled into them in a tangle. He tossed her aside, and she fell backwards, heading for the concrete. Kent reached out an arm before he saw that her staff had rushed forward to break her fall and steady her.

Kent bent over, swearing, grabbing his head and Matt's sleeve as Matt continued to tug until he got the mic set loose. A bubble of panic lodged itself under his diaphragm, stopping his breath. He put his hand to his head to check his stitches after the rough handling.

Then, having what he coveted, Matt shoved the mic to his face and resumed shouting, but spinning toward the crowd.

"Don't believe a word of the lies these shit-disturbing radicals have been telling you!" Matt thrust out an arm, pointing at Kent, who had leapt in Sharon's direction and stopped when he saw she was okay. "This hipster is the least objective excuse for a spokesman as anyone could be. He wants to manipulate you… and the City council to overturn the fair and legal decision made in favour of S & S."

Kent pulled back, his jaw falling open in shock. The son of a bitch, hijacking his rally.

"Who the hell are you?" came a shout from someone in the crowd.

"My name is Matt Seibold, president of Seibold and Sorenson

Developments. It's our company that won the contract to redevelop the City building that this rabble are blathering about. They've distorted the facts. My father is innocent of the crimes he's being accused of. You'll see."

"Are you part of the corruption ring, Junior? Is that how you make your millions?" someone else jeered.

Kent stepped closer to Sharon, tucking an arm around her. "You okay?"

She couldn't answer, shaking her head, her face flushing pink, eyes wide in shock. "I can't..."

"You're hardly objective yourself, son-of-Seibold!" hollered another heckler.

"It's incredible. What a fool," said a man's voice behind them.

"He's undoing your – " Sharon started.

"Wait! Wait! Believe me. Listen. You don't have all the facts. They didn't tell you everything. They didn't tell you who *she* is!" Matt's arm swung to point at Sharon.

Sharon's heart pounded, a bubble choking off her words. Sharon lurched, stumbling as her knees went weak.

She had barely noticed the newcomers who barged through the crowd. Then like a cold shower she awoke to the fact that it was Matt Seibold who had bolted up the stairs, bulldozing straight into Kent.

Oh, no. No, no, no. *This is not happening!* Her arms folded over her stomach, as her heart thudded, and the air whooshed out of her lungs.

The bubble inside her inflated, pressing outward against her ribs and heart, sizzling and surging through her blood. *Noooo!*

"That woman, the fancy lawyer who calls herself Sharon Beckett. Is. A. Liar! She's really the unremarkable little Sharon Brecht, pitiful daughter of the shameful Peter Brecht who cheated and stole from you!" Matt jabbed a finger into the crowd, eliciting a wave of indignation. "She's been lying about who she is, living under a false name. What does that tell you? Talk about lack of objectivity. We went to school together. I know all her dirty secrets."

The expanding bubble pushed her heart into her throat like a cork, choking the breath from her. Her gaze darted to her mother's horrified face. She understood.

Matt persevered over the taunts from the audience. "This is an elaborate ruse to get personal vengeance against my father, who has devoted his life... to serving this community. If you know anything about the beginning of my father's career here at City Hall, you'll remember that he made a name for himself fighting corruption and corrupt politicians..." He jabbed a pointed finger at her again and again like a pile driver. "... like Sharon Brecht's father, Peter Brecht!"

The bubble exploded, releasing panic and terror into her bloodstream like acid toxic waste – seeping into every cell – burning – the primal panic and terror you feel when there is no escape, when you are surrounded, cornered, beaten, and are at risk of being eaten alive by the beast you fear most – when you know you're doomed.

"My father is innocent of the wrongdoing they have accused him of today. But *her* father, Peter Brecht, was a city councillor too! He was so corrupt, he not only lost his position on council, but he lost the respect of all his colleagues and friends!" Matt hit his stride now. The throng had fallen quiet, fascinated by this new twist, their faces one by one registering doubt and confusion. Sharon shrunk under their accusing gaze.

"His crimes were so shameful..." Matt paused for dramatic effect. "So shameful they sold their house and ran away! They disappeared from the community for ever! Then she..." He paused and pointed again, his voice mocking, and waved a hand at her. "She put on this disguise so she could come back and get her revenge on my father!"

Everything slowed down like film stuttering to a halt, separating Sharon from sounds and smells, her limbs numb, her awareness shrinking to her own thudding heartbeat pounding in her temples, her own liquifying bowels, and tense ready-to-spring muscles. She experienced a kind of paralysis, her breath stopped, her heart stuttered in her chest, she deflated like a balloon, shrinking, shriveling, collapsing.

The words that Matthew spoke now were lies, the worst lies. At best, ignorant lies. At worst, selfish, malicious, hurtful lies. Yes, she'd hidden, but it was these very lies she had believed and shied from.

Her true self, the daughter her father had raised, hid behind a mask, cowering from the lies that had made her feel such debilitating shame.

No more shame.

No more lies.

Instinct pushed her into action – flight, or fight. She didn't decide what happened next. It seemed to happen without forethought or logic, without concern for her survival. It was too late for that.

No more hiding.

No more running.

What she was doing was so horrifying, so alien, that a detached part of her mind considered that she was possessed by some demon or gone mad. It was such a desperate act. But she had no choice.

Suspended in her slow motion bubble of hysteria, overcome by a sudden calm, Sharon stepped closer to Matt, staring into his eyes with a dauntless sense of purpose, reached up and pulled the mic headset out of his thick-fingered grip.

At first he resisted, tugging to prevent her from taking it away. His voice faded in his throat. She looked into his pale eyes with a steely, unflinching gaze, piercing through his bravado with her determination, daring him to resist her now that she'd thrown down the gauntlet at last. He flinched and seemed to shrink under her steady challenge, his grip loosening. She pulled the mic from him and set the headpiece over her head, trying to adjust the mouthpiece.

The news station's tech stepped forward to help her fix it. Then she took a step forward in front of the crew, turning to face the crowd, drew a deep breath and prepared to speak.

This was war.

"Lies." The mic crackled, and she froze a moment, the crowd falling silent as the speaker changed once again. "I am so tired of listening to your lies Matthew Seibold. Your lies, your father's lies, and all the cronies and dupes he dragged through the muck all these years to support your father's sinister little fiefdom. It's time for me to tell you the truth."

She turned in a slow circle, blinking rapidly, taking in the stunned faces around her. She saw Kent, her team Ella, Tim, Abby and Dariush, a little behind them City councillors she recognized from the public hearing, and the mayor himself. She rotated, kept turning, looking at all the faces. Not strangers, but friends, colleagues, acquaintances, citizens. People that needed to hear the truth.

"Let me tell you *my* truth." She drew a breath, filling her lungs. "A long time ago. Twenty-four years ago, I was a young girl who believed that her father was an exceptional, principled man, who devoted his life to service, who championed the rights of the people."

"And then something terrible happened." Sharon's panic ebbed, replaced by a clear sense of the rightness and inevitability of what she was doing in this moment. "That wonderful man fell from his pedestal because of lies that were told. Innocent girl that I was, I believed them. Those lies destroyed our life. I thought I suffered, because I had to leave my friends at school, because I had to move away from my home, my neighbourhood, because I had to hang my head in shame when old friends and neighbours taunted my mother and I at the supermarket, when my classmates," she pointed back, turning the tables on him, "like Matthew ridiculed me and jeered at me and made me feel small. But it's my father who suffered the most. He lost his position as councillor representing you, the citizens of the city. A position he prized and gave himself to wholly. He also lost his livelihood, the family home he'd built, the respect of his friends and colleagues. He lost his name. He lost his pride."

Her voice broke, and she paused for breath, her heart thumping a steady drumbeat behind her ribs.

Dad hadn't survived long after the shock of it all. And in that horrible time, while he was slowly dying of distress and depression, she had built a shield around herself, to distance herself from him, to erase who she'd been, to hide from all the pain. A smokescreen. A survival strategy. She'd never had time to contemplate forgiveness. Now, over twenty years on, her grief was mixed with remorse. For though he'd made mistakes, maybe even unforgivable mistakes, he was still her father, and she'd loved him.

That's why his fall from grace had disappointed her so much. More that that, it had broken her. Not only had her wonderful, loving, shining father fallen from his high pedestal, but her entire world had crumbled. Nothing had ever been right again.

"He also lost the love and trust and respect of his only child. And she..." she set a hand over her heart, "... lost her role model. They both lost their identity, their place in the world, and their idealism. They lost their purpose, their legacy, and their trust in humanity." She could hardly see and swiped at her eyes, her hand coming away wet. With a glance at her mother – quickly or she'd lose it completely – she continued.

"And those two broken, downtrodden souls never reconciled." She drew a shuddering breath. "My father died knowing he was innocent and knowing that his daughter did not believe in him. For all that he suffered, I think broke his heart."

The words stopped flowing, her head thick and throbbing. She lifted her wet eyes to the upturned faces around her, her heart squeezing with the pain of all she'd lost. Kent's arm wrapped around her shoulders, and he gave her a squeeze. The fire was gone now. She swallowed and went on, her voice soft.

"It took a long time, and it took the special circumstance of the Pathway Society project, for me to recognize these lies that were told decades ago, and continue to be told today.

"My father was an intelligent man, and when he was ejected from his office, he was smart enough to keep his records. And recently I searched through these records and the scales fell from my eyes. I read about all of councillor Seibold's many crimes and misdemeanours. I saw the evidence that my father kept." A last burst of fiery rage swelled in her chest. "The evidence that was his undoing. Councillor Seibold could manipulate enough people, and enough of the information to fool all of you, and to create in my father the perfect scapegoat."

Sharon glanced to her left and right and saw that her people surrounded her. Kent at her side, her team at her back, the City staff, councillors, reporters, citizens of the Downtown Eastside, and every other neighbourhood of the city who'd come here today to hear the truth. And her mother, her face flushed, her cheeks as wet as Sharon's, pride glowing in her eyes. Sharon nodded.

"That era has ended. No more shall we listen to the lies of evil and greedy men who would manipulate and use us. To steal from us for their own personal gain. To hurt innocent people, to preserve their position of privilege and power.

"My old classmate Matthew Seibold that you see standing here grew up believing that he would be heir to the despicable empire that his father built." She turned to face him, scanning his pale face, the expression frozen into a mask of horror. "But I'm sorry to inform you Matthew that you will get nothing. If you knew of these wrongdoings, sheltered them, took part in any of them, then you will fall too."

She swallowed, her lips trembling. "And if you were innocent, as I was, then I pity you, because you now must face the ugly truth of your own father's sins."

CHAPTER 37

The crowd burst into a thunder of applause and roars and shouts, overlaying a current of discontented murmuring and jeering. People surged forward, moving as one creature, and swallowed Matthew Seibold into its ranks. The crowd jostled and shoved him along, spitting him out at the other side, and he shook himself loose, striding to his car, defeated.

Standing side by side they watched him go. Kent wrapped his arms around her, pulling her back to his chest, holding her tight, tucking his cheek next to hers. "Brava, Princess," he whispered into her ear, his breath hot, enveloping her in a sweet cloud of safety and belonging.

The tension in her frame loosened, and she spun in his embrace, lifting her face and her gaze to meet his, setting her hands on his cheeks. She felt a stunned disbelief, and a dawning realization.

They had vanquished their enemy. Together.

Kent laughed, lifting her and shaking them both with his sudden bark of triumph. "Yes, that was you, Princess." He bent his head and covered her mouth with his, and she felt his pride and relief and love in his kiss. And she received it with a full heart. He kept kissing her until her tension eased, and the beginnings of desire stirred.

She pulled away as he set her down, keeping his arms around her.

Sharon felt a mix of intense pride and admiration for him. This was his doing. This feeling of vindication and release. On the podium, Kent had become impassioned, embracing his role as leader and champion, standing with his long legs set wide. Tall, bold, and so handsome her pulse skittered with the memory of his touch.

A buzz of desire hit her in her back teeth, her breasts, the backs of her knees.

He spoke his truth, and it shone from his eyes. This was his purpose, and it was a crime that anyone would try to diminish its value. His value. How many people had the courage, conviction and passion to stand up, to defy power and authority, to speak the truth that they saw and to fight for their beliefs?

He was one in a million.

All the reasons she had fallen for him rushed at her in a watershed of recognition. This was the class of man that her father was. Dad had taught her these values. He modelled these traits. Kent exemplified them, and she idolized him. They had each helped her become the person she was.

Kent had a natural talent for this, his finger on the pulse of the people. He was like a maestro with his symphony, stirring up a frenzy of violent feelings, and then soothing them with a gentle hand, carrying his audience along with him on this roller coaster ride.

"I love you," she whispered against his ear, and he covered her mouth with his own once more, transferring all of his exuberance and vitality into the connection.

～

Sergé and the other reporters encircled them, volleying questions their way, trying to get one last sound bite for their front-page stories. Kent kept them at bay, reiterating that Sergé had exclusive access to interviews, both before and after the rally. Those conversations were for later.

Sergé confirmed that his paper would publish the interview materials of the case along with the news of today's event, including the full history of Sharon's father. More detail would come out in time.

He turned back to Sharon to find her surrounded by people. Her assistants, a few civic politicians, the Pathway crew, and Carl had all come forward to shake her hand, embrace and congratulate her. She was holding up admirably, but he could see her complexion becoming increasingly flushed, and noticed her hands trembling.

Kent scratched his beard. It was time to take his darling princess home. "All right, thanks everyone. I think we've had enough attention for one day." He bundled Sharon into his arms and turned them, creating a barrier between her and her fans. Bending his head, he whispered, "You okay, Princess?"

Instead of answering in the affirmative, she seemed to disintegrate in his arms. The trembling amplified to an all over shudder, her eyes streaming with tears, gasping and sobbing. He pressed his hand to the back of her head and tilted her forehead to his chest, holding her tight, allowing her the privacy of his embrace for her cathartic release without a word.

Several minutes later, Sharon's shock and relief spent, Kent helped mop up her tears with a hanky and help her dab at her streaked mascara.

"You look beautiful."

She cast doubtful eyes up at him with a side quirk to her lovely pink lips.

"Seriously. I plan to ravish you when I get you home. You've never looked more gorgeous and alive. I love you, Princess."

She thanked him with another brief touch of her lips.

"I apologize for interrupting."

They turned to the voice to see the mayor standing two feet away, a benevolent smile on his face. He stepped forward with his hand outstretched.

"Ms. Beckett. I want to personally thank you for all the work, the research, your records, and everything you have done to purge this criminal organization from the ranks of City Hall."

She swallowed and took his hand, accepting his thanks with a blush. "It was my pleasure, Mr. Mayor, as I'm sure you know. But I didn't accomplish this alone. My team," she gestured to her associates, "did so much of the research and legwork, and Kent." She turned to lay one palm against his chest proudly. "You remember Kent Sawyer from the public hearing, I believe? Well, this rally is entirely his doing. Only half the battle was a legal one. We fight the balance in the street with the help of concerned and passionate citizens. Without Kent and his colleagues paying attention to the needs of the people, a lot more corruption would go unnoticed. And liaison with the press, and multiple community groups that came out to support us today. It wouldn't have been – "

"You're too modest, Princess," Kent interrupted. "Sure I stormed and raged, but you're the one who made this take down a real possibility."

Mayor Taylor smiled at Kent and quietly gripped his hand while keeping his focus on Sharon. They'd had many encounters in the few years Kent had been advocating for street youth and residents of the Downtown Eastside.

She drew a shaky breath, her gaze darting to the side before speaking again. "Actually, I'd like to give the credit to my father, Peter Brecht. If he hadn't challenged Gus Seibold over twenty years ago, he would never have been victim to such a ruthless smear campaign, and might be alive and sitting on council still, in place of his nemesis. Although I prefer to imagine he would have happily retired and spent his days fishing with Mr. Llewellyn." She chuckled softly, then sobered. "And if he hadn't had the conviction and foresight to keep all his files, Mr. Mayor, I wouldn't have had enough evidence to begin this process, let alone finish it. He deserves all the credit."

The mayor nodded thoughtfully, his gaze cast down. Then he glanced up again. "I know the history of that scandal, athough it was long before my tenure in office. But the evidence brought to light today warrants a full investigation into those events, Ms. Beckett."

"Please call me Sharon."

"Sharon. I have a feeling significant reparation must be made to restore your father's honourable name and memory in these halls." He lifted a hand and gestured to the building behind them. "I feel a personal sense of obligation and duty to make sure all the facts come out, and everyone knows the sacrifice your father made, and how he was wronged."

Sharon's chin quivered again, threatening fresh tears. "Thank you, Mr. Mayor. That would mean so much to me and my family."

"Well, I'll let you go. You've had quite a day." He shook her hand again, gripping her shoulder in his gloved hand. "But I want you to know I'll be recruiting fresh talent to help me rebuild a strong, transparent and honest City council. The apple doesn't fall far from the tree and I'd love to have you on board as an alderwoman to help me clean up and begin a new era. I hope you'll consider running with me in the next civic election."

Sharon's eyes went wide, as though despite today's gigantic leap of courage into the pubic eye, such a role had never occurred to her. "Oh, my goodness." She let out a shaky breath. "I don't know about that. I've always been happiest working quietly in the background. But thank you for the offer. I'll give that careful consideration, though I have the feeling my legal career will keep me rather busy." She paused, blinking, then her gaze darted mischievously to Kent's face with a tiny grin. "I know someone else, though, that would be perfect for a dynamic role in public office."

Mayor Taylor chuckled, meeting Kent's gaze with a twinkle in his eyes. "Oh, don't worry, Sharon. I've had my eye on this one for a while now." He waved and moved off, soon swallowed up by reporters as she met Kent's wide-eyed response with a grin.

EPILOGUE

After the official ground-breaking ceremony on the new school renovation and construction project, Kent and Sharon walked hand in hand back to the existing school building where a celebration was already underway.

Reporters had pulled Sharon and Kent aside to answer a few questions about the project and its history, keeping them behind the others.

When they finally walked in the doors, the buzz of conversation from the crowd in the front lobby quieted for a half second before a cheer rose.

Everyone was here. Sharon saw Christine, Van, Sofia, the other staff, a few of the regular street people who volunteered, most of the students, and Harley looking freshly scrubbed and more robust than in recent weeks.

Sharon's phone dinged with a text, and she flinched, remembering the vaguely threatening texts, phone message and stalking that she had recently received. She still found it difficult to believe that Gus Seibold wouldn't be coming for her with revenge on his mind.

But it was Rachel.

Not attending ur stupid party

Ding.

Would be inappropriate and unprofessional

Ding.

Also don't care to see you gloat

Sharon laughed and tilted her phone to show Kent.
Ding.

Pizza and a movie this Sunday?

Some things never changed. And Sharon was glad her friendship with Rachel was one of those things.

Kent's Mom congratulated and hugged him. He glanced around and she said, reading his mind, "Dad had to work... but he wanted me to tell you how proud he is of you and what you've accomplished here."

"Thanks for coming Mom." He hugged her, meeting Sharon's gaze over her shoulder, his expression skeptical.

After his mother left, Sharon slipped her arms around his waist and gazed up into his sexy amber eyes with a question in her own. "I'll be ok," he said. "I think I'll tuck that away and think about it later, when we get home."

The applause died down as everyone had had their fill of speeches at the groundbreaking, replaced by a general festive buzz of conversation with soft guitar music somewhere underneath it all. Sharon and Kent accepted the sodas offered to them by Van and turned to exchange a few words with Christine.

"I know I've said it a million times already, but I can never thank you two enough for all you've done."

"It was our pleasure, Christine. I'm really excited to see the new facility take shape." Sharon leaned in for a kiss and embrace and stepped back, letting Kent get the big bear hug he deserved from his boss and mentor.

"I think we're all rather pleased with the way things turned out," he said. He grinned, self-satisfied, and hooked his elbow around Sharon's neck, pulling her in and planting his mouth over hers in an enthusiastic kiss that sent tingles across her skin, and a jolt of molten heat to her core.

In the weeks since the arrest of Councillor Gus Seibold, many things had advanced. A grateful planning department and City council had expedited development permits for the new school. Contracts were signed with the builder who would oversee the renovation and conversion of the old brick heritage building into state-of-the-art classrooms, offices and residences.

On the legal front, they had filed sufficient evidence to secure several serious charges against Seibold and a few of his key insider colleagues at City hall, including Sam Carter. Even S & S Developments was under investigation to determine whether they were knowingly involved in any criminal activities, or recipient of any contracts through nepotism or misappropriation of City funds. Discoveries would start soon, which would involve Sharon and Rachel on opposing legal teams, which was why she didn't want to be seen at this celebration. In the meantime, Seibold had lost his position and was *persona non grata* in City Hall. She almost felt sorry for him and his disgraced family. Almost.

Sharon brought her attention back to the present at Christine's laughter. "I was referring to the school, you know."

"Oh, I know." Kent joined her with a chuckle. "But we got so much more."

Harley noticed them and ran to Kent with a bright smile on his face, leaning in to head bump Kent's chest when Kent wrapped him in his arms.

"Hey, Sharon," Harley said, turning his face her way with a smirk before racing off again to the buffet where a few other students were loitering, stuffing their faces with party food.

Sharon caught Kent's pensive gaze following the boy. She hoped he could stop worrying about him now that RJ had left town, but also knew Harley was far from settled. Although he might be one of the first residents of the school facility, that would be months off, and he was, despite his past, still too young for independent living. Much could happen in the intervening time.

"Have you thought about taking him in yourself?" she asked Kent.

His head whipped toward her, eyes wide, his expression almost guilty.

"Huh. So you have. Would you maybe foster him?"

He pressed his lips together in a firm line, his earnest golden brown gaze meeting hers with a question.

"Hm. You found me out. I have had preliminary conversations with Harley's aunt, and his current case worker at Child and Family Services. But it would be up to Harley. He might prefer to live in the new housing project, though I hope he'd agree. At least for a few years, to allow him to catch up with schooling, and make a bit of a break from his street life."

Sharon's heart gave a bump of surprise, chased by a thrilling thrum in her belly, her face pulling taut in a smile she couldn't hold back. "That... would be..." She paused, thinking. It would be a wonderful thing for Kent, who watched her now with a worried frown, waiting for the rest of her response.

He wanted to know if she would share the responsibility. If she'd mind.

Although their love affair was still such a raw, new thing, she thought she'd enjoy helping him nurture and protect the wild, clever boy who'd never in his life known a stable home. Though she and Kent still maintained separate apartments, she wondered how much longer they would want to, since they were seldom apart these days. She also wondered whether the look of guilt on his sweet, flushed face had anything to do with his thoughts about their future, and how Harley being part of that would impact them. It wouldn't be easy.

With squeezing ribs and a fizzy bubbling sensation in her head, she sought to reassure him, while daring to risk asking for what she secretly wanted.

"That would be amazing. I'd love to partner with you on that."

THE END

Thank you for reading!

Did you enjoy reading Sharon and Kent's love story?

Please leave a review where ever you purchased the book, as well as other vendors' sites if you find yourself there.

Or on Goodreads: https://www.goodreads.com/review/edit/53979923?report_event=true&survey=1

And on BookBub too!: https://www.bookbub.com/books/before-you-knew-me-an-opposites-attract-romantic-suspense-novel-having-it-all-book-3-by-maryann-clarke

THANK YOU!

First of all, thank you to my readers... that's YOU! Without passionate readers of words, there would be no point in telling stories. You complete the creative process and validate the author's efforts. Thanks especially to those subscribers of my newsletter who stay with me through the process of creating new work for you to read. If you'd like to join their ranks, please subscribe!

For Before You Knew Me, I have a few people to thank without whose expertise, time and sensitivity it could not have been written, or written half so well.

Thanks to Danielle for her legal expertise (not advice!) It was a stretch for my brain but I hope I got all the bits right.

Thanks to Bill for reading and commenting on the social work aspects of the story and my hero Kent's training and character.

Thank you as ever to my first reader and developmental editor Amanda Bidnall for her insight, wisdom, perspective and guidance. You helped take my first bulging mess and wrestle it into shape to make this a much better book. And I'm learning!

Thank you to The Creative Academy mentors, colleagues and

friends for always being there and supporting me and my writing through all the highs and lows. You keep me going!

The Acadium stars Donna, Michelle & Maritza for all their support with market research and book launch strategy.

A huge thank you to my amazing team of Beta Readers who each have the sharpest eye and arenas of expertise that caught all those things to which I seem to be blind: Natasha, Cecelia, Judy, Sophie, Tricia & Ardelle… and especially John (see below.)

Thanks in advance to all the Advance Readers, Book Reviewers and Bloggers for enthusiastically receiving, consuming and sharing this book with the reading community. I value your passion and love you all!

And finally, to my family for always being there and supporting me and my crazy job of writing. I love you always. Special thanks to my partner in all things John who is not only a meticulous proof-reader but this time around a rigorous story editor and collaborator. I'm blessed to have so much of your time and attention.

This one is for Bill.
For your inspiration, and for your dedication
to both creative writing and the downtrodden.

And to the hardworking passionate people who work
in the caring professions without whom we'd be less
human.

MaryAnn Clarke is a Chatelaine Grand Prize winner and Next Generation Indie Book Award finalist for The Art of Enchantment, first in the Life is a Journey series about young women on journeys abroad who discover themselves and fall in love while getting embroiled in someone else's problems. Her Having it All series is about professional women struggling to balance the challenge and fulfillment of their careers with their search for identity, love, family and home.

Always eager to fill blank pages and empty canvases with ideas swirling in her head, MaryAnn set out to write emotionally engaging stories that walk a tight rope between intelligent Women's Fiction and heart-warming Romance.

A polymath who studied Fine Arts, Urbanism, Architecture and Gerontology at university on both coasts of Canada, she turned to her first love, writing stories, when she realized she could have more fun with fewer rules to follow as an author, than working in an office as an architect, or in a university as a researcher. When not writing, she meditates while hiking wooded mountain trails, does yoga and Pilates to fend off decrepitude, reads eclectically, contemplates wormholes, experiments with painting abstract expressionism, kills plants and tries not to burn dinner while solving her next plot problem. Now that her chick has flown the coop, Clarke lives on beautiful Vancouver Island, Canada with her husband and cats. Although she knows she lives in Paradise, she still loves traveling the world in search of romance, art, good food and new story ideas.

Stay in touch to hear book news, special deals and updates about her next release. You can always reach MaryAnn at maryann (at) maryannclarkescott (dot) com

WANT TO READ THE LATEST BOOK IN THE LIFE IS A JOURNEY SERIES?

BUY *A FORGED AFFAIR* : mybook (dot) to/Forged

WANT TO CONNECT WITH ME?
maryann (at) maryannclarkescott (dot) com
maryannclarkescott (dot) com

If you enjoy reading this book, please rate it and leave a review wherever you purchased the book. Your opinion can make or break an author's success, and it means the world to me.

Subscribe & Follow MaryAnn!
maryannclarkescott (dot) com
Question? Fan mail? Sure, you can find me here.

The Art of Enchantment

A Forged Affair

Single Dad in Studio 7D

Alexa sat beside Kate on the edge of her bed, her arm around the hunched form of her friend.

"I would die if anything happened to Simon. I have to be there."

"Don't say another word. I know you have to go," Alexa said. The timing couldn't be worse. But somehow she'd figure it out. She'd done it before. She'd managed to graduate from high school and get into university while helping to raise six kids. This would be a piece of cake.

Kate's eyes filled with tears again. "I do."

"I can do it." It was insane. "How long?"

Kate's mouth thinned. "Two-and-a-half weeks."

"And there's nobody else that can do it?"

"Not… exactly." Kate explained how her own parents were unable, and that Simon's brother Will was away all summer.

"So that leaves me," Alex said.

"And, because you're at the office all day…" she hesitated, hiding behind her cup of tea. "And I know you can't *not* do that. We need someone else to fill in."

"Yeah…?" Alexa prompted.

"Bruce will have to do it," Kate said.

"What? You must be out of your mind!"

Kate visibly deflated. "I knew you'd hate the idea. But he's great with the kids, he really is. They adore him. And he's the only person that's flexible enough to fill in the gaps while you're at the office." She shrugged. "He's already been helping me. And you know you'll need back up. I trust Bruce completely."

"I can't imagine why. That player? How can he take care of the kids? He can't even take care of himself. He's like a big teenager. He won't be any help at all." As soon as the rant had left her lips, Alex wished she could take it back. That was no way to convince Kate to leave her kids and go rescue Simon.

"Someone has to be available and run the whole show while you're working. I already feel terrible that I'm forcing you into this. This isn't a good time for you with the big project and all. You know I wouldn't if–"

"I know, Kate. It's okay. Don't worry about the kids, or me and Bruce - just go get your man and bring him home."

"To be fair, you underestimate him. He's a terrific guy and incredibly smart and talented. Resourceful. He knows how to do everything–"

"Except dress like an adult and behave civilly to women. Well. I'll be damned if I'll feed him and do his laundry," she murmured with a smirk intended to soften her outburst with humour.

They all knew what Bruce was like, didn't they? Ever since Alexa had met him again four years ago, she'd done her best to avoid him as much as humanly possible. He got under her skin like a thorn, a sharp prick and then hours of itching and irritation that made her grouchy as a bear.

She made it a habit never to be in his company that long. But what was the point of arguing? As annoying as he was, they had to make it work. They had to, for Kate.

"Bruce and I will be fine. It'll give us a chance to get to know each other better. We'll work it out." Lord help her, she didn't know how.

The doorbell rang.

"He's here."

❧

His first couple of days as Kate's helper had gone smoothly, and he'd begun to feel complacent that she wouldn't demand too much of him, after all. On the third evening, however, after he'd already crossed the bridge and settled into his boat, he gotten her frantic call to come back immediately. Naturally concerned, he hopped in his truck and raced over. Little did he know that this visit would turn his life, his very world view, upside down.

Ever since they'd met and become fast friends in high school, Bruce had always treated Simon's place like a second home. In fact, it was the closest thing to a real home that Bruce had had since– well, since his Mom had left in the third grade. Simon's parents had been kind to him. It had always been a safe haven from the perpetual state of chaos and persecution that he suffered growing up among his three boisterous older brothers and under the bullying dictatorship of his own father.

Some of his best meals had been shared with Simon and his brother Will as they watched games together. Starting in university, Simon had also hosted their occasional poker nights. Now that Kate was in the picture, and since Markus had been born, Simon's house had taken on a feminine vibe, an atmosphere of domestic harmony and comfort, a qualitative difference from his first less-than-perfect marriage. Something that Bruce found vaguely disquieting, if oddly compelling. It smelled too sweet. And it seemed the last place on earth you'd set up a poker table. He always looked forward to coming, and just as eagerly longed to escape back to his floating bachelor pad.

He both longed for and feared the sense of safety, stability and belonging that it represented. But the price was too high. You just couldn't trust relationships to last, and it hurt too much when you counted on someone to be there for you always, and then they left.

Bruce had stayed for dinner the day Simon had flown to Thailand, and been happy to head home afterwards. Tonight, the moment he arrived, he knew something was wrong.

Kate met him at the door and pulled him into Simon's den. Bruce leaned in, kissing her cheek. "Evening, Beautiful."

She gestured to a chair and sat down. Then she just stared at him. Her eyes were red and puffy.

Oh, dear God. His gut clenched. "What is it?"

"Simon's been in an accident."

Bruce couldn't breath. He was horrified. He was a afraid to ask. "What happened?"

"He was running around trying to make arrangements for his parents, distracted I guess, jet-lagged. He was hit by a motor-cyclist."

He waited, his heart in his throat.

Kate shook her head. "He's okay, I guess. Bruised up. But his leg is fractured. So now he's in hospital, too. But they took him to a different hospital than where his Dad is, so it's impossible. Everything's in chaos. He can't do what he went there to do. He's trying to arrange his father's health care and insurance as well as his own, and keep his mother calm, all from a hospital bed. Travel home at the moment is impossible. None of them can manage. I have to go to him. I need you to take care of the kids."

"What? By myself?" Of course he'd do it if he had to, but… "Wouldn't the kids be better off with a professional? You can hire nannies for temporary gigs, can't you?"

Kate's eyes darkened. "I couldn't do that to Maddie. After all she's been through with her mother. Simon's never left her before, and her first experience with a nanny when she was a baby was… not good."

Bruce remembered. Simon had had some horrific experiences with nannies and sitters when he'd been a single dad, and Rachel was notorious for disappointing Maddie by cancelling last minute. "Don't you have girlfriends? Surely a woman would be a better choice. The kids would–"

She nodded. "Alexa's here, too."

"What... Alex... You're not... That harpy?" He bit back more vitriol. He should know better than to bad-mouth Kate's best friend.

"You don't know the first thing about her."

"I know she's never had the time of day for me. How's this going to work?"

"I know you and Alexa don't have a great history, but... you two got off on the wrong foot years ago. You have to get to know her better."

"Ri-i-ight." Bruce nodded sceptically. He never knew whether he wanted to screw her senseless or punch her lights out, she drove him so nuts.

"Alexa is terrific. She's a smart, caring, funny woman and my oldest, dearest friend. You'll make a great team."

Strange, somehow that had escaped Bruce's notice. The terrific, caring, funny part. Okay, he'd admit she was smart. Too smart. But caring? funny? Nope. She was humourless and abrasive. She was so serious about her career she didn't have time for fun and leisure. Almost a caricature. She was attractive, he'd give her that, in a skinny, dark, exotic sort of way, though not *his* type. Not attractive enough to brave the prickly gauntlet of her personality. They never seemed to be able to get along without bickering. "You expect me to..."

"Cooperate. She has to work full time. What choice do any of us have, Bruce?"

Bruce wanted to run. He knew she needed his help. His, and obviously Alexa's. There was no way out of this. "Of course I'll do it. But you're worried about something?"

"Yes, frankly, I'm concerned that you two *are* going to fight like cats and dogs.

"Calm down, Kate. I promised Simon I'd take care of you and help you. I didn't know it would be like this, but it'll be fine. We'll cooperate. Of course we will." Bruce wasn't sure how, but he'd find a way.

"You need to get along, that's all. Listen and be respectful. Don't be a macho jerk."

"I'm not the one who picks fights with her, you know." Okay, maybe he was somewhat responsible for giving her a certain less-than-favourable impression of who he was. And trying to get a rise out of her. It was so easy to provoke her.

"I really mean it."

"Hmph. Do you remember the time we first met up again, four Christmases ago? She nearly tore me to shreds." Bruce's voice rose an octave remembering. He felt the hair on his arms rise, tingling, and remembered the ache in his groin from their momentary encounter in the darkened hallway.

"You kissed her!"

Bruce grimaced. "There was mistletoe."

Kate rolled his eyes. "That's what I mean. She's not the kind of… tart you're used to dealing with, that's all."

"You can say that again."

"Bruce." Kate shook her head, scowling. "I want your word. Be respectful. Play nice."

"I promise…" Bruce made a pleading gesture with his hands out. "I'll…er, I'll do my best to get along, I'll even learn to like her. Okay?" Even if he had to stop poking fun at her. It might even be boring. He took Kate's hands in his and squeezed them. "And I promise you, Kate, the kids will be perfectly okay. You and Simon don't have to worry about a thing."

Kate stood up. "I knew I could count on you, Bruce." She wrapped her arms around him and held on tight. He returned the hug, but then she clung, and he felt her body temperature rise, felt her shoulders tremble, before he heard her sniffle.

"Hey, hey." He rubbed her back gently.

"I'm so worried about him. I never should have let him go alone."

"He'll be okay. He's a tough guy. Remember he's got a ton of experience travelling around Asia. I'm sure a broken leg won't slow him down."

She lifted her head and glared at him.

"Okay, obviously it will slow him down. I mean, he can cope. He's Sharpy. He can do anything. Right?"

She sniffed again and nodded. "I know. But what if something even more serious had happened over there? I can't bear to think–" Her face buckled.

"Well. It didn't." He set her away from him and looked around for a tissue or something. Finding nothing, he pulled up the tail of his shirt and wiped her cheeks with it. "Look this is a logistical nightmare. And that's why you have to go. But nobody's dying here, Kate. Everything's going to be alright. Okay?"

"Okay."

~

When they entered the hall, Alexa stood there with both Maddie and Markus in their pyjamas, looking scrubbed and combed, with their cheeks glowing pink.

"Koczynski."

"Right." Well, it took two to tango, but he would do his best to lead this dance, and choose his steps carefully. What choice did he have, after all?

"I'll take them upstairs," Alexa said.

Kate's smile was indulgent as she picked up her son. "Say goodnight to Uncle Bruce, Markus."

From her arms, Markus stared at him for a minute, but with a little jiggle from Kate, he finally said, "Night, Boos."

They sure were cute kids. Three-year-old Markus was the spitting image of Kate, with her fine, smooth golden hair. Except he had Simon's blue eyes.

"G'night, little buddy," Bruce said, grinning. "Gimme five." He presented his palm to Markus, who giggled and slapped at it wildly.

"Ouch!" A sharp pain shot through his shinbone. "What the…?" He looked down at Maddie. She'd kicked him viciously with her bony little foot. Simon's seven-year-old daughter Maddie looked more like her mother Rachel, with her thick brown curls and catty green eyes.

"What's up, Scallywag?" He scrubbed the top of her head. "Am I ignoring you?"

She stood with her arms folded, glaring up at him.

"Maddie! Apologize right now," Kate said, frowning.

Madison responded immediately, if half-heartedly, chuffing the carpet with her bare foot. "Thor-ry."

He wasn't convinced. He could see an evil smirk pulling at her lips. Maddie apparently took after her bitchy mother in more ways than one. He pulled a funny face at her, trying to elicit a smile. It'd actually be fun to spend more time with the kids.

"Maddie isn't thrilled with the arrangements," Kate explained as they moved away. "It's not you, though. It's the fact that Simon had to go away in the first place. She has a bit of separation anxiety. He's never left her before, so she's actually furious at *me*. But she's taking it out on you."

Oh, great. Bruce squinted back at Maddie and said in a syrupy voice, "Good night, Madison."

"'Night," she snarled, and stomped upstairs to bed.

Alexa followed her upstairs. "I'll be right down."

"She seems okay with Alexa," Bruce said.

"Yes. They're used to Alex. She babysits pretty regularly."

Bruce was surprised to learn that.

Kate led the way to the dining room, where a casual dinner was laid out on the table. "Help yourself to a beer, Bruce, and some lasagna and salad. I'm just going up to kiss the kids goodnight."

He did, and returned to the dining room, studying the food she set out. When Alexa returned, he ignored her but watched her through his peripheral vision. She sat down at the table, skulking behind a half-empty glass of red wine, like a mean little leprechaun ready to pounce. She scowled at him.

"Hey, partner." He grinned at her. "Looks like we're working together."

"Koczynski." Her husky voice was flat. She glared at him over the dark rims of her angular eyeglasses, obviously no more thrilled at the arrangement than he was.

He offered her a brilliant smile. "None other. How're you doing, Al?" He sauntered around the table, flopped into the chair next to her. He still wondered if it was possible to melt through the ice with sufficient charm. Kate had no idea what she was asking him to do. He threw an arm across the back of her chair and leaned in to kiss her on the cheek.

"Don't get any ideas, Koczynski." She turned her head away, and his face landed in her silky dark hair. It smelled of the tropics. Spicy and sweet. Almost like that cologne he used to wear—what was it called? She may not be his type, but she was like a burr in his hide, small, prickly and stubborn, hard to ignore. She was caramel-coloured with a petite, boyish figure. Kind of cute though. Even though she was the only woman he'd ever met who was persistently immune to his charms. Until she opened her mouth.

That mouth twisted in scorn and she shoved him away, looking like she might hit him with something. Instead, she plucked his arm off and handed it back like it was a rotting log full of maggots. "Do you mind?"

He smiled and shook his head, feeling the first rebellious stirrings from his body. There was something about her throaty voice that seemed to yank his chain.

He took a long draft on his beer, leaning back. "Aah." A small belch escaped. "Pardon."

Alexa shook her head, looking bored with his antics, and slightly annoyed. "So. I'm surprised you agreed to this little arrangement, Koz. You don't strike me as the domestic sort."

You're one to talk. A bark of laughter escaped before he could prevent it. "Like we have any choice."

"What are you laughing at?"

He opted not to reply, instead smiling and taking another sip of beer. She reminded him of Cruella De Ville—hard and mean-spirited. All she was missing was a shock of white in her dark hair and a long cigarette holder. Oh, and a coat made of puppies.

"Nothing at all," he replied, sniggering, then sobered. "You're looking well." She did, too. Her dark hair shone, strands of it somehow sticking out artfully. It managed to look both precise and post-coital at the same time. Everything about her was a carefully considered design statement. It suited her. He flicked the end of her scarf. "Love this, Al. Great colour on you. Matches your eyes." He leaned in closer and flared his nostrils and let his gaze slide over her slender limbs.

Those eyes were narrowed at him now, her suspicions aroused.

There was a vaguely exotic quality about her eyes. They were a strange greyish-green, like a stormy sea, and tilted up at the corners. It might be appealing, if she would smile once in a while. He saw a twinkle of amusement in her eyes, though. Maybe he was getting somewhere.

"That's Alexa to you, Koczynski." She pursed her full lips and eyed his torso.

He sat up taller. "Like what you see?" Raising his arm to flex his bicep, he flickered his eyebrows at her. "I've been working out more."

She let out a gust of air, rolling her eyes. "Nice shirt," she deadpanned. "Not wasting all your time at clubs and parties? I heard–"

He gave her a hard look, his teeth set. "Actually, it's not having to work eighteen hour days that's made the biggest difference." He smiled broadly. "And you could call me Bruce."

She ignored him. "Oh, right. I'd forgotten you were one of the idle rich these days."

His eye twitched with tension, and he forced himself to relax. He tilted the beer bottle back, taking a long drink. "What kind of name is Alexa, anyway? Italian or Egyptian or something?" He'd always wondered if she was mixed race.

Again she ignored his question. No wonder she got under his skin. She retaliated with, "What's with the long hair and Hawaiian shirt? Auditioning for a Hawaii Five-O remake?"

Bruce shrugged, combing a hand through his shoulder length hair. It wasn't that long. "I see you can't keep your eyes off of me tonight, Al." He felt a warm stirring in his trousers. Even though she was trying to goad him, the sound of her sexy voice always had this regrettable effect.

"Hah! In your dreams, Hefner."

He grinned. Feisty little thing. He'd forgotten how she oiled his gears. Her voice was velvety soft and deep, like a spell that spoke directly to his blood, causing it to surge out of control. A Siren's song. He took a page from Odysseus and filed those thoughts away. Far away.

"So. How's this going at work, Ms. Architect?" he asked, with another generous smile.

She sighed. "You're such an ass, Koczynski."

It was sheer torture, being physically attracted to someone you wanted to throttle. She was like a baby panther. Cuddly cute until the claws and teeth came out. *Oh*, that helped. His inconvenient boner eased off a little. That was another good reason to avoid contact with her.

Alexa continued to peer at him with obvious disdain.

"Seriously, tell me about your name—" but she didn't have a chance to reply.

Kate entered the room, flustered, her hair in disarray. Both Bruce and Alexa sat up taller, pasting friendly smiles on their faces. It wouldn't do to advertise their ongoing war of wills to their worried friend. In that respect they seemed to be on the same page. "Well they're down. I guess we'll see tomorrow how they react when I leave."

"Tomorrow?" Bruce said. So soon?

She nodded. "Help yourself to food, you guys." She filled a plate and set it down, pushing at it with a fork, taking tiny nibbles, distracted.

"So, not much time to prepare, but Kate's made a few notes for us," Alexa said, shoving a stack of crinkled papers toward him.

He took them and scanned them. The handwriting was almost illegible. The words seemed almost randomly arranged, as though Kate had jotted down fragments of ideas as they came to her. Not surprising, he supposed. Frowning, he looked up and met Alexa's gaze with a silent question. Was this supposed to make sense? She peered steadily at him, as though trying to convey something telepathically. Again he perused their so-called "instructions." He let out a soundless whistle, smiled again and nodded. "This looks great. We won't have any trouble at all, Kate. Nothing for you to worry about."

Possibly for the first time in history, he earned a smile from Alexa Jenner. What do you know? He did the right thing. He offered a half smile in return.

After a few minutes, Kate picked up an envelope and said, "I got a flight out tomorrow afternoon. You'll pick up Markus from day care, Bruce, at twelve-thirty. Then give him a snack, some exercise, and a nap. Then you pick up Maddie at school at 2:30. She'll need a snack and some down time too. I know it sounds rigid, but trust me, that will make it easier on everyone. I have it all written down there."

Bruce nodded. "I can handle that."

"Don't worry, Katie, it'll be fine." said Alex, her voice soothing and calm. It was almost enough to calm the frenzy of panic rising in his own gullet. But not quite.

Bruce shot a glance her way. He hoped she was as chill about this as she seemed.

Kate continued. "The next part, I'm not so sure about. Alexa, you'll get them ready for bed… you'll have to stay at the house, I guess," Kate said. "Besides, someone has to take care of the kitties, too."

Alexa nodded. "Anything special there? I know Lucy needs her shots." Alexa adjusted her glasses to scan Kate's list.

"Right. Once a day, evenings are fine," Kate said. "And Oscar's no trouble. He's so old, he sleeps all the time."

The subject in question coiled around Bruce's ankles. He looked down. *Fuck, that mangy old cat better not keel over on my shift.*

Kate let out a big breath. "So, Alexa, your mornings will be a bit wild. You'll have to get them up, fed, dressed, and drop Maddie at school for 8:45. Then Markus right afterwards."

Bruce watched Alexa process this information, her eyes cast down at the list, her brow furrowed. "So I won't be able to start my work day until almost nine-thirty," Alexa said, her brow drawing down, her exquisite wide lips pursed.

Bruce studied the long dark lashes grazing her smooth tan cheeks.

She sighed. "With the new Arts Centre project starting, I'll have a team expecting answers from me first thing." She turned to him. "It would be better for me if you could come by here at about seven-thirty, and then drop the kids off."

He froze as her words sunk in. "Do what?"

"Come early and take the kids to school?" She dipped her chin and peered at him over the frames of her glasses, creating the illusion that he was being scolded by a sexy little librarian.

Hell no! He cleared his throat. "It's quite a ways for me to get over here from West Van." His smile felt tight. He could imagine the hours it would take him coming over the bridge four times a day. He'd go nuts. "Morning rush hour traffic on the bridge can be brutal. I couldn't guarantee getting here on time."

Alexa slumped in her chair. "Oh. I see."

The clash of cutlery against Kate's plate jarred his nerve endings as she dropped a knife. He glanced at her, taking in her pinched expression, and remembered his vow to Simon. She offered him a watery smile.

He raised his hands, palm out and responded *sotto voce*. "But don't worry, Kate. Maybe we can take turns or something. Al and I will iron out the details. It'll be fine." He met Alexa's steely eye. "Right, Al?"

"Okay, alright." Alexa nibbled her nail. "I'll have to work longer in the evenings, I guess."

He squinted. Both ends of this stick were getting shorter by the minute.

Kate nodded. "Well, the issue is dinner. I'm sure you'll be home early enough to do the bedtime routine most days, but if they don't eat at a reasonable time, you'll be really sorry. They become unmanageable. It snowballs. If there's one lesson I've learned–"

"I know all about that," Alexa smirked. "A houseful of over-hungry kids is insanity."

How would she know? "What time do they eat?" Bruce asked, frowning.

Kate said, "I'd say, six would be the latest."

"Some days, maybe, I could be off work by five thirty and get here. That makes for a very short work day. I'll draw up a work schedule so you know when you have to cover for me."

"Well, I can feed them dinner," Bruce said. He'd have meals

delivered from that gourmet place. "That's easy." Why that earned him a skeptical glance from both women he didn't know. He was resourceful. They'd see.

"Well don't worry too much, Bruce. Alexa is an incredible superwoman with house and family things."

His head jerked up. "How's that?" It certainly wasn't how he saw her. She was all about her career. He couldn't even visualize her in a kitchen. A bedroom, yes, but…

"Don't you know she practically raised her six younger brothers and sisters while graduating from high school? This woman can do anything!" Kate gushed.

Six? He narrowed his eyes at Alexa, blinking. No, he didn't know that. He tried to picture the shrew caring for six younger siblings and failed. That was a story he'd like to hear. The image didn't fit. "You might have to give me some lessons, then, Al." He shrugged, imagining some up-close one-on-one time in the kitchen, and his body heated. He took a deep breath and let it out through his open mouth. He shut his eyes. *Forget that.*

"I hope I don't have to teach you everything," she said, smirking while she leaned back and crossed her arms. "But I have my doubts."

"Whoah. You underestimate me, sweetheart." Bruce looked for support at Kate. "I have skills, too—"

"He certainly does, Alex. That's why Simon asked Bruce to help me in the first place. He's fantastic with the kids, you should see them together. They absolutely love spending time with him. Nobody does fun and games like Bruce."

"Fun and games," Alexa repeated, straight-faced. Her eyes slid over to Bruce. "That'll come in handy." Her mouth twitched.

He gave her a half smile, cocking one brow. "You have no idea." He'd like to have some fun with her. If only she were capable of letting loose for once. Or maybe not.

Alexa eyed him with flat, grey-green eyes that managed to

communicate her lack of faith in him without a word. Somehow, he felt eight years old again.

He had promised to be nice, *cooperate*. He took a deep breath. "Right. We'll make a plan. "Alexa and I make a great team. She's gonna help me with cooking lessons, and I'm gonna help her plan fun and games."

She nodded, her eyes narrowing.

"Okay, then." Kate stood up, taking her mostly untouched plate to the kitchen. "I'd better pack," she said absently. "I'm exhausted already and I need a good sleep tonight." She turned back. "There's something I'm forgetting…"

Alexa got up and took the plate from her hands. "Let me clean up here. You go to bed. We'll see ourselves out."

Bruce rose too. He couldn't sit while she worked. "I'll give you a hand." He picked up some dishes and took them into the kitchen, then caught her smirking at him, a twinkle in her green eyes. "What?"

"This should be interesting."

"Well good night. I'll see you both tomorrow."

"You bet, Kate." He went to her and took her upper arms in his hands, meeting her gaze. She seemed frail. He wondered what it would be like to find out your one true love was injured half way across the world. "Don't even think about us. We're in control here. You just take care of yourself and bring Simon and his folks home safely." He leaned in to kiss her forehead.

She nodded and slipped away.

A moment of tense silence followed. They stood until they heard her bedroom door close. Alexa's long slow exhale was audible.

Bruce raised his eyebrows at her. "Well?" he finally said, throwing down the gauntlet. Enough pretence—they needed to have this out.

"I get the impression you're not happy about doing this," she said.

"Not at all. I adore Maddie and Markus. We're gonna have a blast," he drawled, leaning towards her ear. His nostrils filled with her sweet, spicy scent, and he leaned back, regretting their proximity, and exhaled slowly.

Her darkened expression said he'd scored a point. "You can get out of the mundane shit like shopping and housework because you're Mister Fun and Games. I have a very demanding job and a huge project starting up, so you're going to have to pull your weight around here and then some, Hefner."

She couldn't be serious. "I don't see a problem. I'll spend my mornings renovating my house and head over here for the afternoons. Easy-peasy."

"I know you. You'll try to weasel out of chores." Alexa said."It will take a little more time management. I have good software for that. We'll make up a spreadsheet, and divide up the responsibilities to make sure everything is covered. I'll have to plan ahead as much as possible and keep you posted on my workdays so you'll know what to expect from day to day."

"Spreadsheets." She was nuts. She was trying to take control of his whole bloody life. He rolled his shoulders and rubbed the back of his neck with a hand, trying to loosen a knot of tension. Next she'd be giving him minute-by-minute instructions.

"You'll have to find time for shopping and chores."

The air in the room grew thin. Did he just get stuck with shopping *and* cooking? He'd have to hire an army of help. "Don't you trust me, Al?"

"No." She blinked. "We're both making personal sacrifices for our friends. You'll have to do your share, Koczynski. Get over it."

"How can we possibly fail?" He offered her a wide smile. "You have project management software. Right, Al?"

She took off her glasses and shoved them into her hair so she could rub her eyes.

"Why are you worried about me, anyway? Sounds like you're the one that's got time management issues. It'll be fine. I can catch up on my construction work on the weekends." Bruce grinned at Alexa, and she stared back.

"Unfortunately, I work most weekends." She pressed her lips together, nodding. "You'll have to stay with the kids during the days and some evenings, too."

"You're not going to dump extra work on me so you can slip a few drinks with co-workers into your week."

Then a slow, inscrutable smile spread across her face, and her voice dropped down a notch, sultry with a hard edge, like the cruel caress of a sharp blade. "Not that it's any of your business, but if I'm working after hours, I'm actually working."

Damn it, that voice! If he ignored her words, it almost sounded like an invitation. For someone else. Not for him. "You mean you have no social life? *Quel surprise!*"

She made a sound, a cross between a scream and a roar, but she kept her mouth clamped tight, so it seemed to bleed out of her ears. God, she was a tiger. Her smoky eyes burned with a fiery light that made him wonder what she would be like in between the sheets. "My personal life has nothing to do with this negotiation. I have responsibilities at work. Period."

Jeezus, she was tense. It's probably because she worked so much she never got any sex at all. Someone should redirect that ferocious energy into bed, and then give her a darn good reason to relax. Not him though. His erection twitched again. Not helpful. It made him so mad he could spit. *Claws and teeth. Claws and teeth.* He sucked a breath slowly in through his clenched teeth and forced a smile.

The stick! "I have to meet tradesmen at my house sometimes. It sounds like you're trying to offload all the work to me."

"Hardly. I'm going to be living here. We'll have to put it on the schedule."

"Right, I guess we will," he replied, grinning past gritted teeth. Despite his promise to Kate, Bruce laughed, because he knew it would annoy her. "I mean what does a thirty-something professional workaholic know about child care anyhow? I'm trying to be helpful, here. I know it'll be a hardship for a career woman such as yourself, honey, but I guess you'll have to pull up your garters and cope with your share of this childcare deal."

"Please don't call me honey." Her shoulders slumped. "I know more than I ever wanted to about childcare and homemaking, thank you very much."

Alexa sliced her hand across her other palm. "All I want is to split this up evenly and disrupt my life as little as possible. If we project manage our schedule and list of duties, we should be fine. I'll put Kate's list in my software and then you can add your constraints. If I can manage the design and construction of an entire civic building, I can handle a couple of weeks co-parenting with you."

Bruce sighed. They were never going to be able to coexist in peace. That much was clear. "Fine. That suits me perfectly."

She crossed her arms. "We'll share the work fair and square, *including* weekends. You do your half and I'll do mine. But let me make myself perfectly clear. I don't care what you think of me, Koczynski. But please *try* not to make this situation any worse. Do your part and stay out of my way."

He nodded. She so totally didn't understand him. He'd do anything for Simon and Kate their kids. "It might be best if we try to stay away from each other as much as possible."

They glared at each other.

"So. We have a deal?" Alexa thrust out her hand like a knife.

He gripped her small, strong hand firmly in his own and squeezed, perhaps a little tighter than he should have. "Deal."

~

End of sample
Get your copy of Making Room For You today!
Click now: books2read.com/BeforeYouKnewMe